Righteous Assassin

A Mike Stoneman Thriller

Righteous Assassin

A Mike Stoneman Thriller

Kevin G. Chapman

Cover design by Bespoke Bookcovers

Other novels by Kevin G. Chapman

<u>The Mike Stoneman Thriller Series</u>

Deadly Enterprise (Mike Stoneman #2)

Lethal Voyage (Mike Stoneman #3)

Fatal Infraction (Mike Stoneman #4)

Perilous Gambit (Mike Stonemen #5)

Other novels:

A Legacy of One

Visit me at www.KevinGChapman.com

For Sharon, whose wit, wisdom, and encouragement make my writing so much easier and whose ideas and suggestions (even the ones I didn't accept) made this book much better than it would have been without her.

Contents

RIGHTEOUS ASSASSIN

Chapter 1 – It's a Jungle

July 29, 2018

CRIME SCENES IN NEW YORK CITY are often bloody, regularly bizarre, and occasionally fascinating to the homicide detectives who are jaded to all but the grisliest circumstances. Detective Mike Stoneman had seen them all in his twenty-four years on the force. Stiffs in swimming pools, stiffs tied up in basement dungeons, stiffs with various parts of their anatomy removed, and stiffs fished out of the Hudson river with their eyeballs eaten away by aquatic creatures. This one, however, was a new variation – what he referred to as a "unicorn." Eaten alive by tigers is not a cause of death often registered by the New York county medical examiner. Mike knelt down next to what was left of the corpse's foot and examined the remnants of duct tape that had bound one ankle to the other. The tigers had left the tape mostly uneaten. Discerning palates, apparently.

"Just another routine murder in the Big City, eh, Mike?"

Stoneman looked up, squinting against the morning sun, and saw Detective Jason Dickson towering over him. Jason was six-foot-three, with broad shoulders that tapered down to a slim waist. Even wearing a suit, it was obvious that he was in great shape and had well-defined muscles across his entire upper body. He was a mountain compared to Mike's five-foot-ten and slightly paunchy frame, even when Mike was standing. On this morning,

Jason was wearing a blue pin-striped suit with a starched white shirt that contrasted sharply against his dark brown skin. His red-and-blue silk tie was expertly knotted and held in place with a gold tie bar, giving him an especially dapper appearance next to Mike's rumpled jacket, wrinkled shirt, and scuffed loafers. Even at 9:00 a.m., the July humidity made Mike sweat as the temperature started its unstoppable rise toward too-damned-hot, but Jason seemed impervious.

Mike looked up at his young partner and smiled, which was a rare occurrence. "What? Never seen a stiff partially eaten by wild animals before?"

"Oh, sure," Jason parried, "just not this early in the morning."

Mike turned his attention back to the remnants of the body. The crime scene team was nearly finished, but the photographer was still taking shots all around the area. Normally, Mike would be worried about people walking around and contaminating the evidence, but in this case the press had been relegated to the spectator area above the tiger enclosure and the zoo security team had not allowed anyone but NYPD into the pit. The whole Bronx Zoo was closed for the day. Mike could hear the faint thumping of a chopper's rotors somewhere overhead, but he ignored it. "Did we get a positive ID on the corpse?"

"Yes, we did," Jason responded with his usual perfect diction. "You were correct, Mike. It's Mickey Gallata. The family has not reported him missing, but his son confirmed that he left home yesterday evening and did not come back. I guess he's not going to make it."

"No," Mike said without emotion. "Slick Mick will definitely not be having supper with his family ever again. It's funny, you know. We've been trying to pin a conviction on him for what, a dozen years? And now, somebody has taken care of all that for us. I guess we should thank them."

"When we figure out who's responsible, I'll send a fruit basket." Jason walked away to talk with the uniformed officer who was patrolling the perimeter of the tiger enclosure looking for anything out of place. Mike was pretty sure that the beat cop from the South Bronx was not going to know whether anything he saw in the replica jungle was out of place or not.

Mike stood up and squinted again as he gazed out of the pit and saw the television news crews positioned along the black iron fence that normally kept the zoo visitors from getting too close to the edge. They had jockeyed for position as soon as the cops had let them in an hour earlier. At the time, the low sun had made the left side of the enclosure the prime real estate for live remote shots. But now, as the sun rose a little higher in the sky, the crews were repositioning, staking out spaces and camera angles with the best backgrounds and lighting. Signs all along the bars reminded the public not to feed the animals. These particular tigers would not need feeding again for a few days.

Several minutes later, Mike and Jason walked together to have a talk with the director of zoo security, Maurice Walker, who was understandably both pissed off and embarrassed by the situation. Walker sported a jacket that could have been navy blue or black, depending on whether it had been cleaned recently. He wore light grey slacks with an elastic waist band that hugged the bottom of his belly, which was spilling slightly over his black belt. His dark sunglasses and open-collared dress shirt made him look like an extra in a gangster movie. He had been working security at the zoo for thirty years and had been promoted up the ranks. This was his home, and it had been violated.

In a thick Bronx accent, Walker explained to the two detectives that there were no security cameras inside the animal enclosures, but there were cameras at the zoo entrances. Jason asked him to provide copies of the recordings so that he could have someone review them as soon as possible. Walker said he would have the tapes sent over.

"Tapes?" Jason asked incredulously. "You mean disks, right?"

"Nah," Walker responded. "This is a City-run operation. C'mon.

You know how it goes. We installed this security system twenty years ago. Ya think City Hall is springing for the latest tech for the fucking zoo? Ha! We got VHS machines and big-ass cassettes. But looking at tape's a waste of time. I know where the scumbags broke in, and there're no cameras there."

"Where's that?" Mike asked.

"Over on the wall, a few hundred yards," Walker pointed toward the brightly sun-lit space overhead and to the right of the tiger enclosure.

"What about the route from there to here?"

"Well, there are a couple cameras, but they're only turned on during the day when there are people here. We don't run them twenty-four hours a day. No reason to record darkness."

Mike looked at Jason and shrugged. "It only matters when it matters. Can we see the entry point?"

Walker led the two detectives out of the tiger pit and up a long ramp past the news crews, who scurried to grab their equipment, thinking that the appearance of the two NYPD detectives might signal something worth recording. When Mike waved them off and kept walking, they set down their cameras and went back to their territories.

Walker guided the detectives to the perimeter wall that separated the zoo grounds from the surrounding city. It was made of concrete blocks that were arranged to mimic stonework, like a medieval castle. Every few hundred feet along the wall, there were steel gates secured with a deadbolt lock and a separate chain-and-padlock combination. Walker explained that the gates were there to allow access for trucks bringing in supplies and large items that would not fit through the public access entrances. They had occasionally had kids climb over the wall and commit acts of vandalism, but nobody had ever broken through the gates before. Walker stopped in front of a gate that was obviously no longer locked. Yellow police tape was strung across the threshold. Its broken padlock lay on the ground, the metal twisted where it had been cut.

"Even with vandalism issues in the past, you didn't keep the security cameras running at night?" Mike was trying to keep a professional demeanor, but his annoyance with the absence of potentially helpful evidence seeped into his voice.

Walker shrugged. "It wasn't my call, Detective. It was a budget decision made by the managing director."

Mike pursed his lips and said nothing. At first, he could not imagine how running cameras could be a budget issue. But, when he thought about the eight-hour maximum duration of a VHS tape, which would need to be changed during the night, he figured it out. No reason to pay somebody to sit in the security office and swap out tapes all night. He examined the broken lock and severed chain lying on the ground. It would have been simple for anyone with some basic equipment to cut the padlock and chain and drill out the deadbolt. "Aren't you worried about somebody stealing valuable animals?"

Walker shook his head. "The only animals here that are really worth anything outside the zoo industry are so poisonous or dangerous that nobody with a brain would try to steal them. And they're all tagged with permanent identification that makes them pretty much impossible to sell."

Mike nodded, then asked, "How did they get Slick Mick into the tiger enclosure without being attacked themselves?"

Walker paused. "Why do you think it was more than one person?"

Mike smiled at Walker's perception. "You're right, Mr. Walker. I shouldn't make that assumption. It's just that, in my experience, one person generally has a hard time dragging a full-grown man around, and it's particularly hard to get someone into a spot like that even if he's unconscious."

Jason interjected, "If this was a mob hit, there were probably multiple goons involved."

Mike frowned. "We're making a lot of assumptions now,

Detective Dickson."

Jason bit back a response and nodded. "Right, Detective Stoneman. Stick to what we know for sure, not what we think."

Mike nodded back. "Right. We'll figure out how the facts fit together later." They walked slowly back to the tiger enclosure, tracing the probable route of the killer or killers and looking for anything out of place, but saw nothing they could perceive as out of the ordinary. At the bottom of the sloping ramp that ran along the side of the tiger pit, they came to a door they had come through before, marked "zoo staff only." The three men paused while Mike examined the broken lock. "Why isn't this door secured with a better lock?"

Walker shrugged. "Who in their right mind wants to break into the tiger pit?"

Mike nodded and said nothing. They walked through the door into a dark corridor, then through another door, with no lock, back out into the pit and the mid-morning sunlight. Mike squinted while Jason smoothly extracted sunglasses from the front pocket of his suit jacket. Jason asked, "Where were the tigers when the killers dragged Gallata out here?"

Walker didn't hesitate. "The animals all stay in their interior cages during the night. We release them each morning, but they're never out here after dark."

Mike nodded again. "Once the perps were past the staff door, was there anything blocking them from releasing the tigers out into the pit?"

"No," Walker replied. "Just a sliding bar on the access door. No lock."

"Pretty easy gig," Jason opined. "Tie the guy up, either ahead of time or when you get here. Cut him a little to get some blood flowing, then release the tigers and walk away."

"Yeah. Very creative," Mike deadpanned. "Jungle Book meets Goodfellas."

Mike walked back into the middle of the pit, scanning the lush foliage and the large rocks hewn from some upstate granite quarry. A small artificial stream meandered across the jungle-scape, ending in a deep pool where the tigers could cool off on hot days. The mangled corpse had been removed while Mike and Jason had been away, leaving only a series of pins in the ground and blood stains to mark the place where Mickey Gallata had met his end. Jason sidled up to Mike as he stood there, contemplating whether this apparent mob hit was worth any time investigating, and kept silent and still for two full minutes. "Good," Mike commended. "That's the longest I've ever seen you keep your mouth shut."

"Thanks. I have two thoughts."

"Great, Kid. Tell me both of them."

Jason paused, frowning down at Mike from his six-foot-three perspective, but he kept his annoyance in check. "First, do you remember what they used to call Slick Mick before he became the boss, back when he was just a goon for the old man?"

Mike smiled and nodded his head slightly. "Oh, yeah. I remember. 'Mickey the Animal.'"

"Kind of poetic justice, don't you think?"

"Sure. Somebody's idea of a sick joke. What's the other thing, Junior?"

"I thought you weren't going to call me that?"

"Sorry. Habit."

"What I was going to say," Jason said softly, "is that last night was the last Saturday of the month."

"Yeah," Mike responded blankly, "I thought about that. This one seems pretty obviously not connected, don't you think?"

Jason turned to his partner and took off his sunglasses, revealing his dark eyes. "Like you always say, Mike, no matter what we may think, what we know is the evidence. What we know is that there was a murder with unusual circumstances on the last Saturday of the month. It could be a coincidence, of course, or it might not be."

"Yeah," Mike grunted, wiping away a trickle of sweat from his eyebrow with the back of his increasingly dirty suit jacket. "Let's see what happens."

Chapter 2 – Genesis

April 1, 2018

*T*ODAY IS THE BEGINNING *of my great crusade. In ten months, I shall fulfill my divine destiny. I did not ask for this. I did not know when I went to Afghanistan for the first time that I would find such inspiration, such meaning. How can a man know? Until God puts that knife in your hand and that evil creature in front of you, how can anyone imagine? I felt the hand of an Angel guiding me and heard the sound of a choir singing in my ears. It was bliss.*

The foolish quote the Bible and say, "Thou shalt not kill." Imbeciles. Over and over, God commands in the Bible that we kill. We must put to death those who have committed sins against the Lord and sins against their fellow man. Thou shalt not kill without justification and reason. Thou shalt not kill in anger or in haste or in the heat of passion. But when divine justice requires death, then death there shall be. I understand that now. Everyone will understand when I am finished.

This journal shall be the scripture I leave behind, to be read and examined and eventually understood by those whose hearts and minds are open to the message of God. He is a vengeful and wrathful God who will punish those who sully this Earth. I am his servant, his Earthly Angel. What else explains this hunger inside me to see the fear and the anguish in the eyes of the evil ones whom God has selected for execution? The righteous of the world will know me and know my story and my inspiration. Let this be known as the first day. The Lord is my shepherd, I shall not stray from the true path of justice.

* * *

April 6

Joy and divine inspiration are mine! The ground beneath my feet seems hardly there as I float on the wings of Angels. As the sun warms the Earth and the buds of spring make their first appearance, so the worm peeks forth from the slime to be plucked from life by a bird. So too has Abel poked his bald head into the rays of the sun and sauntered forth into the jaws of divine retribution. I have him in my sights and without mercy shall I carry out my mission.

Let no man perceive that God is not a just and compassionate ruler of the Universe. For I have seen the toll taken on the families of those who depart from life suddenly. When I returned home after my first tour in Afghanistan, I met the family of my one good friend in the world, who was killed by an enemy bomb and came home in a body bag. His pretty wife and two young daughters were so devastated. The emotional toll was high, but more than that, the reality of living on without a father for the girls and without a breadwinner for the family was terrifying. So many tears, and for no good reason. I understand now that God was teaching me. I understand that when life is to be taken away, it is important to assess the toll on the innocents who face the collateral damage. The evil souls who must face judgment at the hands of the Avenging Angel should not cause wives or young children to suffer for the sins of their parents or lovers. This I understand. This shall I do. None shall be harmed by the removal of vermin from the grass.

And, lo, what God hath laid before mine eyes. A man so vile and deserving of punishment that none could contest the justice of the act. His young trophy wife loathes him and his children are grown and have families of their own. Few will mourn his passing. I have verified all the relevant information, which I first learned about so long ago. He has built a business on the backs and dead bodies of his workers, some of whom he imports from overseas and then enslaves in his sweatshop. Two have died and countless others have been oppressed and abused, yet our acclaimed American justice system has been paralyzed and offers no succor. Criminal charges were brought after the second death, but dismissed. Since when do rich and powerful men do jail time for the detritus they leave behind them in the wake of modern industry? Safety inspectors were no doubt bribed to look the other way. Employees who fear the exposure of their illegal status, or who are too ignorant to make a complaint, cannot stand up to this monster. He feeds on the poor and weak and gives back nothing to the world but pain. He will be the first, after such a long period of planning. I call him Abel, for when Cain killed Abel he was the first to die among all men. This man – this Abel – will be the first to feel the wrath of my glory and my holy mission. He is the first in a cog of righteousness that will crush his compatriots and conspirators as well, all in good time.

Will the patterns of God's glory be perceptible to those who know the details, but who may not understand the profound whole? My sweet inspiration was the voice of God speaking directly to me in my dreams and showing me the path. This scroll is my story, and I the narrator. This is my masterwork, both in deeds and in words. Let those who read this decipher the truth and be lifted by it.

Chapter 3 – Avoiding the Obvious

August 1, 2018

THREE DAYS AFTER finding the partially eaten body of Slick Mick Gallata at the Bronx Zoo, Mike and Jason sat in uncomfortable chairs in a briefing room in City Hall, waiting for the Police Commissioner, the chief of the homicide division, and the Mayor. The meeting was scheduled for 10:00 a.m. It was fifteen minutes past ten. A window-mounted air conditioning unit whirred in the corner, fighting a losing battle against the summer heat. Mike was fidgeting and tapping his finger on the conference room table, feeling like an animal trapped in a cage, which brought his thoughts back to the zoo and the corpse in the tiger pit. Jason was reading emails on his cell phone. Mike thought he looked as calm as a rattlesnake stalking a family of mice. He had been thinking in zoo similes all weekend.

Jason's baritone voice snapped Mike away from his jungle thoughts. "You're going to back me up, right, Mike?"

"Sure, Kid. I agree with you. I don't like it, but I can't deny the facts." Mike turned away and stared out the window. He knew this was not going to go well with the Mayor and the Commissioner. Maybe he should have retired last year, after all.

He had lobbied for the department to let him stay on part-time and teach his classes to the young detectives and the detective candidates. He loved working cases, but teaching the younger cops was more fulfilling than chasing down leads. He knew that the kids called him "Culo de Piedra," which translates to "Ass of Stone." He liked that. As an instructor, he was a hard-ass, but his classes were always full. He lectured on crime scene protocol, evidence collection, chain of custody, how to testify in court, and interrogation technique. He was passing down his knowledge to the next generation. But the Chief said that he could not teach if he was not an active member of the force. Mike suspected that was just a bluff, but he kept both jobs. Today was one of the days he again wished he could just be a full-time teacher. He hated dealing with city politics.

"You should have believed me last month," Jason mumbled under his breath, but loud enough for Mike to hear in the quiet room.

Mike turned his head quickly. "What did you have a month ago, Dickson? Huh? You had three unsolved murders, each with totally different circumstances, victims, methods, and locations. The only things they had in common were that they were unsolved and they all happened on the last Saturday of the month. I'm supposed to go to the Chief and the Mayor with that? It was crazy. It still is, except that I can't in good conscience keep you from taking the theory up the chain now that it's been four months. I'm still not convinced, but I can't say that you're wrong about the pattern." Mike turned away toward the window again, not waiting for any response.

"Why don't you give me more credit, Mike?"

Mike continued to stare out the window at the steamy city. "Because you haven't earned it yet, Kid."

"That's bullshit and you know it!" Jason worked hard to control his tone of voice. Stoneman was his superior, and basically a legend in the department. Jason had attended all of Mike's classes on investigative techniques when he was an aspiring detective. He was hard on all his students, but Jason always thought he was particularly aggressive with the Black officers. "You don't think I deserved my promotion, I know. Fine. I get it. But you have to give me some respect when I'm right."

"You're not right yet. You have a theory. We'll see whether it's accurate, but it's still just speculation," Mike shot back coldly.

"But there is a pattern. I saw it, and you didn't. Nobody did. Am I wrong?" Jason stared at the back of Mike's head, noting the thin patches of hair that revealed the scalp below. He waited patiently, just as Mike had taught him in the classroom, and in their car.

"I can't say you're wrong on this, Dickson. I'm not ready to say you're right, but you might be, and if you are, then it's too important to keep to ourselves. Just don't get cocky, because if you're wrong, the Commissioner is going to remind us both about it for the rest of our careers, and yours has a lot more years left than mine. And if you're right, then we're in for some long nights."

Before Jason could respond, the conference room door opened and three men walked in with sullen looks on their faces. First through the thick door was Police Commissioner Earl Ward. Even with Jason in the room, Ward was easily the best dressed. How he could afford expertly tailored Italian suits on a public servant's salary was a mystery often whispered about around the local station houses. He was as polished in his manners as the mirror shine on his black shoes. Ward was a political animal, and Mike expected a lot of ass-covering from him. He wouldn't know a fingerprint from a blood stain.

Behind Ward was the second Black mayor in the history of the city, Frederick Douglass. He was pursuing an agenda filled with public works projects and social programs. The last thing he needed was a big police matter that would distract the press from his master plan and suck money out of the budget. He frowned, but nodded in Jason's direction. He always supported the Black cops. Always. Jason wondered whether this time would be an exception.

The last man through the door was Captain Edward Sullivan, Mike's unit chief. Sullivan was a ruddy man with large hands and a perpetually red nose. Like every other cop in history named Sullivan, he was called "Sully" by everyone in the precinct. He was a bulldog in supporting his detectives, but he was not the boss in this discussion. Mike correctly anticipated that Sully would have already briefed the Mayor and Commissioner about Jason's theory, which explained why the other two men looked so unhappy.

The Commissioner skipped the formality of introductions and immediately asked Jason to give the Mayor a rundown of his investigation. Jason stood up, buttoned his suit jacket, and began walking toward the front of the room. Ward put up his hand to stop him. "Just sit where you are and give us the facts, Detective."

Jason looked slightly disappointed at being deprived of his moment in the spotlight, but sat back down quickly and began the presentation he had been rehearsing in his head all morning. "Sir, a little more than one month ago there was a homicide involving Pierre LeBlanc, a businessman who owned a drug company. The manner of the killing was quite unusual: he froze to death when he was locked in a cold storage unit in the basement of a restaurant, after first being beaten and tortured. There were no real leads in the case and, after a week, the investigation was turning quite cold, pardon the pun." Jason stopped talking and looked around the conference room. Nobody was laughing.

"One of the detectives handling the case, Steve Berkowitz, mentioned to me that he was frustrated by the investigation. I volunteered to take a look at his file to see if a fresh set of eyes might see something worth pursuing. Detective Berkowitz also shared two other case files that were effectively dormant for lack of any significant leads. When I looked at the files, I noticed something. The LeBlanc murder and the other two all occurred on the last Saturday night of the month. The first was the torture and murder of a businessman from New Jersey named Nicholas DiVito. That one occurred on the last Saturday night of April. Then, on the last Saturday of May, we had the murder of fashion designer Marlene Sheraton. So, we had three unsolved homicides, each one having occurred on the last Saturday of the month for three consecutive months. Although there was nothing in particular about the three cases that suggested a connection, it seemed possible that the timing of the murders might not be a coincidence. And the three murders were all committed under very unusual circumstances."

"Did you report your theory to your captain at that time, Detective?" Ward broke in.

"No, sir," Jason responded meekly. "I discussed the theory with my partner, Detective Stoneman," Jason motioned in Mike's direction. Mike gave no reaction, so Jason continued. "In consultation with Detective Stoneman, we looked further into the three cases and could find nothing about the circumstances, the identities of the victims, the locations of the crime scenes, the murder methods, or anything else that seemed to connect the crimes. The only common factors were that they were each unsolved and with no live leads, and they all occurred on the last Saturday night of the month under odd circumstances. So, we decided that there was not sufficient basis to suspect a serial killer. But, we wanted to see whether the pattern continued this month."

Jason paused, but there were no questions. "Three days ago, on July 28 – the last Saturday night of the month – we had another homicide, and again we have no leads. The circumstances here in the Gallata case are particularly unusual and gruesome. This is consistent with the DiVito murder and with the LeBlanc murder, although admittedly much different from the Sheraton case. We are working under the assumption that the Gallata murder is a mob-related hit on the leader of one of the city's major crime families. For that reason, we suspect a professional killer, and so we're not that surprised that there are few clues and no suspects. We are also getting no cooperation from the victim's family or associates, which makes the absence of leads or suspects, again, not that surprising. While there are reasons to discount this murder as being part of a sequence, we now have four consecutive months with a currently unsolved murder on the last Saturday night. It seems more than merely coincidental, which means that there is a possibility that we have a serial killer on our hands."

Mayor Douglass looked up at the ceiling. Commissioner Ward clasped his hands on the table, then asked, "Detective, is there anything else, aside from the dates of the murders, that leads you to suspect a common perp?"

"No, sir," Jason responded quickly and confidently. "If we had only DiVito, LeBlanc, and Gallata, there could be some commonality in the unusual murder methods and the brutal circumstances. But the Sheraton case has much different characteristics, albeit also out of the ordinary. It's really only the timing that provides the connection."

Douglass now spoke for the first time. "What is your recommendation here, Detective?"

Jason hesitated for only a moment and then responded. "Sir, there is no reason at present to make this public. We don't want folks to panic and start staying home on Saturday nights for fear of being the next victim. I doubt very much that these victims were random or spur-of-the-moment selections. There was far too much planning and preparation needed for each of the cases. But, I think we need to treat this as a possible serial situation and set up a small task force, and we should probably bring in the feds for support."

Commissioner Ward winced visibly. Mike knew well that the Commissioner hated having the feds come in and run his investigations. He also knew that the FBI had resources and manpower that the New York City Police Department could not match under any circumstances, and that putting together an internal task force with the limitations of the City budget would be difficult, if not impossible.

The Mayor was more demonstrative. "I am not having the fucking feds come in and make this into a circus! No. We can never keep it quiet from the press if the goons from D.C. take over. Not happening. Get that thought out of your head, do you hear me?"

Mike nodded and the Commissioner gave his hearty agreement.

Before Jason could even respond with his most formal "Yes, sir," the Mayor stood up and made his way towards the door with Ward on his heels. "Thank you, Detectives," he said, waving his left hand over his shoulder as he disappeared into the corridor.

Dickson, Stoneman, and Sullivan were left alone. "Well, Sully," Mike said, breaking the silence, "looks like we're going to be busy for a while."

"Hopefully not," Sully replied gloomily. "Let's find a perp for one of those homicides and put it to bed fast. Until then, you are now officially a task force of two. I'm reassigning all your pending cases so you can focus on this one. You get nothing new until you close this, so close it quickly."

Mike stood up, stretching his back and craning his neck to the right and then to the left to get the kinks out after sitting for so long. "That would be best, of course, Sully, but even if we don't arrest anyone, the whole thing will die down if we get through the last Saturday of this month without another body."

"Hmmff," Sullivan snorted. "I don't want to wait that long."

Chapter 4 – The Science Never Lies

August 2, 2018

D R. MICHELLE McNEILL pushed her latex-covered hand deeper into the chest cavity, turning her head to the side as she leaned in. She groped around the heart muscle and under the clavicle until she felt a smooth, hard nodule that did not belong there. Carefully pulling it back through the maze of sinew and organs, she extracted the bullet fragment and held it up between her thumb and index finger triumphantly against the harsh, white florescent light. Michelle did not even notice the reddish slime clinging to the metal and the glove as she examined her prize, then tossed it overhand into a metal dish, where it landed with a loud ping.

"Natalie!" McNeill called out.

A diminutive woman of about forty appeared around the corner of the lab, wearing green scrubs that matched McNeill's. She had her sandy-brown hair pulled up under a net, but her clear, hazel eyes sparkled out from behind her rimless glasses. She had worked in the medical examiner's office for just under two years and had proven herself to be diligent, competent, and a pleasant companion, which was just as important as her competency when working in the sterile and never-cheery environment.

"Yes, Doctor McNeill?"

Michelle frowned at her assistant. "Natalie, it's been two years, you can call me Michelle."

Natalie blushed slightly and looked at the floor. "Yes, Doc – Michelle. I'll try to remember."

"Can you please close this up for me? I want to examine this bullet."

"Sure," Natalie responded primly, walking briskly toward the table where the corpse lay with its chest gaping. She picked up a needle and suture and started sewing up Mr. Bernardi, who had been brought in the night before after losing an argument with an as-yet unidentified assailant.

Dr. McNeill scooped up the metal dish containing her prize and walked across the room to a metal-topped table filled with equipment and strewn with notebooks and a few loose sheets of paper. She extracted the bullet fragment with a pair of tweezers and placed it on a microscope slide, which she slid into place under a bulky black instrument. Before peering into the lens, she sorted through the notebooks, looking for one with a fresh right-hand page.

McNeill was pushing fifty, but she refused to admit it. Running five miles three times a week and cross-training at the gym three days kept her in lean shape. At five-three and one hundred sixteen pounds, she could still fit into her college pep squad outfit, not that she had tried it on since graduation. She kept it in the back of the closet with a fantasy of surprising a man someday by popping out of the closet dressed as a sexy cheerleader. But no man had ever lasted long enough to warrant the pom-pom treatment. Her black hair was clipped short, which was practical in her line of work. She kept her nails manicured, but not polished – another concession to the business. If she wanted to, she could paint them red, throw on a skimpy dress, and still turn heads at her twenty-year med school class reunion. Most days, she contented herself with comfortable scrubs and her lab coat, and didn't always notice when male visitors cast interested looks in her direction.

She was just adjusting the light source under her bullet when the swinging doors to the lab burst open, causing her to turn her head and see Mike Stoneman and Jason Dickson walk through. Mike looked around, saw Dr. McNeill, and strode quickly to the table where she was working, with Jason trailing behind. She knew by the look on Mike's face that it was a serious matter.

"Doctor McNeill, can we possibly pull you away from your work for a few minutes on a matter of some urgency?"

Michelle smiled and nodded. "Sure, Detective." She stripped off her latex gloves, set her notebook down on the table, and motioned Mike and Jason toward the back of the room and a well-organized desk with two worn chairs. Mike was a frequent visitor to the lab and made himself at home in the chair nearest to the desk, making Jason walk behind him and slide awkwardly between the chair's back and the wall to get to the far chair. Jason scowled down at the back of Mike's head, knowing full well that Mike could have let him in first to avoid the awkward squeezing, but that he wanted to assert his alpha-dog status in front of the doctor.

"So," Dr. McNeill said as she settled herself into an old leather desk chair, "what brings you in today, Detective Stoneman?"

"We're chasing a phantom," Mike said, "or, rather, Detective Dickson is." Mike jerked his thumb in Jason's direction. "Why don't you fill her in, Kid?"

Jason sat up suddenly in his chair, surprised that Mike was not going to do all the talking like he usually did. "S-Sure," he stammered, composing himself. "We're investigating a possible connection between three murders, or actually four. They all passed through on their way to the morgue and we're hoping that you might be able to help us confirm –"

"—or deny," Mike interjected.

"Right. Confirm or rule out a connection between the cases; something that might indicate a single killer."

Dr. McNeill raised an eyebrow. "You mean a serial?"

"Yes," Jason replied calmly. "I – we – think it's a possibility."

"OK, so which cases do you want me to look at?"

Jason reached into his inside jacket pocket and extracted a list, handwritten on lined paper like notes for a college class. He passed the sheet to the doctor and waited as she perused the information.

"Well, I certainly remember these, Detective. They were unique cases, and certainly high-profile. I gather they all remain unsolved?"

Mike nodded. "Unsolved and seemingly disconnected from everything we have in the files. But Junior here is playing a hunch, so we want to take a fresh look. I'm sure when you were doing the autopsies, they were treated as individual events and you weren't looking for connections. But we want you to review your notes and see if you see anything that might indicate some common component, some possibility that the same killer might have been involved."

Jason jumped back in, trying to reclaim the leading voice in the discussion. "We know that the circumstances of the deaths were very different, and we know that, on the surface, there does not seem to be any pattern or connection. But it's possible, based on other circumstances, and we want to know if you see any physical evidence, or even possibilities." He looked up, hopefully, at the medical examiner.

Dr. McNeill studied the list again, then looked over the heads of the two detectives, deep in thought. On the wall behind the two chairs hung a framed poster of the periodic table of elements. One part of her brain ran through the names of the elements in sequence while another part reviewed her memories of the four murders. They were relatively recent, and they had been memorable. But there was nothing about them that was even remotely similar. "Are you sure these are the right cases?"

Jason sighed slightly and leaned forward in his chair. "There is a pattern – a possible pattern – based on the timing of the murders, certain unusual and brutal characteristics of three of the murders, and the fact that they are all unsolved and lacking any suspects."

"Is that unusual?"

"Well, yes. We don't solve them all, but there is usually at least a suspect, or a theory to explain what happened, and we don't have even that in three of these."

Dr. McNeill looked at Mike for confirmation. Mike shrugged. "It's possible. I'm hoping that you'll tell us that it's not, but I'm still open to all possibilities."

Jason looked at Mike and nodded, almost imperceptibly. Mike nodded back.

"All right," Dr. McNeill said, getting up from her desk chair and walking back toward her microscope. "I'll review the files later today and let you know what I find."

"Let me know when you finish your analysis and we'll come by to get the news."

"I could just send you a report in an email," McNeill suggested.

"No, we'd like to keep away from any paper trail on this and would prefer to discuss it in person, if possible."

Michelle smiled. "That would be fine, Detective." Mike smiled, too. He liked spending time with the M.E. She was smart, and funny, and she looked nice in her scrubs.

Chapter 5 – The Grieving Widow

August 3, 2018

"**A**RE YOU GOING TO LET ME take lead here, Mike?" Jason glanced at Mike, who was sitting silently in the passenger seat of their Ford Taurus. They had left the station seven minutes earlier bound for the New Jersey home of the late Nicholas DiVito.

DiVito's body had been found on April 28th in a maintenance room under the West Side Highway, missing most of the fingers on one hand and most of the other arm. A manual crank meat grinder was left at the scene, filled with the man's flesh and bones. The medical examiner had determined that he was alive when his arms were mutilated and that he bled out, which was the cause of death. They had been reviewing the file, now that it was formally assigned to the Task Force. The murder was unsolved, but during the investigation the detectives had interviewed the office manager at DiVito's factory in New Jersey and learned that one of his workers had died in an industrial accident that had mangled her arm and left her to bleed out.

After completing interviews with the few employees who were available, the prevailing theory was that the dead worker's relatives from Venezuela came up North to take care of the man whom they blamed for the death of their sister, or daughter, or whatever. It had been a professional job, with few clues left at the crime scene. It was a very cold case. The feds were tracking down the circumstances of how the dead woman had entered the country. When Mike inquired quietly about the status of that investigation he was told they had nothing so far, but they were watching a few people. Nothing that would help Mike and Jason.

It wasn't that often that they left New York, but now they were approaching the George Washington Bridge and the silence was eating at Jason.

"It's your theory, so it's your show. You take the lead."

"Okay. Now, she's the grieving widow here, but it's been three months and, from what we know, the guy was not much of a gentleman. So I'm thinking that I don't need to treat her gently today and I can ask her about her husband's activities without expecting a waterworks. You agree?"

"It's your call, Kid," Mike said flatly.

"Why do you do that?"

"What?"

Jason turned toward Mike, careful to keep an eye on the traffic ahead of him on the West Side Highway. "You call me 'Kid' or 'Rook' or 'Skippy' or some shit and I know you're doing it to keep me in my place, to make sure I know that you're the senior detective and you have experience and you're in charge and I'm just the new guy and I get that. But why do you treat me like I'm wasting your time or like you can't be bothered to help me? I'm asking for your advice because I recognize that you have more experience in these situations, and I value your input, and I want to learn from you. Isn't that the way the junior detective is supposed to act?" Jason changed lanes suddenly, prompting a honk from the driver he had just cut off.

Mike sat silently, staring straight ahead. "Most of the time, you act like you already know everything and you don't need my help, so I leave you to it."

Jason slowed to a crawl around the helix leading to the merge onto the bridge deck, and took the opportunity to turn full face toward Mike, more aggressively than he intended. "Are you telling me that I have a bad attitude?"

"Watch the road, Rook."

"See — there it is again. You could call me Jason, or JD, or partner, you know. Every once in a while, just for a change. We've been partners for almost six months."

"You think you've earned that?"

"I think I earned that when I made detective. I'm not some beat cop you can boss around and ignore. Like it or not, I'm your partner and I deserve to be treated like one."

Jason was not looking at Mike now, just at the four lanes of traffic slowly accelerating toward mid-span. He glanced to his left to see the Manhattan skyline and the sun glinting off the Hudson river. He didn't have that many opportunities to see the skyline from this vantage. The tall buildings stretched down the shore until they merged together into a mass, with the tower at One World Trade Center sticking up from the glass-and-metal scrum. He thought that the people living on the Jersey side of the river had a better view than the more expensive real estate on the Manhattan side.

"You think you earned it? You think you deserved to be promoted?" Mike's voice was even and calm, like he was teaching one of his crime scene classes at the police academy.

Jason paused before answering, wanting to control his tone. "Yes, Mike, I'm quite sure that I earned my promotion. I took all the classes — yours included — and I did all the legwork when I was in a black & white on a beat. I passed the exams. I'm a damned good cop and, yes, I deserved the promotion. Why? Don't you think so?"

"It's not about what I think. It's what you think that matters."

"What kind of bullshit is that?"

"The only kind you're going to get today."

"What is wrong with you, Mike?"

"Drop it."

"Fine." Jason eased the car into the left lane, aiming for the express lanes toward I-80. He drove in silence for another five minutes before they had merged onto the Interstate and had a good ten miles before their exit.

"Do you even know why we're doing this?" Mike asked.

"Yes, I do, Detective Stoneman," Jason replied dryly. "We're covering the ground that Berkowitz and Mason already plowed when they were originally assigned to the case. They got nowhere, of course. The relatives of the dead girl with the mangled arm were the chief suspects. The working theory was that they came up from Venezuela and got revenge by mutilating the factory owner. It made sense given that the guy's arm was run through a meat grinder, but they found nothing pointing to any suspects. The woman was not in the country legally. It was not even entirely clear whether she had come to the United States voluntarily. One of the other workers in the factory claimed that some of the women had been abducted and brought to the country in the backs of trucks. They all were forced to work for DiVito under the whip of the plant foreman, a scumbag named Rodriguez who was wanted by the feds on drug running charges.

"The operations of NiDi Exports, Ltd. were shut down and the assets confiscated. Rodriguez was unsurprisingly absent when the detectives showed up to interview the staff. Berkowitz and Mason ruled out the wife, not that she likely would have done it herself, and then the trail got cold and they marked it unsolved and moved on. But now, you and I are coming back and looking at the file from a different angle. What if it wasn't a relative from Venezuela, but rather a serial killer who chose this guy to be his first kill? We can look at the same facts, but now with the context of the serial angle, and we might find things that they missed. That's what we're doing."

Mike scratched his chin and gave a silent nod. He said, "Right," without emotion and then fell silent again.

"So, what do you think about the wife?"

"What about her?"

"About what I was saying before — about how to approach her today. I'm trying to figure out the best way to angle the questions about her dead husband."

"It's not going to matter. You're either going to make her cry or make her scream at you — either way is fine. The more emotion, the better. She'll be more likely to tell the truth if she's upset."

"That's not the standard protocol, is it, Mike? I recall in classes you told us to stay calm and keep the witnesses calm unless we were trying to get a confession or trip somebody up. This woman is not a suspect, so why should I intentionally try to upset her?"

"I didn't say you should try. I just said it's likely that no matter what you do, it will upset her, so don't sweat it."

Jason pondered Mike's advice as they drove in silence. Eventually they reached Montville, New Jersey and pulled into a sleepy side street with huge oak trees lining the sidewalks at precise intervals. The houses were spaced far apart and each sat back on its plot, leaving room for sweeping driveways and rolling lawns of manicured Kentucky blue grass. Jason eased the Taurus to a stop in front of a white colonial with Doric columns framing a massive mahogany-and-glass double doorway. They walked without speaking up a curving stone path to the porch, past carefully trimmed hedges and flower beds rising out of deep black mulch with no perceptible weeds. Somebody was paying the gardener well.

The bell was an imitation of the church bells of St. Peter's in Rome and echoed around the inside of the huge foyer as the two detectives waited. "At least there's no dog," Mike deadpanned.

After a long wait, Jason saw a shadowy figure coming down the hallway toward the door through the frosted glass sidewall. The edifice swung inwards and revealed the slender form of a woman Jason presumed to be Mrs. Helene DiVito. She was wearing tight jeans and a loose-fitting top with spaghetti straps, showing off her toned shoulders and a healthy amount of what Jason assumed was surgically augmented cleavage. Bright blonde hair hung down loosely and pooled beneath her ears. An officer had called the house earlier to confirm that the widow DiVito would be home, and she looked like she was expecting guests. She also sported high-heeled sandals and well-applied makeup, as if planning to go out for the day soon.

"Mrs. DiVito?" he inquired politely. She nodded, but with a quizzical frown. "I'm Detective Dickson, New York Homicide." He held out his badge and ID at full arm's length. "This is my partner, Detective Stoneman," he nodded toward Mike, who inclined his head toward the woman. "We're here to ask you a few questions connected to your husband's death back in April."

The woman standing across from Jason looked much younger than her dead husband. She stepped back, swinging the door open wider, and asked them to please come inside. She led them to a sitting room just off the entry foyer and asked if they would like anything to drink. When both men declined, she said "Suit yourself, but I'm having one." She scooped up an oversized wine glass from a marble counter, half-filled with white wine. She sauntered over to a leather-covered chair, crossed her long legs, and sipped her wine as if they were there for book club.

Mike sat back on a very comfortable sofa and crossed his arms, letting Jason sit on the edge of his cushion and lead the questioning.

"Mrs. DiVito," Jason began in as comforting a voice as he could muster, "I know that you already spoke to Detective Mason after your husband's death, and I'm sorry to have to bother you again, but we're doing some follow-up and just want to go over a few things."

"Of course," Ms. DiVito said, now sitting back in the well-stuffed chair opposite Jason. A glass-and-marble coffee table sat between them, adorned by a Dansk china tea service that appeared to have never been used for actual tea. The room had a hushed and muffled feeling to it, owing to the plush carpet and thick wallpaper. Jason thought that Mike's concerns about the wife breaking into tears were misplaced. He wondered if she would get angry, like Mike had predicted.

"Ma'am, do you know whether your husband ever had any business dealings with Ms. Marlene Sheraton or Mr. Pierre LeBlanc?" Jason reached into a briefcase and hauled out eight-by-ten photos of the other victims. Live photos, with smiling faces. Not the crime scene photos.

Ms. DiVito studied them for a few seconds each before shaking her head and saying, "No, no, I don't recognize the faces or the names, Officer."

"Detective, actually," Jason corrected smoothly. "What about Mickey Gallata, sometimes known as Slick Mick."

Ms. DiVito's brows wrinkled in recognition. "Well, I'm sure I've heard that name. He died recently, didn't he? I heard about that on the news. You don't think that my Nick had anything to do with him, do you? Ha." She laughed derisively, waving a hand in the air and suddenly becoming more animated. "That's rich. Nick always dreamed that he'd be powerful enough that somebody like Gallata would notice him. He watched The Sopranos and The Godfather and all that crap. He wanted to be a Wise Guy. Oh, he'd be thrilled to know that two cops are asking about whether he was connected to a guy like that. Wow."

She paused, looking down at the pristine carpeting. Jason let her have her moment without interruption. It was one of Mike's lessons — never fill the silence. When the witness is in mid-thought, let her keep thinking without the distraction of another question. She looked up and laughed again, harder this time. "Wow. That is a fucking joke. Nick was a wannabe gangster. He tried to act like a big shot at the golf club and pretend that he had connections in New York, but the truth is that he had business contacts and that was it. He didn't really know anybody in organized crime. I'd know. He was a poser. He tried to tell himself that cheating his clients and screwing his employees made him a badass, but it really just made him an asshole. He did some kind of shady business with a guy in Brooklyn who does some kind of business with South America, but he was no gangster."

Jason couldn't help himself and broke into the monologue. "Ms. DiVito, is it possible that he came into contact with Mr. Gallata or someone in his organization sometime shortly before his death?"

"Not a chance," she responded quickly. "If Nick had lunch in the same restaurant as a real gangster, he would have been telling me about it nonstop for days. He wasn't capable of keeping something like that to himself."

"What about his contact in Brooklyn? Do you know the man's name, or anything about the business?"

The woman gracefully crossed her left leg over her right as she pondered the question. She placed her left hand on her knee, flashing a huge rectangular-cut diamond ring below shiny, blood-red nails. Jason tried not to stare. "I can't remember. It was Helman, or Nielson, or something like that. Nick was always trying to make it seem like something important, but he never told me anything specific."

"Was there anything strange about his behavior in the days leading up to the murder?"

She paused and thought for a few more moments, balancing the white sandal that dangled from the end of her left foot. "The other detective asked me that also, and at the time I said no. There really was nothing. He had his routine and he kept to it pretty much like clockwork. He didn't deviate from anything or act funny or concerned. If you had wanted to find him at four-fifteen in the afternoon on a Saturday, I could have told you exactly where to go and you would have found him there. The man was like a human metronome."

Jason broke in again. "So, if I were a killer and I were targeting your husband, you're saying that it would not have been difficult to predict where he would be at a particular time?"

"Hardly! You could have put a bomb in his car on a timer and have it blow up exactly when he turned into the driveway."

"Sounds like you thought of that."

"Oh, you betcha I thought about it. I planned how to kill him a hundred times — not that I would have ever done it, you know, but sure, I thought about it. He was a scumbag and a shitty lover and I'm glad he's dead. He didn't even leave me any money. His business that was supposed to be so great was using illegal workers and the immigration service froze all his assets. They'll probably fine the shit out of the company, which is now totally shut down and filing for bankruptcy. They already shut down the warehouse in Queens and I found out the land has two mortgages and the bank is foreclosing. So, I sleep with the guy for five years and I get squat. Is that not a polite thing for me to say?" She glared at Jason, daring him to judge her.

"Ma'am, I have no reason to doubt your opinion of the man. Nevertheless, we're trying to figure out who killed him."

"Well, if you find out, give the guy a high five for me, will you?" She stood up, indicating that she thought the interview was over. "I'm sorry to say that I have an appointment and really need to get ready to leave, so if there isn't anything else, gentlemen."

The big man stood stiffly and said, "No, ma'am, that's all for now." She escorted them to the door and wished them well in their hunt for her husband's killer.

On the way back to the car, Mike spoke for the first time since their arrival. "What's your evaluation, Detective?"

Jason stopped on his side of the Taurus, looking back over the top of the car at his partner, who was poised with his hand on the door handle. "I think if she didn't have a great alibi, she'd be a suspect, although I would hardly blame her."

"Fair," Mike acknowledged. "What else?"

"The point about the husband being a creature of habit was not in the original report. It suggests that if somebody was looking to ice him, it wouldn't have been hard to ambush him and then drag him away. Not that this really helps us that much, since we already figured that he was taken to the kill site after he was drugged and tied up. But, if we are dealing with one killer, it expands his window of opportunity to have stalked the victim."

"But what about his car?"

Jason blinked blankly.

"The guy's car was found in a lot in Manhattan. If DiVito was taken in Jersey, then either the killer drove it there, or somebody else drove it to that garage."

"True," Jason acknowledged. "I guess that suggests an abduction in New York, then."

"Or a job pulled off by multiple perps, who were smart enough to leave the car in Manhattan to throw us off the trail."

"If he had no connection to Gallata or any of the other victims, then why would a serial killer go to such elaborate lengths to stalk, abduct, and execute him in such a bizarre way? Was he just trying to throw us off the trail by making it look like it was the Venezuelans? Could a serial killer be that smart?"

Mike pondered that for a minute. "Don't underestimate a killer's intelligence, or underestimate how stupid he could be. Maybe he knew the dead girl."

"Then why go on a spree after you get your revenge against Mr. DiScumbag?"

"To cover his tracks and make us think he's not related to her." Mike stood there, dead serious, for five seconds before cracking. "OK, that's not likely."

"Well, if he was knocked off by the pissed-off Venezuelan relatives of the dead factory worker, then that's not consistent with it being the first hit by a serial killer." Jason dejectedly got into the car.

Mike opened the door and got into the passenger seat. Before Jason snapped his seatbelt, Mike spoke again. "I agree with your analysis, JD. However, nothing that happened today poked any holes in your serial killer theory, and a few things actually propped it up a bit. The guy's predictability made him an easy mark for a single killer. A bunch of thugs or angry brothers from Venezuela would not have staked him out, captured him in Manhattan, and then tortured and killed him there. They would have grabbed him here and killed him here and gotten the Hell out of the country. The Venezuela gang theory is weak, which leaves your serial killer as plausible. We're still a long way from making that theory a likelihood, but it's still on the table."

Jason said nothing for a full minute as he maneuvered the Taurus out of the neighborhood and back toward the highway. "Thanks, Mike."

"For what?"

"For calling me JD instead of Kid or Junior, and for keeping an open mind."

"My mind's always open. There's a lot of shit in there, but it's always open for more deposits."

Chapter 6 – The Wicked Shall Perish

April 29, 2018

*A*BEL IS DEAD. *As I sit here in my quiet place, the trumpets of Heaven still echo in my ears and the blood rushing through my body still tingles with excitement. Never before have I felt such a holy thrill. My breathing is controlled and my appearance is normal. None who saw me in the aftermath would give a moment's thought that anything was out of the ordinary. I have no regrets and no doubt that everything was perfect. I wish only that the world knew now what I have done and could appreciate the masterwork. Study and examine my deeds of glory. I know not where I will be when anyone finally reads these pages, but my legacy will survive any travails that might befall me. Even if death shall be my fate, my words will live eternally. And so you shall know the story.*

I knew Able had a rendezvous with his mistress in New York. I knew exactly what parking garage he would go to, where he was so brazen that he rented a monthly space across the street from his paramour's apartment. So many careless fools like Abel chronicle their lives in their emails and on their social media pages where anyone with a brain and a tiny amount of skill can access their innermost thoughts and follow their movements with precision. It was so easy to park nearby, and yet so difficult to wait.

Knowing where he would be, I pulled up to the curb between the garage and the corner and waited for him to emerge from the underground lot. I was outside my vehicle when he came pacing down the sidewalk. I called out to him by name. He came up close to me, relaxed and totally off guard when I injected him with the tranquilizer and hustled him into my car. The perfect abduction.

When Abel awoke, he was still groggy from the drug and only slowly gained a full realization of his predicament. I had tied his hands to the sides of a bulky wooden chair, in an awkward position where the sides of his forearms dug painfully into the arm of the chair. His legs were similarly lashed to the legs of the chair, making him quite immobile. I had secured his midsection to the back with multiple revolutions of duct tape and his neck was pulled back by a similar twine so that his head could not droop, nor turn easily. I had filled his mouth with a wad of handkerchief taken from his suit jacket and then secured it with more tape, so that he could not make much of a sound besides a low whine. When he began thrashing about in an attempt to move the chair and his pitiful moans became louder, I knew that he was fully recovered from the anesthesia and ready for his repentance.

I'm sure that the sight of me confused him at first. The surgical mask covering my face and the matching blue head covering, combined with my white butcher's apron and long yellow rubber gloves, must have made me a shocking sight. His eyes bulged and the veins in his neck throbbed in his anger. How dare I confine him so? Who was I? It was clear to me that he felt anger and rage, rather than fear. That would quickly change.

I had scouted the location carefully and was so happy with the result. There is an underpass beneath a bridge, just off the outskirts of a park. The underpass is never very busy, but after dark on a Saturday night it is fairly well deserted, and if you are inclined to detour around some traffic barriers you can drive a car under the highway and park it there. Embedded in the brick archway beneath the road is a door leading to a small utility room, where there are electrical circuit boxes as well as supplies for cleaning crews, traffic cones, spare light bulbs and grate covers, and other such items for the municipal workers who might need them. The lock on the door was not hard to break, since there was nothing of value inside to protect. I'm sure I could have secured a master key or picked the lock, but in the interest of time I simply brought along a large bolt cutter, which I left in a corner of the room as if it belonged there. I wonder whether the police will even notice it.

The room itself was cramped and stuffy with an odor of mold, but there was a dim light overhead and enough space for me and the chair, which I had purchased from a storefront the day before and left in the bushes next to the overpass. I had a spare folding chair in my car just in case, but this one was so sturdy and solid that I had hoped it would remain un-confiscated by the local street people. The Lord ensured that it was still there upon my arrival.

I explained to Abel that he was to be punished for his sins. He furrowed his brow as he tried to shout at me through his wordless mouth, still angry and not yet fully given over to fear. I spoke of the deaths of his two workers. One fell from the top of a pressing machine that lacked a safety rail. The other had the sleeve of her garment caught between the rollers of a different machine, which sucked her arm into the maw of the grinder. There was no safety guard, and no one monitored the hazard that such a loose-fitting sleeve posed to the worker. By the time the machine was stopped, her arm had been severed and she bled to death before an ambulance arrived. Abel actually looked puzzled as I recited the facts as if he was unaware, which I know he was not.

I explained that although the criminal and civil justice systems had failed to punish him for his sins, God was still watching, and that I was the Angel of Vengeance and Justice who would mete out his punishment. It was at that moment that I saw the expression on Abel's face change from rage to fear. I saw him attempt to shake his head, confined by his bindings. His eyes grew wide and he began to sweat from his temples. He struggled with his arms and legs, but to no avail.

I spoke softly but clearly, so that he would understand and know how to plead when he faced God. I told him that I knew how he exploited his workers. I scolded him for his use of illegals and the payments he made to the couriers who brought fresh meat to his workplace prison. While I spoke, I was preparing. I pulled over a small table and set my meat grinder upon it. Abel again looked confused, but this time a fearful puzzlement. I set down a pair of garden shears and a small hacksaw. Abel's face was white and drained of blood by the time I finished my preparations, and I could see him finally begin to realize that I was not there to rob him or hold him for ransom.

I was taken a bit by surprise at the amount of blood flowing from his mangled arm, but then I understood better how the poor young lady had bled to death so quickly. Abel was crying like a baby. His moans had become soft and muffled, as if he finally understood that he was shortly to have an audience with the Almighty.

At one point, Abel passed out from the fear and pain and loss of blood, but I was able to revive him before the very end. I then left my sign on his body. As he bled from numerous wounds, I took an empty syringe and used it to collect the flow. Just an ounce or so, which I mixed with water from a small bottle I had brought along. Abel was weak by then, and so I removed the tape from his mouth and extracted the cloth. I offered him a drink of water, which he accepted greedily. Then I put the syringe into his mouth, like an infant being fed unpleasant medicine. I pushed the plunger, expelling his blood into his throat, and then held his mouth closed and pinched his nose shut, forcing him to swallow in order to breathe.

My work done, I began to clean up my mess as the life bled out of Abel.

Into a black garbage bag went the tools I had used, his stray bits, and the drop cloth that had captured most of Abel's blood. I removed his bindings and put the used tape into the bag. Finally, into the bag went my gloves, smock, and facemask. Then the first bag into a second bag, all tied neatly with a plastic zip-tie acquired at the Home Depot. The grinder, still dripping with Abel's hot blood, I left on the floor next to the chair so that the people will know the suffering he endured, which may give some small comfort to the family of Abel's victims. I shut off the light but left the door slightly ajar, now having no lock. I walked down to the edge of the river, where I punctured the garbage bags a few times with a ball point pen and dropped the grisly load into the murky water of the Hudson.

When the sun sets, I will watch the news broadcasts at my workplace to see what they say about the evil one who is now gone from the world. And I will watch how the police will be befuddled, and ultimately will not care who claimed the soul of this demon on Earth.

Now I will sleep, peacefully and soundly, having completed my task and feeling beloved in the eyes of God.

April 30

Oh, joy and satisfaction! The press is awash with false grief and laughable indignation over the death of poor Able, whom no one loved. The police have no suspects and no clues. Of course not! I left them none. I can hear the wails of fear bleeding through the newspapers and seeping from the television screen. What a lovely day. Soon, as the police investigate, they will discover his illegal business activities, and perhaps they will even free his captive workers. There will be no suspicion that Abel's death was the work of the Angel of the Lord. But you, dear readers, will know one day. You will understand. You will appreciate the glorious vengeance of the Almighty.

One has met God. Nine more steps lie ahead in my ascension to Heaven. Let the glory of God shine its light on the goodness in the world as evil vanishes. I am eager to continue my quest.

Chapter 7 – Strange Poison

August 6, 2018

"**W**HY ARE WE GOING BACK TO THE M.E.?" Jason asked Mike as they emerged from the subway in lower Manhattan and walked toward the morgue and forensics lab.

"What if I just like visiting?" Mike suggested.

"Oh, I already know that you like visiting the lovely Doctor McNeill, Mike. That's pretty obvious to anyone with eyes."

Mike stopped short, causing Jason to stop and turn. "Is that true? Is it really that obvious?"

"Yes, it is," Jason said. "You get all friendly and casual. You laugh at anything she says that's remotely funny. You lean on her desk. You're a totally different person when you're in that lab, like you've never been near a woman before."

"Wow," was all Mike could say. He resumed walking in silence until they had nearly reached their destination. When they got to the outer door of the lab, Mike rested his hand on the handle. "Do me a favor, will ya? If you see me acting like an adolescent boy in there, cough or sneeze or something to let me know. Can you do that?"

"Sure, Mike. I'll cough a few times as soon as we get inside to establish that I have something going on in my chest, so it's not obvious if I do it again."

"That's pretty devious," Mike said. "Thanks."

Inside, the two detectives stood in silence as they waited for Dr. McNeill to finish dictating the details of the autopsy she was performing. After a few minutes, she clicked off her hand-held recorder, stripped off her latex gloves, and walked away from the steel table and surrounding rolling carts precisely arranged with her tools. She smiled at Mike and Jason as she breezed past them toward her desk area in the corner. Mike and Jason walked behind her.

"You guys always come in at the best times. That poor man there came in last night and the detectives thought that his wife's story about him having a heart attack at the dinner table didn't feel right. I think they may be on to something, although it's too early to make a conclusive determination since I'm not really finished yet, and the tox screen needs to come back first and I need to examine his medical history, which hasn't come over from the hospital yet, but I –"

Jason coughed loudly, covering his mouth with a handkerchief that he expertly extracted from his jacket pocket just in time. "Sorry," he said, "I'm just getting over a cold."

McNeill stopped talking and stared at her two visitors. "Am I babbling?"

"No," Mike said. "I'm sure it's a fascinating case. It's just not ours."

"Sorry. What was it that you wanted to talk about today, boys?"

"Don't you think it's demeaning, to refer to a full-grown Black man like Detective Dickson as 'boy' in the twenty-first century?"

McNeill looked shocked for a moment, then her expression mutated into a scolding frown, followed by a playful smile. "Are you ribbing me, Detective?"

"Well, maybe just a little."

Jason coughed again. Mike shot him a disapproving look, but then steadied himself, realizing that he was smiling at the doctor. He assumed a more professional posture before speaking. "Doctor,

I know we already asked you to look into those four cases, but –"

"Which I will do, but have not had time yet," she quickly interjected.

"Of course, yes, we don't expect you to have done that already. But as you do, we have a few specific questions about one of them because we're re-opening the case and we're going to be interviewing a few witnesses today. I want to make sure I fully understand the M.E. report, and we want to bounce a few ideas off you, if you have a few minutes."

"Sure, Detective. Always happy to spend a little time talking to people who aren't dead."

Mike laughed heartily at the obvious coroner humor, prompting another cough from Jason. Mike pressed on. "We're looking at the death of Marlene Sheraton, the fashion designer."

"Oh, yes, that one was quite unusual. I gather that you haven't figured out who poisoned her?"

"No, we haven't," Mike replied meekly. "That wasn't our case either, until now, so I take no personal offense at that comment."

McNeill now laughed at Mike's weak joke, prompting Jason to roll his eyes, which Mike saw and hoped that the doctor missed.

"In any case," Mike continued, "the M.E. report says that the cause of death was a poison that was delivered by scratching the victim's skin with some kind of knife or sharp edge that was coated with the stuff – like a poison dart. At the time of the original investigation, the exact poison was not determined. The focus was on trying to find suspects who might have delivered the poison, regardless of the exact chemical agent. So, the first question we have is whether you ever got back the tox report to isolate the poison. Our file doesn't list that information."

"I'm not surprised," Dr. McNeill said as she sat down at her desk and reached to open the bottom-right drawer, from which she quickly extracted an orange file folder. She carefully placed the folder on her desk and opened it so that it was perfectly centered on her black blotter. She glanced at the topmost sheet of paper for a moment and frowned. "I do recall that there was still some doubt about the poison. We sent it out to the CDC in Atlanta to get a more definitive analysis and it hasn't come back yet. I guess the detectives investigating the case were not really focused on it. Should they be?"

"We're not sure," Jason interjected. "Every possible suspect seems to have an alibi for the afternoon, except her household help, and they don't have much of a motive to kill their meal ticket. But it could have happened before she even got to the building, so anyone on the street who had contact with her that day could have scratched her."

"I doubt that," McNeill cut in. "Even without a completely definitive ID on the poison, I can tell you that it is very likely something that was fast-acting, not something that could have been administered in the morning that just happened to kill her when she got home. Based on the descriptions of her symptoms, I'd say it is extremely likely that she was poisoned within a few minutes of when she arrived home."

"OK," Jason charged ahead, "so, let's assume somebody had contact with her – maybe right outside the building, maybe in the lobby – the killer scratches her arm and dispenses the poison. What kind of weapon would he need for that?"

McNeill thought about it for a few seconds before responding. "Really, it could be anything with an edge or a point. A small knife, a needle, a razor blade, even something like a belt buckle or a watch band could do it if you put a sharp edge on it. All you need to do is break the skin with a surface that is coated with the toxin."

"How much toxin is required to kill someone?" Mike asked.

"If this is what I think it is, then only a very, very small amount."

"What do you think it is?" Jason asked expectantly.

"Detective, I can't be sure without the supplemental tox report. What we got back didn't match any commonly available poison. It had some very unusual proteins. I would be speculating."

"We're not going to hold you to an opinion, Doctor. Right now, we're open to speculation." Mike leaned forward and put a hand on her desk, but then backed off into a standing position.

"Well, I don't think it's synthetic and I don't think it's plant-based. I'm guessing that it's some kind of venom, which is difficult to isolate."

"Venom?" Jason muttered. "How would someone in New York get his hands on something like that?"

Dr. McNeill shrugged. "I wouldn't have the slightest idea, Detective, but in this world if you have money and an internet connection, you can get pretty much anything."

Mike jumped in. "Doctor, what would be the advantage of using venom rather than a chemical agent or arsenic or something easier to come by?"

Dr. McNeill thought about this question for thirty seconds in silence, and then said, "This was a particularly fast-acting poison, which required only a small scratch to introduce it into the blood stream, unlike a lot of other poisons that have to be ingested. But, trying to find a specific reason why this killer would choose this particular poison is beyond me."

With nothing left to banter about, Mike and Jason said goodbye. Jason coughed once more when Mike lingered behind him in order to say a private farewell to the M.E. Eventually, they made it to the exit and headed up the East Side.

Chapter 8 – All About Eve

May 5, 2018

*T*HE NEXT JEWEL *in my crown of thorns will be a woman. I have waited and bided my time for this triumph. The Lord will guide my mind and my hand, but I must not delay, for more preparations must be made. My path is settled. The method of termination for the second vermin who must die was long ago ordained, and it will establish the pattern that only God can see.*

Among the most evil creatures, men predominate. But down in the slime among them there are some females who vie for dominion over the netherworld. One such creature has made herself known to me, and she is the embodiment of all things in this world that need to die. She is Eve. She will be made to pay for her sins.

She is the embodiment of fashion, style, and wealth, and her sophistication and even philanthropy mask her true nature. She markets clothing to teenage girls and young women who want to emulate her style, but they know not what they covet. She does not design her garments, nor make them. She is merely the figurehead. But she funds the operation and sources the labor to sweatshops in Vietnam and China. Her laborers are often young girls who work sixteen-hour days in awful conditions. Death, disease, and injury are common, and wages are meager. The exploitation of these workers happens without a second thought from Eve, who knows full well what the costs of the manufacturing process are, and yet accepts them as a boost to her profit margin. She does not visit her factory, nor does she impose any standards for the labor force or for safety or benefits for her workers. She is the exploiter and she has no guilt.

Most virulent is the poison that infects virtually every worker. Their sweat absorbs the inks and heavy metals with which Eve adorns her garments of death. They do not drop dead in numbers, nor can you see blood or broken limbs. No, the silent killer infects and poisons over months and years, even infecting the suckling babes whose mothers' milk is tainted with the chemicals of modern luxury. Yet Eve cares not.

I have read Eve's innermost thoughts and private communications. She was easy. Her password is the name of her sister. She lacks common sense as she lacks a conscience. God brought me to her, and I shall bring her to God.

Eve lives the easy life buoyed by wealth and privilege. But she is the virus that infects our society. She is vile and yet revered and admired. Soon her supplicants will understand that justice will not be denied. Her infection shall not incur the pain and agony of her victims, but death is death, and judgment is glorious.

May 19

Eve is not an elusive prey. I can hardly avoid knowing her schedule and movements; there was no need to hack her computer or email, but only to read the society pages. More difficult is to find her alone, which she almost never is. But I have discovered a weakness in her defenses that will prove sufficient for her final downfall. I wonder whether anyone will ever even know. It saddens me that the press coverage may be less dramatic and satisfying than in the case of Abel. But I must be careful.

I needed to isolate Abel and remove him to a private space. This was difficult and dangerous, presenting the possibility of being observed and perhaps even captured. Eve's death will be much less hands-on, and much less of a risk. I regret that I will not be able to enjoy the throes of her death, nor shall I see the fear and anguish in her eyes. I will not be able to mark her body, but that will only further obscure my presence. She will not know that I am the Angel of Death and the messenger of the Lord. I will make up for missing the adrenaline rush later, but for now the mission is the key, and the Lord will reward me a hundred fold.

The beauty of my method is that it both fits perfectly into my pattern and allows me to bring Eve to her end with barely a touch. Contact is required, of course, but contact that can happen casually. I need only a second. It is helpful that her clothes nearly always expose her arms and shoulders, and often her back and legs. Bare skin is all I need. A scratch. It is so easy. I have been tracking her movements and her patterns. I will not fail.

Chapter 9 – It's a Dog's Life

August 6, 2018

THE NUMBER 6 TRAIN pulled into the station at City Hall just as Jason and Mike hit the bottom step after leaving the M.E.'s lab. They were strolling into the plush lobby of 505 Fifth Avenue barely fifteen minutes later. The doorman was expecting them due to a phone call from Steve Berkowitz, one of the detectives who had been assigned to the original investigation. Berkowitz was happy to pass on the very cold case to Stoneman and Dickson and clear it off his roster of unsolved murders. Mike flashed his badge and he and Jason were ushered to the elevator. The bell chimed the tones of Ode to Joy at the apartment of the former CEO of Stardust Fashions. Marlene Sheraton's personal assistant, d'Angela Foster, was already waiting for them beyond the open apartment door.

The interior of the apartment was as lavish as any that Mike had ever seen, and he had seen plenty. A Steinway grand piano was the centerpiece of the living room, which was as large as the entire bullpen at the precinct building and framed by huge windows exposing an expansive and spectacular view of Central Park. Mike could make out the softball fields beneath the apartment buildings on Central Park West. Oil paintings hung on the walls in gilt frames. Mike was no art expert, but he suspected that many of them could have been hanging in the Museum of

Modern Art, although he was not a fan of abstracts. An Oriental rug covered most of the blond hardwood floor and all the furniture was matched to the color of the gold-laced wallpaper. Mike and Jason planted themselves carefully in high-backed armchairs in front of a cut-glass coffee table as the assistant sat casually on the crushed velvet surface of the opposite sofa.

d'Angela Foster was a striking young woman who looked to be in her mid-twenties, but careful makeup and tailored suits can skew such estimates. Her ebony hair was pulled straight back and into a severe bun, which accentuated her long, mocha-colored neck and the drops of diamonds hanging on long gold chains from her ears. A shiny, high-heeled pump dangled loosely from her left foot as it hung over the edge of the sofa; its motion up and down held Jason's gaze as if he were being hypnotized.

Mike was less mesmerized, and so he took the lead in the questioning. I know that you already spoke to Detectives Berkowitz and Mason after Ms. Sheraton's death, but we want to ask a few more questions in light of some new information."

"What kind of new information?"

"I'm not really at liberty to share that with you, Ms. Foster, but it is not directly related to this case so it's nothing that should concern you at this point. If I were stalking Ms. Sheraton, trying to figure out when and where I could get close enough to make physical contact with her, what would I have seen in her daily patterns in the weeks leading up to the assault?"

Foster went silent and looked off into the distance, in the direction of the kitchen rather than out the windows as she thought. She reached into an inner pocket of her tailored suit jacket and pulled out her phone, then scrolled carefully through a number of screens that Mike could not see and started making notes on the paper. Mike and Jason held their tongues, waiting for her to finish her work.

"Detective, I can see from her calendar that she had different destinations just about every night. On each day, she would have left this building by getting into a car at the curb to leave for her office or her first appointment. Someone watching the building might have seen her for a few seconds, but that's it. Each afternoon, she would come back here to change clothes before her evening appointments. Again, she would have arrived by car and walked only from the curb to the door. Then she would leave again, except for the seventeenth, when she stayed home all evening with a migraine headache."

Mike and Jason absorbed the information. "What time of day did she come back to the apartment?" Mike asked.

"It would be generally between five and six o'clock, I guess. Usually on the earlier side, since she liked to relax at home a bit before heading out to whatever event she was attending. Sometimes she even took a bath in the afternoon. So, she liked to get home earlier when she could."

"OK," Mike said with finality. "If we assume, as has been the working theory, that the poison was administered only a few minutes before her death, then it would have been somewhere between four-forty-five and five-fifteen. If I were the killer and I wanted to make contact with her, my best opportunity would have been between the time she stepped out of her car out front and the time she arrived back here in the apartment. Except there's a security camera out on the sidewalk – the video showed nothing. Nobody got close to her in that time."

"What about the elevator?" Jason piped up. "Could someone have been inside the elevator with her and scratched her there?"

Mike shook his head. "Berkowitz and Mason thought of that and checked the video from the elevator. There's a security camera there, too. She was alone."

"What about inside the lobby?" Jason asked. "Is there video between the door and the elevator?"

"Not that I've heard about," Mike said. "The file says that the detectives on the case did speak to the lobby staff, but nobody remembered seeing anything."

"Should we take another shot at them?" Jason suggested.

"Couldn't hurt," Mike replied. "Ms. Foster, thank you so much for your cooperation. If you think of anything else, please give us a call." Mike motioned for Jason to join him at the door, and Jason complied. As they were leaving, Mike turned around. "And, Ms. Foster, one more question, and I'm sure you already were asked this. Did Ms. Sheraton say anything after she got back that day, the day she died? Did she mention any interactions with anyone just before she arrived?"

"No. She didn't say anything. She started to feel bad and then she went to lie down and a little while later we called 9-1-1. She never said anything about meeting anyone."

"That's what we thought," Mike replied. "Thanks." Then he turned and walked out. Jason closed the door behind them and they walked back to the elevator.

Once on the ground floor, Mike walked confidently up to the front desk, which occupied the entire left side of the lobby except for a door leading to some subterranean storage facility. There were two men wearing green-and-maroon uniforms with black limo-driver hats standing behind the desk as Mike approached.

Unfortunately, both men told the same story. They remembered Ms. Sheraton coming home, but did not see her have interactions with anyone in the lobby.

Mike and Jason walked to the door to speak with the final member of the lobby team, whose name was Gerardo, but had to wait while he escorted an elderly resident to the curb and ushered her into a cab, pocketing his tip and waiting for the taxi to pull away as he waved and smiled affectionately toward the lady. When he returned to his post inside the revolving door, he removed his hat and wiped away the sweat that had accumulated on his forehead, then returned the hat to its proper place. He looked askance at the two detectives, but did not speak. Mike asked him the same questions he had posed to the men behind the desk. When they reached the issue of who else was in the lobby, Gerardo had more of a memory.

"I remember that Ms. Sheraton was alone that day, without any guests or her assistant," he offered hesitantly. "It was after five o'clock, so there were many people coming and going at that time, as is usual."

"How do you remember the time?" Mike asked.

"Because I was outside trying to get a cab for Mr. Mendelsohn, who goes to the Jewish Temple every Saturday at five o'clock for the end of Shabbat, and I was having trouble getting a car for him. He was unhappy, but when Ms. Sheraton arrived I asked her driver if he would mind taking Mr. Mendelsohn and he agreed. By the time I got back inside, Ms. Sheraton had already gone through the lobby and I didn't see her there."

"Do you remember anyone else in the lobby that day?" Mike pressed.

Gerardo stopped to think, stroking his chin. Jason reached out his hand, a ten dollar bill folded tightly in his palm. The doorman took the bill deftly and it disappeared into the large pocket of his coat. Mike immediately appreciated the utility of having large pockets as a doorman, although he glared at Jason for offering a bribe to a witness. "Thank you, sir. I do recall that the postman was here at that time, delivering the mail." Gerardo motioned to the rear of the lobby, where a wall was covered with small shiny metal doors bearing the numbers of the apartments, each with a copper keyhole in the center.

"Was it the regular mailman?"

"Oh, yes, Mr. Murphy was here that day."

"Anyone else?"

"There may have been a few other residents coming or going. The dogs were going in and out."

"What dogs?"

"Oh, there are so many dogs. They go out for walks at all hours of the day or night. Always."

"Do you remember which dogs were there at the time Ms.

Sheraton came home?"

"Oh, no, sir. But Shep was there, I think."

"Who is Shep?"

"Oh, Shep is a golden retriever. Very nice and friendly but not well trained. The walkers usually take him out around that time. I remember Shep was in a big hurry that day because he almost knocked over Mrs. Marcovitz when she was coming in. I tell her to use the revolving door, but she likes to use the big door instead. The dog was going out, and the walker was having trouble and didn't apologize, and Mrs. Marcovitz was not happy."

"Who was the walker?"

"I don't know. Shep has had many walkers. They take him out for a few weeks or a month and then a new one comes. Many residents have walkers. Some take out many dogs, but Shep's owners are *un poco* too protective. But Shep is not an easy dog and many walkers don't like to take him."

"Do you know why Shep was so anxious to get outside that day?" Jason cut into the interrogation.

"No, sir. Maybe he needed to go really badly."

Mike reasserted himself as the questioner. "Was that walker someone who walked other dogs?"

"I don't know, sir. I don't remember him, so he must not have walked many dogs, or walked any for a long time. He was new, I think."

"Has he been walking Shep since that day?"

Gerardo again stopped to think. Mike wondered if he was angling for another tip. "I cannot remember, sir. I don't recall whether he was here again after that, but I do remember that Shep got a new walker some months ago. Taryn has been walking Shep and a few other dogs in the building for a while, so the other man was before her. I do not know when he stopped walking Shep."

"Which resident owns Shep?" Jason again interjected, prompting a quick scowl from Mike.

"Oh, the Richardsons. Fourth floor."

"Thank you, Gerardo," Mike said as he stepped away from the door, back toward the front desk.

After having George call up and confirm that there was someone home at the Richardsons' apartment, Mike and Jason headed back to the elevator. They knocked on the door of apartment 4F and were immediately greeted by barking from the interior, low and gruff as befitted a large dog. The door opened a crack and Mike could see a tall, slim, and very blonde woman who looked to be in her early twenties. Her blue eyes peered out through a crack in the door and scrutinized Mike, who smiled soothingly as he flashed his badge. The young woman then opened the door a bit wider. She stepped back and looked scared when she saw the tall Black man standing next to Mike, but when Jason flashed his badge and Mike introduced him as his partner, she relaxed a bit and invited the two men into the apartment. The dog, however, was not impressed by the badges and continued to bark enthusiastically. It was a golden retriever, normally a friendly breed, but clearly in "protect" mode.

As Mike stepped into the narrow entrance hallway past the door, a toddler wearing just a diaper came barreling down the hardwood floor toward the commotion with part of his lunch smeared into his long, curly hair. The woman stooped down and scooped him up, calling out "Joshua!" Mike glanced at the large photograph hanging at the end of the hallway next to the door, showing the child dressed in a sailor suit in the company of a smiling woman in a yellow dress and a serious-looking man in a grey suit.

Mike and Jason followed the nanny (which they both presumed her to be) down the hallway and settled in a toy-strewn living room. Mike and Jason remained standing as the nanny sat down in a worn lounge chair with the child on her lap.

"I'm sorry to intrude, miss," Mike said in his most grandfatherly tone. "Can we ask you whether you have had contact with people who take the dog out – the dog walkers?"

"Sure," the nanny replied in an accent that Mike and Jason would argue about later. Jason was sure it was Swedish, while Mike thought it was Dutch.

"How often is the dog taken out?"

The Golden thumped his tail on the floor, aware that they were talking about him. "I take him for a walk with Joshua in the morning and then walker comes in afternoon."

"Always at the same time?" Mike inquired.

"Not always. Sometimes when Joshua naps. After four, und before six."

"Do you remember a walker who took Shep out in May?"

The nanny, whose name Mike realized he had not asked, furrowed her manicured brows, apparently trying to recall two months earlier. "I think we had two then."

"Right," Mike agreed. "Miss . . . ?"

"My name is Anka," she smiled, happy to be asked, apparently.

"Yes, Anka. Was there a new walker that month?"

"Two new ones," she offered. "James had to move away, and then Nick start. He was nice. Shep like him. But then one day he did not come and Mrs. Richardson had to find a new one. Then Taryn start and Taryn has been walking Shep since then."

"Thank you, Anka. Do you remember when Ms. Sheraton, who lives on the sixth floor, died?"

Anka looked instantly pale. "Oh, yes. I remember. There were ambulances and police cars in front of the building. Mr. and Mrs. Richardson saw them when they came home that day."

"Do you remember whether Nick walked Shep that day?"

"I think so."

"Was there anything unusual about Nick's walk with Shep that day?"

"I don't think so. Nick was always nice. He like to come early and take Shep to the park to run."

"Do you remember when Nick stopped working, after that?"

Anka reached down to the floor where Shep was laying and

scratched him behind the ear. The dog perked up at the attention. Then Anka cocked her head to the side and said, "Yes, it was just after that when Nick did not come."

"That Saturday, when Ms. Sheraton died, was the that last day that Nick walked the dog?"

"I think so," Anka replied. "Maybe he was scared to come here after that."

"Maybe," Mike mumbled, looking at Jason. "Do you know how Nick got hired to be the dog walker?"

"No, sir. Mrs. Richardson is the one who hires the walkers. She puts ads on Craigslist and on the bulletin board in the park. She is very happy with Taryn now."

"I'm glad to hear that. Can I ask you when you expect Mrs. Richardson to return today?"

"Maybe in an hour or so," Anka offered.

"OK. We will go now, but please take my card," Mike said, extending his hand with one of his business cards between two fingers. The nanny took the card and looked at it inquisitively. "Please have Mrs. Richardson call me at the number at the bottom when she gets home. We would like to find out a little bit more about Nick."

"OK," Anka said, once again with a bright smile. "I'll show you out." Anka started to get up with the baby, but Mike waved her back to her chair.

"We can let ourselves out." Mike motioned to Jason and they returned to the door, with Shep trailing along after them, wagging his tail now and not barking. Mike guessed that the casual conversation with Anka established the two detectives as non-threats in the mind of the retriever. They both motioned Shep to stay as they closed the door behind them and walked to the elevator.

"You think?" Jason asked.

"Could be," Mike responded calmly. "Let's see what Mrs. Richardson has to tell us about when this guy 'Nick' got hired."

They left the building and crossed the street to the cobblestone sidewalk in front of the park, bordered by a stone wall overgrown with moss. Mike looked back at the apartment building and tried to pick out the sixth-floor window belonging to the late Ms. Sheraton. Then he noticed the dogs. In the three minutes that they stood on the sidewalk, a dozen dogs and owners – or walkers – passed by on their way up or down Fifth Avenue. There was a gap in the stone wall a half-block north where people came in and out of the park, and it seemed that every third or fourth person had a dog attached to them.

"Looks like walking the neighborhood dogs is a popular activity," Jason observed.

"Yep," Mike agreed. "I wonder how many of them are criminals."

♦♦♦

"I need a few uniforms."

Mike was standing in Captain Sullivan's office. It was after 7:00 but both men had decided to use their personal dinner time eating peanuts at the precinct house and chatting about the potential serial murder case. Mrs. Richardson had called and explained how the family had needed a new dog walker at the beginning of May, when the college student they had been using needed to study for finals and then was going home for the summer. Nick had applied. He was a veteran, he said, and he had an Army tattoo – an eagle on a flag – on his left biceps. He said he was between jobs and they were happy to have him. She didn't remember ever asking him his last name. He was friendly and great with the dog. She paid him in cash every Saturday. He worked regularly Monday through Saturday until after the Saturday when Ms. Sheraton died. Mrs. Richardson did not say "murdered." After that, they never heard from him again. He had given them a cell phone number so they could call him, but after he disappeared the phone had been disconnected. Mike wanted to try to track down Nick the dog walker by having officers flag down and talk to other dog owners and dog walkers around the area.

The cramped space in Captain Sullivan's office was cluttered, with folders and boxes on the floor and bookshelves against the only wall that was not made of glass. On the shelves besides some dusty books that clearly had not been touched in years were photos, all of which featured the Captain either in a sports jersey or a tuxedo and standing next to some local celebrity. Rudolph Guiliani, Ed Koch, Donald Trump, Patrick Ewing, Derek Jeter, and an actress Mike thought was Sandra Bullock were all prominently displayed. The Captain enjoyed traveling in the higher level of New York society as a member of New York's Finest. Mike turned away from the familiar mementos and looked at his friend, boss, and occasional adversary.

Sullivan was rough around the edges, but smart and with a soft heart under a tough exterior. He had a perpetual five-o'clock shadow that he barely tried to keep shaved and a constantly wrinkled white button-down shirt with a thin necktie unraveled to his second button. His face was round, with a thick black moustache under a bulbous nose that had certainly been broken multiple times in his ramshackle youth in the Bronx. He still had a thick accent, especially when he got angry. Behind the desk, his bulk was intimidating, but Mike knew that when he stood up, his five feet and seven inches made him look like a bowling ball with hair.

"You have Dickson," Captain Sullivan grunted back.

"I also need somebody to review a security cam video and it's going to take some time. Dickson and I have some other leads to track down. I need a uniform or two to help."

The Captain scowled. "You are a Task Force of two. You don't get extra resources."

"Think of it as a training experience for somebody who needs punishment."

The Captain couldn't restrain a chuckle, and then a sigh. "Fine. Go downstairs, see who's on the desk, and grab somebody who's in the shop doing paperwork. But don't adopt him, Mike. OK?"

"What if it's a her?"

"Don't fucking bust me on that crap, Stoneman!"

Mike smiled broadly, happy to have agitated his boss. "You really need to be more gender sensitive." Sullivan waved him out of the office without further discussion.

Mike found a rookie in the bullpen named Carla Olson, who was working desk duty after being involved in an accident in her cruiser. Mike explained the security camera assignment to her and she seemed genuinely excited about it. Mike figured that it would not be too hard to identify Shep's dog walker on the security camera video. The guy had been there every late afternoon for three weeks in May. George had already confirmed that the security cameras were connected to a digital storage system that should have video from the past six months. Mike and Jason hoped to find a camera image of "Nick." It was quite a coincidence that he was only around a short time, and then disappeared right after the murder, and he had the opportunity to be in that lobby at exactly the time that the poison was likely delivered to Sheraton. It wasn't enough evidence to convict anyone, maybe, but Mike and Jason wanted to interview the guy. Maybe casing the other dog walkers was just a wild goose chase. He wished they had more resources, like maybe the FBI, but he knew that the Mayor was not wrong about the publicity. Once the feds came in, they would not be able to keep a lid on the story.

Chapter 10 – Eve's End

May 27, 2018

*E*VE IS DESTROYED. *Her demise was much less satisfying than Abel's, but that is the price of cunning. The toxin is fast-acting, so I am sure her struggle was short. I regret that she could not fully understand her circumstances or the nature of her executioner. I am sure she was merely puzzled and confused at the end, rather than terrified.*

The one consistent aspect of Eve's pattern was that each evening she returned to her apartment to change clothes between her daytime activities and her nights out. She rarely stayed in, and certainly never on a Saturday night. On this particular Saturday, it was simple to determine her schedule. She was expected to attend a publicity event for her clothing line in the Fashion District in the early afternoon, and then she was to hand out an award at a gala dinner in the evening. Her pattern was to arrange for a car to deliver her to and from her apartment building so that she could make a grand exit from the back of a black limousine, extending her long, bare leg onto the sidewalk in a glossy or sequined shoe with open toes. She was so glamorous and beautiful. Ha! Her smooth skin will soon be moldering in a coffin.

How would a genius arrange to be in the lobby of her building so that the doormen would take no notice? So many wealthy New

Yorkers need assistance with their dogs. Dogs must be walked, and busy people simply don't have the time. The background checking process for a dog walker? Nonexistent, at least for those who have full-time help already and yet still want a separate employee. The nanny does not leave the apartment, nor does she give a key to the dog walker, so what is the worry? Only that the walker might abscond with the pooch, I suppose, but people are so easily fooled. An army veteran studying for a post-graduate degree could not possibly be a dog thief. He is the most trustworthy person imaginable. Why would you not give your leash to this man and pay him a pittance to pick up dog shit? He is hardly worth noticing. When asked to give a description, the nanny and the apartment owners will have wildly different versions, partly due to the simple disguises I employed, and partly due to their own lack of attention. My work constrains me only during my night shifts, leaving me ample time to plan my victories and set my traps during the days.

In the lobby of an apartment building with an unruly dog on a leash, it is a simple matter to come into contact with a woman walking alone toward the elevator in her afternoon attire. When the edge of the leash brushes the woman's arm, it scratches her. So careless. The woman hardly notices. She glares at the dog-walker as if his actions were intentional and he is an abject idiot. Of course, his actions were entirely intentional, and the small scratch that she barely registered was sufficient to transfer the toxin beneath her skin. It mingles with her bloodstream and infiltrates her entire circulatory system within fifteen minutes.

The first symptom is dizziness, followed by mild nausea. She would then have experienced tingling in her extremities and might have thought that she was having a heart attack – which, in effect, she was. Then difficulty breathing, and her body attempting to defend itself against the invading molecules by inducing a fever. By the time she lost consciousness and somebody called 9-1-1, it would have been far too late for any paramedics to help her. Without knowing the exact toxin and the exact treatment, death was certain.

I returned the dog to its apartment and then lingered, waiting for the ambulance. I watched as they scurried through the lobby with her body on a rolling gurney. It was far too late. I then meandered away, unseen and unnoticed by those whose wealth makes them blind. I was never in the eye of the security camera, and my raised hoodie obscured my face when I entered and exited the building. Eve will have an audience with the Almighty and will plead for her immortal soul, but to no avail. She will burn, and her perfect skin will peel from her flesh. Her cosmetics and perfumes will not save her from eternal torment and agony as her hideousness is laid bare for all to see. Only I see her for what she really is. I, and the Lord.

Chapter 11 – Blood, Frogs, and Lice

August 7, 2018

WHEN MIKE WALKED INTO THE LAB, the lights were dim. Dr. McNeill's assistant was nowhere to be seen, although Mike did not take it for granted that she was actually gone for the day. If she worked half as hard as her boss, she probably never saw the sunlight. Mike had always liked McNeill, partly because she was as dedicated to her job as he was to his. In the lab, on the witness stand, in a briefing with prosecutors, she was never less than perfectly professional. But never cold. Mike was comfortable around her. He didn't second-guess what he wanted to say, like he did around some women. Being around McNeill just felt natural.

Mike lingered over a photo of McNeill and her team accepting an award, displayed proudly on the wall. For the special occasion, she'd wrapped a golden headband around her choppy dark hair and wrapped a dove-grey dress around every curve. He'd never had the chance to see her that way in person, despite their years of working together. All he got was the shapeless lab coat or a conservative outfit in which to testify in court.

"Detective Stoneman," Dr. McNeill said evenly as she walked through the swinging doors, big enough for a gurney and a body as well as a doctor. She had been expecting him. "Thanks for coming in late. I've been backed up with new cases and this was the only time I had for your little side project." She paused and looked puzzled. "Where's your partner?"

"Dickson had a date," "He has a new girlfriend from the traffic division, so I came alone."

"I'm glad you did," she smiled. "Would you like a scotch?"

Mike did a double-take, then brightened and said playfully, "Sure. I'm a little surprised, though, Doctor, that you would have such a thing in a government office."

Michelle spun on a low heel and sauntered toward the grey metal cabinet next to her desk. She bent over, and Mike did not avoid looking at the outline of her backside beneath her smock. She extracted two heavy glass tumblers and a clear, slightly angular bottle with a gold and black label and set them down on the desktop. "It's after hours, Detective. Besides, there's not usually anybody alive in here to complain. Not like your station house, where I'm sure nobody has any bottles stashed away."

Mike laughed and pulled up the same chair he had sat in a few days earlier; the one in which he had sat many times in his years of working with the M.E. "Doctor McNeill, I have always liked the way you think."

The doctor poured them each a few fingers of the GlenFiddich 21, a very good bottle. McNeill had some experience with good scotch. They clinked glasses and each took a small sip, allowing the first sting of the whiskey to coat their tongues and fire off their taste buds. Mike then took a longer sip, savoring the complex, smoky flavor. He looked up at the doctor; she was sitting in a much more relaxed posture than he was used to from her. It was after hours, so he chalked it up to just trying to relax at the end of a long day.

"Very nice," Mike said, holding his glass to the light and admiring the amber hue. "This scotch was in the barrel almost as long as I've been on the force."

"And a little longer than I've been working in this lab," McNeill said wistfully.

"What, you were sixteen when you graduated med school?"

The doctor laughed and turned her head away to hide her blush. "I think we're both just old enough to enjoy this scotch," she said, taking the last swallow from her glass.

Mike drained his own glass and set it on the desk. "I'm assuming you called because you have something to tell me regarding Detective Dickson's connection theory."

"Yes," Dr. McNeill said, then hesitated. She started what Mike thought sounded like a rehearsed presentation. "I reviewed the files, photos, and test results from the three earlier cases. I even re-tested a couple of tissue samples that were in the freezer, since the cases are still technically open. On first look, I saw nothing that indicated a connection. The wounds were different, the causes of death were different, the pathology was different. There was really nothing remotely similar. There was just one odd thing about the first victim, Mr. DiVito, but it wasn't there for any of the others so it was nothing."

"Something other than the absence of a left arm below the elbow?"

"Yes, Sherlock. He had an unusual amount of blood in his stomach."

"Why is that unusual?"

"Well, when people have no injuries inside their mouths, there is generally no blood in the stomach unless there is some perforation and internal bleeding, which was not present here. People bleed on the outside and they don't tend to drink their own blood voluntarily. Sometimes they get blood in their lungs, but stomachs are not generally where I'm going to find blood. But it wasn't there in any of the other victims. If it were some sort of signature, something the killer did intentionally, then I'd expect to see it in at least some of the others, but I didn't."

"So, there's nothing, huh?"

"If this had been just an ordinary case I would have closed it down at that point, but I know that you would not have brought this to me if there wasn't some basis for your – for Detective Dickson's – suspicion about a connection. So, I kept looking and I found something. It's not conclusive, and it wouldn't stand up in court. I'm not even sure I would say that it's really there under oath. But since I was looking for it, I can't say it isn't there either. It's not enough. But it makes me rule out the idea that the cases are definitely *not* connected. Does that make any sense?"

"That depends. You haven't told me what it is yet."

Dr. McNeill smiled and nodded. "It's a cut. You remember that the first victim, DiVito, was tortured and left to die in the mechanic's shed under the West Side Highway, right?"

Mike nodded, not wanting to say anything to break her train of thought.

"Well, the guy had his fingers cut off of one hand and the other arm mutilated in a meat grinder."

Mike said nothing, but marveled at how this diminutive woman could speak so casually about such a brutal murder.

"But there were also some cuts," Dr. McNeill continued. "He had unusual wounds on his upper torso. Not deep, and not really significant. They certainly would have bled some, and they would have been painful, although I expect they were inflicted more for psychological value than physical pain. They were certainly made before death, and they were part of the torture. The second murder victim was poisoned, and there was no evidence of torture or personal contact beyond that one scratch."

"Sorry to interrupt the flow," Mike said, "but speaking of the poisoning, did you make any progress identifying the toxin that was used? You thought it might have been an animal?"

McNeill did a double-take and then re-focused on Mike. "Oh, actually yes. It's not related at all to the cuts, or to anything else, but the CDC finally got back to me and they were able to isolate it. It's a secretion from the skin of a South American tree frog. Very toxic, particularly if introduced directly into the bloodstream."

"A frog?"

"That's what they tell me. I'm a doctor, not a herpetologist."

Mike arched his left eyebrow. "Really? Herpetologist? Did you have to look that up?"

Michelle smiled slyly. "Maybe it was a vocabulary word in my SAT prep course."

"Fine. I'll give you credit for knowing it and I'm going to assume that it means a person who studies frogs."

"Good assumption," she said as she reached for the bottle of scotch and poured both herself and Mike another finger. "The killer had quite an imagination, but it still doesn't seem connected to any of the other three. But, the third victim, LeBlanc, also had the cuts. Again, not the cause of death, but more in the nature of preliminaries – to get the victim's attention and create pain and fear. We catalogued them, as we do with all wounds on a corpse, but they were clearly not the cause of death, and so they weren't scrutinized as carefully. LeBlanc had several. The killer cut his leg and severed both Achilles tendons, which must have been horribly painful. That caused some significant blood loss, but unlike DiVito, the blood loss was not the cause of death. Anyway, when I compared the upper torso cuts on DiVito with the cuts on LeBlanc, I noticed a similarity."

"Were they made with the same knife?"

"Well, that's possible, but not provable. A knife blade isn't like an axe that might have distinctive chips or gouges that could leave a trace. A clean blade leaves a cut that is not distinguishable from any other blade. I can tell the difference between a razor blade and a hunting knife just based on the thickness of the cut, but for the most part, a knife is a knife. No, it's the location. Both victims had a pair of cuts on their upper chest, between the collarbone and the pectoral, nearly making a connection from left to right. Like an inverted letter 'V' or a letter "A" without the cross bar. In both cases, the lines were very straight, indicating that they were drawn carefully and slowly, like a surgeon with a scalpel – not like a typical slash. Here, let me show you."

Dr. McNeill stood up and walked across the room, where she picked up a scalpel from a neatly arranged tray next to the examining table. She returned to the desk where Mike was still sitting with his glass of scotch, which was again nearly empty. "Here, face me in your chair and keep your arms down, like you're tied up."

"I'm game," Mike said playfully.

McNeill smiled and stood over him, glad to be taller than her adversary and in the position of power, with a weapon in her hand. "Now, watch. If I'm just slashing you with this knife, I would make a curving motion, from left to right if I'm doing it backhanded, or from right to left if I'm doing it forehanded." McNeill pantomimed a slash in each direction.

"That's assuming that the slasher is right-handed,"

"True. But otherwise the angles would just be reversed. And even if the killer was trying to be very precise, north to south, the lines would be much more vertical. In order to make the inverted "V" lines, the killer needs to move in close and carefully draw the blade down." She again mimed the motion, with the scalpel blade close to Mike's suit.

"Why downward? "Why not upward?"

"Good question, Detective. An upward stroke is certainly possible, but I think less likely. When a cut is on a vertical surface, most people will cut downward – but it really doesn't matter. The point is that the pattern of the cuts is the same on both bodies. I would never have noticed if I wasn't looking very carefully, since the cuts were secondary injuries. But, it seemed to me too much of a coincidence that two different killers would make the same rather unusual and precise cut marks on two different victims."

Mike sat, deep in thought, as Michelle leaned back in her chair and drained the remaining amber liquid from her glass. "What about Slick Mick, potential victim number four?"

"Well, Detective, there was a little problem making a definitive examination of Mr. Gallata's upper torso, as you may recall."

"Oh, right," Mike conceded. "Was there anything there to suggest similar cuts?"

"I could speculate that any places on the body that were bleeding would have been the first places that the tigers would have gone for. The area where the cuts would have been was certainly chewed up pretty good, while the man's abdomen was untouched. So, it is possible that the cuts might have been there, but it's impossible to be sure."

"So, you think we have a serial?"

"I would not rule it out."

"That is an important bit of the puzzle," Mike said. "I was kinda hoping that you would rule out a same-killer scenario."

"Sorry, Detective."

"Call me Mike. Really."

"OK, then, Mike, but you have to call me Michelle."

"OK, Michelle. But only when we're after hours."

Michelle smiled shyly. "You can come around after hours any time you want, Mike. It's not much of a dance club, I'm afraid."

"Well, at least the company is good." Mike smiled sincerely as he stood up, but before he could take a step toward the door, McNeill spoke up again.

"There was one other thing," Dr. McNeill's voice trailed off at the end, as if she was lost in thought and not sure if she should continue.

"What?"

"Well, I didn't think much of it at the time. I'm not even sure I put it in the autopsy report. But I do remember it. The frozen guy – LeBlanc – he had head lice."

"Lice?"

"Yes. Well, they were all frozen and dead, but I remember seeing them in his hair. Not a lot – not a full infestation – but enough that I noticed. It did seem a little out of character for a man like that, who was wealthy and presumably well-groomed. I remember thinking that maybe he had come into contact with them shortly before his death. Maybe from the killer, or something else in the killer's environment, like a dog."

"And you didn't think it was important at the time?" Mike raised an eyebrow. "That's not like you, Doctor."

McNeill turned her lips into a pout. "And I thought you liked me," she said sadly, hoping to get a reaction that was not coming. "Well," she reverted to a normal voice, "as I said, it didn't seem relevant to the death. Lice don't kill people."

"But they are parasites, aren't they?"

"Sure, but don't start getting all NCIS on me here. We weren't going to be able to get a sample of the killer's DNA by extracting blood from a louse. It doesn't work that way. But nice thought."

Mike opened his mouth, but then closed it again, a tiny bit angry that the doctor had correctly anticipated what he was going to say and shot him down before he got the idea out. He reached around the back of his neck and massaged the muscles under the nape of his hairline, both trying to relax and trying to think. He found himself wishing that he had the same head of hair he had when he was thirty. "Well, you're probably right. That could not have been related to the death. We know the cause of death was exposure – he froze to death. Hell of a way to go. Nobody ever heard of death by lice."

"Well, for that matter, it's pretty unusual to have death by frog or death by tiger. This killer has some exotic methods."

Mike glanced around the lab. The counter was strewn with microscope slides and various sterile containers. Something was pecking away at the back of Mike's brain. He couldn't quite put a finger on it, but something was tickling a memory.

"Doctor – uh, Michelle," Mike stammered, "can you do a web search for me really quickly?"

McNeill sat up in her desk chair and tapped a few keys to wake up her monitor. "No problem, Mike. What do you need?"

"I'm trying to remember something and it's not coming, so I'm ready to cheat. Can you run a search for the words 'frogs' and 'lice' together and see what comes up?"

McNeill shrugged and opened a new Google window. The results popped up instantly, and the first five were all about the same subject: the biblical story of the plagues upon Egypt. McNeill opened the first result link, "Blood, Frogs and Lice" by Dr. Harvey Babich of Stern College for Women, and began reading aloud. "'This article analyses the initial three plagues.'" She stopped reading and scanned down the page. "Mike!" she exclaimed, "the second plague was frogs, and the third plague was lice. Your second victim was killed by a frog, and the third victim had lice. Is this nut trying to recreate the plagues on Egypt?"

Mike stood still, thinking. "The first plague was blood – Moses turned the Nile river to blood, and it killed the fish, right?"

McNeill nodded. "Yeah. The river was turned to blood. Well, the first victim certainly had a lot to do with blood. He bled out, that was the cause of death. And –"

"And what?"

"And the blood I found in DiVito's stomach." McNeill tilted her head back and stared at the ceiling, then sat up and tapped her keyboard a few times while Mike waited.

"So, what are you thinking?"

"Mike, I'm worried that I'm starting to think like a deranged serial killer here, but what if the killer *made* DiVito drink his own blood? What if he mixed it with water and gave it to him to drink? Or forced him, since his hands were either missing or tied down. If he did, then he was very consciously recreating the first plague – blood in the water."

"It makes a weird kind of sense," Mike admitted. "So, what? We have a biblical lunatic who thinks he's Moses?"

"I don't know," McNeill lamented, clicking out of the window with the research results and getting back to the report she had been trying to finish up. "It is just too much of a coincidence."

"What's the fourth plague?"

McNeill clicked her tongue, annoyed that she had closed down the screen with the search results. She opened a new window and ran a new search for "plagues on Egypt" and then clicked on the Wikipedia entry, which figured to be the simplest. She stared at the screen for two seconds and then said, "Wild animals."

"Well, there you are," Mike said conclusively. "There's no doubt about that pattern. Between the biblical connection, the signature cuts you found, and the odd timing on the last Saturday of the month, now we're sure. We have a serial killer on our hands."

"Dickson will be pleased that you confirmed his hypothesis," McNeill offered.

"Hmmff," Mike grunted. "Pleased and insufferable."

"Oh, come on now, Mike. Why do you give him such a hard time? Is he incompetent?"

"No, he's actually a good cop."

"So, is he rude or disrespectful to you?"

"No, he's usually obsequiously polite and proper, especially when there are other people around."

"So, what's the problem?"

"It's complicated," was all Mike was willing to share.

"Mike, he's your partner. If there's something going on there that's going to become a problem between you and compromise your investigation, then you should say something to somebody. I know the somebody is probably not me, of course, but really, don't keep it to yourself." She stopped and looked up at him with pleading eyes.

Mike softened his expression and put on a weak smile. "Don't worry. It's nothing important. And I will give him credit on this one, so that should make him happy. Can I ask you to summarize your findings about the cuts in a report that I can show the Commissioner?"

"Sure, Mike. Give me a few days and I'll send it to you."

"Great." Mike started to walk toward the door, then he stopped and turned back around to find Michelle standing only a few feet behind him. "And, thank you, Doc – Michelle."

"Any time, for you." Michelle took a step back. Mike nodded and turned toward the door. He glanced back as he pushed open the swinging door and saw the M.E. watching him walk away.

◆◆◆

The next morning, back in the precinct house, Mike walked into Captain Sullivan's office and closed the door. He didn't waste any time.

"Sully, we have confirmation that our perp is a serial."

"Oh, Jesus," Sullivan said, dropping his chin to his chest. "Was there another murder?"

"No," Mike responded. "If there had been another so soon it would break his pattern. But we have confirmation from other evidence now that there is a definite pattern – a methodology that cannot be coincidence."

"Shit!" the Captain exclaimed. "Ward is going to split a zipper."

Mike nodded. "Well, whatever the Commissioner thought he was going to do or not do with this case if we got another murder this month, it's time to push up the timetable."

"It's not going to be a good conversation. Where's Dickson, by the way?"

Mike pursed his lips. "I haven't told him yet. But it's going to confirm his theory, so he'll have a shit-eating grin on his face for the rest of the week. I wanted to tell you first, before you saw him dancing a jig in the middle of the room."

"Lay off him, why don't you," Sullivan shot back. "He's a good cop."

"I know that," Mike acknowledged, "but he's got a big head and a big ego and he needs to pay his dues."

"Like you?" Sullivan chided.

"When I was as green as Dickson I did," Mike said. "I knew my place in the pecking order and I waited my turn, most of the time."

"Yeah, right," Sullivan coughed, reaching for a white Styrofoam cup on the desk and taking a sip of his coffee. "From what I hear, you were a pain in the ass know-it-all who always thought that the rules were meant to be broken. Where am I wrong about that?"

Mike scowled and walked to the office door, looking through the glass for Jason's easily recognizable figure out in the bullpen. "He hasn't paid his dues."

"He made detective by the book, Mike. You gotta let that go."

"Hmmff," Mike grunted. "Sully, I never asked you. Why did you choose Dickson for Homicide instead of somebody else? I understand you giving him to me, I'm used to getting the new guys, but why him in the first place?"

Sullivan went silent for a few moments as he formulated his response, then he sat up in his chair and folded his hands in front of him on his desk. "He wasn't my first choice on paper, but when I interviewed him I saw something in him that I really liked. He had a determination and a drive. He convinced me that he could really make a difference here and add something to this team, so I picked him. Nobody told me that we needed a Black homicide detective. Nobody pressured me about affirmative action. It was my call and I decided that he was the best man for the job."

Mike stared back at his boss and friend, nodded slightly, and turned away. He pulled open the door and called out for Jason to come and join them. A minute later, Jason strode in, his suit jacket buttoned and the perfect knot in his paisley tie sticking out from under his collar as if at attention.

"What?" Jason asked.

Mike turned to him and held out his hand for a shake. Jason took the hand with a puzzled look on his face. "Congratulations, you were right. Our guy's a serial."

Jason remained confused. "What happened?"

Mike then explained his conversation with Dr. McNeill, about the lice and how they connected the dots to the first four plagues upon Egypt.

"Damn!" Jason said when Mike finally finished. "This guy is

nuts."

"Aren't you going to say 'I told you so?'" Mike suggested.

"No. Let's catch the bastard first, then I'll rub it in your face," Jason said simply, then turned to Sullivan. "Does this mean we're going to get some additional resources?"

Sullivan let out a sigh that was half a growl. He didn't have more resources to throw at this and he knew he was going to have to be the one who called the Commissioner. "We'll see what the brass says."

"Fine," Jason said, turning to leave and looking at Mike as he moved in the direction of the door. "Come on, Mike. We've got to figure out how to catch Moses before he gets to his fifth victim."

Mike looked at Sully and shook his head slightly. "Great, now we're trying to catch prophets and gods." Sullivan just waved a hand dismissively at Mike, who turned to leave, watching Jason's back as he strode across the bullpen confidently. Mike thought he detected just a hint of a jig in his step.

Chapter 12 – Vive la France

June 4, 2018

*T*HE PUZZLE PIECES WILL INTERLOCK *before long.
Today I launch the third chapter in the epic that is my
genius. Again, I have chosen my quarry carefully so as
not to reveal any patterns that could point toward my true
identity. This third masterpiece has required special planning to
perform the execution in a most unusual manner that will only
later become apparent. All will eventually see how far my
intellect will carry me on my holy journey. I have ached for the
joy of personally administering the vengeance of the Lord since
the death of Abel. My hunger for it is palpable, and yet I must not
let my desire become lust. All must be tempered with the sword of
justice.*

*The next pox upon God's creation is a Frenchman, ensconced
in the decadence of American society. The Frenchman is a vulture
who sucks the blood out of the sick in order to fund his empire. He
raises the prices for his company's drugs while he stifles
competition. He finds markets where his poison is the only
generic option and government programs are obligated to use
them, then manufactures them in cut-rate facilities with
substandard materials without a hint of care about the welfare of
the sick who retch up his swill. I have seen it. I laid in the bed next
to one who nearly died at Napoleon's hands. He is the*

embodiment of greed and excess. He built his Versailles palace on our American soil, importing flowers and grasses as if European lineage is inherently superior. I have dubbed him Napoleon. He shall meet the fate of his namesake's pathetic army. Shall the authorities perceive the allusion? Time will tell. One day the so-called experts will read this chronicle and perhaps understand what was in front of their faces all along, but which they could not see without the wisdom of the Lord.

The chase has almost begun, and I am trembling with the anticipation.

June 11

Certainly, the death of Napoleon will be the most challenging so far. I must also be wary that this third masterpiece may alert the authorities that I indeed exist. I will continue to exult the Lord by carrying out my mission on the Sabbath. My work schedule makes this a joyous fit since I have Fridays and Saturdays off and report back on Sunday night, where I can enjoy the press coverage all night and into Monday morning to my delight and ecstasy. And yet, I am treading such a thin line. I must be so careful, and yet so daring. I could be more random in the timing of my glorious victories, but, it is inevitable that they know. That the people know. The police and the government would hide the truth from the masses, but my glorious tribute to the Almighty cannot be hidden. There will be fear, of course, but good people will understand that they need not fear me.

I must ensure that I am known, even before this journal is published for all to see and understand. I trust that you, my reader, will review the history and the press coverage to fully understand. If I never see the finished product as a mortal man, I shall still thrill at the thought that you will understand my quest and will tremble at the glory of God.

June 22

All the necessary preparations are in place for my encounter with Napoleon. I had to travel outside the City to trap two feral rabbits and then engage in the rather delicate process of harvesting my lovely clues. But latex gloves and spandex sleeves provided a suitable barrier and the cony's eyeball served as an attractive destination. The transmission to Napoleon should be a simple task, which I shall accomplish while blood still flows through his miserable body so that the leaches may feast on his essence before he meets the Lord. This will be the simplest portion of my mission.

The most challenging aspect of the operation will be to convince Napoleon to accompany me to the destination of his demise. I have worked out the details, and I have contingency plans in place. It is divine irony that the location of Napoleon's death is only available to me because of the religious observance of its owner, who keeps the Sabbath holy and does not suffer his employees to breach the law of the Lord. I respect such devotion to the Almighty, but I cannot share the specific observance, although I rest on the Sundays following my Godly efforts. God has provided me with my opportunity; the owner's security system is rudimentary and easily bypassed for my purposes. By the time Napoleon understands the nature of his doom, it will be too late.

Meanwhile I have already started laying the groundwork for the future chapters of my masterwork and have begun securing necessary locations. There is so much to plan that I have already looked well beyond the impending execution of Napoleon. One foul place of business may become the space where darkness shall engulf an enemy of the Lord. I have also secured a location from which I have access to the evil enabler, whose execution shall come very soon. But now that the time has come for the death of Napoleon, I can think of little else. I am fortunate that my professional work is accomplished in seclusion and that the tasks they give me are so simple that most of my work day is free for more significant endeavors. Still, my body is tired and only the strength of the Lord keeps me going. Soon, however, the life blood of Napoleon will give me the power of ten men.

Chapter 13 – Cold Storage

August 8, 2018

"YOU REALLY THINK this is necessary?" Jason asked as Mike pulled their unmarked pool cruiser up to the curb in a no-standing zone on Grand Street, near Lafayette, in Little Italy.

Mike turned his head and shot his partner a disapproving look as he watched Jason exit the vehicle and slam the door. Mike unbuckled his seat belt and locked up the car before joining Jason on the sidewalk. "Are you getting squeamish, Dickson?"

"No," Jason shot back. "I'm just wondering if there is something more productive we could be doing with our time. We've read the reports, you spoke to the M.E., what else is there? The murder was two months ago. This place has been open for business all that time, so the crime scene is going to be nothing like it was then. What do you think we're going to uncover here?"

"Did we uncover anything helpful when we visited Ms. Sheraton's apartment building?" Mike asked in his professorial voice.

"You know we did, but this is different. We know now that we're looking for a serial killer, and we know that this guy LeBlanc was his third kill. We already know there's no video from this kill site, the owners weren't there, and there were no other witnesses, so what the Hell are we doing?"

"Calm down, Detective. I happen to agree with you that there is almost no chance that we'll discover any useful information here. But we're trying to understand this nut and coming to see the scene of his crime may help with that. I'm not sure how, but I think there's a chance. There's no downside to this. And if you felt this strongly about it, why didn't you say something before we left the station? I could have left you there if you didn't want to come along."

Jason stared at Mike, the muscles around his jaw flexing as if he were grinding his teeth and holding himself back from saying something he might regret. After a healthy pause, he replied. "I was thinking about it, but I didn't want to make a scene back at the precinct."

"So why not say something as soon as we got in the car?"

"I was thinking about it then, too, but I didn't want to get into an argument while you were driving."

Mike paused and looked at Jason, cocking his head to the side slightly. "Thank you, Detective. I appreciate that. Now, are we ready to go inside?" Mike walked past Jason toward the door of the restaurant and the big man fell into step behind him.

Mike walked down three steps to the entrance door of the restaurant, making note of the Hebrew letters nailed to the proscenium and the large mezuzah on the door jamb. There were three more steps down inside the door before he arrived at the floor level. A row of small, rectangular windows spanned to top of the wall to let in light.

They introduced themselves to the owner, Mr. Glickstein, who reluctantly led them down a set of narrow stairs to a windowless basement. Ahead of them was a large steel door with a flat handle set midway up. Mike presumed that this was the door to the freezer.

Glickstein stopped a few feet before reaching the freezer door and turned to face Mike. He spread out his arms and said, "This is the place. You wanna see inside the freezer?"

Glickstein opened the door to the freezer and held it ajar, allowing Mike and Jason to walk through. Mike shivered involuntarily in the cold space, lined with steel shelves that were coated with a thin, white sheen of frost and stacked with bags and boxes bearing labels identifying their frozen contents. There was an aisle about three feet wide running down the center of the freezer and going back about ten feet, where a frost-covered steel wall stared back at Mike. Overhead, three incandescent light bulbs sprang to life as the door opened and were ramping up toward full illumination. The floor was also steel, but textured to guard against slipping and covered with a rubber runner mat about two feet wide. Mike visualized the body, slumped against the back wall as described in the case report. He looked around and then turned to walk back out of the cold space.

Back in the relative warmth of the dank basement, Mike asked Glickstein, "Were you the one who found the body?"

"Yeah, that was me. Sunday morning, I came in to open up and noticed that the front door was unlocked. I looked around to see whether there had been a break-in. Eventually, I came down here and saw that the bottles were messed up and the freezer door was open, so I went in and saw the dead guy in the back."

Mike thought for a moment before his next question. "Do you recall bringing anyone down here to the basement to look around in the past few months – someone you didn't already know?"

Glickstein thought about the question for a moment, but then shook his head. "No, I don't think so. But, you know, the men's room is over there at the base of the stairs." The restaurateur motioned toward the far end of the basement space, where Mike could make out a dim light and a doorway with a sign that he could not read. "So, anyone can come down here and take a look around."

"What about your security system?" Jason jumped in. "Have you told any strangers about your security system and how it works?"

"Why would I do that?" Glickstein retorted angrily. "Do I look like a schmuck to you?"

"No, but you look like a man whose security system was bypassed and whose basement was used as a murder site," Jason shot back, taking a step towards the much smaller man.

Glickstein took a step back and looked at Mike. "Hey, I did nothing here. Why're you coming here intimidating me with your big man partner?"

Mike held out his hand, motioning Jason to back off. "Nobody is trying to intimidate you, Mr. Glickstein. I assure you. We're investigating a crime. Nobody thinks that you had anything to do with it."

"You're darn right! Like I'm so stupid that I would kill this man in my own freezer and then call the police. I'm no idiot." Glickstein was getting angrier, waving his arms as he spoke. Mike gave Jason a look, trying to convey that making this man angry was not advancing the investigation. He nodded in the man's direction and mouthed "I'm sorry." Jason scowled at Mike, but took a step back away from Glickstein. He did not apologize for his statement, but he relaxed his posture and clasped his hands behind his back.

Mike reached out a hand and placed it gently on Glickstein's shoulder. "Mr. Glickstein, I'm afraid we're a bit on edge with the murders that we're investigating. My partner, Detective Dickson, raises a valid point. Is it possible that anyone got information from you – without you necessarily being aware of it – about your security system that he might have used to hack into it? Did you maybe have a casual conversation with someone about that subject?"

Glickstein unclenched the fist at his side and looked at Mike with a puzzled expression. "I don't know. I talk. I like to talk to the customers. I tell people about the kitchen and that we get our fish fresh from Long Island. You know, I'm proud of my place, so maybe I say how I don't have bars on the doors and windows like the other places on this street because I have a state-of-the-art alarm system so I don't worry."

"Who did you tell that to?" Mike asked gently.

"Maybe different people."

"You mean more than one? Just in the last few months?"

"Maybe." Glickstein shrugged.

"Do you recall anything about any of the people you discussed that with?" Mike asked, although he expected exactly the answer he got.

"No. You know, it's hard to remember."

"I understand, sir," Mike soothed. "Are there any security cameras inside the restaurant?"

"No," Glickstein said. "There's nothing much to steal, and I trust all my employees."

"OK," Mike said, his shoulders sagging slightly. "Well, if you think of anything specific about any of your conversations about the security system, please make sure to give us a call." He held out a business card to Glickstein, who took it and shoved it into his pants pocket without looking at it. Mike and Jason looked around a little more, making note of where the first cops on the scene had found the victim's blood on the floor and wall. The white chalk marks were still visible, suggesting that there was not a lot of foot traffic in the basement space, and that Glickstein had not bothered to clean it up. They thanked Glickstein for his cooperation and trudged back up the stairs and out onto the street. Mike noted the clear sign next to the door that listed the hours of operation of the restaurant, which included the statement, "Closed Saturdays."

"Not hard for our killer to pick this spot for a Saturday night kill, eh?" Jason noted.

"Might as well have a sign that says, 'Welcome, Moses.'"

"Is there anything about this street?" Jason mused. "This guy is so calculating. There must be something about this spot that he wanted to pick, don't you think?"

Mike shrugged. "Maybe. Damned if I can get inside his head and understand, though. I can't figure why this Jewish guy puts his restaurant in Little Italy, either."

Chapter 14 – Frozen Napoleon

June 30, 2018

I AM BARELY ABLE TO TYPE this entry, my body aches so. I am in need of medical attention and sleep. My personal war with Napoleon proved to be epic and difficult — and yet, as the frost of winter consumed the French army in Russia, so did my Napoleon succumb in the end and there he shall be found. I have no doubt that the authorities and the press will not be able to suppress this death. More details for posterity must wait until strength returns to my bones.

July 1

I am watching the news reports of my success from home today while my wounds heal. I dare not appear in my workplace with obvious scars that might arouse suspicion. A few days of convalescence will diminish any obvious signs of my struggle. Ah, it was so glorious. He was a more worthy opponent than I had imagined, and yet I had the element of surprise, which is such a grand weapon. The media are again awash in their own tears and anger at this affront to the safety and security of the rich and powerful. They shake in their boots at the idea that the Avenging Angel is on the Earth and that the vile and despicable may be called to task not by a ponderous legal system that they can manipulate, but by the hand of God taking direct action. All such evildoers should quake and fear that their sins will be exposed and their souls will be taken.

Napoleon easily accepted the ruse I put forward to lure him to his demise. He revels in publicity, despite the ugly truths buried inside his corporate offices. He was more than willing to meet with a reporter who wanted to interview him for a favorable profile. Two preliminary telephone calls; a cloned website purporting to belong to a major national magazine, altered to include the biography of a fictional writer; and a series of emails sent from a spoofed address – these were all that was necessary to convince the gullible Napoleon.

Only slightly more difficult was hacking into the security system of the restaurant in lower Manhattan that was to be the meeting location. I investigated several likely candidates before I found the perfect dungeon. Gaining access to the building was a relatively simple job, since the proprietors assumed that the alarm would chase away anyone who tried to break through the simple lock. And on the busy streets of New York, a man walking into a restaurant does not arouse any notice. My plan was perfection.

Napoleon arrived for his meeting in the late afternoon, a time when most restaurants were not busy and the absence of other patrons did not arouse suspicion. Before beginning the interview, I invited Napoleon to accompany me to the wine cellar, explaining that I was friends with the owner and had the run of the place. His interest was piqued when I described a particularly attractive selection of French wines, and he calmly followed me into the basement of the cramped space. By the time he discovered that there was no wine cellar, I had rolled a heavy metal cart in front of the exit. He was mine.

I had expected him to be easily subdued under the circumstances, but Napoleon proved to be agile and trained in some variety of martial arts. I was forced to struggle hand-to-hand with Napoleon for a long stretch, resulting in much more damage to the facility than I had intended. The monster landed several blows to my face, leaving me bruised. But I conquered him, incapacitated him with plastic handcuffs, and dragged him to the large walk-in freezer where the restaurant keeps its perishables. I sat him in a chair and bound his legs and arms, at which point Napoleon screamed and pleaded for his life in three languages. I was slightly concerned that his cries might attract attention from the residents of the adjoining building, but inside the freezer his cries were heard only by God and His angels.

We then had a lengthy conversation, although I did most of the talking. I explained his sins to him. I read excerpts from seven lawsuits brought against his company in which the families of injured or deceased children alleged that his low-quality drugs, produced with substandard manufacturing facilities, were either entirely ineffective or caused severe side effects. Napoleon became rich playing off the rules of medical insurance companies, which require the use of available generic drugs rather than brand-name drugs whenever a generic is available. He researched specific medical conditions where no generics existed due to high production costs and low profit margins, and exploited the insurance rules to build an empire of empty generics. Patients were powerless to avoid the requirement to buy his products, and their misery was ensured by Napoleon's careless and malicious business model.

Napoleon attempted to deny responsibility, but his protestations lacked sincerity. He was the mastermind, and he alone bears the responsibility. He was able to avoid criminal prosecution and the civil litigations were all settled, although small solace for the grieving families. No government power was able to stop him from inflicting his damage. The Angel of the Lord, however, has no restriction on the vengeance that can be inflicted upon the unworthy of the Earth.

Napoleon was at first enraged at being bound and subdued, then he attempted to negotiate. He believed that his money could always buy him what he wanted, including buying himself out of Hell. He offered me his wealth. He assured me that he would never go to the police. He offered to give me the account numbers and secret codes that would unlock his bank accounts. He offered to tell me the secret hiding places where he had stashed away gold and diamonds. When he realized that his freedom could not be purchased, he threatened me. He had powerful friends who would track me down and make me suffer for anything I did to him. I think he truly believed these threats. He was puzzled – truly perplexed – that I was unmoved by his bold assurances of my imminent death and dismemberment.

Of course, his bewilderment at his inability to buy his escape was nothing compared to his total lack of comprehension when I planted my little seeds. I pulled out my plastic storage case and held it against his scalp as I hustled my tiny calling cards out from their slumber and into his thick black hair. He could not feel them, of course. He had no idea what was happening. I believe he expected it to be poison or acid or something that would torture him. He did not have long to wait for that, but first I had to ensure my narrative would be properly written.

Freezing to death is not as rapid a process as I had imagined or hoped. I had my thick clothes, but I had removed his jacket and rolled up his sleeves. Napoleon had to suffer before he could meet his ultimate end, and so I made sure that he was weakened by loss of blood. Of course, some of those cuts were my own special marks. I was careful this time to make sure that the messaging was not obscured by surrounding distractions.

I was also rather surprised at the volume of Napoleon's screams, once he realized that there would be no succor for him and no escape. I had to block his mouth with a rag, secured by duct tape, until he was very near his end. It was the snapping of his Achilles tendons that produced the most significant shrieks.

After that, with blood loss setting in and the numbing effects of so much pain rendering him weak, I was not concerned that anyone could hear him outside the thick walls of the freezer.

It was a delicate balance, inflicting pain while not wanting to induce death by ordinary means. It was important that Napoleon die as the troops of France – by freezing. It is both a harsh and a peaceful end, as it turns out; trying to choke out dying words with frozen lips and trying to open eyelids that have stuck together. Trying one last time to strain against the bonds that had held him tight even when he had all his strength. It was slightly pathetic, and at the same time, highly satisfying. His last gasps, the hot steam escaping from his lips in the cold air. When he finally lost consciousness, I checked his pulse and was annoyed that his wicked heart was still beating for a time. I had wanted to be gone from this building much earlier, although I had no worry that the owners would show up even after sundown, for that was not their habit.

At last, Napoleon's evil blood stopped moving through his veins and he was in the hands of God. I removed his bindings and left him there, in a pool of his own blood and urine. As I left the freezer, I whispered to him, "Vive la France."

I slipped out of the restaurant unseen and traveled home unnoticed. I pulled a hooded sweatshirt over my head and, as I expected, no New Yorker on the street noticed a man walking, perhaps with a slight limp, and with the scars of battle etched across his face. Even in the heat of summer, so many young men these days cover their heads in this way. I don't understand this fashion trend, but in this case, it served me well. I arrived home and tended to my wounds. Yesterday, I was able to write only a paragraph, but today my strength has returned and I am able to relate all to you, dear readers, so that you can know the exultation of God and the thrill of righteous victory. For victory I had, and I will have again before my great quest is done.

Chapter 15 – Arrival of the Cavalry

August 9, 2018

MIKE AND JASON had pored over the files for the four murders trying to find some connection, but without success.

Jason pushed his laptop computer away on the conference room table and sighed, arching his back and stretching his arms above his head. "Man, this guy LeBlanc was a real piece of work."

"How so?" Mike asked without much enthusiasm.

"His company manufactured generic drugs at a plant upstate somewhere called Amsterdam. The internet is crammed with stories and chat rooms talking about the lawsuits against him. There are a dozen going on right now claiming that people were killed or seriously crippled because of these drugs. I can't find any record of any trials or verdicts, but there are a lot of pissed-off people out there who think this bastard was a real douchebag."

"Is that the technical term?" Mike asked deadpan.

"Actually," Jason said as he turned toward Mike, "I think scumbag is the technical term, but I prefer the street slang version."

"It's the only thing these four victims all have in common," Mike said as he stood up from his chair and placed both hands on the base of his back. "They're all awful human beings who, at least in the minds of some people, deserved to die. None of them had been prosecuted or held liable for their actions, but it's not like anyone will be all broken up by their passing."

"Does that make our killer a vigilante?"

"Sure. He's Robin Hood. Should we just let him go and figure that he's only going to kill people who deserve it?"

Jason cocked his head to the side as if he was thinking about it. "No, Mike, I think we should bust him, rough him up, and then put him away until he rots."

"That's the spirit," Mike laughed. "If only he would come out and identify himself."

Later that day, Mike and Jason both sat fidgeting in the straight-backed guest chairs in Captain Sullivan's office, listening to the voice of Commissioner Ward through a tinny speaker. Mike had suggested privately that Jason should present the plagues on Egypt evidence that confirmed his original serial killer theory. Jason, however, wanted to make sure that credit went to Dr. McNeill and to Mike and so they agreed to tag-team the presentation. When the Commissioner's reaction was to blurt out "Holy shit," they knew they would not have to fight about the facts. The only question was what action to take next.

Sullivan helped them out by stating the obvious – that they needed to call in the feds now. The Captain told Mike, with the Commissioner listening, that he was putting two more detectives on the Task Force, and that Mike and Jason would have access to whatever reasonable resources they needed. But they all agreed that it would not be enough – they needed help. Regardless of the public relations and communications problems that would result, they needed boots on the ground and the expertise that the FBI could provide. They needed a profiler, and maybe the NSA to give them intel on internet activity. The Commissioner agreed, but he was not happy.

"Do we expect another kill at the end of this month?"

Captain Sullivan held out his hands, palms up, and looked at Mike for a response.

"Yes, sir," Mike responded as calmly as he could. "There is no reason to expect anything sooner, but there is also no reason to expect that this psycho won't strike again on the last Saturday of the month."

"OK. We have three weeks to make some progress and track down this bastard. Do everything you can, and I'll handle the Mayor. I'll call my guy in Washington as soon as we hang up."

There was nothing else to say. Sullivan leaned forward and punched the button to cut off the call. "Set yourselves up in the conference room on the fifth floor, across from the public communications office. That will be your war room until this is over. I'll tell Berkowitz and Mason to clear their cases so they can start helping you out."

"Thanks, Captain," Mike said as he struggled to his feet and stretched his back. "At least we have some concept now of what his twisted plan is. I don't really want to get inside this freak's mind, but maybe we can try to get ahead of him."

Sullivan looked skeptical. "Let's hope so."

August 10

By the next morning, the Task Force had grown to four detectives. Captain Sullivan assigned Steve Berkowitz and George Mason to assist Dickson and Stoneman. They set up in the fifth floor conference room – two floors up from the bullpen – and moved in all the files and research on the case. They had a large whiteboard on one wall of the room that was scattered with notes and pictures of the victims, taped up and linked together by drawn lines in different colors. They had been trying to link the victims to each other and to characteristics they had in common, but without any success other than the obvious fact that they were all awful people.

Jason asked, not for the first time, "How can we use the next plague? This is the concrete jungle, how does he murder someone and make it related to diseased animals? He's already been to the zoo. What's left?"

"If only I had the mind of a serial killer," Mike said, leaning back in his chair.

Before he could go on, however, they were interrupted by an unfamiliar female voice coming from the doorway. "I guess that's where I come in."

Mike turned his head and Jason, who was sitting with his back to the door, swiveled around in his chair to confront the voice, which belonged to a woman neither of them had ever seen. She was quite tall – that was the first thing Mike noticed. She was wearing a pressed white blouse with a blue ribbon necktie, a navy blue jacket, and a stiff blue skirt that ended just above her knees. It struck Mike as being nearly a military uniform. Dark nylons and shiny black pumps, which contributed a few inches to her height, completed the crisp ensemble. Her face was as stiff as her skirt, with the lines of her cheekbones arching upward toward her ears. They were exposed by her black hair, pulled back into a tight bun with not a strand out of place. She had dark eyes that looked right at Mike, seeming to bore through him. She was standing up straight as if at attention, a brown leather briefcase dangling from the end of her left arm. Her air of authority made Mike immediately want to stand up and salute.

"Can we help you?" Mike inquired politely.

"You can if you are Detective Stoneman," she said without taking her eyes off him.

"I am Detective Mike Stoneman. And you would be . . . ?"

"Special Agent Angela Manning, FBI. I specialize in psychological profiling, and particularly serial killers. I have been assigned to work with you on your current case."

"Just you?" Mike asked. "We were expecting the cavalry. Are there more agents coming?"

Manning sized up Mike and the rest of the men in the room before responding. "They are not coming here," she said. "The Director and the Mayor didn't want it to seem like we were taking over your investigation. The Bureau has assigned ten agents to the case, but they will all be working out of the office building in Foley Square. I'll be coordinating their assignments and efforts and they will report to me – to us – here. Whatever we need, the Bureau will provide. All you have to do is ask."

"Sweet," Jason said, getting up from his chair and walking toward agent Manning. "I'm Detective Jason Dickson."

"Yes," she softened slightly and shook his hand. "You're the one who first identified the pattern."

Jason smiled widely. "Why, yes, that's correct." Mike scowled briefly, but caught himself and returned to a professional expression. He introduced Berkowitz and Mason and invited Agent Manning to sit down so they could brief her on recent developments.

"What are you calling him?" Angela asked.

"The Menstrual Killer," Jason chimed in. There had been a heated discussion within the group about the killer's nickname. Mike favored "Travolta" since he was the Saturday Night killer. Berkowitz was a proponent of "Moses" but after some intense discussion they all agreed that calling a serial killer Moses wasn't respectful and if the press caught wind of it they would all look like sacrilegious jerks. So, they all agreed not to call him that anymore. There were a few other ideas, but since Jason had discovered the killer, his preference was allowed to stick. Plus, it was sick, juvenile, and graphically descriptive; all attributes the cops in the bullpen loved.

"That's a sexist nickname, you know," she said without any apparent emotion.

Mike took it upon himself to explain, "Every month, on the last Saturday of the month, he kills. He's very regular, and there's usually a good amount of blood involved. His victims have been male and female with only one common trait – they were all scumbags of one variety or another and we think that, in the killer's mind, they all deserved to die. What would you call him?"

"Batman."

Mike and Jason both broke out laughing, and after several seconds of maintaining her straight face, Angela smiled broadly.

Mike broke the silence. "Well, I guess that would be less sexist, I'll give you that. But, like it or not, he has a nickname and it's going to stick to him – changing names mid-investigation involves too much re-education of the participants. Besides, the name makes the young male cops blush and giggle, so what could be better?"

Angela nodded in acquiescence. "Very well. You were saying that you don't have the mind of a serial killer."

"Yes," Mike said, relaxing somewhat. "We have determined that the killer is linking each murder to one of the ten plagues on Egypt from Exodus. We've been through the first four plagues, and next up is the plague that caused the Egyptians' livestock to become sick and die. Since there isn't a lot of livestock in Manhattan, we're trying to brainstorm how we might narrow down possible targets."

Angela frowned, then agreed, "Yes, it is an interesting question. But the plagues have been linked to the method of death, right? Not so much the location of the murder or the identity of the victims?"

"That's right," Jason said. "So, it's hard for us to anticipate anything that will help us catch him."

Angela opened a leather folio and took out a slender gold pen. She looked up at the very messy whiteboard and shook her head dismissively. "Let's talk about attributes that might actually help us. Detective Dickson, would you please put our notes up on the board, if you can find some free space?"

Jason walked to the whiteboard, picked up the small eraser pad, and cleared off some space at the far right-hand side. "Go ahead," he said when he thought he had enough room and he had scooped up a black marker.

"OK, fire away, gentlemen. What do we know for sure about our killer?"

"He has a fixation on biblical references," Mike offered. Jason hesitated, waiting for some kind of confirmation from Special Agent Manning, but then wrote "biblical" on the board.

Berkowitz chimed in, "He has no problem watching his victims die and getting his hands dirty."

Jason hesitated, uncertain what to write. Angela saved them the time. "Let's just say 'sadist' for now. What else?"

Mason, who was generally pretty quiet, piped up, "His method of killing has been different for each victim, although that's related to the attempt to track the plagues."

"True, and yet still important." Jason wrote "different kill methods" on the board. He looked up at the other three men in the room. They were all deep in thought, as if puzzling over an important test at school. He marveled at the way this woman had taken charge in barely ten minutes, like she was the teacher and the rest of them were scared elementary school students.

After a few minutes of silence, Angela asked a question. "Has he killed or injured any bystanders, or anyone other than his intended victim during any of his episodes?"

"No, none that we know about."

"Has he had the opportunity to kill others who were close to the victims?"

"That's a little hard to say," Mike said in his professorial voice. "I'm sure there were some. The first victim, DiVito, was probably abducted from the street, but nobody saw it. The second victim, Sheraton, had an assistant and a few other people in her apartment, but only she was poisoned. The frozen guy, LeBlanc, was lured either to the place he was found or to some other place from which he was moved, but he seems to have been by himself. As for Slick Mick Gallata, we don't have many details, since the family won't talk to us. Our working theory here is that he targeted these people because he determined that they were bad people who deserved to die. Perhaps it has something to do with his Bible fixation. Maybe he viewed them as sinners."

"That's my analysis also, Detective."

"Have you seen the case file?" Jason asked.

"No, but I've been briefed. I'm looking forward to looking at the actual file now that I'm here. Why don't you gentlemen keep brainstorming the attributes of our killer that we know about. In the meantime, can someone point me in the direction of the restroom?"

When Special Agent Manning had stepped out, Jason turned to Mike. "The Captain did not mention that our FBI liaison was going to be a woman."

"They're mostly women," Mike responded curtly. "It's soft psych stuff and emotions, things women study more. So, let's give her the benefit of the doubt until she does something to suggest otherwise."

Jason nodded silently and went to refill his coffee, bringing back one for Mike as well, but not a third for Angela. He did not want to presume that she would want one, or how she would like it prepared. Mike let his sit, and when Angela returned, he offered it to her. "Two Splenda with powdered cream. You want it?"

Angela smiled and politely declined without explaining why. She removed her jacket and hung it neatly on the back of an unused chair. She pulled a cardboard box full of file folders toward herself and started thumbing through them. The detectives briefed their FBI consultant on everything they knew, and everything they speculated about. The process of re-stating all the facts, the sequence of events, the evidence, the M.E. reports on the victims, and the information they had gathered from the few relevant witnesses proved to be a beneficial exercise in synthesizing the essential elements of the case. Three hours later, amid a backwash of empty sandwich wrappers and discarded coffee cups, Angela rose from her seat and walked over to the whiteboard as if she were going to add another attribute to the growing list. But then she paused and put down the marker.

"He has planned these kills pretty carefully, hasn't he?"

"It looks that way," Mike said quickly. "He has used locations that were deserted and without any witnesses. He managed to get his hands on some very exotic poison, and he took out a mob boss who was very well protected, so these don't seem like spur-of-the-moment operations."

"So, he's been planning this for a while. I'll add that to the list." She uncapped her marker and added a line to the text on the whiteboard. "What else do the victims have in common?"

The four detectives were not quick to respond.

"Were there many people left behind who were sad to see them die?" Angela inquired.

"Not really," Jason quickly answered. "One wife, although she was hardly disappointed the guy was dead. Slick Mick's wife died a few years ago, his kids have their own families now. The other two were unmarried."

"OK, so our killer seems to be careful about not creating collateral damage or hurting bystanders during the kills. He's sensitive, in a twisted way. He has a conscience."

"Sure, he's a real humanitarian," Berkowitz blurted out.

Angela frowned at him. "You may think of him as just a deranged killer, Detective Berkowitz, but he has a plan, and he is thinking carefully about his victims. I'm not condoning that, but the fact that he's not indiscriminately killing innocent bystanders is important. As far as serial killers go, it's a favorable trait."

"As far as serial killers go," Mike repeated. "Pretty low bar."

They all shared a laugh, which broke some of the tension in the room.

"What's the next question, Special Agent Manning?" Jason asked.

"The next question is whether you're going to keep calling me Special Agent until we catch this creep. Can we make it simple?

You can just call me Angela and I'll call you by your first names."

"Go ahead, Angie," Mike quipped back.

"Angela, please," she said with a grimace.

"Fair enough, Angela. Now, how do we can catch our guy before his next period?"

Angela raised her eyebrow quizzically.

"Is that also sexist?" Berkowitz asked.

"Let's not go there, shall we?"

Once again, Mike stepped in. "Right, so from your perspective, what are the significant facts that we should focus on if we want to try to get into this guy's head?"

"Well, normally I would say we need to try to determine what's motivating him, but it seems that he's being pretty transparent about that. He's motivated by a desire to kill off bad people like he's some kind of biblical Avenger, and to do it as a recreation of the plagues on Egypt. But we should confirm. Most of the time, guys like this are also hounds for publicity – they get off on seeing their crimes on television and thinking that they are famous and in the spotlight because of their actions."

Mike jumped on the train of thought. "He has left a few clues, but they were very subtle, even the biblical pattern thing. But we kept all that out of the media, so there hasn't been much publicity. We're trying to maintain that, although it's going to be hard going forward."

"Is there any chance that going more public with the case will help us catch him?" Berkowitz asked.

Angela hesitated for a few moments, then shook her head. "No, if that's what he wants, then giving it to him will only satisfy him momentarily. He's going to keep killing on this pattern regardless of anything else that happens around him. I would bet on that. I doubt that he would change his approach or get careless if there was more publicity. To the contrary, I think he might get frustrated that he's not getting more press now, and he might do things to make himself more obvious in order to get more publicity. Or he might go directly to the press, which might give us a clue."

"So where does that leave us for now?" Mike asked.

Angela smiled and reached to retrieve her jacket from the back of the chair. "It leaves us ready to call it a day and get some rest. We'll have our team ready downtown by next week. I'll see you gentlemen back here first thing Monday morning. Go home, kiss your wives, and clear your minds." And with that, Special Agent Angela Manning strode quickly from the conference room and disappeared into the hall.

The four detectives sat in silence until Angela was well out of sight. Berkowitz spoke first. "Wow, she just came in and took over, and we rolled over like a bunch of schoolgirls, huh?"

"You just hate taking orders from a woman, don't you?" Mason shot back good-naturedly.

"I do not. I mean – I don't mind. I just mean she's – oh, Hell. I'll just shut up before I get hit with a sexual harassment complaint."

Everyone laughed and started to pack up. Mike tossed his garbage into the bin in the corner. "You heard the lady. Let's call it a day and come back fresh on Monday morning." Within five minutes they were all on their way out. Mike stopped off at Captain Sullivan's office on the way downstairs to brief him on the day's events, although he had to admit that they had not only not found any new ideas, but they had not given out any orders to the FBI field agents to do any leg work for them, which was the whole point of calling them in.

"It's the first day," Sullivan stated the obvious. "You're just ramping up. Make sure that you have some action by next week. Even if it's just bullshit, we want to seem like we're using the resources or they'll pull them."

"Right," Mike acknowledged.

"How is she?

"She's good. She knows what she's doing. I like her."

Sullivan gave Mike a nod. "OK, let's hope she tips the balance."

"Amen to that," Mike said without any irony.

◆◆◆

As he walked out of the precinct house at 5:25 p.m., Mike realized that he had no plans and that there were still several hours of sunlight left in the day, which was not the normal situation for him. He had no paperwork to complete, since all his other cases had been reassigned. He had no calls to make and, unless he turned around and went back up to the war room by himself, he had no files to review. Angela was right that it would do them all some good to clear their minds, get some sleep, and start fresh the next Monday. But it was too early to sleep.

Exiting the station and turning right instead of his usual left, Mike strolled down the tree-lined street in the direction of the park. He admired the stoops of the renovated brownstone buildings arranged like dominoes along the sidewalk, some of which were populated by an assortment of children playing and adults enjoying the relatively cool late afternoon. A breeze tickled the boughs of the trees, embedded in their wrought-iron planters every thirty feet next to the curb, sporting signs admonishing the neighborhood to clean up after their dogs. Mike took off his suit jacket and tossed it over his left shoulder, and found himself whistling as he jaunted along. After two blocks he had to wait for the light on Central Park West before crossing over to the edge of the park. He skirted the stone wall separating the greenery from the street until he reached the roadway leading into the park at 96th street, at which point he crossed to the south side and then turned toward the tops of the Fifth Avenue buildings peeking above the treetops. It occurred to him after twenty minutes following the walking path southbound that he was well beyond the cross-street that would take him back to his apartment, but he just kept walking.

At 6:00, a church bell sounded somewhere in the distance, prompting Mike to reach into his pocket and fish out his phone. He may have been taking a carefree walk in the park, but his reflex was not to let the top of the hour pass without checking his email. He frowned when he saw the green telephone receiver icon flashing on the phone's screen, indicating that he had missed a call. Then he remembered that he had silenced the phone during their brainstorming session with agent Manning. He checked the recent calls and pressed the icon to return the missed call. Dr. McNeill picked up on the second ring.

"Hey there, Doctor Phibes," Mike quipped playfully.

"It's about time you called me back."

"Oh, um, I'm really sorry. We were in a meeting all afternoon on the Menstrual Killer case and I silenced my phone."

"You know, for a tough-assed detective, you are so gullible!" McNeill laughed, and Mike was happy that she couldn't see how red his face was getting.

"OK, you got me. But I really am sorry that I missed your call. What do you have for me?"

"Hmm, I have a thick steak in the fridge and a bottle of Cabernet in the cupboard," she laughed again, then cleared her throat. "But first, I have the official written report from the CDC on the poison used to take out your second victim."

"Oh yeah? The frog?"

"Yes, we have confirmation of the species. It's a relatively common South American tree frog."

"Where would our killer get his hands on something like that?"

"Well, I did some digging and made a few calls. It seems that you can actually get the poison on the internet. Or for bonus points, the actual frogs."

"Like Hell, you say?"

"Could I make this up, Mike? Turns out that the stuff is diluted down and refined into a bunch of cosmetic products. The poison, not the whole frog. It acts like botox in certain circumstances and gets injected under the skin, or put into face powders and such. The little critters themselves are apparently exotic pets for rich weirdos who like to lick the skin and get high like some kind of peyote, as long as they don't ingest too much and kill themselves. Can you believe it?"

"Nothing really surprises me," Mike replied. "So, if we try to track down all the sources where the killer could have accessed the poison, we'll end up chasing our tails for weeks with almost no chance of finding him unless he was incredibly careless about having the stuff shipped to his actual home address. Am I about right?"

"You are totally right, Detective."

"Well, what about that steak?" The line went silent for a moment, and Mike wondered if it had been just a joke. He doubled down to avoid stammering. "As it turns out, I am sitting on a bench in Central Park right now enjoying the beautiful day and I have no dinner plans."

"Well, I don't want to be a welcher, so I guess my offer is good if you want to meet me at my place in about an hour."

Mike clenched his right fist and took a breath before answering. "I can't think of anything I'd rather do."

"Great. I'll get out of here and pick up a salad on my way home. It's 319 East Twenty-Third Street, between Second and Third."

"Great," Mike said, perhaps a bit too quickly. "What's the apartment number?"

"7-H," she told him. "Just ring the bell at the door. I'll see you later."

Mike hung up and stared at the phone for ten seconds before sliding it back into his pocket as he stood up from the park bench. He had an hour. He should pick up some modest flowers, or maybe a bottle of wine on the way. He calculated the distance and decided that he had just enough time to hit a market, pick up some flowers, and make it to the number six train. He strolled leisurely toward the south exit from the park and started whistling again.

Chapter 16 – A Tiger's Tale

July 3, 2018

RECOVERY FROM FACILITATING the heavenly judgment of Napoleon has been miraculously swift, and I have returned to full duty and capacity. My verve and stamina have been buoyed substantially by the constant news coverage in print and on television. The frenzy, as it always does, has died away, although one reporter in The Times has continued to doggedly write a story each day as he attempts to interest his readers in the mystery and the unusual circumstances of Napoleon's death. I wish him the best of luck, and I have posted a comment on his article congratulating him on his fine writing and wishing him "bonne chance."

The next soul who shall meet God at my behest has been selected for something I have looked forward to since early in my inspiration. It is simply so perfect, both spectacular and in harmony with the divine theme. I have visited the site regularly since winter. Today I walked through the logistics again, and nothing has changed from my expectations. It is simplicity itself. The handlers are so lax and security is laughable. For who would dare? Who would ever consider? It will be easy, except for the process of bringing the supplicant to the altar of the Lord. Here my preparations have been more difficult and more painstaking, but my focus on this next execution has never wavered, even as *others causes have required my attention.*

With study and thought, I have come to better understand the man and his evil. Unlike Abel, Eve, and Napoleon, this quarry is much more on guard. He worries about electronic surveillance and uses email and even text messages rarely. Determining his routines therefore required more conventional, old-school methods. He has so many enemies, and must be so careful. And yet there are gaps in the armor. There are things that the enemies will not do because of the skewed code of honor that coexists with the fear of reprisals that accompany attacks on the family members of powerful men, and the legal prohibitions that restrict the police. Yet I have no such fears or restrictions.

July 14

The man who rules one side of the criminal landscape is so cruel and heartless that I can hardly conceive of his malevolence. He has no concern for the lives of others and as easily extinguishes the life from innocent people as from mice or cockroaches. He lives off the sweat and toil of others, yet contributes only misery and pain. He views himself as untouchable because he is surrounded by sycophants who protect him and yet fear him. He is Pilate. Justice shall come to him. As nature culls the flock when the predator secures his supper, so shall God thin this scum from the ranks of humankind. I will need to be very cunning and careful, and yet I feel the spirit of God within me and know that I shall succeed.

When I found the key, I felt the joy of everlasting life. Truly, the innocent shall take down the evil. Lo, the entire reality shall be revealed as the plans come together as well as I could have ever expected.

July 29

The logistics associated with the demise of Pilate were truly dismaying to me when I first began the planning process. Entering Pilate's fortress and quietly gliding a knife into his heart would have been difficult, but not impossible. And yet, that would not continue the pattern that the Lord has commanded. No, the site of death has been ordained, and the challenge was to devise a way to bring Pilate to the Lord's altar. And so, the puzzle of puzzles: how to extract a rich and powerful man from a well-secured compound in a highly populated city and move him in isolation to the location? The solution proved vexing and yet, in a sense, simple. What would make a man like this willingly leave his home in the company of a stranger, or travel on his own to the location of my choosing? The answer in both cases is the same – in order to protect a loved one. His grandchild would be the bait that would lead him to his undoing.

On the Saturday before the day of Pilot's demise I watched as the ogre left home with his granddaughter and drove her to dance class. I had no doubt that this was a weekly ritual and I was of course correct.

One week later, with all in readiness, I arrived at the dance studio long before the end of the class. Of course, there would be great risk for me to be seen in this context, but foresight is my specialty and so a disguise was in order. I had easily procured a neat beard, glasses, a stylish bowler hat, and a small scar on my left cheek. Although I doubted that the dance studio would have high definition security cameras, I left nothing to chance. I dressed in a sharp suit and announced to the studio assistant that I was there to pick up the girl and escort her home due to a sudden death in the family. She was at first reluctant since I was unfamiliar but I had correctly deduced that her grandfather, given his business activities, would frequently farm out the task of retrieving his darling granddaughter to his underlings. I was, of course, correct again and she willingly accompanied me.

Once in my car, I explained that I had lied to the nice woman at the dance studio and that, in fact, I was taking her to a surprise party. She was thrilled, if a slight bit put off by the prospect of attending the party in her dance clothes. Still, the plan was successful and the girl was secured. The family no doubt had extreme anxiety concerning her disappearance and I truly regret that other members of the clan were put through emotional distress in order for my grand design to be fulfilled, but in the end only the villain suffered physical anguish. For the girl was entirely safe and well and I revealed her location anonymously to the family before the night was over.

That evening, I telephoned Pilate's home and set my plan in motion. I was certain that Pilate would not involve the police. However, I expected that his own private army would be called into action. I instructed Pilate to leave his home alone and walk to a bodega some ten blocks away – a point easily observable from the elevated subway station nearby – where he was to obtain a burner phone that I had hidden. I observed his approach and watched as he paced the sidewalk, in my complete control. I instructed him to enter the subway and watched as he complied. I easily spotted two of Pilate's associates following once he climbed the stairs onto the subway platform. I called again and admonished him for his violation of my prior rules by bringing henchmen. If he did not order them to leave, I would disappear with his darling granddaughter. He complied.

Pilate was expecting me to ask for money. He was, therefore, convinced that I would do him no harm lest I sabotage my own ambitions for securing the ransom. At worst, he expected that he would pay and then hunt me down later. How little he knew.

I accompanied Pilate through the New York subway system until we finally arrived at our destination in the Bronx. I had him wait while I ventured ahead and then had him meet me in a location where any followers would be fully exposed. I then required him to wade into and submerge himself in a fountain while holding my phone above the water in his hand. He and his associates have means and are sophisticated criminals. Surely they would affix a tracking device to Pilate's clothing, or even hide a simple cell phone with GPS tracking in a pocket or lining. I am not so easily fooled. Water is an effective countermeasure to such devices. He repeatedly offered to pay whatever ransom I demanded in order to get his "grandbaby" back. I gave him encouragement, but continued his trek.

Now, gaining entrance to the Bronx Zoo after public access hours is not a simple prospect. But the facility is not a high-security installation, and with a little surveillance and planning, a gate off a side street can be unlocked. Pilate entered there, just after me. From there, it was only a short distance to the tiger enclosure.

Pilate, of course, wanted to play the part of the tough guy, but the unique qualities of a stun gun subdued him quite easily and rendered him pliable – relatively easy to bind hand and foot and then cut with a simple pocket knife to create a suitable tidbit for the tigers. The beasts don't feed on demand, particularly when they are used to a set schedule. But the smell of fresh blood and Pilate's screams of anguish piqued their interests and led them to their toy.

Pilate went through much the same stages as Able and Napoleon. First, anger and threats of hideous reprisals for me and my family, as if his power would survive his death and strike fear into my heart. Then, bargaining and offers of fortunes, women, and other favors. The man fancied himself as able to bribe anyone, and yet the Lord cannot be bought. Napoleon had begged for mercy, but Pilate would not stoop to that. I admire that about Pilate – he met his death without groveling. I made sure to mark Pilate's body with my sign, although I suspect that my little kitties may have marred my handiwork.

RIGHTEOUS ASSASSIN

I regret that I was not able to be next to him at the moment that Pilate's evil soul drifted from his body and met his Lord. My vantage was more distant than I desired, but self-preservation must play some role. Even with the Lord's protection, there are things on this Earth that one should not tempt. Still, I will always treasure the sound of those muffled screams and the crunch of his bones.

I shall now sleep the untroubled sleep of the righteous.

Chapter 17 – Chasing Shadows

August 13, 2018

O N MONDAY, Mike awoke feeling rested. After a quick jog, a long shower, and a toasted bagel with a healthy schmeer of cream cheese, he arrived back at the war room at just after 8:00 to find Special Agent Manning already there, sipping a Starbucks coffee and staring at an open file folder.

"Good morning, Angela," Mike called out cheerily.

Angela looked up and smiled. "Good morning, Mike. And thanks."

"For what?"

"For calling me Angela. It usually takes weeks for the local dicks to accept me onto the team enough to use my first name."

"Well, we're a pretty accepting bunch here." Before Mike was forced to think of a snappy continuation line, his attention was attracted to the sound of someone tapping on the frame of the conference room door. It was Officer Olson. "Hey, Officer, good morning."

"Good morning, sir. I was hoping to find you here. I've got the results of the surveillance video from the building where the Sheraton woman lived. I think I found your dog walker, but I'm not sure it's going to help you much."

"What do you mean?"

"Come on downstairs and I'll show you."

"You mind if I bring the feds along?"

Olson did a double-take before realizing that Mike was referring to the woman sitting at the table. "Uh, sure."

"Let's take a walk, Special Agent Manning."

A few minutes later, the three of them were huddled around a fourteen-inch computer monitor while Officer Olson walked them through the results of trolling through nearly a month's worth of surveillance recordings. She had been very thorough, cataloguing every instance of "Nick" appearing in the lobby. Olson had noted the time index for each occurrence and saved each as a bookmarked web address on the storage cloud where the management company saved the video. After the third time waiting for the site to load and buffer the video, Angela asked why she had not copied the relevant segments onto a DVD so she could just jump to the next relevant segment.

"Does this look like a high-tech operation?" Olson asked.

Angela looked around at the walls of the tiny room, lined with ancient plywood bookshelves drooping under the weight of file folders, three-ring binders, and VHS tapes. The space was dimly lit by fluorescent lights that flickered slightly every few minutes. The monitor they were staring at was connected by a white coaxial cable to a top-loading VHS machine that easily weighed seventy pounds. "No," she said softly, "I can see that the tech level here is rather low. But, if we need an upgrade for matters involving this investigation, I can make a call."

"Thanks," Mike said. "We'll see if it's necessary in this particular instance, but going forward we'll definitely take you up on that."

As they watched the grainy black-and-white security camera recordings, Olson pointed out the recurring figure coming in and out of the frame, usually with his back to the camera. The person in the video, who appeared to be a male, wore a dark sweatshirt with the hood up over his head, mostly obscuring his face. He also wore a Yankees baseball cap, with the bill pulled down low. The hoodie and ball cap seemed to be especially low when he walked toward the camera. His face was so shaded and obscured, and the quality of the video was so poor, that it was impossible to see any distinguishing features. Each day the pattern repeated between 5:15 and 5:45 p.m. In alone, then out with Shep. In with Shep, then out alone. Olson had identified fifteen instances over a three-week period. And each time, the figure was unidentifiable.

"Do you think your boys at the FBI lab could enhance this at all?" Mike asked Angela.

"I doubt it, but it's worth a try. Forward the URLs to me in an email and I'll send them downtown."

"Thanks. We figured that the dog walker could be the killer, although the surveillance cameras only show the door and not the inside of the lobby. He left a cell phone number that's now dead and no address, and he stopped showing up with no notice as soon as Ms. Sheraton was killed."

"I'd say you have a solid basis to think he's the killer."

Manning and Stoneman walked back upstairs to the war room, where Dickson, Berkowitz, and Mason were sharing a box of donuts and discussing the Yankees' game from the night before. Mason thought that Aaron Judge was a better hitter than Giancarlo Stanton, while Berkowitz held the opposite opinion. They all stopped chewing as soon as Angela and Mike entered.

Angela ignored the men and walked straight to the whiteboard. She wrote down several bullet points.

> 6'0" - 6'2"
> 180-200 lbs
> Right-handed
> Slight limp (left leg?)

"Where did we get those from?" Mason asked.

"From the surveillance video from victim number two," Angela replied, tapping her dry-erase pen against her palm and apparently deep in thought. "What else, Mike?"

Mike sat down and reached for a donut, which he carefully placed on a napkin, and then licked the excess powdered sugar off his fingers. "Glasses," Mike said, just before taking the first bite from his pastry.

"Nose tap?"

"Twice."

"Good call."

"What the hell is happening here?" Berkowitz yelled.

"Sorry, Steve. Angela and I were just downstairs with a uniformed officer reviewing the security camera video from Marlene Sheraton's apartment building. Officer Olson identified the dog walker. We have him on tape fifteen times, but every time he's wearing a hoodie and a ball cap pulled over his eyes. We have almost no chance of getting any usable ID from the video. We sent it down to the FBI's office to see if they can enhance it, but I doubt it's going to be helpful. But, we can figure out a few things about the guy, at least within a range."

"The fact that he made such a concerted effort to evade the security camera, along with the timing of his disappearance and him having no valid contact information, all point circumstantially to him as the killer." Angela turned back to the board. "Now, we know a little bit about his physical characteristics. It won't allow us to put out an APB on him, but when we close in on him, every little bit of information helps."

"OK," Mike said between bites, "what other information can we deduce from what we know? What's in the file that can help us paint a picture of this douchebag?"

"He has a car and drives, so he's probably got a driver's license," Berkowitz called out.

Angela wrote it on the board. "Because we suspect he abducted DiVito from near where he parked his car and transported him uptown for the kill. But he could have had a rental."

"Could happen," Jason agreed. "He's smart, so he might not want his own car to be exposed. A rental seems plausible. But, he would have to have a credit card in order to rent a car."

"He could have a fake identity," Mike suggested. "He wouldn't want to be traced that easily. If he's been planning this for as long as we think, he could have fabricated a few false identities."

"So, you're suggesting that we don't have to check car rentals around the time of those events?" Berkowitz asked hopefully.

Angela jumped in. "I'll put my data miners on it. They'll be able to cross-match all the local agencies faster than we could do it ourselves."

Berkowitz let out an audible sigh of relief.

"What else?" Angela asked to the room.

Mason piped up. "He probably lives in Manhattan, or at least one of the boroughs."

"Why?" Angela inquired.

Mason hesitated and looked around the room. He was typically reluctant to be the center of attention. When he started talking, he spoke so fast he barely took a breath. "He was walking the dog and casing out kill locations in Manhattan, and he had to have had Sheraton under surveillance in order to figure out her routine, and he had to do the same for LeBlanc and for Slick Mick. He had to be both in Queens and the Bronx, so it makes the most sense that he's based here."

Angela wrote down, "Manhattan?" on the board. "It's a likely theory. Um, I'm sorry, Detective Mason – I'm afraid I never got your first name."

"George."

"Really? George Mason, like the University? Your parents either had a sense of humor or grandiose expectations for you."

"Actually, George was my uncle's name. He died shortly before I was born, so I was named after him."

Angela blanched and then assumed an appropriately apologetic expression. "OK, well, fine, George. It's likely you are right about him living in Manhattan. Perhaps not rock solid, but enough to go on for now. What else?"

"He seems to be either very strong or very adept at subduing someone one-on-one. He took down DiVito on the street without anyone noticing." Jason stood up and walked around the table while he talked. "He took down LeBlanc somehow and got him to the kill point, again without anybody noticing. And for Slick Mick, unless he had a helper –"

"He has no helpers," Angela cut him off.

"How do we know that?" Mike asked.

Angela tilted her head to the side and pursed her lips, but then relaxed her face. "I'm sorry, you gentlemen aren't accustomed to dealing with serial killers. I can tell you to a moral certainty based on his behavior so far that he is acting entirely alone. Men like him act out an elaborate self-aggrandizement and never, ever, share the experience with other people. This is a solo operation. Always."

"OK," Jason agreed. "It all makes sense, and it also supports the theory that our killer is a strong guy who probably knows how to handle himself in hand-to-hand combat."

"There's nothing on the video to suggest that he's a particularly big guy," Angela observed. "He's not small, but he's not a monster. So, that suggests some training."

"Could be military," Jason offered.

"That would map," Angela agreed. "He knows how to kill people. He knows how to torture people. He knows how to cover his tracks and how to plan an operation."

"Sounds like Special Forces," Jason said.

"Sure," Mike cut in, "so that narrows it down to a couple thousand possible suspects."

Angela wrote on the board, "Military/Special Forces?" and turned back to the group of detectives.

"Wait," Berkowitz said, "didn't the Richardson family say that the dog walker was a veteran – had a military tattoo?"

"Yes," Mike jumped in, grabbing for a box on the table and

sorting through, looking for a folder. "Yes, they said their dog walker had some kind of Army tattoo."

Angela erased the question mark next to the word "military" on the board and added the name "Nick."

"Wait," Mason shouted out, "wasn't the first victim named Nick?"

Jason slapped his hand on the table. "Yes. Nick DiVito. He was the first kill."

Angela's shoulders sagged. "Did dog-walker Nick have a last name?"

"I don't think so," Mike said. "We were trying to track the guy, but all we had was a first name."

"Well, that's not going to help much," Angela conceded. "It's not likely that he would use his real name anyway, but sometimes serials will use the names of people in their lives, which can help us track them. In this case, it's more likely he's using the name of his first victim, which shows a pretty savvy understanding of how not to get caught."

"Or maybe he just doesn't have anyone else," Berkowitz wondered out loud.

"I'll ask our guys to cross-check military records against what we know about our killer. It will be a long list, but we'll see what we can narrow down from there."

"Sounds good, Angela," Mike said. "It's nice to have the FBI's resources available for stuff like this."

"Our pleasure," Angela replied. She then walked to the board and drew a square in the upper right-hand corner. Inside the square, she wrote "10."

"The number of days before the next murder," Mike said. They all fell silent, wondering if they were going to be able to prevent it.

Chapter 18 – Tick, Tock

August 14, 2018

B Y THE NEXT AFTERNOON, the Task Force had sheets of paper spread out on their conference table, on which were the names and personal data of every serviceman who had been in a special ops unit and who had been discharged during the past ten years. They sorted out anyone named Nick, and identified anyone who had a dishonorable discharge or a psychiatric issue noted on the file, as well as anyone with a New York address. The Task Force then split up the names and contact information and started working the phones. The prevailing theory was that if they contacted a name and spoke to him by phone, he was probably not their man. They excluded all the women. Between the video of Nick-the-dog-walker and the physical requirements of committing the murders in question, Angela was certain they were after a male killer. She also pointed out that nearly all serial killers are male. They enlisted eight FBI agents, working at the downtown federal office, to help sift through the list.

By the end of the day, they had six possible leads – all discharged military men who could not immediately be located. The team, assisted by the FBI agents, worked on tracking them down, hoping to find someone who fit the profile and who could not be contacted. Of course, if they could not contact the right man, then even if he was their killer, they would not know where he was hiding. But they had no other good leads.

The FBI tech team was not able to do anything with the low-quality security camera images from Sheraton's apartment building. There was nothing there that could be enhanced.

"The guy's not stupid," Jason observed.

"That's the problem," Angela sighed.

August 17

By Friday, with the countdown at 8 days, their list of potential persons of interest had swelled to more than 200, and as fast as the Task Force could clear one name, two more were added. At 4:00, they all decided to take a break until Monday morning, having no particularly good leads and with frustration setting in.

Mike met Michelle McNeill for dinner at a quiet little bistro in the West Village. They sat in rickety metal chairs in the outside dining section, which was nearly as large as the tiny inside seating area. Mike kept his jacket on despite the August heat, trying to be a gentleman and not wanting to flash his trusty Glock, which was holstered under his left armpit. He didn't always carry his weapon while off duty, but with a serial killer on the street somewhere, he had decided that he wanted to be prepared.

"Penny for your thoughts," Dr. McNeill said as Mike's gaze had drifted to an examination of the pedestrians passing by their table.

"Oh, I'm sorry," Mike stammered. "I was just thinking about our case and I guess I was wondering which one of those people walking by might be our killer. Pretty silly."

"Not silly, just shows you're dedicated and focused. I know the feeling. Sometimes if I'm in the middle of an autopsy and I take a lunch break, I'll cut my chicken breast down the middle and separate the halves like I'm opening up a chest cavity and review my work in my mind while I eat. Fortunately, I'm usually eating alone."

"You can eat lunch while in the middle of an autopsy?" Mike asked incredulously. "I'm sure my stomach wouldn't take that."

The doctor laughed. "You get so used to it after twenty years that it hardly registers. I'm sure it's like you taking a lunch break during an interrogation."

"I can't believe you've been the M.E. for twenty years."

"Well, actually for the first five I was assistant medical examiner, so it has only been fifteen years."

"Did you have any other jobs before New York City?"

Michelle paused, as if thinking about how much to tell this cop who was interrogating her. "After my residency, I worked for the National Institutes of Health for a while down in Bethesda, Maryland."

"Is that where you got into forensics?"

"Uh huh," she confirmed, as their waiter brought their plates. "I thought I wanted to do research on contagious diseases and help save the world, but I ended up working with dead bodies instead."

"You're still helping save the world," Mike said as he dumped several spoonsful of grated parmesan on his pasta. "You help us catch the bad guys. You don't cure thousands at a time, but you are protecting the City one corpse at a time."

"I guess that's why I like you, Mike. You have the same morose sense of humor that I have." She smiled and Mike dropped his spoon with a clang onto the concrete under the table. He quickly fumbled for it and started to put it back into his food, but hesitated when he saw the doctor's disapproving look and instead held it up for their waiter to see and motioned that he needed a new one.

"Cops tend to laugh at things that would make other people cry, or retch. We have to make light of things or else all the human misery will eat us up from the inside. I've seen a bunch of young cops just bust a gut because they took everything to heart. It's like our current psycho. We call him 'the Menstrual Killer' because it makes light of him and makes him less scary, and because it allows us to laugh at him. I know it's a little sick and gross and probably sexist, but it's part of what keeps us sane."

"I understand. I have to admit that we do the same with some of the bodies in our lab."

"Like what?" Mike asked eagerly.

"I don't think I'm going to tell you that. I need to know you a lot better first."

"That's fine by me," Mike smiled, lifting his loaded fork.

Mike worked on his plate of pasta with Italian sausages and then felt guilty about it, watching Michelle pick at her caprese salad and complain about how she had been trying to take off the five pounds she had gained since the beginning of the summer. Mike could not imagine how her petite frame could ever put on weight, but he didn't need much of a reminder about how his own waistline had been expanding in recent years. But the pasta was really good and he rationalized his enjoyment by taking home a healthy portion in a carry-out container and telling himself he could have it for lunch on Monday instead of a greasy burger. Michelle suggested that maybe burgers were not a terrific choice for his regular lunch diet, and Mike not only agreed, but invited the doctor to help him plan out a list of healthier options. She had barely avoided getting sauce on his coat when she elbowed him and reminded him she wasn't that kind of a doctor.

After dinner they strolled along the sidewalk, watching the many interesting characters who populate the Village on a warm Friday night. Mike could not keep himself from eyeballing every single man who generally fit the physical profile of their killer. Could any of them be their Moses wannabe, just walking freely down the sidewalk? Michelle took Mike's arm with both hands and squeezed him as hard as she could manage, to break him out of his funk. It worked, at least for a while.

Mike suggested that they walk back to her apartment, but she was wearing heels and held out for a cab, telling Mike that she could get herself back home without his accompaniment. "Besides," she'd said, "I don't think I have all your attention tonight. I don't want to keep distracting you." He didn't argue and instead gave her a kiss on the cheek and a smile as he waved through the cab's window. Mike took the subway back to 66th Street and walked home, trying to keep his mind on Michelle, but always finding himself back on the killer.

That night, Mike dreamed about the video of the dog walker. He tried to zoom in on his face, but it was always too blurry. He woke early and decided to go out for a run, to work off some of the pasta. He made it to the park and managed a mile or so before he broke down and walked. Still, the exercise left him dripping with sweat and feeling pretty good about himself. The other runners and bikers in the park did not remind him of his killer as much as the miscreants populating the Village, and he found his mind fairly clear by the time he finished his shower and sat down to read the paper.

The New York Times had an article about the Mickey Gallata murder investigation. The reporter, a veteran of the beat named Dexter Peacock, speculated that the feds had been called in because of the organized crime angle of the investigation. There was no suggestion of a serial killer. He mentioned that Detective Mike Stoneman was leading the investigation for the NYPD. Mike smiled, hoping that the reporter would stick with the mafia angle, at least for a while, and wondered who had given out his name. He made a mental note to ask Sully about it.

♦♦♦

August 20

On Monday, Angela erased the "8" from the whiteboard in the war room and replaced it with a "5." The Task Force continued to work the list of former military possibilities. They finally exhausted the master list and worked on clearing the ones who could not be immediately contacted without having to add any more names. But they were clearing only twenty or thirty names per day, and by Friday, there were still more than a hundred and twenty names on the list. They had no other leads, so they just kept working what they had.

Mike updated Sully over lunch on Friday. He suggested that they go to a salad place on Broadway, which generated a raised eyebrow and a wave of the Captain's thick hand. They compromised on sandwiches from the local Subway, which Mike loaded up with veggies, as suggested by Dr. McNeill. Mike explained where they stood with the list of possible suspects, and admitted that it was a long shot. But at least it gave the Task Force something to do without having any other real leads. "It beats sitting around staring at each other," Mike offered. Sullivan just shrugged and said he would brief the Commissioner.

At 5:00 on Friday, Sully told his detectives to call it a week and to not put in any overtime on the weekend unless there was another murder. Jason said he was planning to meet some of his old college buddies for a basketball game in the West Village. Angela said she was going to try to get tickets to the Saturday matinee of *Wicked* on Broadway. Mike just said "Fine," and then added, "but I have a feeling we'll be seeing each other on Sunday."

"I hope you're wrong, Mike," Sullivan said with as much enthusiasm as he could muster. "But, if you're right, do me a favor and wait until after nine o'clock to call me. My wife hates it when the phone rings early on a Sunday."

"I'm sure we can commit to that schedule," Mike said.

Angela walked to the whiteboard and erased the "1" in the upper right corner, leaving a blank space.

Chapter 19 – Stalking the Devil

August 6, 2018

*T*HE ANGEL OF DEATH *is a discerning and careful servant of the Lord. And now, I have an adversary who can both appreciate and expand my legend. He is a police detective who is investigating the untimely demise of the city's dark lights. According to the newspaper, this man has only recently started investigating the death of Pilate, meaning that he has not begun to truly understand me. He is an experienced and, by most accounts, honest constable. We shall see whether he is intelligent as well.*

It is also reported that the FBI has been brought into the investigation. We shall see if the federal agents can unravel the mystery and piece together all the interlocking parts back to the death of Abel. My glory will only grow in the light that may yet be shone upon my victories.

August 10

The next foul monster who shall die at the hands of God is a man who has accumulated a bounty of sins during his miserable life. He is an abuser of women and is guilty of the sins of avarice, gluttony, greed, sloth, and lust. But beyond this, he has reveled in the infliction of anguish upon others. He is, like Abel, one who takes advantage of defenseless young women who are offered up to him by other vile scum who shall soon feel the wrath of God themselves. He is happy to use them for his own enjoyment and for the pleasure and debauchery of his associates and customers. His sadism knows no bounds. He has no positive or redeeming features. He has made a reservation for his own execution. He is Sodom.

The reach of law enforcement is so limited in cases like this. Sodom has cloaked himself in seemingly legitimate businesses and uses underlings to carry out his most vile commands, shielding him from prosecution. The authorities have identified him and targeted him, but within the restrictions of the law they have not yet built a case that will satisfy those who value rights and process over justice. The Angel of the Lord, however, is not limited by such mortal obstacles as laws. At my hands all are judged, as God judges them. Humans can hide behind the edifices that shield them from each other, but not from the Almighty.

August 13

I have been investigating my adversary, the Detective. He is complex. More importantly, he is from a generation that is less digital and therefore harder to track. Most of the easy methods for infiltrating a person's life are lacking in this case. He has no Twitter account, nor Facebook. He has an email account through the police department, but even accessing his messages fails to reveal the underbelly of the person, since he sends few personal messages and his professional use of email is mostly sterile and uninteresting. It will be risky to track him personally, and yet I feel compelled to understand this man who is to be the vehicle for my brilliance to be understood. I have detected some recent correspondence that may blossom into something interesting.

RIGHTEOUS ASSASSIN

It is now five weeks since I obtained my occasional position at the location of Sodom's doom. With the exception of the Saturday night in July when Pilate met his end, I have toiled in the heat and have come and gone with nary a trace. And yet, in this case it is likely that after the deed is done the police will be able to trace it back to my phantom persona. They will know that there was a man, and that the man is likely the agent of Sodom's end. But they will find only dust and smoke when they attempt to find me. They will know I exist, if they did not already know. My legend will grow, just as I intend.

Chapter 20 – Poor Menu Choice

August 26, 2018

O N SUNDAY, Mike slept late, taking advantage of his day off and figuring that he would probably get a phone call that would wake him. A few minutes after 9:00, he heaved himself out of bed, got dressed in athletic clothes, and headed out the rear door of his apartment building. He jogged slowly east along 69th Street toward Central Park. He had to wait for the traffic lights at Columbus Avenue and Central Park West, but once in the park he had an unfettered route for as far as he cared to run or walk in the slightly humid, but still very pleasant day. The trees in Central Park were thick with leaves and the park was teeming with life and activity. A hundred thousand people at least were running, walking, biking, or otherwise enjoying the park at that moment.

Was the killer here, on the running path with him? Mike shook his head to rid himself of the thought. "I can't even go for a run without thinking of the bastard," he muttered to himself as he slowed to a walk near the southern end of the reservoir. His grey sleeveless sweatshirt had dark stains down the front and under the arms. He could feel beads of sweat trickling down his back, to be absorbed by the band of his shorts.

He made his way southward back toward the 72nd Street entrance to the park. As he emerged from the under foliage he glanced north, toward the Museum of Natural History, which was bustling with activity. A large, red, double-decker tourist bus made a left turn a few blocks away, then kept turning until the driver had executed a U-turn and headed back south. "Nice move," Mike complemented the unknown driver. He meandered back toward his apartment building, stopping at a pushcart parked at Broadway and 70th Street to get a bagel, which he ordered without cream cheese. Then he picked up a copy of the Sunday *Times*. He took the elevator up, but got off on the fifth floor and took the stairs for the remaining five flights. He counted slowly to twenty on the top step as he stretched his calf and waited for his heart rate to slow toward normal, before exiting the stairwell. After a luxurious ten-minute shower, he toasted his bagel and sat down at his small kitchen table with a fresh cup of coffee and the newspaper, and counted his blessings. Such simple pleasures should not be overlooked, he thought.

The paper contained no stories about any Saturday night murders, although he realized that the news deadline for the paper was too early to include a late-night crime story. Mike finished his bagel, washed out his coffee mug, and decided to check the email on his phone. After a quick scan, he dialed Jason.

"Why didn't you call me?"

"I was waiting until noon, Mike. Wanted to give you a few peaceful hours. Besides, there won't be any witnesses to interview until later in the day and there really isn't much of a crime scene to study."

"I appreciate the courtesy, but it would have been fine to call any time after nine. What do we know?"

"The victim collapsed at a steakhouse in the theater district at around ten o'clock last night. The manager called 9-1-1, the paramedics showed up, they worked on him for ten minutes or so, but he was dead on the scene. They don't think it was a choking situation or an allergy, but we won't know for sure until the autopsy. Meanwhile, the responding uniforms saved the remaining food from the table in case anything was toxic and the detectives on the scene took statements and tagged everything."

"Who responded?"

"Jacobson and Melville," Jason recited without emotion. "I'm sure they did a competent job with the scene."

Mike grunted his agreement. Melville was green, but Leo Jacobson was an experienced detective. Mike remembered him as a particularly attentive student back during his first year of teaching aspiring detective candidates. He was confident that there would be no point in re-examining the crime scene. Plus, a restaurant would have cleaned up as soon as the cops left so they could be open for business today. So, he thought, Jason was right – there was no rush.

"What makes us think that this is our guy, again?"

"It was the only death reported last night."

"Really? Slow day. OK, where should I meet you?"

"How about at the restaurant at three? The pre-theater lunch crowd should be cleared out by then. It's called Flannagan's, on 45th between Seventh and Eighth."

"Good. I'll meet you there."

At three o'clock, Mike walked up to the entrance of Flannagan's steakhouse, having taken the downtown Seventh Avenue subway from his apartment. Jason was standing in front next to an ornately carved wooden American Indian holding a tomahawk and wearing a feathered headdress. The entire entranceway was dark wood and could have been the set for an old Western movie, except that there was no hitching post out front where he could have tied up his horse. Jason waved when he saw Mike approaching.

"What do we know about our stiff?"

Jason grimaced and removed his sunglasses. "Robert W.

Sawyer. By all accounts, he was a real shitbag; rich, arrogant, mean, and unfortunately also pretty smart. He has been on the vice radar for years. Apparently, he runs a prostitution operation in the outer boroughs, staffed with undocumented immigrants and runaways. A bunch of the girls have been beaten up and ended up in the hospital, but none of them want to talk about it. He branched out into loan sharking and recently also drugs. We haven't been able to pin anything significant on him personally. He has a million enemies. After reading his dossier, I want to kill him myself."

"Sounds like he fits right in with the other victims."

"Yeah, he does. And get this – his little flesh business operated under the umbrella of a well-known organized crime syndicate in Queens that starts with a 'G.'"

"Slick Mick Gallata." Mike said. It was not a question.

"Bingo. Sawyer was a small-time player in the organization, but I'm told he had his sights set on moving up. I guess that's not going to happen now."

"So, there's a link between Sawyer and Gallata. How does that help us ID our perp?"

"I'm not sure. It can't hurt. It's a connection. Then there's this kill. The method of death matches Ms. Sheraton, sort of. It's probably a different poison, based on the reports of the symptoms, but he certainly fits the profile of victims for our killer."

Mike gave a small nod and walked toward the door. When he got inside, he had to stop for a minute to allow his eyes to become used to the dim light. Despite the bright day outside, the heavy drapes on the front windows blotted out all traces of the sunshine. The place was quiet, with only a few occupied tables and a single waitress walking without urgency toward a couple that seemed to be finishing up their meal. He approached a smartly dressed woman standing near the front podium. She had been expecting them and directed Mike toward the rear of the room. Jason approached a small door, knocked sharply, and then turned the knob and walked in without waiting for an invitation. Mike followed.

The back room was nothing like the richly appointed interior of the restaurant. A metal desk was pushed against one wall, leaving barely enough room for a man to walk past. A fluorescent bulb flickered overhead, brightly illuminating the assortment of papers strewn across the desk and several large three-ring binders stacked up on the floor in a leaning tower. Two plain wooden chairs with bare arms sat askew in front of the desk, facing a middle-aged man with dark hair and a dark moustache, who was smoking the stump of a cigar with the sleeves of his white collared shirt rolled up.

He looked up from some paperwork on the blotter in front of him. "Are you the cops?" he asked indifferently.

Mike gestured to allow Jason to take lead. "I'm Detective Dickson. This is Detective Stoneman. We know that you already met with Detectives Jacobson and Melville yesterday, but we have a few follow-up questions for you, if you don't mind." He didn't bother asking the man with the cigar for his name. They knew from the report that his name was Clancy, although they were not certain if that was a first or last name. He was the manager and had access to the records they needed.

"Sure. Whatever you need, guys. It would be helpful if we could get this situation resolved quickly, since guys dropping dead in my place is not exactly good for business."

"Oh, you never know," Mike retorted. "Tourists may flock here to see the scene of a notorious crime."

"Yeah, but I'm more interested in my local clientele, not so much the tourists," Clancy replied.

"Fair enough. Let's get to it, then," Mike said as he stepped closer to the desk. "We'll need a list of all the employees who were here working last night and when they started, just in case it was an inside job. If anybody from last night doesn't show for work today, let us know."

Clancy looked up and raised his left eyebrow. "If *what* was an inside job? Do you know what killed the guy already?"

"No," Jason interjected, not wanting to be left out of the conversation. "We're waiting for the medical examiner's report, but we're tracking down all possibly relevant information, just in case."

"OK, whatever," Clancy shrugged, turning from his desk and opening the middle drawer of a metal filing cabinet. He ran his fingers across a few manila folders before pulling one out, opening it, and handing Jason a stapled bunch of papers. "Here's the payroll from last week, this has all the names of the staff. You can figure out who worked on Saturday, but nearly everybody does – it's our busiest day. I'll call our Human Resources company to get you the hire dates."

Jason scanned the first page of the payroll report, then flipped quickly through three more pages. "Does everyone who works on Saturday also work on Sunday?"

"No, there are a bunch of people who don't work Sundays, and even some who only work Saturdays."

Jason thought for a moment before asking his next question. "Is there a report that tells us who worked last night?"

"The other detectives wrote down the names of everyone who was there, but if you want to double-check you can pull out the time cards from the back room and see who punched in last night."

Jason nodded and thanked Clancy for the information. "Are there any security cameras in the restaurant?"

"I told the other detectives, there's only one and it watches the cash register. I gave the file to them last night. They said they would have somebody see if they can see the faces of the customers going in and out."

"Nothing in the back rooms where the employees are?"

"Nope," Clancy said briskly, as if he had already answered the question. He glanced at his watch and Jason turned toward the door.

"One more thing," Mike interjected just as Clancy was giving them a hopeful look, like they might be done and he could get back to work. "Who can show us how the kitchen works?"

Clancy looked puzzled. "Why do you want to know that?"

"Just want to understand how someone might have slipped a Mickey into the guy's food."

Clancy shook his head, as if not wanting to comprehend the possibility. "I guess you can talk to Shirley. She's the staff manager. You'll find her in the kitchen, probably."

Mike and Jason found Shirley, the staff manager, who walked them through the procedures used by the waiters and cooks. The place was still old school – paper order slips hung on clips. It was a pretty loose operation. After the tutorial, Mike said, "So, Shirley, in a purely hypothetical sense, pretty much anyone in the kitchen could plant something on any particular plate between the time the order comes in and the time it goes onto the counter. And any waiter could plant something between the time it goes onto the serving counter and the time the runner picks it up and carries it away. And all along the chain, you can tell that the plate is destined for a particular table outside, right?"

Shirley thought about the question and then responded slowly, "Well, yes, I suppose. It would probably be difficult for one of the busboys to put something on a plate – they just don't have access and they should never be hanging around the serving counter. But, anybody else could, I guess."

"And," Mike continued, "if you knew the table number where a particular person was sitting, and you knew what he ordered, anybody in the kitchen or any of the waiters could poison the guy's meal, right?"

After a pause, Shirley agreed, and then Mike thanked her and said that they would let themselves out. At that point, Shirley scurried back through the swinging doors into the pantry to resume whatever she and her clipboard had been doing when

Mike and Jason had interrupted her. The two detectives exited the kitchen the way they came in. As they reached the door, Mike spotted a basket of hard rolls and grabbed two. When he approached the exterior door, he held up the bread so that the hostess up front could see. She smiled and asked him if he wanted some butter, which he declined, handing a roll to Jason.

Then Mike stopped and turned back to the hostess. "Let me ask you something. The man who died, Mr. Sawyer, was he a regular customer?"

The hostess looked to be on the verge of tears. She bit her lip and took a deep breath, then responded. "Oh, yes, sir. He was here most every Friday and Saturday night at least. He loved the place, and we loved having him. The waiters adored him. He was a big tipper."

Mike nodded. "Did he have a favorite waiter?"

"He preferred Dominic or Linda," she quickly responded, "when they were working."

"Who was his waiter last night?"

"Oh, it was Linda. She was so shook up after it happened, I had to call an Uber to take her home. She loved him."

"Thanks," Mike said, turning and heading out the door behind Jason. They both squinted in the late-afternoon sun until Jason donned his ever-present sunglasses. Mike retaliated by crossing the street to the shady side.

"Did the crew last night question Linda the waiter?"

"Yes," Jason muttered as he dug into his inside jacket pocket for a folded sheaf of papers. He pulled it out, then swore softly as he stuffed the papers back into the pocket and dug into the opposite side, annoyed with himself. Mike had caught a flash of the payroll report. Jason produced the correct set of papers and flipped to the second page. "Linda Connors. Worked there sixteen years. Makes a good living working four nights a week. Sawyer was one of her best customers. She was pretty broken up about the situation. Jacobson put the uniforms on her to check out her credit and spending to see if she came into any money recently or if she was deep in debt or something."

Mike pursed his lips. "OK, we'll see if they come up with anything."

"You really think somebody inside the restaurant poisoned the guy's food?" Jason asked. "How could that be our serial killer?"

"I don't know. Maybe this isn't our boy, but remember that the next plague is diseased livestock – so poisoned steak would fit."

"You don't think that could be a coincidence?"

"We can only hope."

August 27

Monday morning at 8:44, Mike's cell phone buzzed. He was two blocks away from the precinct building, walking briskly but not quite sweating. He stopped outside a Starbucks to take the call. It was Dr. McNeill.

"Good morning, Doctor Sunshine," Mike crooned. "Is it possible that you have already completed the autopsy on Mr. Steaksauce?"

"The man has a name, you know," the doctor retorted seriously. "Mr. Robert W. Sawyer's tragic death was not the result of any natural causes. That's what I can tell you for sure. There are no wounds, no puncture marks, his heart was strong and healthy, there are no sign of aneurism, stroke, or other internal injuries. I sent the tox screen out with a rush to the lab, but even rushed it won't come back until Thursday. Maybe Wednesday at the earliest. If I had to take a guess, I would say poisoning is the number one suspect at this point, but we won't know for sure, or what kind of poison, for a couple of days."

"Did you send the food samples out at the same time?"

"Do you really think that I'd send the tox with a rush and not send the likely source of the poison? How long have you known me, Sherlock?"

Mike laughed loudly, drawing some stares from passersby on the street. "OK, I concede to your sleuthing expertise. Call me the minute the results come in, but since we're expecting death by diseased animal, I'm putting my money on the steak." He slipped the phone back into his pocket and continued on to the precinct.

Jason was sitting at the table in the war room, sipping coffee from a take-out cup with a plastic lid, when Mike arrived. "Shocking," Jason deadpanned when Mike relayed the doctor's opinion that the death was not natural.

"Yeah, well, we have three dozen possible suspects among the employees, not to mention the other diners, who could have slipped something into his wine or his food. And that assumes that he was poisoned inside the restaurant and not before he got there. There are plenty of drugs that would kick in after a delay, so nothing is certain."

"Should we spin our wheels based on the assumption that it was one of the employees?" Jason wondered. "We could have the uniforms call on them today to ask follow-up questions, just to see if anybody runs or acts strangely."

"It's a good idea," Mike agreed. "May not turn anything up, but it's about all we can do for now and it has enough potential to be justifiable to the brass. Let's take advantage of our federal helpers on this one and have them do some of the leg work."

Jason turned to his phone, and Mike walked to his usual spot at the end of the table. Before he could sit down, however, he noticed a pink message slip with his name on it. The note advised him to call the Captain as soon as he got in. This was never good news.

Mike walked down to the third floor and then strolled unhurriedly to the coffee machine to pour himself a cup, conscious of the unshaded window of the Captain's office in full view. After carefully adding Sweet-n-Low and skim milk to his paper cup, he meandered to the Captain's door and gave a soft knock on the frame, ignoring the fact that Sullivan was glaring at him already. "You wanted me, Cap?"

Sullivan motioned Mike to a chair in front of his ancient wooden desk. "Mike, the press is on the Menstrual Killer."

Mike hung his head slightly, knowing how this was going to complicate the investigation. "How?"

"We're not sure. The press desk got a call from some reporter at *The Times* named Peacock who wanted a comment on the serial killer investigation."

"That's what he called it, just 'the serial killer investigation?'" Mike cocked his head, thinking about the possible significance of the fact that the reporter had not used the moniker that the investigation team and pretty much the whole precinct had taken up.

"Yes, but we don't have much intel. He was pretty sketchy about what he knew and what he didn't know. The Comms team stonewalled him, but it's *The Times*, so we have to expect a shit show soon. I just wanted you to know."

"Thanks," Mike said sarcastically. "I guess it's better to have a head's up." The Captain just grunted and turned his attention to the report on his desk as Mike let himself out and purposefully walked toward the stairs. He had to go up to the war room and break the news to the team.

Chapter 21 – Steak and Agony

August 26, 2018

I WAS GRATIFIED *to be able to watch from a distance as the poison took effect on Sodom. By the time his guests and the waitstaff realized what was happening and summoned an ambulance, it was far too late. It is a vulnerability that almost all rich and powerful men and women have, but seldom think about. They walk into a restaurant – perhaps, like this, one where they are regular patrons. They chat, and laugh, and drink, and order their food. They eat greedily without giving a second thought to the possibility that someone in the kitchen has tampered with their steak.*

I had observed Sodom's pattern over several weeks from my new place in the kitchen, toiling over the heat. In order to minimize the prospect of another hapless diner receiving the arsenic, I waited until the very last moment before the plates were delivered to Sodom's table to plant the deadly seeds, on the pretext that the meat was not completely cooked to Sodom's specifications. I plucked the entire plate from the serving station and Sodom's waitress waited impatiently as I returned it to the grill and seasoned the bottom from my special bag. Mixed with the other spices and the natural flavor of the steak, the arsenic would not be detected by Sodom as he ate. Unless he shared his meat with one of his companions, no one but Sodom would be harmed, and he would never be so generous.

I calmly remained at my post, cooking various dishes for the busy restaurant and taking a short break only when the commotion out in the main room indicated the impending death of Sodom. I did not flee or give any indication that I was concerned about the night's events. My scheduled shift was over at eleven o'clock, and I was able to exit through the rear employee entrance without a care before the police officer on the scene had a chance to interview the kitchen staff. I strolled from the restaurant knowing that I would never return there.

This is my most exposed position, since the authorities will certainly determine that poison was the cause of death, and will trace it to its source. Those with access will be questioned, and my absence will no doubt be noted. But the establishment's policies are lax and their processes are simplistic. I expected that a much more sophisticated fake ID would be required, but since I have the advantage of being white and lacking a foreign accent, few would question my credentials.

The police will immediately begin investigating my pseudo-self, but all investigations will yield dead ends. This, of course, will make the chief detective and the FBI believe that their ghost is the killer, but that knowledge will only frustrate them. My disguise was so easy and yet so effective. There is only one security camera and it is always pointed at the cash register. As kitchen staff, I was never in view. I avoided any photos with coworkers and kept to myself so that no one will have strong memories of the man who will be the subject of the police search. I am confident that the description of the mystery man will yield no accurate details, since I carefully crafted a backstory to go along with my false identity. I have nothing to fear.

Will they find my fingerprints inside the kitchen? Doubtful. Everything is washed daily. All surfaces are regularly wiped clean. The employees have no private space – no lockers or even cubbies to store personal effects where a fingerprint might be left.

RIGHTEOUS ASSASSIN

Only a doorknob used by dozens of people could bear even a partial print, and that I wiped surreptitiously as I exited the kitchen. No, the police will be flummoxed and unable to find any trace of their ghost.

Chapter 22 – Looking for Mr. White

August 29, 2018

ON WEDNESDAY, Mike felt compelled to call Dr. McNeill to ask about the tox report, knowing that, just like when he called on Tuesday, she would tell him that the rush lab report would not be back until Thursday. He went downstairs to his regular desk so that he would have a little bit of privacy for the call.

"I just thought I'd ask," Mike said apologetically after the doctor told him exactly what he expected.

"You just wanted an excuse to call me, you smooth operator," the M.E. retorted playfully.

"Guilty as charged," Mike admitted. "I just have a feeling that this is going to be more in your ballpark than mine. I think we're going to need you, including your hunches."

The line was silent for a moment and Mike wondered if she was still there. "That's sweet of you to say, Mike," she said softly. "I hope I can live up to your expectations."

"You have never let me down, Michelle." Mike surprised himself by using her first name.

"Thanks, Mike. I appreciate that. I'll call you as soon as I know something."

Mike hung up, wondering whether her tone of voice was as welcoming as he thought. He realized after a moment that he was still holding the telephone handset and staring into space.

His trance was broken by Jason's voice from across the bullpen, "Hey, Mike!"

Mike startled and dropped the handset back into its cradle a little more loudly than he intended. "Yeah!"

"We got something from the feds casing the restaurant employees."

"What?"

"One of them is missing."

Mike and Jason walked back up to the fifth floor and entered the war room together. "What do we have?" Mike asked.

Angela gave him the briefing. "The officers were trying to talk to everybody on the employee list, but when they got to a guy named Charles White, they couldn't find him. The phone number the restaurant had for him is out of service and the address on his employee record is a Post Office box storefront in Harlem."

Mike made a silent "o" with his lips that morphed into a low whistle. "Now that's what I would call suspicious," Mike said. "Any chance that the phone number is familiar?"

"No," Angela said with a shrug. "Not the same as the burner phone number that 'Nick' the dog walker gave to the Richardson family. I'll put somebody on it right away, and I'll see if we have anything in our database for this Charles White – maybe he's someone our perp served with in the military."

"In the meantime," Jason said, "shall we go talk to our friend Shirley?"

"I'd say that would be an excellent idea," Mike said.

A half hour later, Mike and Jason were sitting in the back seat of a squad car that was illegally parked in the no-standing zone in front of Flannagan's Steakhouse, waiting for Shirley to arrive. They had prevailed on the manager to call her in early for the day in order to avoid having their investigation interfere with the normal operations of the house. The Mets were playing a day game in Chicago, which the officer who drove them was listening to while they waited. Todd Frazier had belted a grand slam in the first inning, so the Mets actually had a chance to win a game for a change.

"This one is five, so that's his halfway mark, right?" Jason observed.

"We have to assume that's his plan. But we've only been onto him for a month, so in a way this is really only number one since we've been following."

"I hope we aren't cooped up in that conference room for the next five months with Manning."

"Why not?" Mike asked. "Don't you like her?"

"I like her fine. I don't like the feeling that we're just the supporting cast now with the feds in charge."

Mike turned in his seat so that he was facing the younger detective. "Listen, Kid, I get it. This was your theory. It was your find. You are the one who figured out this guy's pattern, and you want to be the one to bust him. It's a little bit personal now for you, and you don't want to share the glory with the feds. If the feds make the final bust, then they get all the press and the accolades and you're going to be pissed off. It's natural. But we're still on the team. This is still our city and when the time comes to make the bust we still have the jurisdiction, so let's just find the bastard and take him down ourselves. We can share the attention when that happens."

Jason's mouth formed into a combined sneer and frown. "It's not like I'm trying to grandstand here."

"I didn't say you were."

"I'm not a publicity hound."

"I didn't say you were."

Jason turned to stare out the window toward Flannagan's. "You're right about one thing."

"What's that?"

"I really, really want to bust this douche. I can admit that if we miss this one I will be pissed."

"I understand. It feels personal. I remember the first time I had that feeling. Maybe we'll get lucky and he'll dig in somewhere and start shooting so we can take him out."

"I'm not trying to kill him," Jason shot back quickly.

"No, you're just trying to bust him. But keep in mind that if you drag him away in cuffs, then he gets what he wants as much as you get what you want."

The conversation was cut short by the appearance of Shirley, emerging from around the corner and walking toward the steakhouse. Mike said thank you to their blue-clad host and exited the vehicle, rendezvousing with Shirley as she was opening the front door. Once inside, they followed her into the little office where they had spoken with the manager on Sunday. She threw a corduroy handbag onto an empty chair and bent over to open the lowest drawer of the massive steel filing cabinet behind the desk, not offering a seat to the two detectives. She was clearly not happy with being called in early and avoided making any conversation. She combed through manila folders for a minute or two and then rose up, holding one in her hand which read, "White, C." She placed the folder on the desk and opened it, revealing a typed page stapled to the inside cover. There was also some scrawled handwriting that neither Jason nor Mike could make out, even when they bent over for a closer look.

"Have you got an I-9?" Mike asked. Shirley shuffled through a few pages of the thin file and pulled out the form. Mike knew that the work authorization paperwork was supposed to be kept in a separate file, but many small employers did not bother having a segregated I-9 folder and he was not going to give Shirley a hard time about the technical violation. They were not interested in scrutinizing whether any of the workers were undocumented.

Shirley handed over the form without comment and Mike held it in front of him so that Jason could read along. Charles White had listed the same disconnected telephone number and the same bogus address that were listed on the computerized print-out the manager had provided to the FBI. "Well, he's consistent about his fake address and phone," Mike commented. Meanwhile, Jason had pulled out a small notebook and pen and was writing down the driver's license number that was noted on the I-9 form so that they could run it later. The form indicated that he had also shown a birth certificate at the time of hire to prove that he was born in America, although the person who took down the information did not record the birthplace.

"Did he list any emergency contact information?" Mike next inquired.

Shirley shook her head. "There's long-term people here who list contacts like that, and others who just come and go and don't bother. Actors, grad students, stock brokers who get themselves into trouble, you know. White hasn't been here very long. He's a quiet guy. Polite, but doesn't volunteer much information. Keeps to himself, but he knows his way around the kitchen. He did say that he was a cook in the Army."

"Did you ever ask him about his military history?"

"No, I don't get involved with the employees' personal lives if I can help it." Shirley made a face like she had just eaten a bad lemon. Mike could only imagine the kind of crazy shit that a woman like Shirley had to deal with on a daily basis, trying to make schedules and keep an upscale Manhattan restaurant running while keeping labor costs to a minimum.

"Fair enough," Mike conceded. "Can you tell me whether Mr. White has worked since Saturday?"

"No," Shirley said quickly, without consulting any records. "He's one of the guys who only works Saturday nights. It's our busiest night and we have a bunch of people who just work that shift. In fact, I remember that when he started he specifically wanted to work only Saturday nights."

"How long ago was that?" Jason asked.

"Oh, not long," Shirley said, again very quickly and without looking at the file. Mike was impressed with her knowledge of the staff. She flipped to the front page of the file and pointed to his hire date of July 22, just six weeks earlier.

"Mike, that was a week before the last Saturday of July."

Mike nodded silently. Jason made a few more notes of the scarce information in the file and closed his notebook. Then Mike thanked Shirley and requested that she contact them immediately if she heard from Mr. White, and to let them know right away the following Saturday whether he showed up for work as scheduled. They suspected strongly that he would be a no-show.

"Do you have any photographs of Mr. White?"

"No," Shirley said. "We don't use photo ID for the employees."

"What about the camera by the front register?" Jason asked. "Is there any chance that he might have walked through there and been caught by that camera?"

Shirley shook her head. "No, sir. The staff at night doesn't come in the front of the house – they use the rear service door, and there's no camera out there."

"Can you give us a description?"

Jason took notes as Mike methodically walked Shirley through a series of questions about Charles White's appearance: height, weight, eye color, hair color and length, facial hair, noticeable scars or tattoos, type of clothing, hats, logos on his t-shirts, etc. She recalled some kind of tattoo on his arm, but could not describe it well enough for Jason to write down "Army," although that's what they were both thinking. When Mike finished the questioning, he thanked Shirley for her time. Shirley replied, "I hope we never meet again," which made Mike laugh.

Jason and Mike left out the service door, just to take a look around the back alley where the employees came and went. Aside from a rancid dumpster and a homeless man curled up at the side of the building, there was nothing but empty pavement. They circled around to the street and headed for the subway back to the precinct. Both men were silent, but both were thinking the same thing. Jason spoke first. "That's our guy."

"I think you're right," Mike responded without emotion. "If only that information helped us catch him."

For the remainder of the day, the Task Force did what they could to track down Charles White, who turned out to be a phantom. Angela's federal agents and data sources were no help. The driver's license number listed on Charles White's I-9 form belonged to a seventy-five-year-old woman from Albany named Mildred Starkman. A search of the name Charles White in the NYPD database turned up sixteen hits, five of which more or less matched the physical description they had cobbled together. Mike figured that none of them would be an actual match, but Angela had the FBI agents on the case try to track them all down and confirm whether they had an alibi for Saturday night. Meanwhile, a general search of telephone listings turned up sixty-seven Charles Whites who lived in the greater New York area, although only thirty-four within the city limits.

By 7:30, they were all mentally exhausted and called it a night. Dr. McNeill replied to Mike's text message asking whether the tox screen report was back with nothing but a frowny-face emoji. Mike decided to stop by his gym at Columbus and 64th and work up a sweat on the weight machines to clear his head. After a soak in the hot tub and a shower, he was feeling better and ended up going to bed early and sleeping soundly for the first time in several days, dreaming about sizzling steaks.

$\spadesuit\spadesuit\spadesuit$

August 30

The next morning, Mike was up early and went to the diner on 70th Street for eggs and toast before heading to work, skipping the bacon. He picked up a copy of *The New York Times* at the corner newsstand and scanned the front page, but there was no splashy story about a serial killer. Mike was the first person in the war room. He made a pot of coffee and read over *The Times*, cover to cover, despite knowing that anything about their serial killer would have made the front page. He had been in the office more than an hour before Angela arrived, looking less than fresh, with several strands of hair falling out of her usually neat bun.

"Rough night?" Mike asked.

Angela shrugged. "I spent a lovely evening doing laundry in the hotel's guest facility. Nothing like being on the road for weeks at a time."

Jason arrived at 8:58, followed closely by Berkowitz and Mason. At 9:06, the phone on the conference room table rang. Mike picked up before the second ring. It was the M.E. Mike listened, nodded, listened some more, said, "Uh, huh" several times, and then said, "Really?"

Jason was standing up next to the whiteboard, glaring down and holding out his hands in the universal sign for "What's happening?"

Mike ignored Jason and kept listening, then finally said, "Thank you, Doctor," and hung up.

"Was it the mashed potatoes?" Jason asked.

"Nope. Steak."

"What kind of poison?"

Mike stood up, still inclining his head upwards to speak with the taller man. "Good old-fashioned arsenic. She's sending over the report on the fax." Mike walked out into the hallway and across to the communications center. He stopped at an ancient fax machine, stained with brown streaks from long-ago spilled coffee, and waited as the mechanism wheezed to life and started clicking. Jason had followed him and kept asking questions.

"Anything in the other food?"

"She said there was nothing. Only the steak, and the same stuff in his system and inside his mouth and stomach. Can't be much more conclusive."

When the fax machine had finished spitting out the two-page report, Jason and Mike passed it between them and then handed it to Angela, who had followed Jason out of the war room. "Not subtle, was he?" Jason said, stating the obvious.

"No," Mike said, putting down the last sheet of the report. "He didn't care that we would quickly identify poison as the cause of death and the steak as the murder weapon. Maybe he even wanted us to know, like he's taunting us. He's daring us to try to catch him, because he knew that we would figure it out and he thinks he's invisible. Charles White thinks his false identity is impervious, and he thinks we'll never find him. He's an arrogant bastard."

Angela nodded. "The problem is that he's not wrong. We have nothing here."

August 31

On the Friday before Labor Day, the Task Force was no closer to unraveling the mystery of Charles White. All their leads were coming up dead. There was no pattern to the victims that gave them a clue about who would be next, and although they knew that the next method of murder would have something to do with boils, that hardly helped them narrow anything down. The FBI team had cross-checked the name Charles White against military records for anyone who served in the past ten years and came up with a dozen hits, but so far none of them had a clue about who from their military past might be a serial killer using their name. There were still a few names on the list who were being tracked down.

Meanwhile, the dog walker angle was also coming up empty.

The feds had examined surveillance cameras from all around the neighborhood, but none of the buildings had video of the sidewalks across the street in front of the park. There were a few cameras in the vicinity of the steakhouse with eyes on the street, but the FBI team reviewing the video had not conclusively identified the man calling himself Charles White. Mike and Jason were thrilled to have all the federal manpower, but so far it had not helped much.

With the whiteboard's countdown at 29, Angela called the team together. "We need help," she said.

"We have ten FBI agents running down our leads, how many more do you think we need?" Mike asked.

"Not that kind of help, Mike. I think we need to get the general public to help us. We need some tips. We have no good leads, and I don't think we're going to get any on our own."

The detectives were all silent, glancing at each other. After a few seconds, Mike took the lead. "Angela, I don't disagree with you. However, that would require us to publicly acknowledge that we are looking for a serial killer, and the Mayor has unequivocally said that he does not want that message to be disseminated to the public. I don't expect that he will be changing his mind about that."

Angela frowned. "Is it really his call?"

"Very much his call," Mike replied. "It's an NYPD case, not a federal case. You guys are assisting, not leading. At this point, all the criminal activity has occurred within New York City limits. Without any interstate criminal activity and without any federal crime, I don't see how the feds can take over jurisdiction here. It would have to be voluntary, and I doubt that Douglass will go for it."

"But the Mayor doesn't control the press."

Mike's eyes widened and he nodded slightly. "That's true. When the case hits the papers, then the lid will be off, and I expect that the Mayor might have a change of heart. We know that *The*

Times is on the case, but they have not published yet."

"It won't be long."

"Well, we might be able to accelerate the schedule," Mike said with a raised eyebrow.

Chapter 23 – The Power of the Pen

August 31, 2018

MIKE HAD SET UP a meeting with Dexter Peacock, the reporter from *The New York Times,* at a neutral location. Jason thanked Mike repeatedly for including him, knowing that this was a sensitive meeting and that Mike could have easily justified having the rendezvous alone.

"This is part of the investigation. Of course you're coming," Mike had said matter-of-factly. Jason had kept quiet. This was an important moment and he didn't want to blow it. He resolved to not make Mike regret bringing him along. Despite his feelings of disrespect at the hands of the older detective, Jason had enough sense to know that Mike's experience far exceeded his own and that he had better not do anything to mess this up. Then Jason thought about other reasons why Mike might want him along. If it came out later that Mike had leaked the story to the press, there would be Hell to pay. Since Jason was there, he would share the blame. Would Mike try to claim that Jason was the leak? Was he there to take the fall? Jason shook his head and scolded himself for making negative assumptions. But he was going to be careful.

The reporter thought they were meeting in a random Manhattan bar. The truth was that Mike knew the bartender at the Playwright well and could count on his discretion. It would be packed at dinner time on a Friday, especially with the tourists flooding the city on Labor Day weekend. But Mike's guy agreed to reserve the booth in the back for him, as a favor to the NYPD. Mike and Jason were waiting when Peacock strolled in wearing a derby hat, as if he expected Sam Spade to be waiting for him in a 1940s movie. Mike gave a half-arm wave to get his attention and Peacock slid into the booth opposite the two detectives without removing his hat, as if he was not planning to stay long.

"Your communications chief gave me the cold shoulder when I called," Peacock launched into it. "I was surprised when you called me, Detective Stoneman. Why?"

Mike sized up his opponent quickly. He had done enough research to know that Dexter Peacock was a seasoned New York beat writer who covered crime, politics, and scandals of all varieties. He was a New Yorker from Queens and seemed to have met all his aspirations. Mike's contacts at the paper reported that Peacock was a straight shooter, was not on the take, and was an arrogant son-of-a-bitch who didn't back down to anybody from the Mayor to the head of the sanitation workers union. The man sitting across the table from him fit that mold perfectly. Peacock was clearly pushing forty, but he was stylishly dressed in an Italian silk suit with a gold tie bar at the collar of his Custom Shop button-down. The brown hair peeking out from under the hat was styled into a mass of curls that looked natural, but which most people who looked carefully could see was held in place with a gel of some kind that made it look wet when it was really rock hard. Peacock wore a full but well-trimmed beard and rimless, steel-framed glasses, which contributed to the impression of forced hipster. But, his gaze was fixed on Mike and did not waver. There was a toughness under his prim exterior that Mike knew he should not underestimate.

"We're working on the case," Mike said simply.

"The serial killer?" Peacock asked as if he did not already know.

"Yes. As you can imagine, we're trying to avoid a public panic and sense of terror here. Lord knows the City doesn't need that."

"Is that why we're meeting on the cusp of the holiday weekend? So nobody will be paying attention to the story?"

"That's just a side benefit," Mike deadpanned. "We want to share some information with you in the hope that we can work together on this rather than against each other." Mike was calm. Jason thought that he sounded like he was teaching one of his classes to rookie detectives.

"You know that I can't share confidential information about my sources," Peacock shot back, seemingly on the defensive despite Mike's entreaty for cooperation.

"We're not asking you to divulge anything confidential," Mike soothed. "We're pretty sure that you got a tip from one of the beat cops about the fact that the FBI has been engaged to help us with the investigation, and that you were able to put two and two together. The investigation has been going on for a while now and it was only a matter of time before it leaked. Let's start by letting you ask us some questions – off the record. No notes, and no attribution to the department. But, perhaps we can help each other make sure that the public gets facts and not speculation that will only make things worse."

Peacock hesitated, considering his options. "Before that, I need to ask two questions on the record."

"Fine," Mike said, "but I don't promise to answer them."

Peacock nodded. "First, is it true that there have been nine killings that you believe to be the work of the same killer?"

It was Mike's turn to hesitate. Either Peacock had incorrect information, or he was testing to see whether Mike would give him straight answers. "You can say that an unnamed source close to the investigation says 'no,' that number is not accurate." Mike stared at the reporter without expression.

Peacock cocked his head to the side, sizing up Mike's answer. Then he nodded subtly. "Fine. Question two: is it true that the death of Mickey Gallata is part of your investigation?"

"Yes," Mike said quickly, "again, attributable to an unnamed source. Are we clear on that?"

"Clear," Peacock said, raising an eyebrow. "I must say that I'm a little surprised that you're willing to put that on the record, Detective."

"It's not on the record from me. But, like I said, we want to help each other here so that we don't spark an unnecessary panic. We also hope to get some assistance from the public, once they know." Mike held out his hands, palms up. "You know that I can't share information that could compromise the investigation, but since you're on the story I want to make sure that the information you run with is correct. I can live with the public being nervous about good facts, but I want to avoid unnecessary anxiety based on bad information. So, now we go off the record and you can test your information on me."

Peacock looked wary of this invitation, but put his clasped hands on the table and leaned in towards Mike. As he hunched over the table, the padded shoulders of his suit jacket peaked up like he was wearing football shoulder pads. Jason make a mental note that Peacock was wearing clothes that he hoped would make him look bigger and more impressive, but underneath he was probably scrawny. "OK, let's start with the victims of the serial killer. Nicholas DiVito?"

"Yes," Mike said calmly.

"Pierre LeBlanc?"

"Yes."

"Howard Wiseman." This time Peacock didn't state the name with the inflection of a question, but rather seemed to be gathering steam and made it a statement.

"No, not him," Mike responded. "He's the banker who was fished out of the river a few months back, right?"

Peacock looked puzzled. "Yeah, that's him. He had his fingers broken, similar to DiVito. Since it was still unsolved we – I – assumed he was part of the serial killer's group."

"No, we don't think so."

"Why not?"

Mike paused, thinking about how much information he wanted to share. If the reporter thought that Howard Wiseman was on the killer's list, then he did not understand the timing of the kills, and he was looking for patterns in the methods. Since the timing was critical, there was no need to reveal everything. "Not the killer's type of victim," he said simply. "Here's the scoop for you, Mr. Peacock. All the victims were scumbags of one variety or another. We think this guy sees himself as an avenger, a kind of fucked-up Batman going around killing people whom he determines deserve to die. Your basic, law-abiding, non-scumbag citizen doesn't have to be afraid of this guy – he is not killing randomly, or on a spur-of-the-moment rage. He's a planner, and he carefully selects his victims as people who, in his view, have it coming to them. Wiseman was a banker, and he had some debts, probably to the wrong kind of people. But he was not the kind of person we think our killer would go after."

Peacock looked surprised. He glanced at Jason for confirmation, and got a small incline of his head, affirming that he was on board with what his partner was saying. "So, Barbara Nevin?"

"No."

"We already know Mickey Gallata."

"Correct."

"Robert Sawyer?"

"Yes."

"Jackson Renfroe?" Peacock paused, then added, "or was he not the right type of vic?"

"No," Mike said, "I mean, no, he's not on our list for the serial killer, and yes, he doesn't fit the pattern for the type of victim."

"So, not Abigale Werner, either?"

"No," Mike replied, trying to keep a mental count. That was seven names that Peacock had thrown out. He had not mentioned Marlene Sheraton.

"So, just the four?" Peacock turned his head, as if listening more clearly with his left ear than with his right.

"We can confirm those four, off the record," Mike said, careful to say nothing that was not true. He could, in fact, confirm those four. He did not say that they were the only four.

"Have you got any leads?"

Mike thought for a few minutes about how to answer this one, wondering who the other two dead people on Peacock's original list were. "There are a few things we're running down, but it's far too early to know whether they are going to pan out. We don't know who this guy is yet, but we're obviously working on it. We would appreciate it if *The Times* did not write anything that will spook people into being terrified, and we don't want you to send people into a fervor over one-upping each other to call in tips on their no-good brother-in-law or their bastard ex-husband as a way to make their lives miserable." Mike paused to take stock of the reporter. "This is all off the record, but we want you to be able to verify facts so that you don't go chasing shadows – and so that you don't do anything to impede our investigation."

Peacock looked offended at the suggestion. "I would never knowingly impede a police investigation," he said indignantly.

"I know you wouldn't *want* to impede the investigation," Mike said, "which is why we're having this conversation – to help you avoid doing something that you would not want to do."

Peacock remained silent for a minute. "I have two more names: Christopher Sullivan and Isaac Winters."

"No, and no," Mike replied.

"Hmm," Peacock murmured with his head down, "So you're telling me that I'm chasing up the wrong tree with more than half of my supposed victims, but that there really is a serial killer out there somewhere?"

"Yes, we think there is a guy," Mike replied. "Off the record."

Peacock placed both hands on the top of the table and pushed himself up, causing the rickety structure to wobble precariously, sloshing some of Mike's Diet Coke out of his glass and onto the dark surface. "I'll be going now, Detectives. But one thing – if I get more leads that I want to verify, will you be available – to make sure that I'm not chasing more shadows?"

"I can't promise anything, but you call and I will get back to you. That much I can say for sure, as long as we're chasing this bastard."

"Fair enough," Peacock said, as if he needed to have the last word. He held out a thin hand and shook with Mike, then with Jason.

"One more thing," Mike interjected. "We have a name, but we're sure it's a fake. Still, it's possible that someone out there who reads *The Times* might help us track it down. Charles White. The killer used that alias during one of the murders. You can use that, but don't quote me."

"Good. I'll make sure it gets in the article." Then Peacock turned and walked out of the bar, without looking back.

"Well, that was enlightening," Jason said, his first words in twenty minutes.

"It was, indeed," Mike agreed. "And let me say, I'm impressed that you managed to hold back and not insert yourself into the conversation. Well done, Detective."

Jason suppressed a smile and tried to look serious. "So, you think that Peacock has no clue about Sheraton or the last Saturday pattern?"

"Yes, I'm pretty sure of that. He wouldn't be blowing smoke about the other possible victims if he knew."

"Let's see if we can keep two steps ahead of him from here out."

"Sure," Mike agreed, "let's see. We'll also see if an article in the paper yields any useful tips, and we'll see if the Captain crucifies us for helping the process along."

Chapter 24 – Internet Exposure

September 2, 2018

D EXTER PEACOCK'S STORY about the serial killer hit the streets in the Sunday *Times* the day before Labor Day and did not make the Commissioner happy. "**Serial Killer Stalks New Yorkers**," was attention-getting. Mike was pleased to find that Peacock had focused on the similarities between the victims, and even used the Batman analogy. He made it clear that the killer was focused on a particular type of victim and that citizens who were not criminals need not be worried. But the story was nevertheless sensationalistic and the gory details of the kills – at least as much as had been made public – were repeated as Peacock attempted to merge them into one seamless modus operandum.

Peacock was not entirely successful, but he did spin a good yarn, in Mike's opinion. He also indicated that the police were hot on the case, but that they were not yet ready to provide details about potential suspects – which anyone with a brain could easily read to mean that they were stumped and grasping at straws. He mentioned that the killer may have used the name Charles White, and encouraged anyone with information about someone suspicious using that name to contact the police tip phone line. This was fine with Mike, but Commissioner Ward was livid that someone in the department had leaked that detail without authorization. Mike was not asked whether he was the source of the leak, and he felt no compulsion to volunteer the information.

Of course, the Task Force had no success tracking down Charles White, who had predictably not shown up for his next scheduled shift at Flannagan's. None of the other employees could say anything about "Charles" except that he kept to himself, didn't say much, and was a pretty good cook. Nobody ever hung out with him, or went home with him, or even knew where he lived. He'd only worked four shifts before the murder, having called out for the last Saturday in July. Then, after Sawyer's murder, he never came back. As far as anyone knew, he had never gone out to the front of the house and had never had any contact with Robert Sawyer. The trail was as cold as the refrigerated room in the back where they kept the steaks.

All the local papers ran with the story the following day, after the NYPD held a press conference to confirm the story from *The Times* and reiterate the fact that average citizens had nothing to be afraid of. This was not some kind of Jack-the-Ripper knockoff picking off random New Yorkers. This killer was selecting his victims carefully and long in advance. The public relations guy giving most of the briefing did not say anything about the last Saturday night of the month, and refused to confirm or deny whether any particular recent murder was believed to be connected to the serial killer. The headline in the *Post* made Mike laugh loudest: "Rich Scumbags, Beware!" *The Post's* angle was that ordinary citizens, and even low-level criminals, could rest easy, but that if you were rich, high-profile, and a real menace to society, you should be nervous.

"Amen to that," Jason said when he saw the paper on the conference table. "I hope the guy scares them all straight."

"That would be the best gift this guy could give us," Angela agreed.

That day, the calls started coming into the police tips hotline. Seventeen men named Charles White were reported as suspects, but after the federal agents tracked them down, all of them were cleared based on rock-solid alibis for at least some of the murders. Nothing brought them closer to finding Charles White, or Nick the dog walker.

◆◆◆

September 5

Two days later, the Task Force had several dozen more called-in tips, but no real leads, and was no closer to identifying Charles White. Berkowitz and Mason had been dispatched to an apartment in Washington Heights rented by a man named Charles White who did not have a listed telephone and whose landlord was not able to provide a description or a work address. They were not really expecting to find their man there, but they needed to check it off the list of Charles White sightings. Angela left mid-afternoon to go downtown for a briefing with the FBI team. The daily grind was getting to them, and the clock was ticking again toward the next expected kill date. The calendar was their friend this month, since the last Saturday of August had been the 25th, leaving five weeks before the killer's next period (as they had all taken to referring to the last Saturday, despite the universal acknowledgement that it was both sexist and gross). But, even with the extra week, the number in the corner of the whiteboard already was down to 24.

The local and national media outlets were all over the story, of course, prompting briefings every day by the department's communications director and, at the first press conference, Commissioner Ward and Captain Sullivan. Mike and Jason were introduced as the detectives leading up the Task Force and Mike's face was all over the video, along with a few notes about his past successful cases. Jason got few mentions and, although he didn't say anything, Mike could tell that he would have liked more recognition since he was the one who first detected the killer's pattern. The City offered a $10,000 reward for a tip leading to the arrest and conviction of the killer. Between the NYPD uniforms, several of whom had been loaned to the Task Force, and the FBI agents, they were fully engaged in following up on what were all still useless tips. The heat was definitely on.

At 6:30, Mike snapped off the light in the war room and watched as the blue screen on his laptop computer monitor faded to black. The whirring sound of the cooling fan inside the machine expired, leaving behind a pronounced silence. He was just pulling on his sports jacket when Jason appeared at the door and scanned the room.

With the lights off and his computer shut down, Mike was in shadows, but he called out, "Hey, Dickson. What's up?" Mike walked toward Jason, skirting between chairs in the dim illumination seeping through the frosted windows from the hallway lights.

Jason stood still in the doorway, waiting for Mike to arrive, not speaking.

Mike stopped a few feet away. "Alright. Spill it."

"What?" Jason asked innocently, raising his eyebrows and holding out his hands in front of himself, as if perplexed by the question.

"You gotta work on your poker face, Kid. You look like the cat that swallowed the canary and you're just busting to tell me about it."

Jason scowled. "I thought we weren't doing the 'Kid' thing."

"Yeah, well some habits are hard to break, especially when you're pissing me off."

Jason smiled. "Fine. You're right. We got something that you're not going to believe."

"Try me, I'm very suggestable."

"We found the killer's blog." Jason broke into a full grin as he watched the confused expression on the older man's face.

"What the hell? Are you telling me that the bastard has a website?"

"Essentially, yes. He has an online diary in which he has chronicled his entire spree."

"Who else knows about this?" Mike asked in a low voice, despite the absence of anyone else in the vicinity who could overhear.

"It came in through the public information hotline – a tip from some kid looking for reward money. You know that most of them are crackpots or useless. This one, though, was a bullseye. The reviewing uniform immediately recognized it and called me right away. I think we're the only ones who know."

Mike looked at the floor, lost in thought for a few moments. "Have we gotten back to the tipster?"

"No, we've done nothing yet."

"Who's the uniform?"

"A girl, er, female officer. She's pretty young. Who else is going to get assigned to screen the tip line?"

"When did this happen?" Mike asked, suddenly more animated.

"Just now," Jason responded.

"C'mon," Mike said, grabbing Jason's arm. "Let's go talk to the officer, where is she?"

"Down in the basement in the communications center."

As they walked to the elevator, Mike dug out his phone and dialed Angela. It rang through to voicemail, so he hung up and dialed again. The second time, she picked up after three rings. Mike didn't wait for her to say hello. "Angela! Do you have a computer guy there? Someone who knows his way around websites?"

"What? Why?"

"Do you have one?"

"Sure. I'm sure we do. Tell me what's going on."

"Get him, and get his and your asses up here to the precinct as fast as you can. It's an absolute emergency. I'll explain when you get here. Don't say anything to anyone."

"About what?"

"Exactly. See you in a half hour." Mike hung up just as the elevator door opened.

Within ten minutes, Mike, Jason, and a very nervous-looking young woman in a police uniform were sitting in an interrogation room under the harsh fluorescent lights. The female officer was short but looked to be solidly built under her tightly fitted blues. She had dark hair and eyes and the caramel coloring of a Latina. She was looking around the room, focusing on the two-way mirror on the wall, which she knew led to an observation area where someone usually was watching. Mike noticed and tried to calm her.

"Don't worry, Officer Rodriguez, there's nobody behind the glass. I'm sorry that we're in here, but I didn't want to be obvious about this and I want to keep it quiet."

"I understand," Rodriguez said, without much conviction, her eyes darting back and forth between the two detectives.

"How long have you been on the force?" Mike asked soothingly.

"Um, just six months, sir," the woman said with a quavering voice.

"That's, great," Mike smiled like a proud grandfather. "I'm really happy that you were so quick to recognize the significance of this issue. Very good job."

Officer Rodriguez blushed slightly, inclining her head and looking down at the table briefly, then back up at Mike. "Thank you, sir."

"Please, it's Mike. We're all on the same team here . . . uh, I'm afraid nobody has told me your first name. It's . . . ?"

"Maria," she said haltingly.

"Great, Maria. You call me Mike, and this is Jason," he said, motioning to the big Black man, who was glowering at Mike. "Now, please just tell me what happened when you listened to the tip in question."

Officer Rodriguez took a deep breath and then started speaking, getting more confident as she went along. "I was listening to the recorded calls. I've been assigned to this duty for the past two days and there have been a lot of calls. Most of them are pretty crazy, but I log them and pass the report along to Detective Dickson." Rodriguez paused and glanced up at Jason, looking for some kind of approval or confirmation that she was telling the truth. Jason gave her a subtle nod of encouragement.

"So, this afternoon I listened to three or four and then I got one that was really different. The voice sounded young, like a teenager. He spoke very clearly, although you can tell that he was pretty excited. He said that he found a blog that he thinks may be written by the serial killer that we're looking for. He didn't say why he thought that the site was related to the killer, he just gave the URL. He repeated it twice because it's a long string of numbers and not a normal name. Then he left his name, address, phone number, and email and he hung up. It was a pretty quick call – much shorter than most of the ramblings I listen to."

Rodriguez stopped and looked up expectantly, then continued. "I thought it was credible, so I opened my browser and I brought it up and, well, it's pretty bizarre. But there are a lot of details, and, well, I thought that it seemed just crazy enough to be legitimate, so I didn't want to wait for the daily report and I called Detective Dickson and told him about it. That was about a half hour ago. Then Detective Dickson came down and I showed it to him and then he left and told me not to tell anybody else about it and to wait for him to come back. That's about it, sir – Mike."

Mike smiled kindly and reached across the metal desk to pat her hands, which were entwined in a tight ball. "That's great, Maria. Very good work. Now, Jason and I will take it from here, but I want to impress on you that we need to keep a very, very tight lid on this. We don't want the public to get to this. If it is legitimate, it will compromise our investigation if it gets to the press. You need to keep this entirely to yourself – I don't want you to even tell other officers here in the precinct. Not your best friend on the force, not anyone, do you understand?"

Rodriguez looked frightened, again darting her gaze back and forth between the two men. "Um, I guess. I can do that."

"Have you told anyone else about this yet, Maria?" Mike's voice was urgent, but still soothing.

"No, sir, Mike. No, nobody except Detective Dickson."

"Did you write down the URL anywhere?"

"Just on the report sheet, which I gave to Detective Dickson."

Mike looked over at Jason, who held out a sheet of paper that he handed to Mike. "Great," Mike said, scanning the information on the page. "What about the recording of the call? Where is that?"

"It's in the answering system. When I finish with them, I press the code to save the message to memory so it disappears from the inbox."

"Did you do that for this message?"

"Yes, right after I finished the written report."

"Can you get back to it if you need to?"

"I'm sure I could, I would just need to figure out the number assigned to that one or listen to the saved messages for that hour."

"OK. Please do not do that. Please just leave it in the saved messages file and do not access it and do not tell anyone about it. Understand?"

"Yes, sir."

Mike gave Rodriguez a fatherly smile and slumped back into his chair. "Great. That's great. As long as we can keep this quiet, it may be the break in the case that we've been looking for. Thank you so much. We'll take it from here." Mike stood up and extended his hand to the young officer, who gave him a weak shake. "Jason, why don't you escort Officer Rodriguez back to her work station?" Mike nodded at Jason knowingly. Jason lead the way out the door of the small room, leaving Mike to his thoughts.

Mike pulled the laptop toward himself and examined the website, which Rodriguez had scrolled down to the entry describing the most recent kill. There was just a date at the top and then text. It looked like a diary. He scrolled down further, noting some of the key dates. The writer had chronicled each of the killings, including details that Mike immediately recognized as things that had not been reported in the press and that nobody but the killer and the police could possibly know. It seemed authentic. It was him, and Mike could not believe their good luck. They needed to keep it under wraps while they used it to track him down.

Jason returned after a short interval, standing in the doorway silently. Mike was on his phone. "Yeah. Good. See you in ten."

"Manning?"

"Yeah. She's in a black & white and should be here in ten minutes with her tech guy."

Jason nodded. "I'll go see who we have down in IT who knows how to grab the data off the saved telephone messages."

"Good. Then as soon as Angela gets here, we've got to get out to Queens."

Chapter 25 – The Kid Stays in the Picture

A N HOUR LATER, Mike, Jason, and Angela were parked in a no standing zone in front of a post-war apartment building in Flushing, Queens. It was just after dark, and the red brick façade was pockmarked by a checkerboard of lighted windows looking down over the semi-circular driveway in front of the complex. A trickle of water seeped weakly from a fountain, overgrown with unkempt flowers and a few stray weeds.

Jason suggested that he and Angela should go inside, figuring that a Black detective and a woman would be more welcomed inside than a White cop. Mike reluctantly agreed.

After knocking on the door of their target's apartment, a thin Black woman with streaks of gray in her hair answered and identified herself as Mrs. Jackson. Angela explained that they were there to see Donyell Jackson.

"Is he in trouble?"

"No," Angela tried hard to avoid anything that might spook the boy. "We just need to ask him a few questions about something he might have seen."

Mrs. Jackson looked skeptical, but told the cops to wait. She re-emerged a few minutes later, dragging a very confused teenage boy behind her. The boy was skinny as a rail and was wearing New York Knicks gym shorts, a plain black t-shirt, and Nike sneakers that were as white and shiny as the day they came out of the box. He glanced at Jason and Angela, then at his mother, who was frowning menacingly. Jason said, "It's about the call you made to the Tip Line."

"Oh. Cool," Donyell said.

"Do you have a laptop computer, son?" Angela asked gently.

"Yeah," Donyell said, recognition dawning in his brain. "Do you want me to get it?"

"Yes, please."

Donyell disappeared into an interior room, while Jason explained to the mother that they would just need a few minutes with Donyell. Angela took Mrs. Jackson into a small kitchen and sat in a metal chair while her host made tea. Angela told Mrs. Jackson that they were investigating gang-related violence and that Donyell was not at all involved, but that he had been a witness to an assault by several gang members and called it in. They needed to speak with him about it, but his involvement needed to be kept very confidential and quiet, lest the gang members find out who was ratting them out. She impressed upon the nervous mother how her son might be in danger if she should speak to anyone, even her friends and neighbors, about his involvement.

Mrs. Jackson was frightened, but Angela praised her son's courage and urged her to be as strong and brave as Donyell. She was confused, but seemed to understand. Most importantly, she bought the whole story. Angela had not identified herself as an FBI agent, nor as an NYPD officer. She had simply remained silent on the subject.

When Donyell returned to the main room with a bulky laptop under his arm, Jason sat with him on a threadbare sofa. "Son, we got your call on the NYPD Tip Line."

Donyell beamed. "Did you see the blog?"

"Yes, we looked at it."

"So, is it real? Is that the Scumbag Killer guy?"

"Well, Donyell, we haven't yet begun our investigation into it. It certainly seems possible, but we need to do some more work and track down the owner of the blog and such. You understand?"

"Sure!" Donyell responded quickly. "I'm cool with that. When do I get my money?"

"Slow down, Buddy," Jason said. "We have to verify it, and it has to lead to a conviction for you to collect the reward. But there's something even more important."

"What?" Donyell said, puzzled by the prospect of not immediately receiving the Tip Line reward money, which he had already started spending in his head.

"You have to keep this under wraps. If it hits the press, the killer will know that we're on to him. He'll stop posting and burn the site, and we won't be able to catch him. You understand?"

"Yeah," Donyell said reluctantly. "I get it."

"So, who else knows about this? Who have you told?"

Donyell suddenly seemed to understand, and his face lit up like a Christmas tree. "Oh, man, that's no problem. I ain't told nobody. I'm not sharing that reward."

"Good. That's good," Jason said. "Are you sure that you haven't told any friends, like a girlfriend?"

"No way," Donyell quickly retorted. "I found that crazy site last night and I knew it was that serial killer guy, so today when I got home from school I looked up the Tip Line number and called. That's it. Nobody else knows."

"Not even a post on Facebook or Instagram?" Jason pressed.

"No way. Not me. I know better than to blab something like this all over the net."

"Did you write down the URL?"

"No way, it's crazy long. I just bookmarked it."

Donyell explained how he found the website by accident when he clicked on the "next" button at the bottom of a friend's blog. He showed Jason where he kept his bookmarks. All but one of the bookmark labels were the names of people – presumably Donyell's friends. The last one on the list, however was just a web address with a long series of numbers, but no recognizable words.

"Is that it?" Jason asked.

"Yeah," Donyell answered.

Jason reached over to the finger pad and maneuvered to the link, then right-clicked and selected the "delete" option. The web address disappeared from the screen.

"Hey!" Donyell exclaimed, reaching toward Jason's hand, but too late to prevent the damage. Jason then navigated to the computer's internet log files and deleted them.

"Now, you need to forget that blog address."

"What?" Donyell furrowed his brow and looked confused.

"You need to forget it. Don't search for it, don't tell anybody about it, don't talk about it – you need to pretend that you never knew about it. If you want to collect that reward, you need to help us keep it a total secret. If word gets out, we will assume that it's you who leaked it, and you will not get any reward money. You got that?" Jason gave Donyell his best serious cop look.

Donyell was wide-eyed, but he took a deep breath and said, "Sure, I get it. I don't say nothin' to nobody."

"Now, clear the data in your trash." Donyell looked annoyed, but complied. "Good boy," Jason said, patting him on the arm. "I will let you know as soon as we catch the bastard, but until then, you know nothing and you say nothing."

"Right."

"Are you sure you didn't write down the URL for that blog anywhere else?"

"I'm sure."

Jason told Donyell the cover story about the gang violence, and how he was helping the police and needed to lay low and say nothing lest the gangbangers find him and hurt him for snitching on them. He was not to tell even his mother any of the real details. His mother had been told the same story and she was not supposed to ask him about it. Donyell said he understood. Jason and Angela made their good-byes and walked out, satisfied that they had scared both the boy and his mother into staying silent about their find.

In the building lobby, Mike said, "Well?"

"I think he's on board. I wiped his browser history. He says that he didn't write down the web address anywhere and he hasn't told anyone about it. I told him he would get no reward money if he visited the site again or told anybody about it. He said he would keep it to himself. I think he'll do it."

"Good. Maybe we'll get lucky on this one." Then he turned to Angela and asked, "Did you talk to your forensic IT guy?"

"Yes, he has it. With any luck, we'll be able to trace it."

"Well," Jason said, "don't they say that true sociopaths want to be caught? Perhaps this is his way of ensuring that he does."

"I'd say instead that this is his way of making sure the world knows his perverted story," Angela offered. "The subconscious desire to be caught is all tied up with the desire for fame and acclaim for their actions. He wants to be sure that his story gets told, so he's telling it himself. Welcome to the internet age."

"Great," Mike grumbled, "now we have serial killer psychos self-publishing."

Chapter 26 – Tracking the Invisible Man

September 6, 2018

THE NEXT MORNING, there was a new face sitting at the table in the war room. When Mike arrived, Angela introduced him to Alberto Simpson, the forensic IT expert whom Angela had brought in the night before. While Angela had joined Mike and Jason in Queens, Simpson had stayed in the war room, scrutinizing the blog, with his laptop in front of him and a pad of notes slowly filling up the table at his elbow.

"Have you been here all night?" Mike asked.

"Sure," the thin man responded. His white dress shirt was wrinkled and frayed around the collar, as if it were one of two or three that got worn to work every day for a year or more. He had a wispy beard that he intended to be a goatee, but which was so thin that it resembled dark cobwebs more than a proper beard. His hair was thick and black, but disheveled and badly in need of a barber. He wore khaki slacks and black tennis shoes with white socks, and could not have looked less like a federal agent if he had an eye patch and a hook for a hand. But, Mike noticed, his eyes were sharp and clear and he had a sense of urgency when he spoke that belied his unkempt exterior. "You told me that this was top secret, and I have told no one about it, just like you asked."

"Good," Mike responded. "So, have you had any luck tracing the source?"

Simpson frowned and bit his lower lip before responding. "Well, I have to say that this guy is good. Normally it's not that much of a problem tracing back a blog like this. There are two easy ways. First, the registration with the site host, which we can't immediately see, but which we can usually get with a subpoena. Second, the IP address of the computer that uploaded the text. Here, the visible name on the account is fake and the email address is at Hotmail so it really can't be traced anywhere. So, nothing useful. The IP address used to upload the text is no help. Every upload used a different address, a different computer each time. I tried to trace back the addresses, but they're all over the world – some in Europe, some in Asia, one in Brazil. I think the guy is hacking into remote machines and using them as proxies to upload his stuff. It leaves no trace to where he actually is, which is really brilliant, when you think about it."

"Can't you trace it?" Jason asked, incredulous that the IT genius could be stumped by a psycho killer.

"I just told you, I can trace each entry back to a different PC – and they are spread out all over creation. I expect that they belong to innocent civilians who don't have any idea that he's using their computer to upload his crap. He makes the host computer a slave and operates it remotely, leaving no trail."

Jason paused. "If you had one of those computers, could you use it to back your way into where he was hacking in from?"

Simpson ran his left hand through his tangled hair as he thought. "I can't be sure, but it's possible. But, if this guy is as good as I think he is, it's quite possible that he uses a clone or another slave to hack in so that he wouldn't be that easy to catch."

"Well, do you have any better ideas?"

"No, not really. We could try."

Mike decided it was time to chime in. "Mr. Simpson, why are you so sure that the identity used to set up the account is a fake?"

"Well, Detective, I guess I can't be sure that the guy's name is not really Ronald Reagan with an address of 1600 Pennsylvania

Avenue in Washington, D.C., but I'm pretty confident."

Mike nodded and remained silent. Jason then said, "OK, let's track down a few of the host computers and see if we can find one that we can get our hands on."

Simpson nodded and said, "Will do. Anything else you need for now?"

"No," Jason said, "we'll read through the blog to see if there's something there that we might be able to use to catch the bastard."

"What was the name of the blog?" Mike asked, scolding himself for not already knowing that information.

Jason answered before Simpson could open his mouth. "It's A-O-D."

"What the Hell does that mean?"

Angela chimed in. "It looks like an abbreviation, but who knows of what. Maybe after we have more time to read his journal we'll get a clue."

"Could it be his monogram?" Mike asked.

"Is it ever that simple?" Jason retorted.

"Probably not, but who the Hell knows with a guy like this."

"I'm going to guess it stands for "Angel of Death," Simpson cut in.

"Why is that?"

"I've been reading his stuff all night. He writes a lot, but there are a bunch of references to himself as the Avenging Angel and the Angel of the Lord and the Angel of Death. It fits. I'm guessing that he's using the initials with periods and the zero to hide it from search results."

"What do you mean? What zero?" Mike hated feeling like he was not clued into technology discussions.

"If you look carefully," Simpson explained, "the middle letter is not a letter O, it's the number zero." Mike looked where Simpson was pointing and saw, "A.o.D."

You see, if you give a website a name with normal words in the title, anyone running a search for any of those words would pull it up as a search result, even if they aren't specifically looking for your blog. In this case, the title of the blog is not a word – it's not even an abbreviation because of the zero. Plus, he has inserted periods between each character. So, this title is not going to come up on any search results, and even if somebody is searching for a word that happens to occur in the text of a post, it's not going to come up among the early search results, certainly not on the first page, because the search engines prioritize titles. It'll be way down the list where nobody is likely to see it. Normally, when you have a blog, you want your posts to be findable so that you get hits and comments and find readers. The guy does not want this to be found. At least not for now. He can always edit the title later when he's ready to publish."

"What do you mean by publish?" Mike inquired.

"Well, I expect that at some point – when he's done with his project – he will change the title so that people will be able to find him. He clearly wants this to be widely read eventually. I wouldn't be surprised if he copies the whole thing and moves it to a different URL that he can name something easy for people to remember and find, instead of this string of random numbers."

"Project?"

"Sure," Simpson said. "If you read this through you'll see that he has a master plan, although he doesn't disclose exactly what it is. He has some specific blueprint that he's following, and he is clearly not done yet."

"Great," Mike sighed. "Well, at least we'll have something to work on. Has he been posting in advance of all the kills?"

"Oh, yes," Simpson responded quickly, "He almost always posts information about the upcoming kill, and then he talks about it after the fact. He posts a few times a week at least. He's careful not to write anything that could get him caught, or might tip us off about the identity of the intended victim, but he always talks about them."

"Good," Mike said, turning to get ready to leave. "At least that will give us something to work with, and we'll know if he kills again whether it's him."

"One thing to keep in mind, gentlemen – and Agent Manning – is that the killer may well be watching the traffic on the blog."

"What do you mean?" Angela asked.

"Well, for a blog like this, the owner can see statistics that show how many visitors have clicked on it – how many page views. Every time somebody accesses the URL, it will be recorded. If the killer sees a bunch of hits on the site or on the individual posts, he'll know that somebody is reading."

The room went silent. Then, Angela offered, "Well, he probably wants readers, so he'll figure that some people just stumbled on his site and are following his story, which he might actually like."

"Or," Jason said, "he might get spooked and abandon the blog if he thinks we might be on to him, or start a new one on a different site that we won't be able to find easily."

"How can we avoid that?" Mike asked.

"Well, we shouldn't visit the site."

"What the fuck?" Mike blurted out. "We find this trove of information and you're suggesting that we not use it?"

"I'm not suggesting you don't use it," Simpson said, more than a bit annoyed. "I have already copied all the material so that we can pore over it as much as we like." He gestured to a small pile of paper next to his laptop. "But going back every day to check to see if he has posted anything new is likely to tip him off. It seems that he does not want people reading this until he's ready."

Angela put her hand on Jason's arm and nudged him aside so that she could get closer to Simpson. "Alberto, is there any way to bypass the system that records the hits, so that we can look in on the blog without him knowing?"

"I don't think so. Maybe if we got the site host to alter the counter."

"Would that work?"

"Sure, it would work, but it would require them to cooperate in hacking into a user's site statistics, which they don't usually do without a court order."

Mike coughed loudly. "Sorry. But if we can't get a court order for this, then I'll eat this computer."

"Sure. But how are we going to get the court order without revealing the big secret? I mean, we'll have to tell the court why we're asking, and that's a public filing, so the press will be all over it. And then we'll have to explain to the host what we want them to do and why, and so we'll have to swear them to secrecy. But how much control will we really have over that?"

"What if we try it without the court order?" Jason suggested. "What if we reach out confidentially to someone high up and explain what we need and why we need it to stay under the radar? Maybe we could get some citizen cooperation."

Angela shook her head sadly. "Jason, I wish the world worked that way, but when the FBI shows up on the doorstep of a tech company asking for secret access to a private account, we don't generally get a friendly welcome. But, I'll have the legal guys put the petition together for a court order anyway. Maybe they can get it filed under seal or something to keep it quiet."

"OK. Let's start reading this pile of shit and see what information we can glean from it. Simpson can try to track down the clone computers that were used to post to the site and we can see if that leads anywhere. We have some homework to do, so let's get to it." Mike picked up the stack of printouts and motioned toward the door.

Jason said good-bye to Simpson and asked that he call immediately if he found out anything about the host computers, and reminded him about keeping everything quiet and out of the press. Simpson said that he understood, then Jason followed Mike out the door, with Angela on their heels.

Mike was waiting in the hallway. "You believe this shit?" he said calmly.

"Oh, yes," Angela jumped in right away. "This guy wants fame and recognition. A blog is perfect. Normally I'd expect him to leave a diary, but a public blog is so much more efficient for getting his message out to the world. It makes sense."

"Yeah," Mike replied calmly. "It all makes so much sense. The guy is smart, and seems to be a computer whiz. That's not a good combo for us."

"Let's hope the press doesn't find it," Jason muttered quietly.

"Thanks, you're just full of sunshine," Mike replied sharply. Mike walked into a small interior room where a bulky copying machine stood waiting for its next job. He set the papers in the hopper and the machine started to churn. "Just three copies, for you two and me."

"What about Berkowitz and Mason?" Jason asked.

"We'll let them see these copies, but no more get made. We have to keep an air-tight seal on this."

"OK," Jason agreed. "Let's start with the three of us and go from there."

"Bedtime reading, eh?" Angela quipped.

"This guy is already starting to haunt my dreams," Mike replied. "I might as well take him to bed with me."

Chapter 27 – Anticipation

September 6, 2018

*H*ALF OF MY DIVINE PLAN *has been executed. Although not every aspect of every event has gone exactly as I planned, on the whole the Lord has guided my hands with great precision and success has resulted. Five devils have left the Earth. Five plagues upon the face of God's perfect world are no longer scourges upon the firmament. I remain healthy and fully capable of completing the glorious road. My resources remain adequate and the plans already laid will bear fruit in due time.*

The next mission is one that I have planned since the very beginning of my quest. The evil that will be eliminated from the world is a man who hides behind a mask, and yet his foul stench precedes him. He is Pharaoh. He enslaves those unable to fight back against him. He traffics in human misery. Pharaoh embitters their lives and cares not when they die at the hands of those to whom he sells them.

I have known of Pharaoh for some time. One of his taskmasters recruited me to join the vile trade after my military service was ended. My former comrade showed me a part of the operation as if I was bound to keep his secret solely by virtue of our shared combat. I came to know Pharaoh and I have been planning for this moment ever since.

Even before the death of Napoleon, I secured entry into the building where Pharaoh runs his seemingly legitimate business. His company gives to charities and sponsors a little league baseball team. He acts as if he is a pillar of the community, but I know better. His company imports many products that are entirely legitimate. Ships enter the port with loads of containers. Most are filled with goods beyond suspicion. Some containers, however, have a false partition. Behind the legitimate goods Pharaoh hides his most valuable and most reprehensible cargo. From his comfortable office, he sends out instructions to his devils.

I now have access. His security guards recognize me even now as a fellow businessman, working late hours on Fridays and Saturdays and coming in and out during the week. I have tracked his routine. He will accompany me voluntarily to his doom. The countdown has begun.

I know that I must be careful, for the authorities are trying to track me. I knew, of course, that the death of Sodom would leave a trail. It would not be difficult for the police to deduce how Sodom met his end and the universe of people who had access to his steak was quite limited. I could not, of course, hang around to be questioned by the police, and so I bid a sudden farewell to the place of business, leaving a fairly obvious hole in the personnel roster. But I knew this would be the case, and I took precautions to ensure that my face would not appear on any security camera, and my disguise will prevent the general description of my character from yielding any useful identification. My faux name and address and telephone number will not provide any hint of my true identity. Chasing that ghost will be a useless process.

But still, the police are on the hunt, so I must be careful. Pharaoh will meet his end at the appointed time, despite the hunters. I will ensure success, and the divine quest will continue.

Chapter 28 – Shedding Light

September 7, 2018

MIKE WAS THE FIRST ONE to arrive in the war room on Friday morning. After hanging his jacket on the back of a chair and getting his first cup of coffee, he erased the countdown number in the corner of the whiteboard and wrote in 22. After the rest of the team assembled, Jason closed the door and Angela dialed Simpson and put him on the speaker phone.

Simpson confirmed his total failure in tracing the origin of the killer's blog. Since it was a free site, there was no credit card to trace, and it was easy for the killer to use a disguised email address. It was, in a nutshell, a wild goose chase trying to find him through the front door. Angela thanked him for his efforts and suggested that he get some sleep.

Jason, Mike, and Angela had each read the entire blog front to back and they compared notes. They had many.

"The guy's a complete freak show," Jason spat out disgustedly.

"Keen insight, Detective Dickson," Mike said flatly. "What other pearls of deductive reasoning did you manage to glean from his magnum opus?"

Jason showed Mike his middle finger playfully, then consulted his notes and began a recitation of his key findings. "First, the guy is a total narcissist with a God complex."

"Whoa, such big words, Doctor Dickson."

"Screw you, Mike," Jason said with a good-natured grin.

"Go on."

"Stop it," Angela broke in. "We're all on the same team." She erased the notes they had posted the day before on the whiteboard and started making new ones as Jason rattled off his observations – keeping her own opinions to herself for the moment.

"He's got to be like a med school exam for a psychiatrist." Jason paused to give Angela a knowing look. "Second, he's a sadist. He really seems to enjoy killing people, and not just killing them, but making them suffer. He gets off on it. He plans it and executes it like it's an opera."

"I concur with that," Mike agreed easily. "He's a sick bastard."

"I feel like he's totally out of his mind with all this Avenging Angel shit and being on a mission from God, and at the same time he's so calculating and carefully planning each kill that he seems completely in control of his emotions and his actions. He's nuts, clearly, but he's smart. Within his own delusional world, his actions make total sense. He also seems very conscious of police procedure and what he needs to avoid in order to get away with his murders. The question I have is: who does he think he's writing this for? He has kept this blog invisible, so why write it?"

"That I understand," Angela volunteered, still scribbling furiously on the board. "Like you said, he's a narcissist, and he thinks he's on a mission from God. He wants people to read all about it. He wants this to be a sacred text for the church of psycho killers. He's making a record. When the time is right, he'll show it to the world. For now, he knows that this can get him caught and he's hiding it – but it's intended for the world. I would expect that in the end, when he's caught, he will trigger some automated email message that will go out to every news outlet on the planet. He wants to be the most famous man on Earth, and this is his manifesto."

"I know that we assume these guys want to get caught, but why not get away with it all and then publish the journal without being in prison, or dead?"

"He wants the spotlight. If he's a fugitive, then he's famous, but he has to hide. He doesn't want to hide. He wants to step up to a bank of microphones and speak to his adoring supplicants. He wants to write his life story and have biographers fight over the right to interview him in prison. He wants to be Charles Manson, but with a higher IQ. He wants to be Hannibal Lecter and consult with the FBI on future serial killers. He has to get caught, or surrender himself at some point, in order for this to work out. He's going to kill as many people as he is going to kill, and then he'll be done and he'll walk into a police station or a court with a high-profile lawyer on his arm like he's going to the fucking Oscars." Angela popped the cap back onto her marker with an exhausted sigh.

"It doesn't really matter," Jason offered. "We can't prevent him from talking. All we can do is catch him and put him away for the rest of his life, or until they fry him. That's our job."

"I'd like to pull the lever and fry him myself." Mike was still staring out the window.

"Alright," Angela interrupted. "What do you two have to contribute here that can help us catch the son-of-a-bitch?"

"Well, from your perspective, what are the significant facts that we should focus on if we want to try to get into this guy's head?" Mike asked.

"Normally I would say we need to try to determine what's motivating him, but with this journal we don't have to speculate."

"That's assuming that he's not just bullshitting us and that these journal entries really reflect his state of mind," Jason observed.

"Do we have any reason to suspect that he's not being totally honest in his journal?"

"Everything he has written so far matches factually with the murders, so he's not feeding us false information. But that doesn't mean that the rest of it isn't just an act – something to help him get off on an insanity defense when he gets caught." Jason looked up at Angela, hopeful for some affirmation.

"Jason, do you really think this killer is hiding perfectly sane ulterior motives behind the journal as a defense exhibit?"

Jason looked annoyed at having his observation turned into another question. "No, not really. I just don't want to make assumptions and take things at face value. This guy is slick and smart and it's not out of the realm of possibility that he's leading us down a garden path."

"You're entirely correct, Detective, to take nothing for granted." Angela stepped away from the whiteboard and sat back down at the conference table. "Based on my reading of the journal text, I would put that theory on the scale of possible, but not likely enough for us to waste time following it."

"Good," Mike said. "I really want him to be just crazy and hungry for glory and fame, or totally off the rails and really thinking that he's the Angel of Death."

"Good, because that's where I think he is," Angela concurred. "Like many serial killers, he thinks that he's justified in his actions and that he will be a hero. He wants everyone to know his story, and in this internet age, he can write his own story in real time. I believe that he is writing his own version of truth and that he would be quite offended if he knew that you were questioning his veracity."

Mike chuckled. "My fondest wish is to confront this bastard and let him be offended."

The Task Force members spent the next three hours dissecting the killer's descriptions of his first five kills, pulling out tidbits and speculating about the significance of facts that the killer had let slip into his descriptions. In the end, the list of significant facts was not particularly long:

Veteran - Afghanistan

Army cook - restaurant job
Night job - does not work Saturdays
Religious (extreme)
Planned kills carefully
Single-handedly subdued victims
Enjoys torture/killing
Connection between victims?

"What about the next kill?" Mike asked in a tired voice as he poured himself another cup of coffee from the ancient steel urn in the corner of the room. He carefully added two packets of artificial sweetener and two shakes from the non-dairy powdered creamer. "We have three weeks until his next murder. What do we know?"

"He calls this one Pharaoh."

"Right. Another biblical reference. What's the significance?"

Jason puzzled over the possibilities. "Pharaoh presided over the slavery of the Israelites. We already know that our guy has an Exodus fixation, so he's trying to free the slaves. He made a reference to the victims being slaves. Sounds like our Pharaoh is engaged in human trafficking of some kind."

"All plausible," Mike said softly, thinking about something that he could not quite catch in his brain. "What did he call the other five?"

Jason rattled them off. "The first was Abel, who was the brother of Cain and the first murder victim described in the Bible. That doesn't really tell us anything. He was the guy who was kidnapped and held in the chair under the West Side Highway and tortured to death. Remember, he had his own blood in his stomach."

"Yes, there was a lot of blood involved there. Cause of death was blood loss."

"Second kill, Marlene Sheraton, he called her Eve just because she was a woman and Eve was the first woman. Again, no real information there. She was poisoned – South American tree frog venom."

"Yes," Mike mused. "Death by frog, but that has nothing to do with the biblical story of Eve. The method relates to the plague, so he's mixing his metaphors."

"We'll cite him for bad grammar," Angela quipped.

"Right. OK," Jason continued the rundown. "Number three was Napoleon. That was Pierre LeBlanc – tortured and frozen to death. He made a comment in the blog about whether we would figure out the significance of the name. I looked up Napoleon and he did not die from freezing, but he did lead his army on a march into Russia where a large portion froze to death, or died of disease on the march. I guess the name relates to the cause of death, not so much the identity of the victim."

"Wait," Angela broke in. "Napoleon is not a biblical reference. He broke the pattern there. He was still working on the plagues theme with the method of death, but he chose a name for the victim that was from outside the Bible."

Mike reached for the box of donuts in the middle of the conference table and held one in his hand without taking the first bite. "He thinks he's so clever. He must have something obtuse in mind." Mike picked up a photo of the frozen victim and tried to remember the autopsy report. "The guy was French, like Napoleon, so maybe that's the hook there."

"Number four was poor Slick Mick – mauled by tigers," Jason continued. "The killer called him Pilate. There were several references in the blog that we can now relate back to Mick, but nothing that would have pointed to him in particular before the kill. There was a reference to Queens and a man with a granddaughter, so not much to narrow down the field. Pilate was the judge who sentenced Jesus to death by crucifixion, and Slick Mick certainly had ordered plenty of hits in his miserable life, so I guess that was the connection. The nickname has more to do with the victim's identity and nothing to do with the manner of death. But being mauled by tigers is absolutely tied back to the plague of wild beasts."

"OK, what about number five?"

"The douchebag pimp was called Sodom. It's another biblical name, obviously, but a city instead of a person so it's harder to pinpoint. Sodom is connected to excess and debauchery, which seems consistent with the victim's personality. Who knows? Again, after the fact, we got the clues about him working in a restaurant and poisoning the guy's steak, but by the time he wrote that, the kill was over."

"What about the kills themselves?" Angela asked. "What information from the blog entries might have helped us figure out the methods if we had been reading them in real time before?"

Jason got up and stared at the bullet points Angela had scrawled on the board. "The guy is no dummy," Jason said as he turned away from the board and toward Angela. "There's nothing really there in the blog that would have pointed us to DiVito or Sheraton in particular. I guess if we had been expecting death by frogs, we might have guessed the poisoning angle, but that wouldn't have helped us figure out who he was going to target. That seems to be the case for all of the kills. He's very careful about what he writes."

"What about the third kill, LeBlanc?" Mike asked to the room. "Anything there in the blog entries that might have helped us?"

Jason turned his attention to the print-out of the blog posts. "I guess we could have figured he was targeting somebody French, but that wouldn't have helped us. I'm still not entirely sure what the big reveal is regarding Napoleon. Our killer's blog makes these references about how he's wondering if we're going to figure out his secret meaning? What is that about?"

"It's a puzzle," Angela said, tapping the board. "He's matching wits with us, trying to play a game where only he knows the rules. Why would it really matter whether we solve the puzzle? It probably won't help us find him, but he's amusing himself by setting up some hidden connection that he can laugh about."

Jason stepped up to the whiteboard and selected an orange marker. He started writing bullet points about the LeBlanc murder and Napoleon. He wrote "frozen army – Napoleon" on the board. "Napoleon's army had 10,000 soldiers freeze to death the night of November 8th and 9th, 1812. So, freezing to death and Napoleon go together."

"Yeah, but remember that the hook back to the plagues is the lice," Mike said while looking down at the pages of the blog. "We found lice on the corpse. That must be what he meant by going out and catching a wild rabbit. He must have harvested lice from the rabbit and then transferred them to LeBlanc. But why?"

"Try searching 'Napoleon' and 'lice' and see what you get," Angela suggested.

"Why not?" Jason muttered while punching in the search on his laptop. He paused, swiped through a few screens, then exclaimed, "I'll be damned."

"What?" Mike and Angela said in unison.

"It says that in the summer of 1812, Napoleon's army had an outbreak of Typhus and an infestation of lice, which ended up killing a lot of the army. Do you believe this?"

"So, Napoleon's army froze to death and died from lice. I guess that's close enough for this guy to call his freeze-out the third plague." Mike stood up and stretched his back. "Did you know that one way to get rid of lice is to freeze them?"

Jason exclaimed, "No way."

"Well, according to Doctor McNeill, it's considered one of the most effective methods. The critters freeze up, die off, and let go of their little clingy things in your hair, and you can brush 'em out."

"How does she know that?" Jason asked, skeptically.

"I asked her the same thing. She says that it's a mom thing."

"I didn't think she had kids?"

"She doesn't. Maybe she means her mom."

"Oh," Jason said, mouth open, thinking about how he would have responded to that line if he had received it from the M.E. He realized that there was no response. "OK, so the guy had lice, and froze to death. This crazy bastard thought that we would be able to put those two facts together and come up with Napoleon?"

"No, he didn't," Angela said. "He figured that it would stump us. I'm guessing that he doesn't even expect us to work out the plagues. He's writing his blog so that after the fact, we'll go back and slap our heads and say, 'of course that's what the evil genius had in mind.' He's being intentionally vague because he thinks he's the only one clever enough to work out the puzzle, and he knows that even if we figured it out, it won't really help us catch him."

"Well, now we know his pattern. The next kill should have something to do with boils," Mike cut in, trying to keep the conversation going in the right direction.

"What does that even mean? Death by boils?" Jason said, making a disgusted face.

"Maybe he's planning to boil somebody – a nice juxtaposition to the frozen guy," Mike offered.

Jason grimaced. "This guy is sick and sadistic, so I don't put anything past him. But that's not going to help us much. How do we anticipate where he's going to be when he boils some dude?"

"We watch the blog and see what he writes," Angela said. "Well, Simpson watches the blog and we read it after Simpson uploads the text for us. Our killer always gloats in advance about what a perfect victim he has found. Maybe he'll give something away."

"Yeah, maybe." Jason stood up and stretched, yawning. "But so far he hasn't divulged anything in advance of any of the kills that would have helped us."

"What do we know about why the killing started when it started? Was there a precipitating event that launched this man on his spree?" Angela looked down at Mike and Jason as if a lecturer in a college seminar, waiting for a bright student to raise his hand.

"That's a blank," Jason mumbled. "All he says in the journal is that his mission was inspired by God – that he is called to do the

Lord's work on Earth and to cleanse the world of the filth that has evaded judgment by law enforcement, or some crap like that. It's not like he's telling us that some creep criminal killed his mother and he's out for revenge – that would be too easy."

"Well, Detective Dickson, while we may not completely understand the significance of the statement, there is a statement." She turned and wrote on the board: "Avenging Angel – Work of God."

"There has to be some reason why things started. We know that he served in the Army, but the killing didn't start immediately after his return. He seems to have found a job and worked for some time – enough that he has an established schedule and he is allowed to work alone, without supervision. Probably at night, except that he doesn't work Saturday nights. So, he got a job, presumably a pretty good one, and yet something triggered him to start this blog and to start planning his kills. What was the trigger?"

"The last blog post mentions something about when he got out of the Army, that he got recruited by his comrades – his old army buddies – to get involved in the dirty operations of this guy Pharaoh." Mike was sitting back in his chair, staring up at the ceiling, which for unknown reasons was splashed with several brown stains that Mike guessed were coffee. "He says," and Mike had to pause while he dug through a pile of print-outs looking for the right page. "He says, 'I came to know Pharaoh and I have been planning for this moment ever since.' So maybe that was the trigger – maybe this whole thing started with him getting involved with this Pharaoh character, and he has been building up to this one for a long time."

"Why does it matter?" The frustration in Jason's voice leaked through. "He's out there, he's planning his next kill, and we have to stop him. That's all that really matters."

Angela shot Jason a disapproving look, but then softened. "Detective Dickson, the more we understand about the killer, the more we'll be able to predict his next move. I know it's frustrating, but I can tell you that I've been on enough of these cases to know that it's always helpful to ask the question, even if we don't know the answer yet."

"What about what he said about his first guy, Abel?" Berkowitz asked.

"What do you mean?"

"Well, he said that Abel had co-conspirators. Wait." Berkowitz shuffled through his pile of papers to find the blog entry he was looking for. "Yeah, here. He wrote *'This man – this Abel – will be the first to feel the wrath of my glory and my holy mission. He is the first in a cog of righteousness that will crush his compatriots and conspirators as well, all in good time.'* It seems like his plan included targeting people who are connected to DiVito. So, how are any of the other victims related to the first guy?"

Everyone sat in silence, unable to offer any suggestion.

At that moment, Mike's cell phone started vibrating and buzzing in his pocket. He excused himself from the conference room and extracted the phone in the hallway. The number displayed on the screen was not familiar. "Stoneman," he barked.

"Detective Stoneman, it's Dexter Peacock, from *The New York Times*. I'm working on a story that will be published tomorrow on the serial killer situation, and I would like to give you an opportunity to weigh in on a few facts and to give me a quote on the record if you are so inclined."

"Did you call the department's communications office already?"

"No, not yet. I figured after our conversation that you would want to have the first shot at a comment. But more importantly, I want to honor your request that I check with you to make sure that all the important facts are correct."

Mike pondered the possibility that the reporter was actually well-intentioned, then dismissed it as unlikely. Still, it could do no harm to listen. "Go ahead," Mike replied.

"First, I want you to know that I interviewed the operations manager at Flannagan's Steakhouse, a woman named Shirley Ellison. She confirmed that a man going by the name of Charles White worked at the restaurant for a little more than a month leading up to the death of Mr. Sawyer, and that he has now disappeared. Also, she says that the police are very interested in finding this Mr. White. I want to confirm that you have not yet found the man who used the name Charles White."

Peacock paused, waiting for a confirmation from Mike. "I have no problem with your facts there, Mr. Peacock, but I have no comment about the progress of our investigation."

Peacock pressed forward. "It seems that there is a substantial gap in time between each of the murders, probably because the killer is carefully planning each one, targeting a particular individual. Immediately after each kill, there is very little chance that there will be another one right away. Would you agree with that analysis of the killer's pattern, Detective?"

"I will have no comment on the record regarding that. However, I will not disagree with you."

"Excellent. Thank you. And do you want any comment on the record regarding the investigation?"

"No, thank you," Mike said curtly.

"Very well. Thank you for your time." Peacock hung up and Mike went back to the war room to brief the rest of the team.

"The Commissioner is going to blow a gasket if he finds out that you're talking directly to the press," Jason observed.

"True. It's a good thing that nobody is going to tell him." Mike looked around the room as everyone nodded their silent agreement.

Chapter 29 – Racing the Calendar

September 8, 2018

THE TASK FORCE MEMBERS straggled into the war room on Saturday. By noon, Dickson, Stoneman, Mason, and Manning were assembled. Overtime on a Saturday was not entirely unprecedented, but this many detectives all working on a weekend made Sully cringe, thinking about the budget. Nobody talked about the new article in *The New York Times*. It had not exactly accused the NYPD of being incompetent, but it strongly implied that it was only the presence of the feds on the case that gave the police any chance of catching the clever serial killer whose name was probably not Charles White. The Task Force tried to ignore Dexter Peacock.

"Did Simpson come up with any way to suppress the hits on the Menstrual Killer's blog?" Mike asked Angela when she arrived.

"Well, he has a few ideas, but he says it's not really possible to suppress the data. We're supposed to call him this morning."

Mike walked to the corner of the table, set down his coffee cup, and hung his jacket on the back of the chair. He was whistling softly.

"And why are you so happy this morning?" Jason inquired.

"Do I look happy?"

"Yes, you have a shit-eating grin on your face."

"I do not."

"Oh, Jesus Christ, you look like you got laid!"

"That's ridiculous. I most certainly did not," Mike huffed, and then added sheepishly, "I did have a date with Doctor McNeill last night."

"No shit?"

"No shit," Mike confirmed. "We went to dinner and I then walked her home and said goodnight, as a gentleman."

"Did you kiss her goodnight at least?"

"Gentlemen do not kiss and tell, Detective Dickson."

Before Jason could press him further, Berkowitz arrived and asked whether they had heard anything from Simpson. Mike motioned to him to close the conference room door as Angela pressed the button on the speaker phone in the middle of the table and dialed Simpson's number. Simpson picked up, and quickly got down to the point of the call.

"Guys, there is no way to prevent the owner of the blog from seeing the number of hits he's had. At least not without cooperation from the blog host, which we're not going to be able to get without a court order. Our legal guys are working on it, but we're going to hold for now so that we avoid any publicity. The best we can do is limit the number of times that we access the site so that the owner of the blog might think that the hits are random – like the kid who stumbled on it by accident. That won't give us any guarantees, but it will limit the chances that he notices the traffic. We should only access the site once per day, so we might miss a few hours of information. But he tends to put them up mostly in the middle evening hours, so we'll try to access early in the morning to make sure we get that night's information."

"What are the chances that the killer will notice the extra traffic?" Jason interjected.

Simpson was silent for a moment, then began haltingly, "Well, I can't really say. It depends on how much traffic he already has. He's been hiding the blog, so he probably does not really want to see traffic. Of course, that assumes that he's checking. He might just figure that he's behind a curtain and not bother checking his stats much. Even if he felt one way or another about more hits, he might not notice for a while."

Mike chimed in at this point. "What if we just access the site from a computer and leave it on, connected to the site, so that it's just one instance of access and we keep it running?"

"Sorry," Simpson replied quickly. "In order to see new posts, you have to refresh the site, and when you do that it counts as a new hit. It's a good idea, Mike, but it won't help."

"So, not really a good idea, just an idea that won't work," Mike responded.

"Well, yes."

"Thanks," Mike said. "Can you take care of setting up the daily access to see if there are any new posts, and immediately let us know if there's anything new?"

"Will do."

Jason punched the button to hang up the phone and turned to Mike. "We have no choice here, Mike. We can't not look at the site. If there is something important there, we have to know. We'll have to take our chances that he won't pick up on the fact that we're watching."

"Unless he already assumes that we are watching. Remember how arrogant this guy is. He might believe that the whole world is already reading his statements. We should consider the possibility that he's already feeding us misinformation through the blog and trying to send us on wild goose chases. We need to take nothing for granted, but I agree that we need to read it and see what he's saying."

"Damn, Mike, you are so cynical. But probably right."

"Yeah, sometimes I hate it when I'm right."

"I hate it, too," Jason said, smiling to himself and turning his back on Mike.

Mike put his palms on the conference table and leaned in, putting most of his weight on his arms. "We caught a break here, folks, finding this blog. We have to use it to our advantage while our killer doesn't know that we're reading."

Everyone nodded.

"Now, how can we use it? What can we do with this information that will help us catch this miscreant?"

Nobody said anything. Then Angela walked to the whiteboard and uncapped a fresh marker.

Chapter 30 – Holding Pattern

September 10, 2018

O VER THE NEXT TWO DAYS, the Task Force continued to sift through the blog posts in search of something significant that they didn't immediately see, and also to chase down the additional tips that continued to pour in from the hotline. They evaluated and dismissed several dozen more leads about men named Charles White, most of which involved real people named Charles White, none of whom ever worked at Flannagan's Steakhouse. One of the leads was a guy named Charles who was white, but whose last name was Johnson. Jason then ran a search just for the hell of it and determined that there were more than 120,000 people living in the New York area with the first name Charles.

There were 19 days before the last Saturday and they had nothing new from the blog. They kept trying to glean information, but the vague references and biblical rantings did not provide anything specific.

Dr. McNeill called Mike on the pretext of providing information about the final set of lab tests on Robert Sawyer, the most recent victim. There was nothing important, but it gave her a chance to ask some questions that she knew Mike could not answer about the case, and to tell him what a nice time she had at dinner the prior Friday. At the very end of the call, Mike suggested that they should do it again sometime. Dr. McNeill asked, "When?" Mike paused, having half-expected her to be too busy, and tried to calm his heartrate before suggesting Thursday night. She agreed and they planned to meet, as before, at the M.E.'s lab at the end of the day. Mike went to the barber that night on the way home, having noticed that his hair was getting a little shaggy.

On Thursday, with 16 days to go before the killer got his period, Mike was awakened from a sound sleep by a call from Angela. There was a new post on the blog. Mike booted up his laptop and navigated to the secure website that Simpson had set up to house the confidential documents they were sharing as part of the investigation. Copying the text into a file prevented them from sending more hits to the blog than absolutely necessary. Mike had wanted Simpson to just send them by email, but Simpson was paranoid that the killer could be hacking the email accounts. He had insisted that this was easier for everyone. Everyone except Mike. It took him three tries to get his username and password right in his half-awake state, but he eventually got into the site and navigated to the new document. It was not a long post. Mike read it through twice before taking out a pen and making some notes.

September 9

I am now the Chief Executive Officer of an internet start-up company developing apps to aid child safety. An irony, given Pharaoh's business model. The Saturday night security guards expect me to arrive late and stay late, as I've been doing. They think nothing of it. They are completely fooled and on my side. I bring them food and they thank me profusely for my kindness.

I have secured the proper elements and power source. There is a security camera in the hallway leading to the health club, where I intend to see him meet God. I would not expect the security guards in the lobby to even notice that camera during the hours when the club is not open for business, but just in case, I have hacked into the system so I can freeze it when the time comes. The security system is simplistic and easily manipulated. The only challenge is to induce Pharaoh to willingly follow me.

I have already planted the seeds of my plan. I have befriended Pharaoh. We are both late-night denizens of the office building. He appears to work hard, although much of what he does during the long hours bears little resemblance to work. Pharaoh has even invited me to visit him in his office, but so far I have declined. The day, however, is not far away.

After a half hour, Mike picked up the phone and dialed Jason, who answered on the first ring. "You want to talk?"

"Not really," Jason replied sleepily. "I'm going to need to read it again when my mind is fully active. On first read, I'd say we have some leads here – or at least some possible leads. I'll see you in the office, and we'll read it together and see if we can make any sense of it."

"Right," Mike answered, then hung up. He turned off the computer, turned off the lights, and got back into bed, but sleep would not come. His mind was contemplating the post, wondering who Pharaoh could be. Now, the investigation team knew that they were looking for a Manhattan office building with a health club. How many of those were there? Could they possibly narrow it down? Eventually, the alarm sounded and he startled. He had not realized that he was sleeping, and had no idea how much additional sleep he had managed after the call from Angela. He only knew that he wanted to roll over and find more, but he dragged himself into the shower instead.

Two hours later, he and Jason were back in the war room. "Well, shit," Jason said, "we don't know who, where, or why. We know when, but we've always known that. Aside from the fact that our killer has had personal contact with his next victim and has made friends with the security guards in whatever building he's using for the kill site, he hasn't tipped us off to anything we can use."

"Not true," Angela disagreed. "He mentioned that he brought food to the nighttime security guards. This was probably on Saturday nights, after he finished the dinner shift at Flannagan's. That's something that the guards would remember, if we could ask them."

"How many possible buildings are there that would fit the description?" Mike posed the question, dreading the answer.

"The folks downtown are working on it," Angela replied only slightly more hopefully. "It's a lot."

"He probably knows that," Jason said softly. "He's taunting us, although we have to believe that he doesn't know we're watching – at least, I hope he doesn't."

"Well, at least we have something to try to track. We might get lucky," Angela tried to sound optimistic.

"Speaking of getting lucky," Jason sat up straighter in his chair and looked at Mike, "how's it going between you and the M.E.?"

Mike frowned. "That's personal."

"I know, but I'm still asking."

"Detective Dickson, I am not at liberty to discuss details."

Jason laughed loudly. "I really like Doctor McNeill. I hope you can keep it going with her."

"Thanks," Mike said, with a suppressed emotion that Jason picked up on. Mike felt himself blushing. Blushing, for goodness sake! But he also smiled to himself and returned his attention to the blog post. "Do we know anything else that could help us?"

"I don't see anything, Mike. He mentions that he rented an office in this building. Trying to find the guards he fed will be easier for us than trying to find every single white male who rented office space."

"I agree," Mike sighed. "It's so damned frustrating to have a window into the creep and still be chasing shadows."

"At least we have shadows," Angela said, picking up her phone. She dialed her contact at the FBI field office to check on the progress of the research. By that evening, ten FBI agents and six uniformed NYPD officers were splitting up lists of buildings and making phone calls. Every beat cop in New York was alerted to chat up night security guards to ask if their building had a health club, and whether they knew of a recent tenant who brought them (or their weekend counterparts) food late at night. It wasn't exactly a needle in a haystack, but it was a long shot.

By the end of the day, Mike, Jason, and Angela had covered the whiteboard with lists and notations, but they felt no closer to unravelling the killer's mysteries. Mike excused himself at 5:00 so that he could go meet Dr. McNeill. He got off the subway at Franklin Street to give himself a chance to walk a little extra on his way to the M.E.'s office, which helped clear his head, breathing in the crisp September air and feeling his blood circulate through limbs that had been sedentary all day. Despite the relatively cool temperature, Mike was just on the verge of breaking into a full sweat when he arrived at the lab, which was deserted.

Mike called out for Michelle, but got no response. He was wondering if she might have forgotten their date, or left already, when the small door at the back of the room opened and McNeill walked out. She was already out of her smock and looking fresh, with neatly brushed hair and a tasteful gold necklace that Mike was sure he had never seen her wear in the lab. She smiled and walked up to Mike, planting a quick kiss on his cheek that he wasn't really expecting. He caught a whiff of her perfume.

"I'm ready, Mike."

"You sure are," Mike quipped back, then he realized that the comment might be misconstrued. He quickly tried to retract it. "I mean, er, you look nice, and I'm glad you're ready to go. Because I've been cooped up all day and am really looking forward to a glass of wine."

"You suave Devil, you," Michelle said playfully. "Just shut up and let's get out of here."

They stopped in Chinatown at a little dim sum place that had signage only in Chinese characters. Mike waved to the stooped Chinese man standing in front, and they were quickly ushered down a flight of stairs to a table by the window, with a view of the legs of passing pedestrians.

"This is cozy," Michelle said, trying to get a conversation started.

"Yeah, I – I think so, too," Mike responded haltingly. "I had a cousin who showed me this place a long time ago. It's a hole in the wall, but the food's great and it's dirt cheap. Uh, not that I'm taking you here because I'm trying to be cheap."

"Don't worry," Michelle said with a light laugh, "I'm all for high-quality food that isn't outrageously expensive. There are plenty of pricy places. I like finding the secret bargains." She raised her manicured eyebrows to indicate that she was sharing a secret, and it made Mike's skin tingle just a bit behind his left ear. "What was your cousin's name?"

"Louis. We called him Louie. He was a kind of genius. He taught mathematics at City College, but he couldn't ever remember where he parked his dumpy car on the street. I had to bail his jalopy out of impound more times than I can remember after he forgot to move it to the other side of the street. He was a character, but he knew the City better than anyone I ever met outside the force. I guess he spent a lot of time walking around."

"That's ironic, since he had a car."

"Well, yeah, I guess it is." Mike chuckled, more to himself than as a response to Michelle's comment. "I really liked him, but he got cancer and died a few years ago. But I keep coming to this place, kind of in his memory."

"That's sweet."

"I dunno. I don't have any family here in New York anymore, so it seems like a way to – it's stupid."

"No, it's not," Michelle quickly replied, reaching out a hand and putting it on top of his, which was lying on the bare table top. "I'm sure it can get lonely in your business without a family to come home to at night. I often feel the same way."

"Yeah?"

"Oh, yes. My mom moved to Florida about five years ago and my sister and her family live in Connecticut. I see her and her kids every once in a while, but mostly I hang out with my friends and I have my work. But I get it about wanting to remember your cousin Louie."

Mike smiled and squeezed her hand. "I have a hard time figuring out how somebody as intelligent and charming as you can be single."

Michelle dropped her head and then looked out the window at the passing pedestrians. "Well, that's a long story and one that we probably should not get into right now."

"Oh, I'm sorry."

"No need to be sorry. It's just that I've had a few, well, let's say unfortunate experiences in the dating area in the past few years."

"Yeah, well, I know how that goes."

"Really?" Michelle sat up a little straighter in her chair. "Have you been dating?"

"Not really dating," Mike said, perhaps a little too quickly. "I had a – how can I put this in a way that will not make me seem like a pervert . . . ."

"Mike, that's the last thing I would think."

"OK, well, I had a very small fling with a much younger woman. It was a few years ago. I guess she kind of seduced me."

"Uh huh?" Michelle mumbled skeptically.

"No. You see, it turned out that she was involved in a murder, and she seduced me so that I wouldn't pursue her as a suspect."

"Did it work?"

"Unfortunately, it did. At least for a while. I'm not proud of it. In fact, it's probably the most embarrassing thing I've ever done.

Since then, I've been kind of out of commission when it comes to dating."

"By out of commission, do you mean . . . ?"

Mike quickly leaned forward over the table. "No, no, not physically out of commission or anything like that. I mean, I'm capable. I mean, well, I chose not to get involved with anybody since then."

"OK," Michelle said comfortingly. "I get it. I'm glad you told me about it."

"I haven't told anyone about it before. Not even my partners."

Michelle reached out again for Mike's hand and gave it a squeeze. "I won't mention it to anyone."

"Thanks." When the waiter came around, Mike selected various plates of dumplings and buns as they passed by and they laughed and talked through two glasses of white wine each. Mike had not felt this comfortable with anyone in a long time.

After dinner, Mike walked Michelle back to her apartment building. They lingered in front of the elevator opposite a bank of mailboxes inside. After an awkward minute, Mike leaned in, and Michelle wrapped an arm around his neck as they kissed, then kissed again. Mike said good night and waited for the elevator door to close before turning and exiting back to the street, with a bit of a spring in his step. A few minutes later, a man in a dark jacket and a New York Yankees baseball hat approached Dr. McNeill's building. He keyed in an access code at the outer door, then opened the door and went inside. He examined the names on the mailboxes in the lobby for a few seconds, and then exited back out the door and turned left, back toward Canal Street.

Chapter 31 – Cat and Mouse

September 17, 2018

O N MONDAY, Mike, Jason, and Angela were back in the conference room, drinking bitter coffee and trying again to puzzle out the information in the killer's journal. They went back to the beginning and read through every kill, taking turns reading the text aloud. Angela thought that hearing it read might trigger thoughts and reactions that they did not have just reading silently. They noticed speech patterns and the repetition of certain phrases, but it was all consistent with his delusions of grandeur and ranting. Nothing suggested anything about the identity of his next victim. Nor did the expected cause of death provide much to narrow down a search. The sixth plague was boils. Jason was sure that the death would be by electrocution, while Mike expected a literal boiling. Angela tended to agree with Jason, which pissed off Mike much more than he realized it should.

By the end of the day, they all agreed that until they got more information from the next blog post, they had nothing that they could follow up on. It was twelve days to kill day, and the killer's posts always became more frequent in the days leading up to the murder as he worked himself up into a froth of expectation. It was in those last few posts that he sometimes let slip details that, after the fact, they had been able to connect to the actual deaths. It was all they had to hope for.

Meanwhile, the Task Force and the FBI agents working under Angela followed up on the only lead they still had going; the description of the building where their killer was planning his next execution. They had beat cops helping canvas buildings to establish whether they had basement health clubs and weekend night security guards. Many of the buildings contracted out their security, so there was another layer of follow-up needed to identify the weekend guards and track them down to ask about a tenant who brought them food on Saturday nights. Mike was happy to have all the federal boots on the ground because there was a lot of ground to cover. Unfortunately, they had not yielded any buildings that met all their criteria.

That evening, Mike sent Michelle an email, updating her on their lack of progress and telling her how much he had enjoyed their date the night before. It had been a casual dinner. They talked about the investigation and the plagues on Egypt. It was a short note, but he got a knot in his stomach as he hovered his cursor over the "send" button. "This dating thing requires way too much mental energy," he mumbled to himself. He commanded the attention and respect of New York City cops and detectives. Was he really nervous about whether he would have another date with the M.E.? That was crazy. And yet his palms were sweating.

The next morning, Mike's cell phone buzzed in his pocket when he was two blocks away from the precinct building. He was so close that he decided to let it roll into voicemail and check it when he got to the war room. Four minutes later, when he walked in, he saw Jason and Angela hunched over the table. As soon as Mike walked through the door, Jason grunted at him.

"Good, you got my message. Grab a chair and a copy."

"Copy of what?"

"Seriously?" Jason looked up at his partner. "How do you not answer your cell or listen to your messages?"

Mike sat down and saw a sheet of printed paper on the table in front of his regular seat. He grabbed it and dispensed with any further banter. The killer had posted something overnight:

September 17

I talked to Pharaoh. He is supremely confident in himself, and a salesman for his economic interests. He asked me about my start-up company and listened for perhaps sixty seconds before he cut in and talked about how the smart phone app I was supposedly developing might have an application in his import/export business. He thought the child-tracking app could help root out fraud and skimming of product, and could be used to track employees without their knowledge. He wanted me to consider marketing the product more broadly. He wanted to invest in the business. He probably saw this as a way to launder his blood money, but I smiled and nodded my head and cemented my ability to approach him as a businessman and colleague. He had no idea that he was speaking to his executioner.

I told Pharaoh that I would think about what he said and thanked him for taking the time to speak to a novice businessman. He was gracious, but I knew he had ulterior motives. He thought he could fleece me and steal my ideas. He invited me to join him and his associates on Saturday night, when his co-conspirators and their women transform his business into a den of iniquity to rival Sodom and Gomorrah as they hold a party in Pharaoh's offices. I said I would think about it and bade him farewell, but told him that I looked forward to seeing him again as we both burned the midnight oil at the office. He smiled and shook my hand. I grasped his firmly and left him to take the other bank of elevators up to his high-floor office, with the beautiful view, as I proceeded toward my humble space. I knew that Pharaoh's days were numbered. It was thrilling, and it makes me look forward to his end that much more.

When Mike looked up, Jason and Angela were looking at him, having had a head start reading the entry. "Well," Mike said as he put his sheet down on the table, "we now know that the victim, Pharaoh, is a criminal who runs an import/export business out of a high-floor office in a building with a health club. Do we think that might narrow our search?"

Angela was smiling. "I already ran this by my guys and they are cross-checking for references. Assuming our killer is giving us accurate information, it should narrow the search. Jason asked your captain to run the same information past all the NYPD units who might be involved in investigating criminal activity in that kind of business. Who knows, maybe –"

"Maybe we get lucky," Mike finished. "We keep saying that, but so far it hasn't happened. Any progress on the other leads?"

"Nothing yesterday," Angela grumbled. "Now we can add an extra question for the building security guards – whether they know anybody who hosts parties in his office on Saturday nights and who is in the import/export business."

"What is he importing, or exporting, I wonder," Jason mused.

"Maybe it's South American tree frogs," Mike shot back.

"Or plagues upon Egypt," Angela added. They all chuckled.

"Why is it that cops can make jokes and laugh at this sick shit?" Jason wondered aloud.

Angela's expression turned suddenly serious. "It's a coping mechanism. If we don't laugh a little bit, all the stress and dead bodies would eat us up inside and we'd go nuts."

"Is that the clinical term?" Mike asked seriously.

Angela smiled. "Actually, 'bat-shit crazy' is the formal diagnostic phrase."

They all burst out laughing.

Chapter 32 – Voices and Shadows

September 24, 2018

AFTER A FRUITLESS WEEK of chasing down possible office buildings and talking to security guards, combined with more unsuccessful combing through military records, the Task Force was beaten down and tired. Angela suggested that they all take the weekend to recharge. The killer's blog had been quiet for several days, but since his pattern was to post at least some descriptions of his preparations for the next kill, they all expected to see something soon.

Mike had requested to not be awakened before 6:00 a.m. to be told that there was a blog post. For a dead body, he would gladly rouse himself from deep sleep and head out to a crime scene, but an electronic message from their serial killer could wait until morning since there was nothing that could be done sooner anyway. He checked his phone before entering the shower on Monday morning and saw that there had been activity. He then rushed through his personal hygiene and got to the war room at 8:15. Angela was already there when Mike arrived, but he was happy to have out-hustled Jason for a change.

RIGHTEOUS ASSASSIN

September 22

I am sitting in my tiny office one week before my planning and preparation will result in the righteous death of Pharaoh. Tonight was a dress rehearsal, and it was splendid. I have confirmed that Pharaoh and his wretched gang will spend next Saturday night in this very building, entertaining. I have been invited to the party, and this time I will accept.

But tonight, I had work to do. I hacked into the security system and planted my false image. I then descended to the basement and visited the altar where Pharaoh will be sacrificed. I practiced the removal of my equipment from its hiding place behind a wall panel. The time it will take to bring Pharaoh to the point of death it is entirely within the window of my opportunity. Yes, his compatriots will eventually miss him, but he is such a headstrong personality that his minions will not immediately report his absence. I planned and practiced three different exits to ensure that I will have multiple options for escape into the night.

The guards look forward to my arrival with their treats each Saturday. Yes, they will remember me, and there will be images of my false face on the security cameras – I have chosen not to try to avoid them or erase all the video. The images will be useless to the police as soon as I shed my skin and resume my normal appearance. The police will identify the man the guards know, the man who rented the office space. But since this man does not exist, it will not matter.

I am consumed by the divine rush of adrenaline. I will return home to sleep, knowing that my mission will succeed once again, and the Devil will be erased from the evil world.

"I wonder why he waited until Sunday to post this when he clearly wrote it on Saturday?" Mike mused.

"Maybe he was worried about a trace. He says he was in his office in the building where he plans to carry out the kill, not in his usual office or home or wherever he normally is when he makes his posts. Perhaps he needed to be somewhere else in order to post using the slave computers."

Mike nodded. It sounded plausible, although he did not fully understand the IT issues. "What do you think he means by 'equipment'? He's got a health club as the kill spot and we're expecting something to do with boils. What equipment does that suggest?"

"Suggest what?" Jason panted as he stormed into the room, frowning at the sight of Mike already there sipping his coffee. Mike and Angela pointed to the printout sitting at his regular seat at the table, but Jason had already read the post. Mike shrugged. Mason and Berkowitz arrived shortly afterwards, and the process of poring over the blog post began anew.

"It's like we're cramming for a literature test and trying to glean the deep meaning of some obscure author's novel," Mason complained. "I always hated English."

"Well, the language always hated you back," Berkowitz joked.

"What about the reference to the three exits?" Mike said, cutting off the jabs. "He's planning alternate escape routes. I don't recall him mentioning that kind of planning in his entries discussing any of the earlier kills. Does this mean that he's worried about getting caught, or getting cornered? Why the careful attention to detail?"

"And does it help us narrow down the building? Do all buildings have three or more exits?" Angela looked around the room, expecting that someone from New York would automatically know the answer. Nobody spoke up.

"What's the fire code say about that?" Mike posed to the group. When nobody answered, Mike looked at Mason. "George, why don't you go check that out – see whether code requires three exits or more from a high-rise. It wouldn't surprise me, but if it doesn't, maybe we can use that to narrow down our building search."

Mason nodded as he got up and left the war room to make some calls. How hard could it be to find a building inspector?

"What else is there in this that we can use?" Angela said as she meandered in the direction of the whiteboard. She erased the entire left half of the surface and picked up a marker, writing in "escape plan" and "three exits."

"What about the reference to timing?" Berkowitz posed. "I know this guy likes to torture his victims, but how is that related to timing? How can you practice killing someone and time it out?"

Angela wrote "timing of kill" on the board, then offered her thoughts. "I agree that it's an odd reference, and not in keeping with the others. Maybe he thinks that the victim will be missed and that he has to hurry the process. He talks about this party." Angela paused to write "party" on the board. "He's telling us that the victim, Pharaoh, has an office in the building and that he hosts parties on Saturday nights with other people there. The killer intends to lure Pharaoh away from the party, bring him to the basement, and kill him. Since he will be gone from the party, the other guests may miss him, so the killer needs to be quick about it. Somebody may come looking for him, which is maybe why he needs an exit plan. But there is some kind of equipment involved, and then some amount of time, perhaps related to the equipment."

"What does he have to do, warm up the chainsaw?" Jason said mockingly.

"No," Mike said softly, holding up a finger as if to take over the floor. "No, not a chainsaw, but warming something up is possible. Remember the boils angle – boils are like blisters. He might be heating up something to cause blisters or burns. He may indeed need to literally heat something up to be part of his torture. He had to test out how long it took to heat up whatever equipment he's using to burn the victim."

"That makes sense," Angela agreed. "How does it help us?"

"No idea," Mike conceded, slumping against the back of his chair and rocking backwards, nearly losing his balance in the process.

"What about the reference to his false face?" Jason said, changing the subject. "He plans to change his appearance right after this kill so that we won't be able to recognize him, even if we have him on a security camera? What do we know about what Charles White looked like when he was working at the restaurant last month?"

Angela drew a line down the whiteboard to mark off a new column of information. She wrote as she spoke. "We know that he's pretty tall – at least six-two or so. He had a scruffy, blondish beard and long, stringy hair." She listed the attributes.

"So, he plans on shaving his beard, cutting his hair, and maybe changing the color so he looks different and we can't catch him." Jason paused, not sure whether he was finished or not.

"Which means that he's not as sophisticated as he thinks he is," Angela interjected. "He's a hacker, but he doesn't seem to be familiar with facial recognition software."

"What do you mean?" Mike asked.

Angela shrugged. "If we have a good image of his face, we will be able to run it through the facial recognition database. We might not know what his new appearance will be, but we might be able to identify him. It doesn't matter whether you shave a beard or grow one, or change your hair color or even eye color. The software makes a match on your face like it's a fingerprint based on the space between your nose and eyes and the angles between your eyes and mouth – things you can't change without surgery. If he really was in the military, and if we can get a good image of him, we can make a match."

"You FBI guys have all the good toys," Jason pouted.

"But it still doesn't help us find him before the kill." Angela tossed her marker into the gutter underneath the whiteboard in frustration.

Chapter 33 – Close, but No Cigar

September 29, 2018

MIKE, JASON, AND ANGELA had agreed to bring in some Chinese food and have dinner together in the war room, where they had spent so much time together over the past two months. The other members of the Task Force, who had been working earlier in the day on Saturday, were home with their families.

Doctor McNeill's mother was in town for a visit and they were having dinner in Times Square before going to see *Kinky Boots* on Broadway. She had invited Mike, but he had begged off based on it being the last Saturday of the month, and he secretly had no desire to spend the evening with his girlfriend's mother. He realized that he had never articulated Michelle as his "girlfriend" to anyone, and in fact not even to himself, but he could find no other way to describe Mrs. McNeill when Jason had asked. Now it was too late. The moniker was going to stick between them, although Mike asked Jason not to tell Angela, which he immediately did.

"It's not a big deal, Mike," Jason chided in between bites of chow fun. "She's a lovely and intelligent woman, and she's very attractive. You like her. She likes you. You've gone out a bunch of times, and you'll probably go out again the next time you're both free. So, even without getting into the details of your comingling of bodily fluids, anyone watching would say that she's your girlfriend."

Angela pursed her lips disapprovingly. "Let's not talk about Mike's bodily fluids while I'm trying to eat." She then calmly dipped a steamed pork dumpling into its thin black garlic sauce and popped it into her mouth expertly with her chopsticks, smiling while she chewed.

"Fine," Mike shrugged. "Let's just drop it, shall we?" He pushed back from the conference table, which was strewn with white cardboard containers, chopstick wrappers, and crinkly waxed paper from the fried noodles. He put his hand on the table to balance himself and it came away sticky from spilled duck sauce. He struggled to his feet, listening to his left knee crunch under his weight. He avoided reaching down to massage it, despite the pain.

It was about 8:30 when the phone rang. It wasn't any of their cell phones, but the land line – the old, boxy black phone with the loud, shrill bell sitting on the little table in the corner of the conference room. It was the precinct line, so nobody jumped to answer it. A call to the local police precinct could be anything from a cat stuck in a tree to a domestic dispute. Then Jason asked the question that was just jumping into the minds of the other two: "That phone doesn't generally ring, does it?"

Mike shook his head and, since he was already standing, walked over and picked it up. After a moment, he said "Yes, this is Stoneman." Jason and Angela stopped eating and trained their eyes on Mike in the corner. "Wait a minute," he said and looked down at the phone, hovering a finger over the line of little buttons along the bottom. He finally selected one and pressed down, activating the speaker. He carried the speaker box and the phone set over to the conference table and set them down. "Agent Forrest, I have you on speaker now. I'm here with detective Jason Dickson from the NYPD and Special Agent Manning from the FBI. Can you repeat what you just told me?"

The voice coming out of the box was tinny and the volume fluctuated up and down. The three of them stared at the tiny black holes in the silver box as he spoke. "This is Agent Everett Forrest. I am part of an FBI Task Force working on an investigation into suspected human trafficking coming through New York harbor. I monitor wire taps that we have on a couple of suspects and a little while ago, I listened to a conversation between a suspect and a man who was arranging a meeting. The other guy said his name is Charles White, and I remember seeing a bulletin a while back that you were looking for a suspect by that name. And, well, I have nothing better to do here in the box so I figured I have a bad guy connected to a guy with the name of your bad guy, so I'd give you a head's up."

Mike made eye contact with Jason and then spoke into the silver box. "Agent Forrest, thank you for being so on the ball. Even if it's just a coincidence, that's good police work."

"Thanks."

"What can you tell us about the suspect you're monitoring?"

"Well," Agent Forrest hesitated. "I'm not sure what I can tell you, since you're not on the case."

Angela broke in, "Agent Forrest, this is Special Agent Angela Manning from the profiling team at Manassas, Virginia. I have level 2 security clearance and I'm working on a serial killer case with these detectives. Let's not stand on protocol here."

There was a pause before Agent Forrest's voice creaked through the box. "OK, well, I don't want to mention his name, but he's a pretty slimy character. He has an organization of ex-military thugs who kidnap young girls in South and Central America and then cram them into shipping containers and bring them into Miami and New York. They end up as hookers or worse. The guy looks legit on the outside, but he's a real scumbag."

Mike looked up at Jason and Angela. "Sounds like someone who could be one of our guy's targets." Both nodded.

Jason spoke loudly into the speaker box. "Agent Forrest, when your suspect talks about his business, does he describe it as an import/export business?"

"Actually, yes," came Forrest's surprised reply.

"Listen, Agent Forrest," Mike said, speaking quickly, "our guy has a pattern of killing on the last Saturday of the month, and that's tonight. He has a pattern of killing people who, in his mind, deserve to die. He calls himself the Angel of Death. Our guy recently used the alias Charles White and he has described his next victim as being an evil man who says he's in the import/export business, who traffics in human misery and who enslaves people. So, there are a lot of connections here. Why don't you tell us where this meeting is going down so that we can get over there and see if your Charles White is our Charles White?"

Again, the speaker box was silent. "Um, Detective. I know that I called you, and I'm not exactly sure what I expected you to say, but I don't think that I can tell you anything that might compromise our operation, at least not without the permission of my Director. We've been on this guy for a year, so we can't just storm the building and tip him off that somebody is tapping his phone."

"I get it," Mike barked into the speaker box. "But if your Charles White is our Charles White, and if your guy is his target, then your year of work will be moot in a few hours because your guy is going to be dead. I tell you what, you give us a general idea of the part of town where they are now and we'll start heading in that direction. You get your Director on the phone and have him call me on my cell, and we'll see if we can work something out. In the meantime, we won't be wasting time and we'll be able to move fast if we get permission. How about that?"

Agent Forrest agreed and told Mike that the building was in Brooklyn Heights. As they rushed to the area in a black & white with its lights on, Angela got on the phone with her Director in Washington, who was sensitive to not wanting to blow the other operation. Meanwhile, Mike was on his cell talking to the New York Regional Director of the FBI, who was having dinner at a very expensive Manhattan restaurant and was not happy about being pulled away. After five minutes and some technical frustration in trying to get all the parties connected on one conference line, the Regional Director agreed to let Agent Forrest give them the address on the condition that they only go in looking for Charles White. They were not allowed to ask about the FBI's suspect, and in fact the Director refused to even give Mike his name. Mike was admonished to take no action that would compromise the FBI's surveillance operation, and he agreed.

As they sped toward the address, Angela said, "We want the basement!"

"Right," Jason chimed in. "In the blog he said the kill would happen in the basement."

"OK," Mike shouted over the car's siren. "Listen, when we get there, let's not even ask about Charles White. Let's just head for the basement and check it out." The others nodded and they all fished out their guns to check their safeties and inventory their spare ammo.

They pulled up to the front of the office building with the lights and siren off and piled out of the squad car. They hurried into the lobby after waiting for the security guard to come to the door and eventually let them in. When Jason asked the guard how to get to the basement, he asked whether they meant the storage level or the health club.

"Health club," Mike responded quickly. The guard directed Mike and the group of cops toward a bank of elevators at the far end of the lobby.

The uniformed officer who had been driving their squad car emerged first from the elevator at the health club level, followed by Jason, Mike, and then Angela. The building security guard stayed with the elevator, happy to let the real cops handle the search. He gave the uniformed officer a white plastic key card to get them past any locked doors. "Should we turn on the lights?" the officer asked Mike.

"No," Mike whispered. "If our killer is down here torturing the FBI's guy, we don't want to tip him off that we're here."

The uniform swiped the key card at the glass door leading to the gym, and the four walked quickly down the carpeted corridor past inspirational posters about eating less fat and taking the stairs instead of the elevator. Mike couldn't stop himself from whispering a pledge to get to the gym more often. At the end of the corridor, another set of heavy doors insulated the interior of the gym from the exterior hallway. The leading officer pressed carefully on the metal bar in the center of the door. The latch gave way with a loud click and he slowly eased the right side of the double doors open with a slight creak. As soon as the door was open, Mike heard a low humming sound.

The space on the other side of the door was an expansive exercise room, filled with weight machines, treadmills, ellipticals, and stationary bikes. To the left was an alcove with free weights and barbells, and to the right was another corridor guarded by a desk area, with computer monitors and a large pump-action bottle of hand sanitizer. The entire scene was illuminated only by the eerie, yellow glow of a single emergency light in the corner, next to a pile of foam mats. Mike could make out the hulking shapes of the equipment and was sure nobody was tied up and being tortured in the dim space.

The officer took a few steps into the main room, executed a slow 360-degree turn, and then shook his head at the trailing detectives while motioning toward the desk area with his gun. When Angela came last through the door, it slammed shut behind her, making them all jump.

"Sorry," she said, embarrassed that she had allowed the door to close so loudly.

At the end of the hallway next to the desk, another yellow security light cast dim shadows and a reflection into a mirror at the far end. The group carefully crept down the second hallway. On their left were two openings in the brightly painted cinder-block wall: the women's locker room to one side, the men's to the other. Mike could still hear the humming sound, and now it was accompanied by a gurgling noise coming from the direction of the locker rooms. Mike motioned to the uniform and Jason to take the women's room, while he and Angela would take the men's. He briefly caught himself thinking that he should send her into the women's room, but then shook his head and ignored the instinct.

Mike led the way into the locker room, slowly creeping past dim lockers and avoiding knocking his shin against the low changing bench. He carefully continued to the end of the row of lockers, then past the entrance to a lavatory area, turning with his gun outstretched as he checked the space for signs of life before moving on. The gurgling sound was louder here. Two steps later, he saw a line of showers to his right. He pointed his gun toward the empty space, then looked to his left and saw the hot tub – and the slumped head of a person leaning back against the lip with both his arms extended, as if in a deep lounging position. Or maybe dead.

He motioned to Angela to cover him and scrambled quickly to the edge of the pool. Bubbles erupted all over the surface and steam rose up around the area like a cauldron. At first, Mike assumed the hot tub was just in normal operation, but as he got closer he could feel the extreme heat emanating from the water. Mike dropped to a knee behind the figure and quickly determined that his arms were tied to the ground with plastic straps. He fished into his pocket for a boy scout knife and opened the blade with his teeth, keeping his gun in front of him in case the killer was lurking nearby. He cut the straps and reached down to haul the body out, but then drew back, yelping in pain as his fingers touched the fabric of the man's suit jacket, which was saturated with boiling water. He shook off the pain and grabbed the man's hair, which was above the water level and, while hot, did not scald Mike's hand. He heaved the heavy body halfway out, and then called to Angela for assistance. Angela grabbed a white towel from a nearby shelf and used it like a potholder as they managed to pull the man out of the water and onto the tile just as Jason and the uniform dashed in.

"Did you see anybody?" Mike barked at Jason.

"No," the detective panted. "The women's room was clear."

"Search the rest of the place, fast!" Mike ordered as he hurried to a nearby sink and turned on the cold water, holding his burned hands under the flow and cursing under his breath. "Get the security guard," Mike told Angela as he winced at the pain.

After a minute of bathing his burned hands, Mike walked back over to the limp, soaked figure laying on the tile next to the still-boiling hot tub. He had seen the condition of the body before he went to cool his burns and knew that hurrying was not necessary. He did not know the name of the dead man, but he was pretty sure he was the one whom the FBI had been surveilling for the past year. He knew the man was a despicable criminal, and yet he could not help but recoil from the gruesome scene. When the state puts a criminal to death, it's a quick and relatively painless process. There is no suffering, lest the execution be deemed "cruel and unusual." This poor son-of-a-bitch had been boiled alive in a two-thousand-dollar suit. He glanced quickly down at the man's face, which was relatively less burned than the rest of his body. It was a mask of agony just the same, with a huge blister bubbling out from under his left eyeball, which was enlarged beyond all possible proportions and cooked to a sickly green hue.

Mike looked away and sat down on the nearby bench next to a white towel. He gingerly reached into his jacket pocket and extracted two blue latex gloves, which he slowly worked onto his hands over the still-sensitive burns. He rose from the bench and walked back toward the entrance, searching for a light switch, which he found just inside the exit to the hallway by the desk. The lights flickered on and hummed to life, giving a cheery and clean feeling to the locker room. Mike extracted his cell phone from the holster on his belt, but saw that he had no service in the sub-basement of the building. Just then, Angela returned, leading the building security guard.

"Call for back-up and a coroner," he instructed, "and lock down this building – nobody goes out or comes in. Understand?" He glared at the guard, who nodded silently, then removed his radio and squawked to his companion upstairs to call 9-1-1 and initiate lock-down, active shooter protocol. Mike turned back to his crime scene.

There was no need to put up restraining tape or secure the area against pedestrians. They were very much alone. Within thirty seconds, Mike heard the squealing of a siren and saw the reflection of flashing lights out in the main exercise area as the building's alarms sounded. He took a few steps past the hot tub, where there was a short passageway leading out to the exercise room. He looked past the treadmills aligned along the far wall to a bank of mirrors. He could see the reflection of a uniformed officer, who was leaning against the white desk and talking into a telephone handset. He had crept past that desk just a few minutes earlier. He realized his reflection would have been visible in the mirror to someone standing here, just out of sight in the darkness.

Mike walked back to the hot tub and all around the area, trying to avoid looking at the scalded corpse. He followed the snaking path of two black rubber cords that emerged from the water near the wall, and then unplugged the industrial cord connected to an electrical panel that had been removed from the wall, behind the mechanism for a chair lift used to heft disabled patrons into the tub. When he pulled the plug, the low humming sound that had been coming from the water ceased, and the bubbling subsided slightly.

He continued around the perimeter of the tub with his head down, looking for evidence. He examined the plastic zip-ties that he had cut away, which had bound the dead man to the ground and effectively kept him inside the tub. There was little chance of getting a print from the rough plastic. Then he looked up and noticed that one of the lockers on the higher tier of the two-level setup was slightly ajar. He carefully opened the metal door until he could see inside, where he found a plastic bag partly filled with additional zip-ties, the kind you can buy at any Home Depot. Also in the locker were two neatly folded white towels, the kind the gym probably used for its showers. He lifted the towels and peeked under, but saw nothing but grey metal. He scowled and turned to complete his sweep of the area. He found nothing helpful.

Mike left Jason to supervise the crime scene and had Angela come with him to see if they could track down their killer's office space, which they assumed existed somewhere in the building based on what he had written in his blog. They returned to the elevator, where the same building security guard who had originally led them to the health club was still acting as the elevator attendant shuttling police up and down from the lobby. Mike asked him if he knew where Charles White's office was.

"Who?"

"Charles White," Mike repeated.

The guard looked confused. "I'm not sure who you mean, Detective."

Now it was Mike's turn to be confused. "He's the guy we came here looking for. Tall guy, six-foot-two or three, works late hours, brings in food for the night security guys on Saturday nights."

"Oh!" the guard said with a flash of recognition. "You mean Charles Gordon. He's a really nice guy. He brings us take-out from a steak house. Yeah. He works on weekends sometimes and comes in really late sometimes. That's the guy, his name is Charles Gordon."

Mike looked at Angela and shrugged. "Has to be the same guy." Then he turned back to the guard. "OK, do you know where this Charles Gordon has his office space?"

The guard said that Gordon's office was on the sixth floor and led them back to the lobby and then to an adjoining bank of elevators that covered floors 2 through 15. Once on the proper floor, the guard, whose name was Gerard, let them into the suite of offices with his pass card.

The name of the company, Angel Enterprises, was emblazoned in gold letters on a white cardboard sign hanging on the inside of the door. Inside, the office was as spartan as if it were vacant. There were four cubicles of office space inside the main door, each with a black leather desk chair. Each grey desktop sported a fourteen-inch computer monitor and a pull-out keyboard underneath. Mike could not see any computers, but he figured that they were under the desks on the floor. The walls of each cubicle were made of dark cloth. A few push-pins dotted the surface of one partition, but there were no notes attached to them. Mike saw no papers, no trash in the cans, and generally no signs of life. There were telephones on each desk, and Mike wondered if their killer would have used one of them to make calls to his victim.

Mike asked Gerard to let them into a different office across the hall, where he grabbed a sheet of paper from the tray of a fax machine and tore off two strips of tape from a desktop dispenser. He fashioned a makeshift sign marking the Angel Enterprises office as a crime scene. He'd send in the forensic unit later to scrub the place for prints that he doubted they would find.

Twenty minutes later, Mike, Jason, and Angela were in the building lobby with a dozen uniformed officers gathered at one end of the marble expanse, interviewing angry and frustrated men in business suits and ladies wearing party dresses and excessive makeup. None of them claimed to know what happened to their host, whose name was Justin Heilman. The cops conducting the interviews had not been told that Heilman was the target of an FBI investigation so that they could not inadvertently blow the cover of the federal operation.

After satisfying themselves that the interviews with Heilman's party guests was under control, Mike left Jason in charge of the interviews while he and Angela wandered over to the main security desk to see whether there was any security video that might shine some light on the events of the evening. "Can you play back the security video from this console?" Mike asked. The guard at the desk was older than Gerard. As Mike talked to him, he came to the conclusion that the man was a retired cop, or maybe retired military. He looked to be in his early sixties, with a bushy grey moustache but a clean salt-and-pepper crewcut and clear, brown eyes. His uniform was smoothly pressed and his tie was perfectly knotted and tucked into his starched tan shirt. His building ID card, bearing the name Edward Felton, was clipped neatly in position on his front pocket next to a shiny silver pen. Mike could not see his shoes, but he guessed they were polished to a mirror shine.

"Sure," Felton said, "what camera do you want to see?"

"I don't suppose there's a camera inside the men's locker room down in the health club?"

Felton chuckled. "Ha. No, not in the women's room either. Just the entrance hallway to monitor who goes in and out."

"OK, let's see that." Mike walked around behind the desk so he could see the small monitor on which eight squares showed the views from different cameras. Felton paged through the options for video on the security system. He clicked a button and the eight small squares were replaced by one larger image, showing the hallway just inside the main door to the health club. The camera was mounted on the ceiling inside the door so that the image would show anyone coming in. "What time is that?" Mike asked.

Felton clicked his mouse and a date and time stamp appeared in white characters along the bottom of the screen. 9-29-18: 8:35:14PM. Another click of the mouse caused the time stamp to spin forward at six times normal speed. As the minutes sped by, the image on the screen remained the same, an empty hallway and a closed door. Mike and Felton watched the absence of action in silence for a few minutes.

"Who are we looking for?" Felton asked.

Mike turned to him abruptly, somewhat confused by the question. "What do you mean? We're looking for Charles Gordon."

Felton looked back at Mike, impassively. "Nobody told me who you were looking for."

Mike hung his head, as he realized that he and his team, in their efforts to maintain the FBI's cloak of secrecy, had never explained to this guard who they were chasing. The guard named Gerard knew because Mike had asked him to take them up to Charles Gordon's office, but nobody had clued in Felton. He was not a cop, so he didn't need to know.

"I'm sorry, Officer Felton," Mike said.

"Sergeant Felton," the older man corrected.

Mike raised an eyebrow. "Army?"

"Twenty years and out," Felton said proudly.

"Well, Sergeant Felton, I am indeed a dipshit for not realizing that we had an asset here in the lobby that we did not utilize. The man we came here to find is Charles Gordon. He might have also been called Charles White. Do you know who we're talking about?"

"Sure," Felton said. "Very friendly guy. Been here a few months." Felton manipulated his mouse again, shaking his head. He stopped the image of the health club hallway and pulled up an image of the front door, viewed from the inside of the lobby. As he scrolled through the video, Felton told Mike that Charles Gordon had come in earlier in the evening, as was pretty normal for him on a Saturday night, and that he hadn't seen Gordon leave yet. "There!" he exclaimed, clicking his mouse to freeze the image. "That's him arriving."

Mike looked at the monitor and saw a clear image of a man's face as he walked calmly through the door and across the marble-tiled lobby carrying a large white paper bag. "Can you capture me an image of that face?"

"Already doing it, sir," Felton replied smartly as he tapped a few keys.

Mike looked over to where Jason was standing, listening to one of the uniforms take a statement from one of the partygoers. "Hey, Jason!" Mike shouted, his voice echoing across the empty space.

"What?"

"We got him."

Chapter 34 – Rough Workout

September 30, 2018

I AM STILL TRYING *to make sense of the way in which the Lord nearly abandoned me during the execution of Pharaoh. My planning was indeed essential, and I escaped capture by the police by using one of my alternate exit routes. I had to run as if enemy fire was at my back and hidden IEDs lined the sidewalk all around me. My instincts – the instincts of a soldier – saved my life as God reached out his hand and guided me to safety. I know now, more than ever, that the Lord is watching over me. And yet, my own skills and powers were tested. I cannot understand how events came to this end. There is work to be done. Fortunately, my body is not damaged and I can resume my normal appearance and normal routine without suspicion.*

My plans went perfectly, in the beginning. I arrived in my small office earlier than usual and called Pharaoh's office. My business phone line had been one of the small details that I did not neglect when setting up my office environment. The number is not listed in any directory and known only to me and listed on my business card, which I also created to make my façade more realistic. I gave the card only to the security guards in the lobby so that they could ring up when my non-existent guests and clients showed up. I told Pharaoh that I wanted to take him up on his offer to attend his Saturday night party. But first, I wanted Pharaoh to meet me downstairs in my office, where I had something important to show to him. I implied that it was related to investment and financing, safe in the knowledge that Pharaoh's greed would bring him to me alone, not wanting to share the potential windfall.

Pharaoh arrived as scheduled and I explained that I had discovered a brilliant new use for the software I was developing, and that I needed to show him downstairs in the health club, where I had set up an experimental application. We bantered casually as we descended in the elevator. Pharaoh talked about himself, of course, and how much he was going to help me with my business. I knew that he was salivating over the prospect of cheating me out of my life's savings. I was salivating over the prospect of taking Pharaoh's life.

We exited into the basement health club where my access card opened the door. We walked down the health club hallway and I was confident in the knowledge that even if the guards were glancing at their monitor, they would see only empty space. I guided Pharaoh into the men's locker room and to a seat next to the hot tub, where I had already placed a towel on the wooden bench. Pharaoh was oblivious to the heavy-duty, 120-volt electrical cord running from a panel in the wall and into the water. I positioned myself behind him and reached into a locker where I retrieved two extra-long plastic zip-tie cords. I quickly slipped the first cord between Pharaoh's right arm and his back while I grabbed his left arm, pulled it behind him quickly, and secured the cord, pulling it tight and drawing his upper arms together in a painful clench as his shoulder blades compressed backwards.

Pharaoh cried out in his annoyance. He must have thought that his binding was merely a part of my demonstration. He was unhappy only that he did not know what was happening. There was no fear in his voice, only the frustration of a man who thinks himself powerful and in control, and who has suddenly found himself in a subservient position. When he opened his mouth to scold me for failing to properly explain what I was doing, I stuffed a rolled-up athletic sock into his mouth, then quickly secured it with a length of duct tape.

Now, Pharaoh was angry. His eyes bulged and his forehead turned red with the flood of blood to his face as he grunted wordlessly through his binding. He stood up, straining against the restraints on his arms and trying to wriggle free. But his arms were pulled so far behind him that he had no leverage against the cord. As he stood, I pushed against his chest with two fingers, sending him toppling backwards onto the tile floor. The thud of his skull contacting the inflexible surface left Pharaoh stunned, and I quickly used a second cord to bind his ankles tightly together, rendering him effectively immobile. I saw flecks of blood marring the white tile of the floor.

I swung his bound feet toward the hot tub and pushed him into the water, watching the surprise on his face and, for the first time, seeing fear in his eyes as he moaned through his gag and shook his head violently. He submerged briefly, but bounced back to the surface quickly, since the pool was only three feet deep at its center. Pharaoh breathed heavily through his nose, ejecting water from his nostrils. His eyes showed rage now, as if he would rise from the water and kill me with his bound hands. I smiled at him soothingly as I began the recitation of his sins.

"I am the Angel of God," I said to him, prompting a look of contempt mixed with confusion. "I know your sins and your wickedness. You import not only coffee and cocoa and sugar, but also young girls, who are abused and sold into bondage." Pharaoh's face turned to perplexity and doubt. "How can this man you do not know possibly understand your deepest secrets? It is because I am the agent of the Lord. I know the darkness in your heart."

As I spoke, I retrieved two more zip-ties from the nearby locker and used them to secure each of Pharaoh's arms to grommets embedded in the floor around the hot tub. The steel arcs were used to secure a cover, but provided an easy way to immobilize Pharaoh so that he could not possibly struggle out of the water, even if he were to free his legs. I walked to the wall and plugged in the heavy black cord. The room was then filled with a humming akin to a choir of angels. The heating elements beneath the water began to turn red, creating tiny bubbles that clung to the metal. Pharaoh had no understanding of what was happening.

I had observed the same behavior from Pilate, who expected that his abduction was a precursor to a ransom demand. He had never considered the possibility that he was there to die, and Pharaoh was much the same. He was pained, annoyed, and angry, but he was not yet afraid. I was required to explain.

"The Lord will wreak vengeance upon your vile soul. Your sins have brought you to this end. No more shall you spread pain upon the land."

Still, he looked only confused, perhaps thinking that I was some crazed, but ultimately harmless religious zealot.

At this, I was the one annoyed. I revel in the pain of the wicked. "Pharaoh, you must understand your fate and why you are here. Within the next twelve minutes, my heating element will boil the water around you. You will start to develop second-degree burns on all of your skin. Blisters will sprout from your fingers, your blood will start to boil, your eyes will expand to twice their normal size, and your brain will burst. There is no force in the universe that can stop this from happening. You will meet God and face judgment for all your transgressions, and I shall watch you die."

Finally, I saw true fear in Pharaoh's eyes. I reached down, ripped the tape from his mouth, and removed the sock. I had no worries about anyone hearing his cries here in the sub-basement.

As soon as his mouth was unbound, Pharaoh began such a vile torrent of obscenities and threats that even Pilate would have been embarrassed. As the water around him frothed and heated, he began to scream, from the pain and the fear and in the vain hope that someone would hear. I laughed and advised him to make peace with his death.

As the steam rose from the angry water, Pharaoh ceased his screaming and lost consciousness as he succumbed to the call of the Lord. In the moment of Pharaoh's departure from the mortal world, I heard a sound. The humming of the heating element was a low groan, accompanied by the bubbling of the water, but I heard a metallic clang, as if a heavy door had slammed shut. I froze for a moment, listening intently. I knew that the guards did not patrol the health club at night, and I was confident that no other denizen of the building would be here this late, unless one of Pharaoh's minions had come looking for him. God's hand guided me to be careful.

I backed away from the pool and walked down the passageway leading to the main exercise room. I carefully peeked around the corner where I could see the mirrored wall beyond a row of treadmills. In the reflection, I saw them. There were three or four figures, and at least one held a gun in his hand. The last one in the line turned his head and I saw a face I recognized from the television – the lead detective investigating my case. Police! But how?! It was not possible, and yet there they were. The exercise room was dark and vacant, and they were carefully walking toward the main entrance into the locker rooms. Within a few minutes, they would find what was left of Pharaoh.

I dashed across the darkened space to the emergency exit door, which I had scouted as one of my escape routes. It led to a painted concrete stairwell and a fire door that emptied onto the sidewalk at the rear of the building. I had earlier disabled the alarm connected to that door. A quick dash around the corner took me to the subway, my heart pounding in my chest.

I do not know how the police could have discovered the location of Pharaoh's demise. I must study my movements and retrace my steps. I must be even more stealthy. I cannot allow the work of the Lord to be stopped by these misguided fools. I will not post this entry to my blog right away, just in case the police have stumbled upon my writings and are watching my website. If they are, I will use that to my advantage.

Chapter 35 – Overtime

September 30, 2018

THE TASK FORCE did not normally work on Sundays, but they had anticipated the possibility that they might all be "on the rag," as they mockingly called it in honor of the menstrual killer. They had expected to be combing over a crime scene, and Berkowitz was still in Brooklyn supervising the forensic unit and watching the remaining security video. The rest of the team was back in the war room.

"Do we have any information on whether this Charles Gordon persona is real or not?" Mike asked in Angela's direction.

"Not yet. It's a pretty common name. We'll probably have a confirmation on his identity through the facial recognition review sooner than we'll be able to verify whether this Charles Gordon name matches any other information we know about him."

"How confident are we that the facial recognition will get us a positive hit?"

Angela had sent the security cam image to her boss at Manassas, where the FBI's database would go to work as quickly as the weekend shift could process it. "If he really was in the military, then we'll definitely have his face in the system. It shouldn't take long."

"Let's hope so," Mike said, "but we're talking about a guy who's arrogant enough to be live-blogging his kills. I hope he's not smart enough to figure a way to beat the facial recognition software."

"I wonder why he used the Charles White alias when he was talking to Heilman?" Jason mused as he wiped donut powder off his fingers with a napkin.

"I've been wondering that, too," Angela replied with a puzzled expression. "He used Charles Gordon as his persona with the building security guards, but told Heilman his name was White. I'm not sure whether it was just a slip, or if he was playing a game with Heilman, figuring that even if Heilman recognized the Charles White name from the newspapers, he would not figure out that he was about to be a victim. Either way, we caught a break, and hopefully soon we'll know his real name."

"Just remember that having his real name doesn't mean it will be easy to find him. We know he created at least two false identities, so he might have others and may be living under a totally different name."

"Don't listen to him, Angela," Jason cut in, "he always throws cold water on any anything positive during an investigation."

Mike shrugged. "I just don't want to let ourselves believe that getting an ID on our killer is the end of the road."

"We know," Jason grunted. "But every piece we put together will help, like Manning says. We need to understand him, and each bit of data builds his profile."

"The voice of experience," Mike muttered.

Jason spun toward Mike, his eyes betraying his anger even as he worked to keep his face neutral and his voice normal. "You know, Mike, you have twenty-something years of experience and that counts for a lot, but don't discount training and education and intelligence. There are many ways to attack the same problem."

"I never said Manning isn't intelligent."

"No, but you always imply that I am not intelligent, like because I'm Black I can't be smart." Angela could see Jason's neck bulge under the pressure of a throbbing vein.

"That's bullshit, Rook. I never said you're stupid."

"No, you're too savvy for that," Jason's voice was rising slightly. "You never say anything outright. You just cut me down and call me Junior and Rook and Kid and let everyone know that you think I didn't deserve my promotion because I'm not smart enough to be a detective."

Angela was turning her head back and forth between the two detectives like she was at a tennis match, not understanding where this was coming from. She tried to turn down the temperature. "Hey, hey, now, boys, let's stay focused here. Nobody said anything about anybody being smarter than anyone else."

"You're right," Mike agreed. "Nobody said any such thing. The fact is that Detective Dickson had the twelfth highest score on the detective exam and he got one of the six promotions that were available. All of the six cops who had higher scores, but didn't get the promotion, had more years on the force than Jason and all of them were white, so you do the math and figure out whether Detective Dickson deserved his shot."

Jason was silent for a moment, then opened his mouth, but closed it again without saying anything. Angela addressed said, "Mike, there are a lot of factors that go into promotion decisions besides who scored higher on the test, you know that."

"Of course there are," Mike agreed. "In this case, the other five cops who got those promotions were all white. If one of those other six guys ahead of Jason had been selected, then the whole class would have been white males, even though twenty-nine percent of the force is Black and seventeen percent Hispanic and eight percent are women. So, yes, there were other factors."

Jason finally cut back into the conversation. "You know what, Mike. You are right."

"About what?"

"You are right that it would have looked bad for the department to have a whole class of detective promotions that were all white males. Selecting me made the demographics look better. But there were four hundred cops who took that test, so my score was higher than ninety-seven percent of all the applicants. And I have military experience and I have a college degree, which were also factors on the list of established criteria, so don't quote just the racial statistics and imply that I got some kind of undeserved special treatment and that I don't deserve to be a detective!" Jason was shouting by the end of his statement and he had taken a step toward Mike.

"And I suppose that a detective with less than two years in the job gets assigned to the Homicide Division all the time?" Mike growled.

"No, Mike. That does not happen all the time, but there was an opening and I applied and Sully picked me, so take it up with him!"

"Drop it, you two!" Angela shouted.

"Why?" both Mike and Jason said at the same time, looking at their FBI colleague.

"Because I just got an email from Manassas," Angela said excitedly as she tapped her laptop's keyboard. Mike and Jason both surged toward the chair where Angela was now sitting in front of her laptop. Their fracas was immediately forgotten.

"Did they ID him?" Mike asked in a perfectly normal voice, as if he and Jason had not been nearly ready to brawl on the conference table.

"Yes," she said, reading off the message. "1st Lieutenant Ronald Joshua Randall. Born February 19, 1989. 6'2" and 225. Raised in Dallas, Texas. Joined the Army right out of high school. He was a football player and had some background with computers.

"He served two terms, including three tours in Afghanistan. It says he's a good shot with a rifle, but his specialty is hand-to-hand combat, particularly with knives. In his first tour in Afghanistan, he killed six people in close combat. His officers were concerned that he liked it a little too much. He seemed to seek out opportunities to not only kill enemy soldiers, but to brutalize them. Recommendation was to keep him out of combat situations.

He was reassigned to the kitchen and turned out to be a pretty good cook. High marks for social interactions.

"During his last tour in Afghanistan, he was in a convoy that ran into an IED. Two of his companions were seriously maimed. He suffered a concussion and a few broken bones. He recovered but was discharged due to his injuries. While in the hospital in Kabul, he connected with another soldier who was the son of a minister and he found God.

"Now, this is interesting. It says that he became born-again and started fanatically attending church services in camp. His reviewing psychiatrist said he talked about the radical religious underpinnings of the enemy and became a fanatical proponent of the Christian God as the solution for all ills. The shrink recommended a psychological discharge if he didn't qualify for an injury discharge. He was labeled as a high risk for Post-Traumatic Stress Disorder. He was sent home with a full military benefits package.

"When he got home, he immediately got a job in the IT department of a big financial services operation that was keen on hiring vets because they are a government contractor. He has records at the VA hospital in New York, but the most recent record is from four years ago. Since then, he has no records. He hasn't filed taxes since 2013. No recorded Social Security contributions. They're trying to trace his bank accounts and credit cards, but it looks like he dropped off the grid." Angela turned her laptop sideways and looked up.

The team sat in silence, trying to take in all the new information.

"So, we have confirmation that he really was military, and he's a big guy with hand-to-hand combat skills, which jibes with his ability to subdue his victims." Mike paused, trying to connect dots in his mind.

"And he was a cook in the Army, so that explains the restaurant job as a cover. Something he's good at," Jason added.

"Is there any indication of counter-intelligence training?" Mike asked.

Angela scanned the report on her laptop, but shook her head. "Nothing I can see. But that doesn't mean he didn't pick some up along the way, which would provide him with the ability to manufacture fake identities and documents. That, combined with his computer skills, would allow him to drop off the grid and live under assumed identities."

"Anybody serve with him named Charles White?" Mason asked.

"Don't know yet," Angela replied, her eyes still scanning her computer screen, "but they're cross-checking names now and we should have that pretty soon."

Mike reached for a pad of paper and started scribbling some notes. He looked up at the whiteboard, which now had "27" written in the top corner. "We should check the IDs for anyone in his units who died over there. If he was looking for identities to assume, the easiest are dead soldiers. He could have collected dog tags and Social Security numbers from dead comrades. We should get a list and run them to see if any of them seem to have come back to life."

"Good idea, Mike," Angela said as she typed into her computer.

"If he found religion, that explains all the biblical references, but there's nothing there to explain why he suddenly decided he needed to start killing people," Jason mused. "None of his victims were military, or middle-eastern, or Muslim, or had any other attributes that would make them targets of the average ex-Army guy."

Angela stepped away from her laptop and walked to the board. She erased a section where they had listed the attributes of the victims and wrote "Lieutenant Ronald Randall." Under that, she started making bullet points:

Army

Knives

Cook

Psych discharge/Injury discharge

Born Again

Buddies died - IED

"He says he's the messenger of God," Jason pointed out. "Maybe he really is just psychotic."

"Is it ever that simple?" Mike asked.

"No," Angela responded. "But there's a first time for everything."

"OK," Mike said as he pulled out his phone and rolled up the cuff of his shirt. "Let's track down this bastard."

Chapter 36 – Countdown

October 1, 2018

O N MONDAY MORNING, Mike was not at all surprised to see the now-familiar text message on his phone when he woke up, letting him know that the killer had a new post up on his blog. When he walked into the war room, he was expecting the usual stack of pages to read. After every other kill, their boy – Lieutenant First Class Ronald Joshua Randall – had given them a long and detailed account of what happened and Mike expected no less after the excitement of the prior Saturday. He was surprised to see only one page, and with very little text.

October 1

> *The Lord has made the river boil, and with it the wretched refuse that was Pharaoh has been cleansed from the Earth. I cannot now provide the explanation for and glorious narrative of his death, but suffice to say that he is done, and the glory of God is manifest. Evil cannot win against good. Evil will perish. Evildoers should beware the wrath of God and the blade of the Avenging Angel.*

"That's it?" Mike asked to the group rhetorically.

"It's certainly a break from his pattern," Angela said, stating the obvious. "Perhaps the near capture is causing him to be more circumspect with his posts. This could be a problem; he may be cutting off our information supply."

"Great," Mike sighed. "Any information from the landlord yet?"

"Yes," Jason said, pulling some notes out from under his leather folio. "We woke up the rental agent first thing this morning and the lady there had heard about the activity on Saturday. She was kind enough to share the information without a subpoena. It turns out that Randall rented the space under the name Charles Gordon. We looked up the corporate registration for Angel Enterprises and it's listed with Charles White as the CEO. It has a federal employer ID number, but no record of actually paying taxes. The agent says that Mr. Gordon gave her a line about how the corporation did not yet have an official seal and so couldn't set up a bank account. He gave her a money order for the first month's rent and security deposit. No red flags about the agent. The building has tons of empty space, so they're happy to rent to just about anybody. Angel Enterprises rented one office in a suite of shared offices that had a common receptionist, kitchen, copier, and other office necessities. Mason and Berkowitz are over there now with a search warrant to go through the office, not that we really expect to find much."

Jason paused and looked up at Mike, expecting some praise for making quick work of the research. Mike nodded, but said nothing.

"Great job, Detective," Angela said enthusiastically, flashing a scolding look at Mike. "So, let's try to see if there's anything here that helps us. Randall works a job with late-night hours. He formed this dummy company and rented space in this building a few months ago. He was making plans. He was targeting this guy. It was fortuitous for him that there was a health club in the basement.

"He's a hacker, so he hacks into the security system. He gets to know the guards who work the night shift on weekends, so they aren't surprised to see him there working all hours. But where does he get the big heating coil that he stashed in the health club and used to boil the hot tub?"

"Not hard," Jason said. "It's a big building. He orders the equipment and has it delivered to the office suite. Building security isn't inspecting delivery boxes to see what kind of equipment he's having delivered. I'm sure when we trace it, there will be a totally legitimate dealer who sold it to Angel Enterprises. Nothing odd there."

"Let's try to track it down, just to see if it takes us anywhere. Have Mason see if the building's shipping and receiving office has any record."

While Jason was in the hallway on the phone trying to raise Mason, Angela sat back down at the conference table. "It reinforces that our guy is a planner. He's renting office space and ordering industrial equipment months in advance. This is like a business plan for him."

"Yes," Mike agreed. "He's planning two kills ahead. He has no fear of being caught."

Jason reentered the conference room and announced that Detective Mason was going to look into the delivery angle. Nobody thought it would amount to anything, but it was another loose end that needed to be tied up.

"We never figured he'd be in Brooklyn," Jason lamented. "I was so sure he would be in Manhattan."

"We all did," Mike soothed. "Don't beat yourself up over that one."

"Thanks, Mike."

"Don't mention it." Mike got to his feet and stretched his arms over his head, leaning to the right, then to the left, listening to his back crack loudly. "I can't remember a case where we had so much information and so few actual leads."

◆◆◆

The morgue was quieter than normal at 4:00 on Monday afternoon when Mike walked through the swinging doors. Dr. McNeill, as always, had her blue gloves on and was peering intently into a microscope. Mike stood quietly, allowing her to finish what she was doing before trying to attract her attention. After a full minute of silence, she said, without removing her eyes from the lens, "I know you're there, Detective. Just give me a minute and I'll be able to give you my full attention."

"No worries," Mike said casually, "I'll just stand here and enjoy the view."

"You are incorrigible, Mike."

Mike enjoyed the fact that the doctor had dispensed with the formality of title and called him by his first name, even during work hours.

She stood back from the microscope and reached behind herself with her left hand to massage her lower back. She then leaned forward again to make some notes in what looked like a college essay notebook. When she finished writing, she clicked her pen closed and turned to face Mike.

"You said that you finished the analysis on Mr. Heilman."

"Yes, I did, but you didn't need to come in person to get that from me, Detective."

"Well, I was ready to leave the precinct anyway and I thought if you're not busy with any other dead bodies tonight, you might be interested in stepping out for a bite of dinner with me."

Doctor McNeill raised one eyebrow and a sly smile tilted the corner of her mouth. "I shall gladly accept the invitation to join you for dinner."

Mike sat down on a metal chair a few feet from the doctor. "What's your pleasure? Mexican? Chinese? Italian? I know a great place in Little Italy that's off the beaten path where the owner loves to serve cops."

"That sounds lovely, Mike. Let me just go clean up and I'll be ready in a jiffy."

"OK, but before you go, can you tell me about the autopsy on Mr. Heilman? I'd rather not make this a working dinner."

"Of course," Dr. McNeill said, smoothing down her smock as she walked to her desk, where she scooped up a file folder and flipped it open. "There's really not much to say, aside from the fact that he was burned over 100% of his body below the neck and he was covered with blisters and third-degree burns. It's really a wretched way to die." She looked up at Mike and saw a grimace on his face.

"Yeah," Mike croaked out.

"The cause of death is technically cardiac arrest caused by trauma. His tox screen shows traces of cocaine and amphetamines, but not enough to have contributed to death, nor enough to have rendered him unconscious. I find no evidence of him being drugged, but there is a serious contusion on the back of his head, in an area that was not burned. It's consistent with a solid blow with a blunt object."

"What about hitting his head on a tile floor?"

"Oh, yes. That would be consistent. That's a pretty specific guess."

"Well, we found blood and hair on the floor a few feet away from the hot tub."

"Then I expect that you are quite correct, Mike. In the meantime, I found nothing on the body that wasn't boiled clean."

"I know, Doctor McNeill," Mike parried. "But you know what I really want to know." He raised his eyebrows and leered suggestively. "Come on, give me what I want."

"Yes."

"Yes, what?"

"Yes, he had them."

"Both sides?"

"Yes. I will say that they were not as clean as on the others. It was like the killer was in a rush. I suspect that the deceased was already in the water when the cuts were made, in which case our killer is a true fanatic – his ritual was important to him."

"Thanks. It's not a surprise, of course, because we knew it was him even before we got there. But thanks for the confirmation. If we ever have a trial, there will be no doubt that this is the guy, and if there are any copycat attempts, we'll know they're fake if they don't give us the cuts."

"I think that's what he wants," McNeill said. "I think this is truly a signature, so that nobody else can falsely claim his fame and glory. It's his way of telling you that it's really him, even if you didn't already know. He wants you to know. It's a bloody calling card."

"OK, enough morose conversation. Let's try to go out and forget about work for a few hours. What do you say?"

"I say I love the idea, and I love Italian food. I'll be right back." She sauntered through a small door in the back of the room and disappeared. Mike stood looking around the lab and sniffing, trying to smell her perfume. Then he wondered if she would wear perfume in the lab while she was working and whether that would potentially contaminate evidence.

Three minutes later, the doctor returned wearing a grey dress that, despite its simplicity, showed off her toned torso and bare, well-muscled arms. Mike could not help but smile and force himself to stare directly into her eyes.

"You look nice."

"Why, thank you, Mike," Michelle said as she held his eye contact longer than was really necessary. "I'm glad you approve."

"I do," Mike responded quickly, then worried about the implications of the comment and sputtered, "Uh, not that you need my approval."

"Of course I don't. But it's still nice to hear." Michelle then dropped her eyes and went silent. Mike, in his practiced way, did not fill the void and just let the silence hang between them. "You know who could use some approval, though?"

"Who?"

"Your partner, Detective Dickson."

Now it was Mike's turn to look away. "I don't know what you mean."

"Oh, c'mon, Mike. You know exactly what I mean. I see how you treat him. You act like you're the President of the frat and he's the freshman pledge who needs to be hazed and kept in his place."

Mike stood with his mouth slightly open, unsure how to respond. Finally, he blurted out, "I do not."

Michelle just looked at him with penetrating eyes. "Then what am I seeing?"

"I don't know. He's a new detective. I'm teaching him the ropes, that's all."

"Are you teaching him, or testing him?"

"What?" Mike was seriously confused by this turn of the conversation.

"I get the impression that you don't think Jason is worthy of being your partner. It's little things I've seen and heard between the two of you. You had a different partner last year, if I recall. What happened to him?"

Mike fell silent. "I'd rather not discuss that. But I really don't think I'm treating Dickson badly. I treat him the same as any new detective."

"Really?" Michelle pressed.

"I don't know," Mike admitted. "I guess if you're picking up on something then maybe subconsciously I'm pressing him a little. I don't think he deserved to be promoted, if you want the truth."

"Why not?"

"He was not at the top of the detective applicant class, but he got the promotion. I think it was partly a racial balance thing. All the other detective promotions were white men. I think he got some special consideration. And he got assigned to Homicide way earlier than most detectives. Sully says it was his call, but I still think Jason got some special handling." Mike finished as if his explanation was the end of the discussion.

Michelle, however, was not satisfied. "So, how is that Jason's fault?"

"What do you mean?"

"Was Jason eligible to apply for the promotion? Did he have sufficient experience?"

"Yes, but not as much as some of the other candidates."

"Did he do all the necessary training and pass all the tests?" Michelle continued.

"Well, sure."

"So, he applied for the promotion in good faith, and somebody else decided to give it to him. What was he supposed to do, decline the offer?"

Mike paused to formulate his response. "No, but he should understand that he's in a position where other people are going to question him and wonder whether he deserved it."

"And you're one of them?"

"I guess I am," Mike conceded.

"Well, maybe while you're holding him to a higher standard, you might consider cutting him some slack. It can't be easy for him, you know. You might think about being a supportive partner instead of just *la Culo de Piedra* all the time."

Mike was surprised. "Where did you hear that?"

"Oh, I hear things," she said coyly. She took Mike's arm and led him out of the building. They strolled together up the sidewalk, chatting about subjects other than Mike's relationship with his partner, then turning north toward Canal Street.

Mike's attention was firmly fixed on Dr. McNeill as they meandered along amid the usual pedestrian traffic of lower Manhattan during the afternoon rush, in no particular hurry. He did not pay any attention to other people on the street and did not notice the non-descript man in the New York Yankees hat, blue jeans, and black windbreaker. He was not moving quickly or slowly, but simply flowing with the other walkers on the opposite side of the street from Mike and Michelle. He watched them without needing to look very carefully. He stopped at the corner and waited for the green light, even as others dashed across whenever there was a gap in the vehicular traffic. He approached a garbage can and pretended to deposit some unseen trash, which delayed his progress for a few moments. He remained on the opposite side of the street and a half-block behind until Mike and Michelle entered a small restaurant on Mulberry street.

The man in the jacket took a chair at an open table in the outdoor seating area of a bakery across the street from the Italian restaurant, where he had a view through the window. He could see Mike and Michelle sit down at a table against the far wall. When they sat, he could see only the doctor, which suited him just fine. He ordered a coffee and a cannoli and settled in.

Chapter 37 – Tracking a Ghost

October 5, 2018

THE SEARCH FOR RONALD RANDALL/Charles White was coming up empty day after day. The feds traced the money order used to pay for the office space in the Brooklyn building to a check cashing store in lower Manhattan, but since they already knew who he was, there was no point to trying to pull security video. Randall had paid with cash, of course.

The guy was a ghost, but a ghost with a blog. On Friday, with the countdown to the next period standing at 22 days, the next blog post hit the net.

October 4

My quest to fulfill the glory of God has progressed to this point without significant interference. The police continue to search in vain to find me. They will fail now as always, for the Lord protects me and shields me from their sight.

My plan evolves and the Lord guides my way. The light of God continues to shine upon me and I shall proceed upon the appointed plan. I am even now formulating my plan for the demise of the next blight upon God's firmament. But even as I continue, I am puzzled about how the authorities were able to come even close to intercepting the execution of Pharaoh. I have devoted myself to solving this mystery for the past few days and I have uncovered the truth. The constable involved is careless with communications that are as transparent to me as a neon billboard in Times Square. Such is the ease with which I peer into his world. It was he who brought the authorities to our little pool party. I can hardly fault him, for the task of the Centurion is to keep the peace for Caesar.

Now I know Centurion's actions and movements as well as God can know. I need not fear further interference. God's plan will be revealed in its glory and I will be revealed and revered as the oracle of the Lord. Centurion is an ant crawling through the mud and grime of the world thinking that he has a purpose and a plan, when in fact the plan is mine and he shall be crushed under my sandal.

In the stark light of revelation when this scroll is made known to the world, all will understand the full scope of my greatness and God's plan. The faint of heart and weak of faith will question me, but I am resolute in my belief and my knowledge and my skills. It is inevitable that I will succeed, for even if I fail I will succeed. It is impossible for Centurion to stop me. It is impossible for anyone to stop me, for it is not possible to fight God.

When Mike finished his first read through the text, he looked up to find both Jason and Angela looking back at him. "So?" he asked, without further explanation.

Angela was the first to reply. "There are some significant deviations from his usual pattern here."

Jason nodded his head vigorously. "Damned right. Our killer is gloating, which is normal for him, but he's not telling us about how awful his next victim is. Usually, he starts to justify why the intended victim deserves to die and how he is the avenging angel of God sent to wreak justice on the unrighteous. But not this time. This time he's telling his readers about this Centurion, who seems pretty obviously somebody in law enforcement who was involved in his near-capture during his last kill. Hell, he could be talking about Agent Manning."

"What about the name, 'Centurion?' What do we think of that?" Mike asked.

"It's not strictly speaking biblical," Angela observed, "but it's consistent with the general New Testament time period under Roman occupation."

"He seems to be implying that he has intercepted communications from this person. Could that mean he has hacked Centurion's emails?"

"It seems logical," Mike agreed. "We know he's a computer guy. Is there any chance he got access to the FBI's emails from the surveillance team that was watching Heilman?"

Angela thought about it for a moment. "They tell me that our email is secure, but who the Hell knows. I have an account and I have to log in on a secure server with a password and a secondary confirmation, but if the Russians can hack into government emails and systems, it's probably possible for anyone with enough experience to do it."

"Great," Mike sighed, "now I guess we'll need to go back to using Morse code."

Jason chuckled, but then got serious. "Do we need to be worried that Centurion is one of us and not the FBI team?"

Angela moved to the whiteboard and started another list. She wrote down the names of every member of the FBI's surveillance team.

"I still think our names should be on the list too," Mike said, looking at the messy board. At the bottom of the board, Angela squeezed in the names Manning, Stoneman, and Dickson.

"Why not Berkowitz and Mason?" Jason asked.

"I don't think they've been mentioned by name in any of the news reports," Angela responded. "How would Randall even know who they are?"

"He's a hacker, right?" Mike said, not so much a question as a statement. "He could be hacking into our emails for all we know."

"I agree," Angela shrugged. "It could be any of us, but we don't have any more room on the board."

Chapter 38 – Getting Personal

October 8, 2018

"**W**HAT HAVE WE GOT?" Mike said as soon as he arrived in the war room on Monday morning. He was not happy that he was not the first one there. When he was younger, he had always been the first one in the precinct. He had no wife or kids, he didn't go to the gym in the mornings, and he didn't sleep particularly well. Having nothing better to do, he would routinely arrive at 6:30 and enjoy the solitude of an empty office while he ate his morning bagel and got caught up on paperwork. Now, he seemed unable to get in before 8:30, and the younger cops were already there. He wondered whether Angela got in early in Manassas or if she came in early on this assignment only because she had nowhere else to go and nobody waiting for her back in her hotel room. It didn't matter, but still it nagged at him. Tomorrow, he was going to set his alarm for an earlier wake-up.

Angela reported that the FBI was tracking down leads on their man now that they had a positive identification. "I have a hard time believing that somebody can stay totally off the grid for long in 2018."

"What about tracking down dead comrades?" Mike asked.

"We're on it. Or, rather, we've reached out to the armed forces to get a list of soldiers killed in action who were in Afghanistan at the same time as Randall."

"Doesn't that expand the list, opening it up to anyone in Afghanistan and not just guys assigned to his unit?" Jason asked.

"It's true," Angela agreed, "but the way these guys come in and out of central bases, particularly if they get injured, we wanted to cast a wide net. If he was in a field hospital at the same time as somebody brought in from another part of the country, who then died in the hospital, he could grab the guy's tags or copy information from a chart even if he never knew the guy and never actually served with him. If he was already thinking ahead, we can't limit ourselves."

"Fair enough," Jason conceded. "If one of those guys springs back to life to get a credit card or rent an apartment, we'll have a bulls-eye."

"Or get a job," Mike interjected. "We know he has a job, and we're sure it's not under his real Social, so he has to be using a fake. If we can find his current employer, then we'll be able to track him."

"What about the number Charles White used when he got the job at the restaurant? Did we ever track that one down?" asked Detective Berkowitz, who had just arrived with a sesame bagel in his hand.

"Nah," Jason quickly cut in. "We already checked that. It was a fake. The restaurant never checked it and he wasn't there long enough for anything to come back to them from the tax folks. They don't verify the numbers at the time of hire. So, that one is just a dead end."

"What was he going to do if the restaurant checked?" Berkowitz wondered.

Angela chimed in with a reply. "If he's as organized as we think he is, I'm sure he has a list of valid numbers. He would have apologized for getting the number wrong and given out a different one. Maybe he changes the number by one digit so he can say he just wrote it down wrong. Happens all the time."

"How are you so well-versed in Social Security fraud?" Mike asked.

Angela shrugged. "When you're coming up through the Bureau, you get a lot of small-time cases. I had a few of those before I got into profiling."

"So, Ms. Expert, tell us how hard it is to use somebody else's Social Security number to fake their identity. How many identities could this guy have?"

Angela stood up and walked toward the grimy window that was letting in its filtered light. "Well, obviously you need the number, but the number by itself is not enough. If you're applying for a credit card or renting an apartment or opening a bank account, you need an address that matches the history of the Social, and you may also need another ID for verification. Sometimes you can use just the Social and the address to get another ID like a credit card, and then you can establish a new address under the assumed name and use that to open other accounts. If you set up utilities or voter registration, you can use them to get a driver's license, in which case you have a permanent false identity. If the Social belongs to someone who is dead and there are no alternate records being created simultaneously, you can carry forward with that identity indefinitely."

"So, let's say our guy Randall has established a solid false identity based on a dead soldier," Mike said as he also stood up and started pacing the room. "He could get a job, pay taxes, rent an apartment, and basically live this other guy's life. He could be totally on the grid, with electronic records and bank accounts and internet service and the whole shebang, and we would have no idea because we don't know who we're looking for. Ron Randall may be off the grid, but we could find him if we only knew the name he's using. Is that about right?"

"Exactly," Angela gritted her teeth. "I guess we could have been doing this same search two months ago, if we had decided to just assume he was actually military and that he might have stolen identities from other soldiers. But now we have him narrowed down to a specific period of time in Afghanistan, so our chances are better."

"How long until the federal computers can spit out some results for us?" Mike asked.

"At least a few days to get the lists and start cross-checking them against tax records and credit card databases, but they're rushing it as much as possible."

"So we wait," Jason said angrily as he pushed his chair back from the conference table. "Damn, I hate this! I want to be out there chasing leads and instead we're just sitting here waiting for the feds to save the day. What the fuck!?"

"I agree with you, Jason." Mike said without emotion.

"What?"

"I agree with you. We should be out chasing down other leads. Do we have any?"

Jason held out his hands with the palms up. "We have Charles White, but all the dead ends there have been chased. We know that he rented the offices in Brooklyn under Charles Gordon, so that gives us one more thing to chase. We know who he is, so there's no point in going back to the dog walkers. What about trying to find guys in his Army unit who knew him and who might have kept in touch with him? Maybe one of them has an email address for him that we can trace?"

Mike nodded. "Angela, when your guys are looking into the dead soldiers, can they also look into getting us a list of his buddies – the guys he actually served with?"

"Already on the agenda," Angela answered quickly. "We're also trying to track down any family members, but that may be tough since his parents are both dead."

"Those guys and his family are probably spread out all over the country, so we can certainly use the federal help chasing them down." Mike sat back down. "Which still leaves everything to the feds and gives us nothing to sink our teeth into."

"What about the shitbags who were involved in the operation that Heilman was running; that the feds were watching? What happened to them?"

"The operation was pretty much blown up when Heilman got himself killed," Angela explained. "The agents picked up a bunch of known associates while they could, some here in New York, some down in Miami. None of them seem to have any connection to Randall."

"There's always the 'next plague' angle," Berkowitz offered.

"What's the next plague?" Mike asked as he struggled to remember the list.

"A storm of fire and hail," Jason responded, flashing Mike a condescending look.

"Any chance that's going to help us?"

Nobody said a word.

"Great. Just like the others. We know the method, but it doesn't really help us narrow things down. We don't know how his twisted mind is going to kill somebody with hail." Mike hung his head and leaned on the conference table. "Any other ideas?"

"What about going public again?" Angela asked softly, and there was an immediate silence in the room. "We got help from the public once before. Maybe somebody out there in New York knows him. We can release his photo and his real name, and fire up the hotline. What about that?"

"It would show the public that we're making progress," Jason offered.

"It would spook the hell out of our killer," Mike countered. "But maybe it would cause him to stop killing if he thinks we're getting close."

"Doubtful," Angela interjected. "Our guy is fanatical and feels invincible. He thinks he's three steps ahead of us, and he's not entirely wrong about that. We know that he intended to alter his appearance after the last murder, so if we send out the photo of Charles White to the public, we'll get tips on guys who look like

Charles White and not really like Ronald Randall. We can send out his name without the photo, which will tip him off to what we know, but that might cause him to clam up on his blog. And that's our only window into his mind."

"But how does seeing his name in the paper tip him off that we're on to his blog?"

Mike cut in. "Any decision to go public will need the Commissioner's approval, and the Mayor's. On the one hand, they may want to show that they're doing something. On the other hand, I'm sure they don't want to do anything that might be second-guessed later. I'll have Sully float the idea."

Everyone nodded. Mike got up and walked toward the door. Then he stopped at the threshold and turned around. "Are you coming, Dickson?"

Jason turned his head, surprised. "Sure," he said as he hastily got up and grabbed his jacket.

◆◆◆

Later that afternoon, Mike got another call from Dexter Peacock. The reporter wanted to get confirmation that Heilman was another victim of the serial killer. Mike conceded that he was, and that he fit into the killer's profile of taking out scumbags. Mike could not say that Heilman had been the subject of an ongoing FBI investigation and surveillance program, but he did confirm that he was a likely criminal, off the record. Peacock also wanted confirmation that the police were at the building while the killer was still there, but that they missed him. This confused Mike, since that fact had not been disclosed. He wondered if one of the building security guards might have let that information slip. "No comment on that," Mike responded.

"Can you confirm that the victim was bound and boiled to death in a hot tub?"

Mike paused. He did not think that the police had released the cause of death, and wondered who could have leaked that information. "No comment on that," he said.

"I have reason to believe that the killer had stalked his victim for several months and had access to the building because he had rented an office there. Can you confirm that information?"

"No," Mike said, probably too quickly. "I cannot confirm that information, but may I ask where you got it?"

"I'm sorry, Detective. I cannot reveal my sources, as you know."

"Not even if it might help us catch this guy before he kills again?"

"Detective, I'm sure you have access to the same information. I will make sure that you know anything important that I know."

"I'd like to think that," Mike said, then he hung up.

When Mike relayed the content of the call to the rest of the Task Force, they all speculated about how Peacock could have obtained the information. It was all plausibly available if he knew the right people to ask and could get them to talk, including some of the uniformed officers on the scene and the security guards.

"He's either very diligent about tracking down witnesses," Angela said, "or else he's getting information from another source. He could have been tipped off by Randall."

"You think?" Mason asked.

"It has been known to happen," Angela said. "When a serial killer wants publicity, sometimes he goes to the press himself to get his message out – to start getting a taste of the fame he craves. I've seen it happen."

Jason walked to the whiteboard, erased the number in the corner, and wrote in 19.

Chapter 39 – Watching the Watcher

October 9, 2018

I'M TELLING YOU, I still think the feds who were on the surveillance detail monitoring that Heilman guy have to be high on the list. They are here in New York. They are law enforcement, and he has every reason to be pissed at them." Jason was pacing the war room as the group continued to puzzle over the possible identity of Centurion, and how it might help them find Ronald Randall.

Angela sighed. "We have talked to them. Agent Forrest was the guy in charge. But there's no way that Randall could even know who he is or care that much about him."

Jason scowled and sat down. "Don't underestimate this guy."

"He's still on the list," Angela said as a peace offering. "We haven't ruled him out, but there's no reason to think he should be high on our radar."

"Look, it's been a long day. Let's all take a breath and a break and we'll get back to it tomorrow." Mike looked around the room. Nobody seemed to have a contrary opinion. It was 5:15 and Mike wanted to get out of the building.

"So, Mike, if we need to get you on the phone tonight, shall we call your cell?"

"Why ask that, Detective Berkowitz?"

"Oh, just want to make sure we're not interrupting anything.

We could leave a message on your precinct number if you would prefer. You know, just in case you and the good doctor are getting busy."

"You're a dick, you know that, Berkowitz?"

"Thanks, Mike. I appreciate that you're paying attention."

"I think it's time for me to leave now," Mike said, reaching for his jacket.

"I'm tired," Michelle said as soon as Mike walked in the door of her lab.

"Sorry to hear that," Mike said soothingly. "Were your patients talking back to you today?"

"Yes. One of them called me a bitch."

"Well, I hope that made it into your autopsy report," Mike said totally seriously.

Doctor McNeill tried to keep up the straight banter but could not keep herself from giggling. "OK, you win that one, Mike. But, seriously, it has been a brutal day. I don't think I'm up for going out in public tonight."

"That's fine," Mike said, smiling. "How about you let me pamper you? We can go up to my place and I'll cook you dinner and rub your tired feet. What do you say?"

"I say lead the way, Mister Police Man!" McNeill giggled again. "Give me just a minute to throw this lab coat in the bin and grab my purse."

Five minutes later, Mike and Michelle were getting into a cab on Pearl Street. Mike told the driver to take them to 68th and Amsterdam, and Dr. McNeill leaned over to put her head down on Mike's shoulder. She closed her eyes and Mike stayed quiet to let her nap. He gazed out the window as the cab crawled toward the West Side Highway.

He did not notice that another yellow cab was directly behind them all the way to the exit at 59th street, through the light at West End Avenue, and onto Amsterdam. Mike nudged Michelle awake when the cab pulled into the semi-circular driveway at his apartment building. It took a few moments for her to rouse herself. He helped her out and nodded to his doorman as he and Michelle squeezed together through the revolving door and disappeared into the lobby.

The cab that had been behind them had discharged its single passenger at the corner and immediately caught another fare without a second thought. The man in the leather jacket loitered on the corner, tossed a bit of trash into the can under the pedestrian walk signal, then reached down to pet a golden retriever who was being walked along the sidewalk before continuing casually toward a bench next to a small fountain. He sat down and crossed his legs, looking across the street at the white brick façade of the apartment building on the opposite side. He caught a glimpse of Mike and Michelle through the wall of windows as they turned left past the front desk and toward the bank of elevators on the west side of the building. The man then looked up, counting the windows up the side of the building until he stopped on a darkened pane on the tenth floor. He waited, and after three minutes, the light came on behind the glass. The man stood and stretched his arms above his head, then walked east to Broadway and hailed a cab heading downtown.

Mike got out of his third cab of the day outside his apartment building at 2:32 a.m. He had insisted on accompanying Michelle back to her apartment after they had stayed up late watching one of Mike's favorite movies and sipping red wine. They had both dozed off and missed the end of *A Few Good Men*. Mike had suggested that Michelle could sleep on his couch, but she insisted that she needed to be in her own bed and needed her own toothbrush. It occurred to Mike that he could suggest staying at her place, but he could not seem to find the right opportunity, and she did not offer. So, he walked her to her apartment and gave her a kiss that lingered long enough for him to want more, but not long enough for her to invite him in. He caught another cab and returned home, where he waved to the same doorman who had been on duty when he and Dr. McNeill had arrived earlier that evening. The doorman smiled and waved back. Mike wondered when his shift ended and how he got home to wherever he lived in the middle of the night.

When he got back upstairs, it was so close to 3:00 a.m. that he decided to wait up just in case he got a text message. He got into his bed with the light on the side table still on and his phone perched on the edge of the maple tabletop and switched on the television. The local cable channel, New York One, was running its normal, repetitive half-hour news summary, recorded sometime the night before.

Just after the blonde anchorwoman finished reciting the top story of the day, a fire in Queens, his phone buzzed and Mike reached awkwardly to grab it. He was glad he had stayed up. There was a text from Simpson. Randall had made a new post. Since he was already awake and didn't want to wait until morning, Mike navigated to the secure Dropbox location so that he could read the latest.

October 9

I have experienced great joy when reading the newspaper coverage of my conquests and watching the local news broadcasts as they recount the deaths of those who have met God at my hand. Although the press always gets the facts wrong, the world has learned of my prowess and you will ultimately understand the full narrative. The press coverage, of course, has failed to make the connection that the Angel of Death was responsible for all the executions. And, also inevitable, the media made no effort to unwrap the puzzle of my genius. I cannot blame them for their inattention, since they were not even aware that I was the architect of the pattern. And yet, I can't help but admit a certain disappointment.

But I am expecting an improvement in the press coverage quite soon. I have decided to disclose my scripture in confidence to one person who is in a position to spread the Word of God at my direction. Time will tell whether this gambit will succeed, but I am, as always, two steps ahead of the witless police and FBI. I shall continue watching. I shall not make the mistake of underestimating my enemies. I shall find their weaknesses and exploit them.

I shall not allow the intervention of the FBI to interrupt the grand narrative of my story. I have selected next for judgment a man who facilitated the evil activities of Pharaoh. Haman will feel the wrath of God when he dies. Haman shall not escape judgement. His sins are more pernicious and subtle, but no less deserving of justice. The will of God shall not be thwarted by mortal men who are oblivious to the divine plan. No one can escape the judgment of the Angel of Death. Let him lust after the sins of the flesh, and then let him burn in a hail of wrath.

Chapter 40 – Counting Down

October 10, 2018

"HE'S NOT GIVING US as much information about this Haman person as he has about his prior victims." Mike paced around the conference room as he talked. Manning, Dickson, and Berkowitz were listening closely; Mason was on assignment chasing down another possible Charles White sighting. Mike was animated, waving his arms as he continued. "But we now know that this guy is somehow connected to Heilman. Are there any other connections that we missed?"

"We weren't really looking," Jason pointed out. "Once we had an ID on Randall we weren't that concerned about making connections between the victims."

"OK, fine, but now we know that there is a connection. If we can find that person, maybe we can intercept Randall when he tries to get to him." Mike continued pacing the small room as if movement would make answers appear.

"I've already got the guys downtown running searches and trying to see if adding Heilman to the group of victims would yield any common results."

"What about the characteristics of Haman? That's another biblical name, right?" Jason asked.

"Sure," Berkowitz cut in. "Haman is one of the great villains in the Bible. He was a minister under the reign of King Ahasuerus of

Persia. The kingdom worshiped a bunch of Gods but there was a significant Jewish population. Haman hatched a plan to kill off all the Jews because they refused to bow down before him. Haman convinced the king to sign a decree and set a date for all the Jews to be executed, but it turned out that the king had married a Jewish girl named Esther, who pointed out that she would have to be killed also. So, the king had Haman executed instead. Jews celebrate the deliverance every year during a festival called Purim."

"Are there any Jews here?" Jason asked sarcastically.

"Screw you, Dickson. I'm just trying to help," Berkowitz shot back.

"Is there anything in the story that might help us predict the identity of this victim called Haman?" Angela asked as she stepped toward the whiteboard.

"We've been down that road," Mike interjected before Angela started making a list on the whiteboard. "Let's hope that the feds can help us find this Haman, but in the meantime we have other leads to chase and we're running out of time. What about the Centurion angle? Randall has never given two names at the same time. Is he planning to kill both?"

"That would be a feat of strength," Jason observed. "His master plan seems to be a little jumbled since we nearly caught him."

"Well, if we have him a little shook up, then that's fine," Mike added. "Let's keep him on the run. The more we throw him off his game, the greater the possibility that he'll screw up."

"If Centurion is someone involved in the Heilman investigation, maybe he'll show himself there. Should we be coordinating with Agent Forrest? I want to make sure he's not potentially in danger." Angela looked around the room for some support.

"We've got him covered," Jason blurted out.

"What do you mean you have him covered?" Angela asked, turning her head sharply in Jason's direction. "Don't tell me that you have an FBI agent under surveillance without telling him?"

"He's not under surveillance," Mike quickly interjected, shooting Jason a look. "We have his *building* covered. We have a rotation of plainclothes cops watching the area, looking for Randall. We're not following Forrest, although if he happens to be in the area that we're watching, our guys know who he is and they will be especially vigilant looking for someone following him."

Angela stared at Mike, mouth agape. "And when were you planning to tell me this?"

"I wasn't planning to tell you, but I wasn't hiding it either. You'll notice that as soon as it came up today, I told you about it. It's not a secret, but I was worried that you would tell your guy and then he would act squirrely."

"He's a federal agent. You don't think he could walk down the street without tipping off the killer?"

"He's an electronic surveillance expert – a wire guy. He specializes in bugs and recording equipment. He sits in a van or a vacant building and listens to a microphone. He's not a field agent and has no experience with live surveillance. So, no, I don't think he would handle it well. Are you going to tell him?"

Angela gave Mike a burning look. "I'm going to tell my Director and let him make the call."

"Mind if I participate in the call you make to the Director?"

"No, Mike. I don't mind." Angela spat out, clearly irritated. "You're a member of the Task Force and you have a right to be involved. I would not exclude you from the process."

Mike shrugged. "I'm sorry, Special Agent Manning. I regret not telling you about it."

"Fine," Angela said stiffly. "I'll send him an email and set up a time for later today."

"Are you sure using email is wise?" Jason asked. "Aren't you worried that Randall may have hacked our email?"

"No. I'm not worried. I asked Simpson and he said our servers are totally secure and that if there was a hack, it had to be the

NYPD."

"Like Hell!" Berkowitz shouted, standing up, clearly agitated.

"Alright, let's calm down," Mike cut in, motioning to Berkowitz to sit down. "Let's not turn against each other. Now what else should we be doing?"

Jason broke in by asking, "Do we have the list of dead soldiers from Afghanistan yet?"

"No," Angela said with some annoyance. "We're still waiting for that, but even when we get it, the FBI is going to chase them down and research whether their Social Security numbers have been used. So that's not something that we're going to have to do ourselves."

Berkowitz scowled. "Damn it! I feel useless just sitting here trying to decode this bastard's blog posts."

"I agree," Angela soothed. "But that's the deal. We do what we can do, and we wait."

"Shit, I can do that downstairs at my desk, and I can do some paperwork I have piled up. So that's where I'm going." Berkowitz stomped out of the war room.

"Any more lists to make?" Jason asked. Mike couldn't tell whether it was a serious question or just Jason being a smart-ass.

"None that I can think of," Angela replied without enthusiasm or rancor.

"How about we take a walk, get some air, and see if inspiration hits us outside this shit-hole?" Mike suggested. The others nodded, and fifteen minutes later, the room was dark. The whiteboard countdown stood at 17.

Chapter 41 – What's in a Name?

October 13, 2018

"IT'S JUST SO FRUSTRATING," Mike said in a hushed whisper across the small table. He and Dr. McNeill were seated at an outdoor table, separated from the passing pedestrians by a brightly colored curtain attached to a three-foot high metal frame. They and the diners packing seven other small tables were enjoying an unusually warm Saturday evening in October at El Caballero on 12th Street, just west of Sixth Avenue. The one harried waitress responsible for the sidewalk dining area swept in and set two large, frosted margaritas on the table next to the wicker basket of tortilla chips and then rushed away to another table. A little frozen slush sloshed into the white ceramic bowl of salsa. Mike pushed one of the glasses carefully in Michelle's direction, then lifted his own and slurped a large sip from the edge, enjoying the large crystals of salt clinging to the glass.

Michelle pinched a paper napkin from a metal dispenser perched on the edge of the table and carefully wiped the spillage off the side of her glass before leaning down and sipping through her straw. "I know, Mike. I keep going over the lab reports and the autopsy records and trying to find something that I missed the first time through. I just get nowhere. I wish I could point you in some new direction, but I've got nothing."

For a few days after the original article by Dexter Peacock in

The Times, the major New York daily newspapers sparred over the moniker that would stick for the killer. The *Post* started out calling him alternatively "The Mob Hunter" and "The Scumbag Assassin." Apparently, there was not enough consensus even within the paper to decide on only one name. *The Times* had first called him "The Bad Guy Stalker" and then *The Daily News* started referring to him as "The Devil-Killer," which got picked up by the local television news broadcasts for a while. But then *The Times* pivoted to "The Righteous Assassin" and that moniker stuck. Mike always preferred "Scumbag Assassin," but he supposed that language was too vulgar for *The New York Times*.

"I just feel like he's out there, laughing at us. We know that he's going to strike, and he's made us feel like we know his intended victim. And yet there is nothing we can do, and it just eats at me."

"You need to clear your head, Mike," Michelle soothed. "Have a few drinks, have some good food, and just try to relax. Give your mind a rest, that's doctor's orders."

Mike chuckled. "Well, if my doctor says so." He lifted his margarita and took a healthy slurp.

"There. Feel better now?"

Mike took another swallow and then put down the glass suddenly, clamping his left hand over the bridge of his nose and grimacing. "Brain freeze!" he choked out, holding up his right hand toward the doctor, who was halfway out of her chair. "I'll be fine." A minute later, Mike sat back and took his hand away from his eyes.

"Do you need anything?"

"Just some tender, loving care," Mike said, trying to smile through the remaining pain in his head.

"I can do that," Michelle said softly.

"Can we eat first?" Mike winked.

Michelle chuckled softly and picked up her menu.

◆◆◆

When they finally left the restaurant, they walked unsteadily back toward Third Avenue and then turned north toward Michelle's apartment. When they reached the front door, Mike said, "I'm not sure I'm in shape to drive home."

"Good thing you don't own a car, then," the doctor said as she punched in the code to unlock the main lobby door, which buzzed loudly until she pulled on the handle. They wobbled to the elevator and rode up to the sixth floor, Michelle leaning against Mike's larger frame, which was itself leaning against the side of the elevator car. Mike stood silently behind Michelle as she fit the large, double-sided key into the security lock on her apartment door, then followed her inside. He closed the door softly behind him and twisted the lock until it closed with a satisfying *ker-chunk*.

When he turned around, Michelle was missing. He heard the sounds of a zipper and rustling cloth from the bedroom, and froze. He figured he should wait for her to come back out. Unless she wanted him to follow her in? His brain was still whirring when she stepped back through the doorway, and his jaw nearly dropped. She'd slipped a ribbon into her short hair and was wearing a cheerleader's uniform, complete with pleated skirt and a pom-pom. "Is there anything I can do to take your mind off your troubles, Detective?"

"What troubles?" Mike said, covering the distance separating them in two long strides and lifting her off the ground.

Chapter 42 – A Crack in the Armor

October 18, 2018

O N THURSDAY, with the counter at 9, Angela got a call on her cell phone and left the war room. She came back four minutes later with an excited look on her face. "We have a hit on the Social."

"Where?" Jason asked.

"New York City," Angela replied with a smile.

"Bingo!" Mike exclaimed.

"We gotta update your vocabulary," Jason quipped playfully.

"Whatever," Mike shrugged. "What's the scoop?"

Angela filled the group in on her call. "The agents downtown finally tracked down the one other Social Security number that they had been chasing. The number belonged to a soldier named Charles Cooper who died in an IED incident in 2013."

"Charles?" Mike interrupted.

"Yeah," Angela confirmed. "The guy's number was used to set up a bank account and there have been federal tax returns filed every year since then by our dead soldier."

"Do we have an employer?"

"Not exactly. The guy, Charles Cooper, filed tax forms from a bunch of different companies, all of which issued him 1099 forms as a contractor, not W-2s. He had seven different 1099s in 2014, five in 2015, nine more in 2016, and five last year."

Berkowitz jumped in excitedly. "Seems like half the City works now in this so-called gig economy as contractors. Most of them should be classified as employees, probably, but they like writing off all their expenses."

"Take it to the Department of Labor," Mason said dismissively, "what matters is his current job. Do we have that?"

Angela looked down at her notebook. "It's not quite that simple. Tax records don't specify the dates of employment. There were five different companies that issued 1099s to Charles Cooper in 2017. We've got to start calling those companies to see when he worked there and whether they have contact information."

"OK, now we're getting somewhere," Mike said as he stood up.

"Where are you going?" Angela asked.

"I'm going to get some sandwiches. We're going to be busy this afternoon."

By the end of the day, the war room was littered with semi-empty food containers, paper coffee cups, and note pads. Berkowitz and Mason had moved down to their desks in the bullpen because they could not hear themselves think with five people in the same conference room all talking on the phone at once. Angela moved a chair over to the far end of the room to have some semblance of quiet while Mike and Jason sat at the conference table. Each of them had taken one of Charles Cooper's employers and was working through various human resources and finance department employees who did not want to give out personal information about their workers.

"We have to find his current employer," Mike said.

"Of course," Angela agreed. "We know from the blog that he is currently working a night shift Sunday through Thursday, with Friday and Saturday nights off. It's some kind of IT position, but it seems to be located in an office. Remember, he was unable to go to work when he was beaten up after killing LeBlanc. He had to take a few days off. So he's working in an office. If we can figure out where he's working, we can arrest him when he shows up for work."

"I hope it's that easy," Mike said without conviction.

"You never know. Sometimes you catch a break."

"Yeah, but in my experience, one break leads to ten new leads to chase down."

Jason had been trolling job listings for contract IT guys. "There are a shit ton of these guys," he said in frustration. "The listings are for just about every company in New York, and they can't help us figure out who applies or who gets hired."

"We've got the whole team searching," Angela said, trying to keep up an optimistic attitude. "We know who we're looking for. Charles Cooper doesn't seem to have any credit cards, at least not any that are being used. He has to be leaving some footprint somewhere."

"Sure," Jason agreed, "but we're on a deadline."

Chapter 43 – Cornered

October 22, 2018

"**WE FOUND RANDALL!**"

Mike and Jason, who had arrived at the front of the precinct building at the exact same time and walked up to the war room together, stopped dead in their tracks at the doorway. Angela was staring at them with an expression of mixed happiness and anticipation.

"What?" Jason exclaimed.

"How?" Mike asked at the same moment.

Angela started to talk quickly, very animated. "The agents downtown have been running web searches for Charles Cooper every day. Until today, they were just finding hits for other guys with the same name along with our guy's Linked-In page. But today we got a hit on a corporate website announcing the launch of a new intranet system and thanking all the people who had worked on the project, including a contractor named Charles Cooper."

"No shit?"

"We caught a break."

"What's the company?"

Angela consulted the notes she had scribbled on a legal pad. The Task Force had become paranoid about email and so had taken to receiving important communications by telephone. "It's a small software security company called IT Intelligence. They have an office in midtown. We're trying to get contact information for their internal security guys, but we're worried about somebody in the company tipping off Randall so we want to be careful."

"Makes sense," Mike said as he hung his jacket on a chair. "Unless he's lying in his blog, he works nights, so if we can get there tonight when he shows up for work, we can nab him."

"Let's hope," Jason said as he crossed his fingers.

"Who's our potential contact there?" Mike asked.

"A guy named James Havens," Angela said without consulting her notes. "He's the head of the company's security team, although it's a small company so I'm not sure how big the team is. We told the receptionist that we have a potential hacking situation involving one of the company's employees and that we want to consult with their security chief. That's all we said and now we're waiting for a call-back from the guy."

"Is he calling us, or the agents downtown?"

"He's supposed to call me," Angela replied, standing up and beginning to pace. She walked to the whiteboard and stared at it for a moment, but did not pick up a marker.

Mike whistled softly. "What are we going to tell this Havens guy? Are we going to come right out and tell him that we think his contractor is our serial killer and we want to send in a SWAT team tonight to capture him?"

Angela shook her head. "No, we don't want to risk that. It's doubtful they could keep that quiet. We want Randall to come in for his night shift just like always like nothing special is going on. Once he's in the building, we should be able to cover all the exits and then send in a small team to confront him at his work station. It will be after normal hours so the building will be pretty much deserted."

"What about building security?" Mike asked. "We'll need to clue them in at some point, right?"

"Already on that," Jason said, looking up from his laptop,

which he had booted up during the conversation. "IT Intelligence is located at 285 Lexington, at 37th Street. I'll track down the building security folks and let them know to be expecting some police activity tonight, but without giving them any details. I'm sure that when the uniformed officers show up, the evening building security guys will cooperate."

"You think we should grab him in the lobby?" Mike asked.

Angela thought about it. "We don't know for sure what he's going to look like. If we grab the wrong guy, that might tip him off. I'd rather let him get inside and grab him in the office."

"I don't know," Jason cut in. "Remember how much of a planner Randall is. He had multiple escape routes from that basement health club, and that's not his normal base of operations. If he's thinking like a soldier, he'll have figured out contingency plans for what might happen if his cover gets blown while he's at his office. Letting him get inside the building could be a mistake."

"He won't be expecting us," Mike retorted. "We have the advantage for a change."

"It's still his home turf," Jason cautioned.

"There also might be bystanders in the lobby. We don't want to let him have a hostage situation," Angela added.

"What about the elevator?" Jason suggested. "We could have somebody in the elevator car and when he gets in to go up to his office, we've got him trapped."

"That assumes only one elevator," Mike said. "Or we have guys in every elevator car, which would arouse a lot of suspicion from the building security guys. What if Randall has paid them off to alert him if the cops show up?"

"I'd still opt for taking him inside the office," Angela finally said as if it were her final answer.

"Me, too," Mike agreed.

"OK," Jason conceded. "We'll cover all the exits. I'm sure Sully will free up as many officers as we need for this."

"Let's not blow it again," Mike said softly.

At 7:50 p.m., the Task Force and a squad of twelve uniformed officers were huddled around an unmarked sedan parked two blocks away from the building where IT Intelligence had its offices. After a lot of badge flashing, the security director had given Mike and Jason a list of all the employees and contractors who worked overnight shifts. Without telling Havens which person was the target of the investigation, they knew that Charles Cooper's shift started at 8:00 p.m. and ran until 4:00 a.m. They could have waited until midnight, when there would be even fewer people in the building, but Captain Sullivan would not authorize the overtime in the absence of a good reason to wait four extra hours. Mike could not think of a good reason, and so the operation was planned for 8:15. Angela had wanted the feds to provide officers for the event, but the Commissioner wanted it to be purely an NYPD capture, so all the personnel except for Angela herself were New York's Finest.

Berkowitz was stationed in a Starbucks across the street from the building and was keeping an eye out for Randall's arrival, although they were not one hundred percent certain of what he would look like given his past pattern of wearing disguises. But, a six-two ex-soldier would tend to stand out from the crowd, and there were not that many people entering the office building at this hour. At 7:55, Mike's cell rang.

"Steve, what have you got?"

"Big guy wearing a black hoodie and a Yankees cap just went inside."

"Hoodie? Not a very professional look."

"Yeah, well this guy maybe didn't want to show his face." Berkowitz paused. "I didn't get much of a look at him, but he breezed past the security desk and went to the elevators."

"OK. Keep on watch and let's see if anybody else fitting our general description comes in."

"Roger that."

Mike nodded toward Jason, Angela, and George. "Our guy just went in, we think. Give it a few more minutes, but so far, so good." Nobody spoke, but everyone nodded back to affirm their understanding and readiness. "Keep your radios on channel three."

Ten minutes later, Mike got another call from Berkowitz. "Nobody else matching our boy's description has entered, Mike."

"OK. Stay put for now and when we go in you come join us in the lobby."

"I'll be there."

Mike motioned to the uniformed officers, who had drifted away into several clumps, that they should come back to the lead car. "OK, folks. Let's make this quick and clean." Mike, Angela, and Jason piled into the back seat of the lead car, with two uniformed officers in the front. George rode in the next car, a black & white with three more of the uniforms. The rest of the officers were to deploy around the building, covering all the exits.

The two cars pulled up to the front of the building and the uniformed officers led the way into the lobby, causing the two sleepy building security guards to snap to attention. Jim Havens, the security guy, was already standing by the reception desk. The officers explained the situation and advised the building guards that they were going in to make an arrest, showing them the arrest warrant, which Mike had obtained that afternoon. The guards stood aside as the team moved to the bank of elevators. Three officers stayed in the lobby to guard the exit and the emergency stairs just in case Randall tried to bolt.

"Which floor has the IT department?" Mike asked Havens.

"Twenty-three."

Berkowitz, who had made his way into the lobby, joined the other Task Force members and three uniformed officers at the elevators. The group rode in silence to the twenty-third floor, where the man they had been hunting for two months was presumably waiting, oblivious to his impending capture.

The group exited the elevator and Havens asked, "OK, now that we're here, who are you going to arrest?"

"The target is a man your guys know as Charles Cooper, who works the night IT shift. I'll ask you to open the door for us and tell me where we can find the space where this guy Cooper works."

Mike heard a distinct click next to the glass door emblazoned with the IT Intelligence logo as a small LED light flashed green under a black sensor pad when Havens waved his master key card next to it. Havens led the team down a long corridor and around a corner before stopping in front of a set of double-doors marked "Command Center."

"He should be in here, monitoring our systems for problems during the night."

"Anybody in there with him?"

"I don't think so, but it's not my department, so I can't be sure. This is the only IT operation that works after normal hours."

"OK. Everybody ready?" The team all nodded. The two uniformed officers positioned themselves on either side of the double doors, ready to burst inside with guns drawn as soon as the door was unlocked. Mike, Jason, George, Steve, and Angela would come in behind them. They expected that the surprise entrance, combined with the strength of their numbers, would prevent Randall from attempting to shoot his way out. But, they were prepared for anything.

Mike motioned silently to Havens to unlock the door. The security chief complied by swiping his key card in front of the sensor pad. Mike watched for the red light to turn green, but instead it flashed red several times. There was no clicking sound. Havens swiped the card again, but got the same reaction from the red light. Mike motioned to the uniformed officers and one of them grabbed the steel handle of one side of the double doors and pushed down, then pulled up, but got no movement. He pulled hard outward and the door moved a fraction of an inch before catching on the lock with a creaking sound. Mike and Jason exchanged a puzzled look as Havens continued to flash his key card in front of the pad with increasing frustration.

"This is a master key. It should work every lock in the place," Havens muttered.

"Could our guy have accessed your security system and locked this door from the inside?"

"I don't see how. He'd have to reprogram this key pad, and he doesn't have authorization for that."

Mike glanced up and down the hallway, assessing their situation. "What are our chances of breaking down this door?"

Havens paused for a second, then shook his head. "They're high-security steel doors and the magnetic lock can withstand 1,000 pounds of pressure. You'd need an explosive charge to get it open."

"Is there another exit out of that room?"

"Sure," Havens said. "You can't have a locked room with only one exit. There's an emergency fire stair in the far corner. The fire alarm would go off if anyone opened the door."

"Can we get to the fire stairs without getting into the room first?"

"No. There's no access from the hallway – only from inside."

"Where does the stair lead?"

"Down to the street. I think there's an exit door onto the sidewalk."

Mike pulled a radio unit from his belt and pushed the talk button. "All units. Operation Exodus. Suspect may be on the move on the fire stairs. Be ready for him to exit the building on the sidewalk on 37th Street. Lobby units, stay sharp – he might try to double-back to the lobby."

Mike turned to the Task Force. "Jason, George, Steve, you guys take the elevator down. Cover the lower floors, try to get ahead of him. See if you can get into one of those floors and access the same fire stairs."

The three detectives instantly turned and retraced their steps toward the elevator lobby. Mike, Angela, and Havens stayed at the command center doors with the two uniforms, stymied.

"How could he have known we were coming?"

Angela furrowed her brow. "Maybe he didn't. Maybe he just always has this door locked when he's in there by himself at night working and writing his blog and hacking into people's emails. He doesn't want anyone walking in on him, so he keeps the door locked."

"So, you think it's possible that he doesn't know we're even here?"

"I don't know. We tried to open the door. He might have heard that, or he might have the sensors programmed to alert him if someone tries to come in."

Mike turned to Havens. "Are there security cameras in these hallways?"

"Sure," Havens said, pointing up to a small, smoked plastic dome on the ceiling at the end of the hallway. "We have security cameras at all the entrances and in the hallways so we can prevent equipment from walking out."

Mike pondered that. "If he has access to the security camera feeds, then he would have seen us coming."

Havens grunted. "I don't see how he could see the security cameras. It's a pretty secure system."

"Yeah, so is the lock-out on the doors, I'm sure," Mike said glumly. "We need to get in there. Havens, how long will it take you to get into your security system and re-enable your key card?"

"Maybe ten minutes. I have to go down to my office on twenty-two."

"Do it. Call me on my cell when you've got it done. Leave me your key card."

Havens hesitated, not wanting to give up his master security key, but he reluctantly agreed and hurried off around the corner.

Mike paced in front of the door while Angela pressed her ear against the gap between the double doors, listening for any noises inside that might indicate that Randall was still there. The uniformed officers holstered their guns and stood on either side of the doors like wooden soldiers, waiting for instructions. Angela shook her head silently to indicate that she did not hear anything.

The radio on his belt squawked, "Mike!" and he quickly grabbed it.

"Stoneman!" he shouted into the box.

"It's Lopez, sir. No activity on the street or in the lobby. It's all quiet."

"Thanks. Stay sharp." Mike returned the box to his waist. "Where the Hell is he?"

Just then, Mike's cell phone rang, and after answering quickly Mike swiped Havens' key card in front of the pad. The light turned green and the door clicked. The uniformed officers drew their weapons and pulled the door open, rushing in with Mike and Angela close behind, also with weapons drawn. The shock-and-awe approach of arriving with eight people was down the drain.

The four of them fanned out around the room, searching for any possible hiding places, but Randall was not there. The room contained banks of computers and monitors arranged on desks in a semi-circle in front of a tall wall full of television screens displaying the status of various company systems in different locations. Mike couldn't make any sense of the information, but didn't really try. He was there for Randall, and Randall was gone. They carefully examined the work stations and found one with a cup of coffee sitting next to it, still hot under its plastic lid. The desk chair was pushed back from the working surface, unlike all the others that were neatly pushed in. The monitors were all dark. When Mike tapped the space bar on the keyboard with a ballpoint pen the monitors flashed to life, but showed only a start-up screen. Randall had rebooted his desktop before he left.

"Find that fire exit!" Mike barked and the uniforms dashed off, one in each direction. One of them shouted a few moments later and they all gathered around the door. There was a metal push-bar in the center and a large red and white sign reading "Emergency Exit – Alarm Will Sound."

"I guess it's not that hard to disable a fire alarm, eh?" Mike asked to nobody in particular.

One of the uniformed officers responded. "Nah, I've seen that a lot. Guys use the fire stairs for smoke breaks and stuff. It's pretty easy to rig the sensor so it thinks the door is closed even when it's really open."

Mike did not respond immediately, but pushed open the door with his jacket sleeve to avoid smearing any fingerprints and peered into the stairwell. It was a standard concrete stairway leading both up and down, with an iron handrail running along the walls on both sides. The whole interior of the fire stairs was painted a dull gray. Mike listened, but heard no footfalls. He reached for his radio again. "All units, this is Stoneman. Randall has left his work space on twenty-three and has likely used the fire stairs to leave the floor. I want this building locked down. Nobody goes in or out without being questioned. Anybody taller than five-eight gets detained. Male or female. Randall is here somewhere and we're not going to let him get away."

Mike returned the radio to his hip, pulled out his cell phone, and dialed Jason. "Where are you?"

"I'm on the fourth floor. I started on six but couldn't get in. I'm inside the office space now and approaching the fire stairs."

"Good. Take the stairs up when you get inside and clear the stairwell. Check the doors on every floor going up to see if there are any signs that Randall exited the stairs on another floor."

"Got it."

Mike snapped his phone back into its holster angrily as he paced around the command center. After a minute, he turned to Angela. "Can you get Simpson or somebody else from your team up here to look at Randall's computer?"

"Sure." Angela pulled out her own phone and started scrolling. Just then, Havens came into the room slowly, making sure that he was not disturbing a crime scene.

Mike walked toward him. "Mr. Havens, thanks for solving our lock problem. It appears that our man has fled down the fire stairs. We've got all the exits covered and we're locking down the building. He has to be here somewhere. In the meantime, we'd like to get a forensics unit in here to look at his desktop computer to see if we can determine what he was working on and whether there is any useful information to be gleaned from that machine. Can I have your consent to that search?"

Havens paused. "Detective, I think it's fine under the circumstances, but I'm going to need to get authorization from my Head of IT and probably from our legal counsel before I can allow that."

Mike scowled, but held back from swearing. "I understand. Can you start that process right now? In the meantime, we'll make sure that the machine is not touched. I'd like to have an FBI expert here looking at this tonight."

"OK, I'll start tracking people down." Havens once again left in the direction of his office.

"This guy is like Houdini," Mike mumbled.

Angela walked over to him. "I've got Simpson on his way. I remember what he wrote in his blog about the building in Brooklyn with the health club. He said he planned out multiple exit routes just in case he needed them. He has things under control, but he is still thinking ahead, like a soldier. He wants a back-up plan and a back-up to the back-up. He comes into this office to do his work and also to work on his planning for the next kill and he wants to make sure he's completely alone and nobody walks in on him, so he hacks into the security system to lock out everyone but him. We don't know that he also hacked into the security cameras, but let's say he did. When we tried to swipe in, he might have gotten some notice, or maybe he just heard us jiggling the door. He sees us on the camera and realizes that he's blown. He quickly reboots his computer to wipe out anything he was working on and puts plan A into motion. So, what's plan A?"

"Plan A is to get out of here via the fire stairs," Mike answered.

"Sure, but if plan A is to run down the fire stairs and exit to the street, when he sees two uniforms and five detectives in the hallway he has to know that we're not alone and that we're going to have the street exits covered."

"Yes. He's smart, and that's pretty obvious. So, what's plan B?"

"If it's my plan," Angela said haltingly, "I would have a place on one of the other floors that would give me an exit route, or where I could hide."

"That makes sense," Mike agreed, but he hesitated. "And then there might be plan C. If I were trying to outfox the cops, maybe instead of going down, which is where they are expecting me to go, I go up."

Angela raised an eyebrow and looked interested. Mike walked back to the door to the fire stairs and once again peered in. He heard footsteps and went into a crouch, drawing his gun. He kept the door open a crack so he could see, and then relaxed and opened the door wide as Jason emerged up the steps, slightly out of breath.

"Nothing?" Mike asked.

"Nothing. No sign of him, and no sign of entry on any other floors. All the doors were locked, but all of them have keypads, so he might have been able to get in on another floor."

Mike quickly explained his plan C theory to Jason, then called to one of the uniformed officers and the three of them entered the stairway and started slowly climbing. Angela and the one remaining uniform stayed put on the twenty-third floor command center in case Randall tried to come back from wherever he might be hiding on a different floor, and to keep the scene secure. Angela even speculated that it was possible Randall was still in the command center somewhere in a hiding place from which he might emerge if he thought everyone had left. She wanted to test that theory by announcing that she and the uniform were going to check out the workspace beyond the wall of the command center along with Havens. Then, she planned to open and close the door, while actually staying in the room and sitting silently in a corner waiting to see if Randall crawled out of some spider hole under the floor or inside a server tower.

While Angela worked her theory, Jason, Mike, and their accompanying uniform, Officer Gary Rose, cautiously climbed up the fire stairs, checking on each landing to see if there were any signs that the access door had been opened. Jason had barely caught his breath from his twenty-floor climb, but he was still doing better than Mike after seven more flights. On the landing for the thirty-second floor, Mike paused and bent down. There was a pile of cigarette butts on the floor, under the large number "3" stenciled on the cement wall. Mike fished his cell phone out of its holster on his belt and fumbled with the screen before locating the flashlight app icon. The bright light instantly illuminated the area. They could all clearly see the scuff mark, where someone's shoe had disturbed the butts and ashes, sending a corner of the pile spilling off toward the "2" and leaving a small trail of soot along the painted floor. The direction of the scuff mark was toward the access door, but was also the direction someone would have been moving if climbing up the stairs.

"The scuff mark could have been made by one of the smokers," Jason pointed out.

"Yeah, but dogs are careful not to step in their own shit, so I'm going on the assumption that our boy may have come this way."

"Should we call for more back-up?"

"No. All the others are watching exits or searching other floors, and there's no time. If he came this way, he probably has an escape route, so we need to move."

The three men covered the next ten floors as quickly as they could, checking each access door to confirm it was locked and showed no signs of a recent opening. Every door had the same steel handle shaped like half a staple, which was firmly locked when one of the cops pushed down to confirm their lack of access to the floor's office space. At what would have been the forty-third floor landing, there was no number painted on the wall. Instead, a small red sign with white letters informed them that roof access was restricted to authorized building staff. Mike and Jason exchanged a glance and a nod, both thinking that they needed to proceed carefully. Mike again pulled out his cell phone and this time quickly found Havens' cell number in his recent calls list. The security chief answered on the first ring.

"Yeah?"

"Stoneman. We're at the roof entrance for the fire stairs on the forty-third floor. We think our guy might have gone up. Can you unlock the door up here remotely?"

"I can't. That's building access, not us, but I can call the building security office. Hold on."

Mike could hear Havens place a call from his office phone. The building's security director was already aware of the police activity, so he did not need much of an explanation. Within half a minute, Mike heard a loud click come from the door. Officer Rose reached out and pushed down on the handle, which released. He pulled the heavy door open a crack to confirm that they had access to the roof. Havens' voice then came back on the phone.

"The door should be open."

"It is. Thanks. Leave it unlocked so we can get back inside."

"Will do. You guys want some more bodies up there?"

Mike paused, then said, "We're good on the roof, but if you can get a few people into the stairway up on forty-two just in case he gets around us and tries to get back down the stairs, that would be helpful. But tell 'em to be careful; this guy is a killer."

"Got it."

Mike reached to return his phone to its holster, but then

changed his mind and reset the flashlight function in case they needed some extra light. Officer Rose extracted a military-grade flashlight from his belt and, on a silent count to three, he pulled open the door and went through, followed quickly by Jason and Mike. The three stood back-to-back, scanning the rooftop to make sure Randall didn't get the jump on them. Seeing nobody, and few hiding spots, they then fanned out to check the space. The roof was typical of a high rise, covered with a thick coating of rubberized tar to keep out the rain and snow and dotted with vents, large air-conditioning condenser units, and other mechanical equipment. A stiff breeze blew across the expanse from west to east, whipping a small pile of plastic bags and discarded paper that had gathered in one corner. Mike didn't really expect there to be a coating of dust that would show him footprints, but he still cursed the wind.

Jason carefully moved toward the eastern edge of the roof, checking behind each mechanical structure that could serve as a hiding spot, while Mike went south and Rose went west. The stairway they had emerged from was on the northern edge of the roof, looking across 37th Street toward the buildings on the other side of the street. After several minutes of tense silence, Mike called out, "Over here!"

When Jason and Rose arrived, Mike was talking into his radio. "Yes. The building adjacent to this one to the south. Get officers on the exits to that building and put out an APB to all officers in midtown to be looking for our guy, last seen wearing a black hoodie and a Yankees baseball cap."

Mike turned to Jason and just said, "Shit!"

Jason looked past Mike and immediately saw the reason for Mike's frustration. The roof on which they were standing had a short wall all around its edge about four feet higher than the rooftop. Looking over the edge, Jason could see to the south another office building about two stories shorter, with a similar rooftop twenty feet or so below where they were standing. The two buildings abutted one another. On the top of the short wall next to Mike, a shiny metal oval stuck up out of the concrete. It was a carabiner, attached to a Piton spike that had been pounded into a crack in the concrete wall; the kind you'd see used by mountain climbers – or soldiers. Looped through the carabiner was an orange nylon rope. When Jason looked over the edge, he could see the end of the rope puddled up on the roof of the adjoining building.

Chapter 44 – Identity Crisis

October 23, 2018

THE TASK FORCE GATHERED very early the next morning, still second-guessing every move from the night before and kicking themselves for allowing Randall to slip through their fingers again. Naturally, by the time the officers on the street were told to cover the exits from the building next door, it was too late. Security cameras from the lobby showed Randall strolling out, carrying a small gym bag. They had no idea where he went after that.

Mike was particularly depressed. He, Jason, and Angela had briefed Sully and Commissioner Ward about the operation and what happened. Nobody blamed Mike or the Task Force. It wasn't the first time an operation had gone sideways. But they were all unhappy. When they left Sullivan's office, Mike told Angela that he and Jason would meet her back upstairs. Despite their disappointment, they had leads to follow to keep their minds focused on the continuing chase, rather than on the recent failure.

After Angela left to hit the stairway, Mike asked Jason to join him in a small huddle room just off the bullpen. The legend around the precinct was that the tiny room had been the home of the switchboard operator back before the desks had direct dial lines. The building was old enough that it might have been true. Mike closed the door and turned to Jason.

"I just wanted to say, before we go back upstairs, that I appreciate you not rubbing my nose in the fact that you were right."

Jason just looked back calmly. "You mean about letting him get up to his office instead of taking him in the lobby?"

"Yeah."

"Well, I'm not going to second-guess you on that, Mike. It could have gone either way. I didn't fight that hard for taking him in the lobby after Angela pointed out that we could be setting up a hostage situation. You made a tough call. I agreed in the end. There's no point in me saying I-told-you-so."

Mike held out his hands at waist level, palms out. "I think there might be times when I discount your instincts, JD. I know that I've been pretty tough on you, and you've taken my shit like a trooper. I should listen to you more sometimes."

Jason looked surprised at this admission and didn't know what to say immediately. "Mike, thanks. I know I've had a chip on my shoulder – a bit – and despite my high self-esteem, I do recognize that I have a lot to learn from you."

"OK," Mike said, moving to the door. "Let's both work on that." Mike led them to the stairway and they walked in silence back to the war room, where Manning, Berkowitz, and Mason were all hunched over file folders and note pads.

Charles Cooper's employment records were the first vein to be mined. He had an address listed with IT Intelligence, but like all his prior employers that they knew about, the address was a storefront Post Office box. Each time he took on a new job, he used a different box, which provided a street address and an "apartment" number corresponding to the box number. He had used three different storefronts, all in different parts of town. In the case of his IT Intelligence address, the storefront was in Queens. They dispatched two FBI agents to the store to see if the owner had any records and to stake out the place in case Randall showed up to pick up his last paycheck. Since he was not on the regular payroll for IT Intelligence, he did not have direct bank deposit, which foreclosed another possible lead. The telephone number listed on the Independent Contractor Agreement form with IT Intelligence was predictably not in service. The Social Security number he used on the form was the same one they already knew about from the 2017 tax records and led them nowhere.

Angela was not surprised to find that there were several hundred people named Charles Cooper living in the greater New York area, not that they figured that their man would have listed his telephone number or otherwise made it easy for them to track down where he lived. They kept an officer in the lobby of IT Intelligence's building and had Jim Havens on high alert in case Randall/Cooper showed up back at his office, but they were not expecting him to walk right into their arms again. A dozen FBI agents were tracking down any appearances of Charles Cooper or his Social Security number. Meanwhile three of New York's finest were interviewing employees at IT Intelligence to see if anyone knew where Charles Cooper lived or anything else about him. A forensics team was combing through Cooper's desktop computer, and a separate team was collecting evidence inside the command center where Randall/Cooper was last seen.

"If he can't come back to his workplace, then we have disrupted his routine," Angela said to the Task Force assembled in the war room. "Guys like Randall have a routine. We've seen it in his blog. Now he has lost his refuge, the place he went to watch the media coverage after his kills, and the place he used to upload his blog posts during his overnight shifts. The forensic guys have not confirmed that his posts came from that desktop, but we can assume it for now. The question is how this disruption will affect him."

"You're the expert," Jason observed. "We're all just guessing. You have some experience to draw upon, right?"

Angela hesitated. "Actually, I can't say that I've had a case like this before, where a killer's life has been disrupted like this, but he has not been captured. Based on what I know and what I've read, I would guess that he could go one of two ways. Either he'll run and hide, or he'll go all-in on his next kill with the intention of going down in a blaze of glory."

"A rather polarized range," Mike said, stating the obvious.

"Of course, there could be other options for him, but it's impossible to say for sure." Angela threw up her hands in frustration. "This guy is not typical. A lot of his behaviors are outside the lines, so I'm not going to bet the ranch on any option."

"OK, so we watch the blog, we try to track down where he's living, and we hope we can find him before his next – kill date," Mike said, opting to not use the crass term that Angela didn't like. He thought that Michelle would be happy with him.

Berkowitz then jumped into the discussion, "If Randall purchased an apartment or home, there would be real estate records. We could check those to see if Charles Cooper, Charles Gordon, Charles White, or Ronald Randall had any recorded transactions. It's a longshot, but worth tracking down."

Mike agreed that it was worth a shot and Angela made a call to dispatch a few agents to contact the records clerks in each county to see what they could find.

"What about rentals?" Jason asked. "Is there any repository of records of the names of people who have rented apartments?"

"The City doesn't keep track," Mike responded, looking out the window. "The feds have already looked at income tax returns for the Social Security number we know Randall used, but the addresses listed are all different and all bogus. The government doesn't really care where you live as long as you pay your taxes, so that's no help. What else can we check?"

Angela moved to the whiteboard and started making a list.

Utility/electric/Gas

Internet provider
Cable TV

"There are a bunch of different providers that he could use for these, and they may not want to give up their information without a subpoena."

"Can you get your legal guys to prepare subpoenas?"

"Sure, but it will take a little time."

"Then let's get cracking," Mike said with renewed energy. "If we can find his apartment, maybe we can avoid screwing up the capture this time."

"Assuming that he hasn't already ditched it," Jason put in pessimistically. "Now that he knows we're getting close and that we know his Charles Cooper identity, he may figure it's time to get a new alias and erase his trail. That's what I'd do."

"Then we need to move fast," Angela shot back, insisting on keeping at least a cautiously optimistic attitude.

Then George, who seldom spoke up during their group discussion, suddenly stood up, his mouth wide open like he was waiting for somebody to lob a grape in his direction. "They're connected!" he exclaimed.

"Who?" Angela asked as everyone turned in George's direction.

"Pharaoh – I mean Heilman, and DiVito, and Sawyer. That's the link!"

"What are you talking about?" Jason asked dismissively.

George began to pace as he spoke. "Heilman was part of an operation that was kidnapping girls from third-world countries and bringing them to the U.S. He was an importer. He brought the product in. So, who did he sell to? He sold product to guys like DiVito, who used the women in his sweatshop in Jersey. And he sells product to scum like Sawyer, who takes the pretty ones and makes them into sex slaves for himself or his customers. I'd bet that both DiVito and Sawyer bought merchandise from Heilman.

You see! They're connected."

"What about the others – LeBlanc and Sheraton? How were they connected to Heilman?" Jason asked, but nobody had an answer.

"Maybe they're not," Angela suggested. "Even if Randall selected some of his kills because of the connection to Heilman, that doesn't mean all of them had to be. Remember in his blog he talked about not wanting to have a clear pattern and about how he was trying to throw us off his trail. He may have targeted unconnected victims just so that we wouldn't see the pattern."

"What did his blog say about how he found out about Sheraton's overseas sweat shops?" Mike asked to nobody in particular.

It was Berkowitz who found his copy of the blog printout first. "He says something about reading her private communications. I always figured that he had hacked her email, although I never understood why he was looking at her in the first place."

"Wait a minute," Angela said very slowly, as if a light bulb had just illuminated over her head. "What was the name of Marlene Sheraton's company?"

Jason remembered without having to consult his notes. He had a very clear memory of his conversations with Ms. Sheraton's lovely assistant, d'Angela Foster. "It was called Stardust Fashions."

Angela was already digging through a folder. A few seconds later, she held up a sheet of white paper. It was a tax form. "We never really cared where Charles Cooper worked before 2017. We were focused on finding his most recent job. It doesn't much matter now, but here he is – he worked for Stardust Fashions, Ltd in 2015. They paid him $42,500. That's when he had the chance to hack Marlene Sheraton's emails, when he was working in their IT department."

"I'll be damned," Mike sputtered. "How did we miss that?"

"It wouldn't have helped," Angela said. "By that time, we already had him pegged as Charles Cooper, so finding a connection between Charles Cooper and Marlene Sheraton would not have advanced our ability to find the mythical Mr. Cooper."

"Unless he listed his real address when he worked for Stardust Fashions."

"Well, not much chance of that."

Everyone in the room was silent for a moment, before Berkowitz asked the next question that they were all thinking. "Do you think there's some connection to LeBlanc, the third victim?"

"We haven't found one yet," Mike said.

Angela did what she always did – she walked to the whiteboard. "LeBlanc's company made drugs. That's what Randall railed about in his blog. The drugs were substandard and messed up people who took them. Our guy was injured and was in and out of the VA hospital. Maybe he took some of LeBlanc's bad drugs?"

"Or maybe somebody he knew from the hospital?"

"Holy crap!" Jason burst out. "Remember what he wrote – that he had witnessed firsthand someone who nearly died because of one of Napoleon's – LeBlanc's – tainted drugs. When he was in the hospital! He picked up his grudge for LeBlanc and held onto it until he put together his hit list."

"That leaves only Slick Mick," Mike observed.

"If there were criminal enterprises involved in Queens, then Slick Mick must have had his finger in them," Berkowitz said simply. "We know Sawyer was in his gang, so Randall probably could have gotten a bead on him through the prostitution ring."

Angela started erasing some of her notes from the whiteboard. "Many serial killers pick their victims based on personal interactions or grudges. In this guy's case, he has pumped it up into this quest as the Angel of Death, but in the end all the victims are people he targeted because he had some very individual reason to hate them and want them dead."

"So, how does all this help us?" Mike asked.

George spoke up again quickly. "I remember a reference in his blog about his Army buddies inviting him to get involved in

Pharaoh's operation. He said something about knowing Pharaoh's secrets and then planning to eventually kill the guy. I'm thinking that Randall got recruited out of the Army to join up with the kidnapping ring. Remember, one of the FBI agents said that they use ex-military guys for their muscle. Maybe Randall even worked with them for a while, who knows? That's how he found out about DiVito and Sawyer and started thinking about targeting them. And if Slick Mick was connected to Sawyer, then maybe Randall stumbled on him along the way."

"It makes sense," Angela agreed. "And he recently made a reference to a new guy he calls Haman, who is also somehow connected. If he's part of this same operation, then Randall is going to have a problem because this party is blown now. Our guys have arrested anybody that we have enough dirt on to justify it, and the rest of the operation is going to go underground, at least for a while. Whoever this Haman is, I doubt he'll be hanging around New York."

"Well, let's follow that angle," Mike suggested. "Can we get a list of the guys that got arrested, and maybe the guys they are still chasing, who were connected to Heilman's operation?"

Angela was already dialing the phone.

Chapter 45 – Connections

October 24, 2018

THE TASK FORCE, aided by ten FBI agents, was evaluating the movements of every person of interest who had been identified during the surveillance operation surrounding Justin Heilman's import/export business. The FBI's code name for the program had been Operation Marlin, partly because it had a base in Miami and partly because of the idea of catching the big fish. Now it was routinely referred to as Operation Tuna Salad, since it had been torn to shreds by the death of the head douchebag. Still, there were ships in transit and customers who still expected to get their goods. The underlings were still pressing ahead with the business, hopeful that there were promotional opportunities available in the near future.

Mike and Jason focused on the ex-military guys who worked security and logistics. The feds didn't have deep files on these guys because they were never considered important. As military grunts, they were impossible to flip as witnesses, and they were so far down in the operation that they didn't have much information that the guys listening in on the wire taps didn't already know. But, the feds did have names, general descriptions of their jobs and territories, and photographs. Predictably, there were no photos or names that matched their killer, Ronald Randall. They had already figured that Randall's connection to the operation was so far in the past that it was not likely to have been captured by the FBI surveillance, which had only been in place for twelve months.

"What makes you think there's any chance that one of these goons has been in recent contact with Randall?" George asked when Mike handed him a new stack of folders.

"Not a thing," Mike responded gruffly. "It's a long shot, but we have no better leads at the moment, so we track them down."

"But they're not going to talk to us even if we can find them. It's a waste of our time."

Mike sighed. "You're probably right, George. But, if there's a guy out there who solicited Randall to join up with this operation, then that guy was probably close with Randall at one time, and there's a chance he might have had some communication with him. Maybe he has a good cell phone number, or an email address. If we can get that kind of information, then it's worth trying. And if you're the guy who finds the golden egg, we'll all buy you a beer and I will tell the press that it was your superior detective skills that broke the case."

"That's such bullshit."

"I know, but it sounded good. Now hit the phone." Mike smirked and patted George on the shoulder, then went back to his own pile of folders.

"I have one," Jason said as he slipped his cell phone back into his pocket. "It's pretty thin. The guy's Army discharge was two years before Randall's, and his address is listed as Los Angeles. Are we chasing these guys ourselves, or are we passing them off to the feds?"

"It's your call if you want to work a particular lead yourself, but otherwise the feds have enough boots so go ahead and call it in downtown."

Jason held up his flat hand and wavered it back and forth to indicate that it was a so-so proposition. "It's not that hot, so I'll pass it."

Angela hung up her phone and made a motion mocking a

quarterback throwing a pass in Jason's direction. "That's the stuff, Jason. Send the Bureau the crappy leads and let us run with them."

"Happy to help keep your boys busy," Jason quipped back good-naturedly. Jason and Angela had developed a comfortable pattern of banter. At this point, they could say almost anything to each other and neither would take it seriously or personally.

Just then, Angela's attention was diverted to Steve Berkowitz, who had his hand raised and was waving it from side to side as he spoke on the phone. "Uh huh. . . . Yes. . . . I think so. . . . OK. Thanks." Berkowitz dropped his hand and looked up at Angela. "This is a hot one. Guy was in Afghanistan the same time as Randall, but more importantly he was injured and in the same field hospital as Randall. He's also from Brooklyn."

"Sounds like a prospect," Angela said.

"Steve – you and George pay a visit to this guy's last known address and see what you can dig up. If he's home, bring him in."

"With pleasure," Steve said as he got up from his chair and headed for the door, with George close behind.

"Every time we get a little lead, our guy seems to stay just ahead of us," Mike observed glumly. "Maybe we're due for a break."

"Oh, we're due," Jason agreed. "But being due doesn't mean it's going to happen."

"Well, let's be good scouts and be prepared just in case," Angela said. "I'll have the guys downtown put together everything they can on this guy so we have as much background as we can get."

Two hours later, with no good leads coming through in the war room, Mike got a call from Berkowitz. They had been lucky and found their guy at home. He had tried to bolt, but he and George had managed to persuade him that coming down to the precinct house was in his best interests. He could hardly object at that point since he was handcuffed. When they arrived back at the station, they deposited the guy in an interrogation room, cuffed him to the table, and went upstairs to consult with the team.

Angela took charge immediately. She had already made notes on the whiteboard based on the information the FBI was able to put together with an hour's notice. "Harry 'Hank' Carson. Thirty years old. Born in Mobile, Alabama but moved to Brooklyn when he was five years old. Mother brought him to New York when the father moved out. Two brothers and a sister. A few minor juvenile arrests for petty crimes. Graduated high school, then spent a year in auto mechanic trade school before enlisting. Spent six years as a Marine including two tours in Afghanistan. Turned out that his auto mechanic skills were decent because he ended up working in the motor pool keeping the trucks and tanks running and didn't see much actual combat. Got clipped by an IED during a convoy mission and ended up in the field hospital, which lead to his medical discharge. Looks like he and Randall were in the hospital together for about three weeks. Carson was discharged three months before Randall, but that's not a surprise since Randall's injuries were more severe and he had to go through the psych evaluation."

Angela paused as if waiting for some response or questions, but she got only polite attention, so she continued. "After he got back stateside, Carson was treated at the St. Albans VA Hospital in Queens for six months, then was deemed fully recovered. At that point, he dropped off the grid. There is no record of him holding a job, at least not under his own Social Security number, and why wouldn't he use it? He's picked up on the radar of Operation Marlin when he is photographed on the docks unloading a shipment. The agents eventually verify his identity and start tracking him. He seems to stay in New York and work on this side of the import business. He's basically security and muscle for the underlings who deliver the human goods to Heilman's customers. He traveled as far as Chicago with the women, who were shipped in trucks if they were being taken outside the New York area. He was an escort. It's not clear how much he knew about the operation."

"Anything else?" Mike asked.

"That's it," Angela said, putting down her black dry-erase marker.

Mike then turned to Berkowitz and Mason. "How did Mr. Carson react when you requested his voluntary presence in our interrogation room?"

Steve chucked. "We got lucky in that he was at home when we came calling. He lives in a shit-hole apartment in a public housing building in Queens. When we knocked and identified ourselves as NYPD, he decided to inspect the structural integrity of the fire escape. We heard him open the window so we made a lawful entry through the front door. It turned out that the building needs to do some work on the fire escape maintenance plan, because Carson was not able to get the ladder at the bottom of the fire stairs to deploy and we caught up with him on the second floor. He didn't have a weapon, and we explained that we would be forced to put a bullet in his leg if he resisted arrest. He asked us why we were arresting him, but didn't otherwise talk once we read him his rights."

"He's not really a suspect, why did you read him his rights?"

"Sorry, Mike. Habit."

"OK. Jason, do you feel up to taking point on this interrogation?"

Jason sat up straight, a little startled by the question. "Sure."

"Good. You've got the ex-military background. You might be able to connect with this guy."

"Understood," Jason responded confidently. Mike and Jason walked down to the interrogation room in silence. At the doorway, Jason paused and turned to face his partner. "Thanks, Mike. I appreciate you letting me lead this."

"It makes sense," Mike said without emotion. "You're the good cop in this scenario. Let's hope we don't need me to be the bad guy, but I'll be ready if needed." Jason nodded and opened the door.

The interrogation room was painted an off white, with bright lights on the ceiling. There was the expected two-way mirror on one wall, behind which other officers could observe and listen. A camera was mounted in one corner. Carson was seated in a metal chair in front of a white table with metal legs, which were bolted to the white tile floor. His left hand was handcuffed to a steel bar embedded in the center of the table. Carson looked bored, sitting slumped forward with both arms resting on the table. He wore blue jeans and a black t-shirt with very short sleeves, which showed off his biceps muscles. His file listed him at six feet one inch and two-fifteen, but he had obviously been hitting the gym since that report. He was easily a solid two-fifty, with bulging veins in his thick neck and running down his impressive arms. His head was shaved smooth. Mike wondered if he was on steroids because his head seemed particularly large. He had an American flag tattoo on his right forearm and a black snake encircling his left. He looked up at the two detectives with dark eyes that betrayed no particular emotion. He was an impressive physical specimen, and certainly someone you would not talk back to if he gave you an order in a dark alley.

Jason sat down in a chair across the table from Carson. Mike stood a few feet behind Jason and off to the side, leaning against the wall next to the two-way mirror and scrutinizing the suspect. Jason was a big man, but looked ordinary sitting across from Carson, who had his head down, staring at the white table surface.

"Mr. Carson, my name is Detective Dickson. This here is Detective Stoneman." Jason motioned toward Mike, but got no response from Carson. "May I call you Hank?"

"No," came the sharp response. "You can get me a lawyer. I asked for a lawyer, but here you are questioning me without my lawyer." Carson looked up and met Jason's eyes for the first time.

"Well, Hank. Let me tell you first that you are not here because you are a suspect in any investigation. So, you are not under arrest, which means that you don't really have a right to a lawyer. But, in the meantime, nothing you say can be used against you since you did ask for a lawyer and now I'm talking to you without one, so you can relax. The camera is recording this, so there will be proof of what I just told you."

Carson squinted skeptically. "Detective Barko-whatsit sure as shit told me I was under arrest when he cuffed me and dragged me down here."

"Let's just say that you were under arrest for resisting arrest, but we're willing to let that go, and we're willing to talk to our friends at the FBI about getting you some slack in their investigation into your participation in Justin Heilman's human trafficking operation."

"I don't know nothin' about that."

"I think you do, Hank. The FBI has photos of you on the docks, and accompanying the truck to Chicago, and off-loading the van in Brooklyn, and I have to tell you that the pictures are pretty clear, so you're in a heap of trouble."

"How do you know about an FBI operation?" Carson cocked his head, and Jason shot a quick side glance at Mike. This was the opening.

"Hank, do you read the papers?"

"Not much."

"Well, maybe you've seen a big headline in the *Post* or the *Daily News* before you read the football columns?"

"Maybe."

"So, Hank, have you heard that there's a serial killer that the papers are calling the Righteous Assassin?"

"Yeah, I might have heard something about that." Carson seemed confused. He had obviously not put two and two together yet.

"Well, Hank, Detective Stoneman and I are the lead team

working with the FBI on the serial killer case. That's how we have connections with the FBI."

"What's a serial killer got to do with . . ."

"With what?" Jason prodded.

"Nothing."

"You're wondering what our serial killer investigation has to do with Heilman's little import/export business, which is a fair question for you to ask, Hank. You see, the connection is that Mr. Heilman is no longer the head of his business because he was knocked off by the serial killer."

Jason paused for effect and watched Carson's face, as did Mike. He was confused and scrunched up his face, deep furrows appearing on his forehead. He was muscle, not brains, and he was trying to process this information. Jason stayed quiet and let him think. After a minute of silence, Carson looked at Jason with one eye half-closed and said, "What's any of this got to do with me?"

Jason smiled. "Great question, Hank. You would think that your small role in Heilman's operation has nothing to do with why a psycho serial killer decided to target your boss for a murder."

"I didn't say he was my boss," Carson interjected.

"No. No, you didn't. That's true. But you see, Hank, we know that you were military. Marines, right?"

Carson nodded silently.

"I was Army," Jason said, looking Carson in the eyes. "402nd Field Support in Iraq." Carson did not show any recognition. "When I got back stateside, I didn't know what to do with myself. I got drunk and chased some women and I worked for a while in a bar where I got into a bunch of fights. I was a little messed up." Carson didn't speak, but nodded again and the hard lines on his face softened slightly. "I finally got my shit together and got into the police academy, and now I'm a detective, but I know how hard it is to figure things out when you get out. Some of my buddies ended up on drugs or got in with some bad dudes. I think that's what happened to you, Hank. Somebody came to you and offered you a job and it turned out to be supporting this scumbag Heilman. You took it because it was good money and you felt like you were back in a unit with other ex-military guys. It felt pretty good and you went with it. Is that about right?"

Carson fixed a hard stare at Jason, searching for indications of bullshit. Jason stared him right back, without blinking. After twenty seconds or so of the stare-down, Carson said, "You don't know nothin' about me."

"I know enough. I know that you're not a big player in Heilman's gang. You don't deserve to do time for it. I know you probably didn't know any better when you tried to recruit Ronald Randall to join the operation."

Jason paused. He saw a flicker of recognition in Carson's eyes when he mentioned Ronald Randall. Mike saw it, too. Carson didn't say anything, so Jason pressed forward. "You were in the field hospital outside Kabul after your IED injury back in '13. Ronald Randall was there, too. He was more banged up than you. You met him there and made friends, and after you came home and got hooked up with Heilman you hooked back up with Randall. I'm guessing maybe at the VA Hospital, but it really doesn't matter. You figured he might be a good guy to invite into the business, so you showed him around and tried to get him to get in. You didn't really do anything wrong there. You were trying to do a favor for him – get him some good work. Nothing wrong with that, right?"

Carson was closely following Jason's recitation and did not interrupt to correct or contradict anything. He still looked confused.

"Hank, there's nothing criminal about offering a job to a military buddy. We know that Randall did not want to take the job, so he walked away. You're not in any trouble because of him. Remember, I can't use anything you say against you because you don't have a lawyer here. So, just help us out a little and confirm for me that you know Ronald Randall. Can you just say that?"

Carson hesitated, seemingly unsure about how he was being tricked, but then he nodded again and said, "OK, fine. I know who Ron Randall is. So what?"

"Hank, we're trying to find Lieutenant Randall."

"Why?"

Now it was Jason's turn to pause. He glanced over at Mike, who gave Jason an almost imperceptible nod of his head. "Hank, Ronald Randall is the serial killer we're looking for. He is the Righteous Assassin. When you knew him, had he started to get heavy into religion?"

"A little," Carson offered reluctantly. "He said that God had saved his life."

"Well, Hank. Now he thinks he is God's Avenging Angel and he's out trying to kill off people who he thinks deserve to die for their Earthly sins. I doubt that he's coming for you next, but he has already taken out at least three people connected to Heilman, including Heilman."

Carson just sat looking at Jason, still with a rather confused look on his face. "Are you shitting me?"

"No, Hank. I'm not shitting you at all. I'm as serious as a heart attack. I'm telling you as a soldier that finding Randall is all we're interested in. We're not trying to trap you and we're not trying to pin anything on you."

Carson sat still, deep in thought. Then he said what Mike and Jason most hoped for. "If I talk to you about Randall, what kind of deal can I get?"

Jason and Mike excused themselves and left the room, going next door to the viewing room behind the two-way mirror where they found Angela already on her cell phone. She held up a hand to Mike to indicate that he should not talk yet. When she hung up, she turned to Mike and said, "Full immunity for any crimes committed in connection with Operation Marlin." Mike and Jason turned around, having not spoken a word.

Over the next hour-and-a-half, Jason and Hank Carson shared

a pepperoni pizza, a six-pack of Coca-Cola, and a bunch of stories about their Army exploits. Jason presented Carson with a written statement granting him full immunity for any crimes committed in the employ of Justin Heilman. Carson seemed fully satisfied by the document and immediately began spilling everything he knew about Lieutenant Ronald Randall. Most of what Carson had to say was information they already more or less knew. Carson confirmed Randall's sudden religious zeal and confirmed that he had recruited his former hospital mate to come into Heilman's gang, but that Randall had declined. He had brought Randall along on a job for Heilman and explained how the operation worked. He was not worried about Randall taking the information and going to the cops, partly because he figured that there was a bond of honor between soldiers, and partly because Randall had technically been a participant in the criminal activity, so if he went to the cops, he would have to admit his own involvement.

The one piece of information that they did not already know, or guess, was that Carson had met up with Randall not at the VA Hospital, but at a veterans' club in Manhattan. The club met in the back room of an Italian restaurant in Greenwich Village. Carson said that, even after Randall turned down the opportunity to join the Heilman organization, Carson saw him sometimes at the club. Randall had given Carson a cell phone number, but Carson said he didn't still have it anywhere and that the phone where he had the number stored was long since thrown into the harbor. Carson had not seen Randall around the veterans' club in a few years. Carson had no idea what Randall's address was, but he was pretty sure he lived nearby to the club.

"Why is that?" Jason pressed.

"The day I finally got him to come along with us to see the docks it was cold and he was wearing just a light jacket. He said he needed to run home and get a warmer coat, so he took off and was back inside of five minutes wearing a big parka, so he had to be pretty close by."

"Did you see what direction he went from the club?"

"Nah. I wasn't tailing him. He went out through the front of the restaurant, not out the back door, so probably heading out toward 10th Street and not downtown, that's about all I can say for sure."

Jason and Mike made eye contact and Mike left the room to consult with Angela about starting to canvas the buildings in the area, looking for an apartment rented to Charles Cooper, or Charles White, or Charles Gordon, or Ronald Randall, or some variation of those names.

Carson had nothing else of value to add, so Jason called in a uniformed officer and had him escort Carson to a holding cell. Jason had already explained to Carson that they did not want him communicating what he had told the cops to anyone, and that if anyone in Heilman's operation got wind that he was arrested and then released too quickly, they would suspect that he was talking and his life would be in danger. He agreed to spend a few days as a guest of the hotel NYPD in order to preserve his long-term prospects.

Chapter 46 – Storming the Castle

October 25, 2018

THE NEXT DAY three FBI agents, along with Berkowitz and Mason, tracked down anyone who had been a member of the veterans' club back in 2013 or 2014 to see if they had any memories of Ronald Randall, or any of his aliases, but their efforts came up empty. Meanwhile, Angela had a group of agents calling up the landlords and management companies that ran every apartment building within a three-block area north of the restaurant where the veterans club met to see if they could get a match on a tenant. With the universe of possible buildings narrowed down, it was only a matter of time, assuming that Randall had rented the apartment using one of his known aliases.

At 3:00, Angela's cell phone rang in the war room. When she hung up after a short call, she told Mike and Jason to get their jackets. They crammed into the back seat of a squad car and raced to a squat building on 11th Street, two blocks from the veterans' club. The landlord was not one of the big real estate management companies, but rather a Jewish grandmother who had inherited the building from her father and rented out the six units as her sole means of support. Without a bit of luck, the feds would not have been able to identify any of the tenants, who were not listed in any database.

The little old lady was happy to cooperate with the federal

agents and explained that none of her tenants matched any of the names they were looking for. But, she did rent her third-floor walk-up to a nice young man named Ronald Gordon. After getting a general description of her Mr. Gordon, including that he paid his rent in cash, they were pretty sure they had their guy. Upon some further questioning, the landlord mentioned that all the utilities and internet were included in the rent and they were in her name, not in the tenants' names. The agents thanked her and helped her back into her ground floor apartment.

By 4:30, the building was surrounded by cops and the FBI agents had quietly removed all the other residents for their own safety. They had been watching for an hour and there was no sign of movement through the one set of windows in the upper floor flat. Mike, Angela, and Jason decided to risk storming in, understanding the risk that Randall might have some kind of booby trap or military-style defensive installation in there. They called in the S.W.A.T unit, which brought along a battering ram with a full body shield. Getting the contraption up to the third-floor landing was an operation, but by 5:30 they had everything in position.

The team burst through the ancient wooden door like it was made of matchsticks, then swept the two-room space in thirty seconds. Randall was not there. The apartment was sparsely appointed. The main room featured a wooden desk and chair, a small table next to the efficiency kitchen, and a floor lamp. A solitary picture hung on the wall behind the desk. It was a photo of a group of soldiers against a desert background. There were six in the group and all were smiling as they jostled for position in front of the camera.

A layer of dust covered much of the surface of the desk, but near the chair a rectangle of clean wood marked where an object once sat, about the size of a laptop computer. A CAT5 cable hung limply from a wall outlet and snaked away along the floor, underneath a six-outlet plug extender. Mike walked to the adjoining bedroom where a battered mattress took up much of the floor space, strewn with a pile of blankets and two old pillows missing half their feathers. A small lamp sat on the floor next to the mattress. On the wall above the bed the paint showed a shadow where a large cross had hung.

The bedroom closet held a decent collection of jeans and khaki pants, polo shirts, and mid-range sneakers. A chest of drawers held socks, underwear, and t-shirts. Randall had not packed up all his clothes. The kitchen cupboards held plates and glasses, and there were freshly washed dishes in a drying rack next to the sink. The place was clean to the point of sterile. The fridge held yogurt, fruit, juice, and an assortment of neatly packaged containers that appeared to be leftovers.

"It looks like he plans on coming back," Jason observed.

"Except that he took his computer and his cross."

"Well, there's that. So, he figured we were coming for him."

"Yep," Mike snapped as he opened the cupboard under the sink and inspected a fresh, empty trash bag lining a circular bin. "He took out his trash before he left, so he wasn't in a hurry. He must have cleared out yesterday. Let's check the dumpsters out back and see if we can find his garbage. You never know what might be in there."

The agents combed through the apartment but did not find anything useful. They retrieved the garbage and spilled it all around the alley behind the building, but it yielded no clues to Randall's whereabouts. No discarded matchbook with the name of the bar where he hung out. No scrap of paper with a half-written note. He was just gone.

Chapter 47 – Missing Michelle

October 26, 2018

E ARLY FRIDAY EVENING, with the countdown reading 1, Mike, Jason, and Angela were in Captain Sullivan's office on an interminably long conference call with the Mayor, who wanted to know what they were doing to make sure that the killer would not strike again the next day. They gave Frederick Douglass the full briefing, but of course they had no idea if they would be able to prevent the next kill. They had an APB out on Randall, but they did not know who his target was or where the strike was likely to happen. All their efforts to track him down had failed. The feds had arrested several people connected to Operation Marlin and they had a few low-level members of Heilman's organization under surveillance, but they doubted that any of them was Haman. Randall's blog had gone dark again and was giving them no clues.

"So, we've got nothing," said Commissioner Ward, who was in the downtown conference room with Mayor Douglass.

"We've got quite a lot," Mike said, trying to sound optimistic, "just nothing likely to allow us to catch him before tomorrow. We're closing in, sir. He knows it. He has abandoned his apartment and he can't go back to his last job. But, he may have an alternate location where he can stay and he may have other false identities to use. He has shown that he's a planner and has escape routes, but he's on the run. There's a chance that he will go into hiding and not try for a kill this month."

"A chance, but nothing we can bank on, right?" Mike did not respond. "That's what I thought." The Mayor hung up, leaving the Task Force sitting in silence.

A frustratingly unproductive hour later, Mike hurried out of the precinct house and hailed a cab on Columbus Avenue. He had made plans and was looking forward to seeing Michelle instead of staring at Jason and Angela all night. This figured to be his last quiet evening for a while if Randall struck again the next day. He dialed Michelle's cell phone, but it went to voicemail.

"Hey, it's me, Mike. I should be at the restaurant in fifteen minutes or so. If you're not there yet, give me a ring back and let me know your timing." He pushed the END button and frowned down at his phone. It was 6:56 and it was not likely that she was still at the lab. She had texted him at 4:30 that day to say that she was probably going to be early for their 7:00 dinner reservation. Mike had texted back to let her know that he might be running late, and she had responded "OK." So, where was she? Maybe her phone battery was dead. He shook his head and shoved his phone back into his pocket. Why was he so concerned? It didn't matter. He'd be there in a few minutes. He could not wait to kiss her again.

He got out of the cab at 7:20 after cursing the New York traffic all the way downtown. He paid the driver and took a mental note of the fact that he had been giving larger tips to cab drivers since he had started seeing Michelle. He walked quickly to the doorway of the Greek restaurant, pulled open the flimsy screen door, and walked inside. It was another beautiful fall day in New York, but the weather forecasters were predicting frost inside of a week. For tonight, though, Mike wore only his sport jacket. He scanned the crowded tables but did not see Michelle. He waited several minutes for the hostess standing at a battered wooden podium to finish talking to another customer before he could get her attention.

"Hi. I'm here to meet a woman, Doctor Michelle McNeill. I'm late for a seven o'clock reservation that was in her name."

"Oh, yes!" the hostess exclaimed. "Are you Mike? I have a message for you." She didn't wait for Mike to confirm his identity or show her any identification. She reached under the lip of the podium and pulled out a small envelope. He took it from her and thanked her, turning back toward the door as he squeezed between two elderly women who were directly behind him and anxious to get their name on the waiting list. Inside was sheet of paper that looked like it had been torn from a small notebook. As he cleared the ladies, he started reading the note and stopped in his tracks.

> *Hello, Detective Stoneman. You know me as Charles White. Dr. McNeill has made a house call for me and cannot come to your dinner. I will guarantee her safety as long as you follow my instructions. I am watching the restaurant. You will exit the building and stand next to the tree to the left of the door. I have access to your email, text messages, and telephone calls. Do not make any calls or try to send any messages, or I will disappear and you will never see Dr. McNeill again. If you are not outside within five minutes of entry, I will assume you are attempting to circumvent my instructions. Hurry.*

Mike glanced back at the hostess at the podium, where she was talking to the two old ladies. He wondered how much time had passed since he walked through the door and felt a bead of sweat slide down the side of his neck. He did not have much time. He scanned the group of people waiting for their tables who were milling around in the small foyer of the restaurant. He quickly picked out a woman who was looking at her phone. He took a step and was next to her.

"Excuse me," Mike said in a quiet but emphatic tone. He fished his wallet from his pocket and flipped it open, exposing his badge. "I am a detective with the New York Police Department. This is an emergency. I need you to call 9-1-1 right now and tell the operator that Mike Stoneman told you to call."

"What?" the startled woman responded, stepping backward.

"I have to go, right now," Mike said urgently. "Just call 9-1-1 and tell them Mike Stoneman told you to call. Mike Stoneman. Detective Mike Stoneman."

The woman looked shocked and confused.

"Just do it!" Mike shouted as he bolted for the door. He hurried outside and saw the tree planted in a square of unpaved ground next to the curb. In three steps he was standing next to the tree, and immediately his cell phone rang.

"Hello," Mike barked.

"You are tardy, Detective," a calm voice replied. "You were inside for seven and a half minutes. I assume that you have violated my directions. I'm sorry, but this is not acceptable. You will have to find a new Medical Examiner."

"Wait!" Mike shouted into his phone, glancing around at the people walking past on the sidewalk who were giving him puzzled looks. "No, wait, please. I had to wait for the hostess and it took her a while to find the note. I'm here. Don't hold that against Michelle."

Mike listened intently to the silence coming from his phone. After maybe twenty seconds, the calm voice spoke again. "I don't believe you, but it won't matter. Please raise your left arm over your head."

"What?" Mike replied, confused.

"Detective, I am a patient man, but I need you to follow my instructions without question. Raise your left arm."

Mike hesitated. What was Randall playing at? He had his phone in his left hand, pressed against his ear, so he raised his right arm over his head, feeling foolish.

"That is your right arm, Detective. Do you think I'm not watching? Do you think you can disobey me and I won't see?"

Mike quickly switched the phone to his right hand and thrust his left arm toward the branches of the tree. The sun had long since set, but the ever-present light of the City allowed Mike to see all around the vicinity. He scanned the sidewalk on both sides of the street, but saw nobody who looked like Randall.

"That's better. You will keep this line open on your phone. You will not try to send any text messages or emails or I will see them. You will not speak to anyone. You will follow my instructions exactly as I tell you. I will be watching. Doctor McNeill is safe, for now, and I'd prefer to keep her that way. But that's up to you."

"What do you want?" Mike said, trying to engage Randall in conversation, as he knew he should according to the hostage negotiation manual.

"I'm sorry, Detective. I neglected to explain that you are also not to talk. You will listen only. And right now, I want you to walk toward Sixth Avenue. Do not stop. Do not talk to anyone. Put the phone in the front breast pocket of your jacket while you walk, and take it back out when you get to the corner."

Mike stared at the phone screen. Did he dare try to send a text message despite Randall's instruction? Was the maniac really capable of killing Michelle if he violated his rules? Of course he was. And how the Hell was he able to see what Mike was doing?

"You're not walking!" the voice barked, loud enough to be heard without speakerphone. Mike stuffed the phone into his front pocket and started walking, trying to think, and starting to sweat even more. He reached the corner of Sixth Avenue and stopped, then extracted the phone and held it to his ear without speaking. He tried to hear any background noise that might tip him off to Randall's location, but heard nothing at all. Was he still watching? Mike turned around in a full circle, scanning the sidewalks and the parked cars while holding the phone in his left hand. He did not see anyone watching him.

"That's very graceful, Detective. Can you spin around again for me?"

"No, I'm dizzy," Mike spat out. "Where are you? Come on out and we can settle this like gentlemen." It was worth a try to see if he could get under the guy's skin a little bit, as long as Mike didn't piss him off to the point that he'd take it out on Michelle.

"We will, Detective. All in good time. Right now, I need you to stand right there and keep your eyes out for a blue Honda Civic that will be approaching from the south in about one minute. You will get into the back seat and say nothing to the driver. Do you understand? No talking at all, and do not contact anyone. Do you understand?"

"Yeah. I got it." Mike let the phone drop from his ear and scanned the northbound traffic, looking for his ride. He correctly figured that Randall was done talking for the moment. Within a minute, a blue Honda pulled up to the curb in front of Mike with the familiar Uber symbol displayed in the passenger-side window. Mike waved to the driver and got into the back seat.

"You Stone?" the driver asked.

"Yeah," Mike grunted.

"No talking!" Mike could hear Randall call out, although the phone was far from his ear.

Mike returned the phone to his ear and whispered, "Sorry."

"Put the phone on speaker," Randall ordered. Mike put the phone on his lap and pressed the speaker icon. "Juan, please drive," Randall's tinny voice called out. The driver pulled away from the curb.

Mike sat back, saying nothing and trying to think. He watched the traffic, looking for a police cruiser. When the Honda stopped at a red light at 21st Street, Mike saw a cab pull up on his right with a lone male passenger. Mike waved his hand back and forth in front of the window, trying to get the man's attention without making any noise. After a few seconds, the man looked toward Mike with a puzzled expression. Mike was about to start mouthing for the man to call 9-1-1 when Randall's voice crackled through the speaker. "I see that!"

Mike froze, spinning his head toward the front of the cab. Then he saw the driver's phone, mounted on the dashboard so he could see his GPS directions, except that instead of the usual electronic map on the screen, Mike saw a photograph of the gothic entranceway of what he recognized as the cathedral of St. John the Divine. A church. Mike concluded with a shudder that the phone was connected to a video chat of some kind, and the caller on the other end had substituted the church image for his own face. Randall could see inside the cab! Mike sat back again, not saying anything. He continued to scan the traffic around the Honda, now trying to figure out how to get a message to a passing cop without speaking or waving. Randall went back to silence, and the driver pulled forward with the green light.

Pedestrians dashed in front of the Honda whenever it was stopped at a light, but Mike could not figure out how to get their attention. He put on a poker face, knowing that Randall was watching. He tried to make eye contact with the driver whenever he glanced into his rearview mirror, but Juan did not seem interested in holding Mike's gaze. Mike surmised that Randall had given the driver instructions not to talk to Mike and to keep the phone pointed at the back seat. He wondered whether the video chat might drain the phone's battery, but then he saw that it was connected by a cord to a charging port. No possibility that it would fade out.

The thought prompted Mike to glance down at his own phone. The battery charge indicator was red, listing fourteen percent power remaining. With the call to Randall continuously connected, the battery would quickly drain. Mike wasn't sure whether that would help him or not. It would cut Randall off from the call, but he would still be connected by the video call on the driver's phone. He decided to risk picking up the phone, and held it up so that Randall would be able to clearly see him as he brought the speaker's microphone to his mouth and said softly, "I'm running out of battery."

"Of course you are," Randall's voice replied. "Please let me know when it is at two percent."

Mike frowned but kept quiet. He replaced the phone on his lap and looked up as the driver made a right turn on 57th Street and began heading east. He saw a black & white police cruiser pass by on his left, too fast for him to make any eye contact. At Third Avenue, a traffic enforcement agent in the middle of the intersection directed the vehicular flow, but Mike was not able to get more than a nod out of her before she turned her attention to the oncoming cars. Then the Honda turned left onto the ramp toward the Queensboro Bridge. Mike knew it had been renamed as the Ed Koch Bridge, but he refused to call it that. They were heading toward Queens.

The clatter of a subway train moving along next to the slow-flowing traffic created a racket. Mike quickly put his thumb over the phone's microphone and attempted to talk softly like a ventriloquist, without moving his lips, to communicate with his driver without Randall seeing anything suspicious on the video link.

"I'm a cop and this guy is a killer. Call 9-1-1 as soon as I'm outta the car."

Juan looked at Mike in the rearview mirror, holding his eyes longer than previously. Mike removed his thumb from the phone as the subway train pulled away, traveling faster than the vehicular traffic. He wasn't sure that Juan had understood him, but he was reasonably certain that Randall had not been able to hear or observe his communication.

The Honda crawled along Queens Boulevard for another twenty minutes, then picked up the Brooklyn-Queens Expressway before exiting onto the Long Island Expressway. The driver exited at Borden Avenue in the area known as Maspeth and followed the surface streets for another twenty minutes. They were making a series of left turns, going in a square pattern and covering the same ground. When they got to the second pass across Maurice Avenue, Mike looked down at his phone, which was at three percent battery.

"My phone battery is down to two percent," Mike said loudly, breaking a long silence within the car.

"Fine," came Randall's electronic voice. "Juan, please proceed to your final destination."

Juan made an unfamiliar turn down a side street and drove on for several minutes. The incessant glow of New York's artificial illumination lit up the landscape around him, but he was not familiar with this part of town. The clock on his phone stood at 9:42. Juan finally pulled to the curb in front of a nondescript building with a neon sign in what looked to Mike like Chinese characters. The building had no exterior windows, but a large door with leather padding dominated the front entrance, covered by a dark awning.

"Time to go, Detective," Randall's voice called out. "Please give Juan your phone."

Mike hesitated, trying to think what Randall was up to and how he was going to communicate with his Task Force without his phone. On the other hand, when he left the car without his phone, Randall would not be able to see him or hear him. Assuming he hadn't been followed somehow. "How will we communicate when I give up my phone?" Mike asked.

"You will go into the club and sit down at a table by yourself. I will contact you there."

Mike furrowed his brows but could not figure any way to avoid following the instruction. He handed the phone forward to Juan, once again placing his thumb over the microphone and mumbling "nine-one-one" without moving his lips as he turned his head away from the camera on the dashboard. He then nodded at the camera, opened the door on the passenger side, and exited the vehicle onto the sidewalk. He was still wearing his khaki slacks and blue sport jacket, his white dress shirt with a sweat stain around the collar, and his blue-and-orange striped tie slipped down several inches above the unbuttoned top button. He looked like any New York businessman after a long day at the office. He looked around, hoping to find someone on the sidewalk he could quickly talk to, but the place was deserted. He wondered if it got busy late at night, but for now it was empty.

Mike walked through the heavy, padded front door into the interior of the building, which turned out to be a nightclub where all the signage was in Chinese. There was music playing that Mike did not recognize and a dancer was gyrating on a raised stage at the back of the place, wearing a bikini with tassels on her breasts. There were a few dozen people in the place, all of whom appeared to be Asian, including the bartender, a strikingly tall woman wearing a black leather corset. It appeared to Mike to be a typical strip club, except that no hostess accosted him at the door and tried to interest him in a private dance. He looked around and easily found an unoccupied table far from the stage where he sat down, looking around to see if there were any cameras through which Randall could be watching.

After a minute, a waitress in a skimpy, kimono-like robe walked over with a black tray in her hand and asked Mike a question in Chinese. Mike looked at her, expressionless, then shrugged and held up his hands to indicate that he did not understand. She then tried again in heavily accented English.

"You Stone?"

Mike paused, then figured that this was part of Randall's plan so he nodded. He didn't make any attempt to talk to the waitress to get her to send a message to the police. Randall probably had a camera in here somewhere, and she probably didn't speak English well enough to make it a worthwhile attempt even if Randall wasn't watching. Given the shady nature of the establishment, she was likely very reticent to call the police here for him. Randall had planned it out well. Before he had a chance to consider any other options, the waitress was back with her tray held up. She plucked a small object from its flat surface and deposited a cell phone on the table. Mike picked it up and examined it. No manufacturer's logo was obvious; it was certainly a pre-paid burner. Totally untraceable. It was already turned on, with a call in progress.

"Yeah," Mike said loudly into the speaker, needing to shout above the music.

"You didn't tip your waitress, Detective."

"I'll get her when she brings me a drink. Are you going to join me?"

"Soon, Detective, very soon. Now it is time for you to take a little walk. Please exit the club the way you came in, and we can talk when you get outside the door. Leave the line open."

"I need to take a leak first."

"Hmm. I suppose that can be permitted. Keep the phone line open."

"You're going to listen to me piss?"

"I promise not to be embarrassed."

"Fine." Mike held the phone by his side as he walked toward the back of the club, where there was a neon sign with two sets of Chinese characters. He wasn't sure which was "men" and which "women," but he was pretty sure it was pointing him toward the bathrooms. He really did need to pee after spending nearly two hours in the cab, but he was in more need of time to think before he went outside. He guessed that Randall would have him walk around for a while until he got close to wherever his nemesis planned to spring his trap. What he needed was a way to get a message to Jason or Angela. He took a wrong turn on purpose when he got to the back of the room and glanced down at the phone's screen. He mashed a few buttons to bring up a browser, but the phone had no data service and could not connect to the internet. No way to send an email.

Mike slowly found his way to the bathroom and, helpfully, there was a stick figure on the door in addition to a Chinese character. He guessed that if Randall had tapped into the security cameras inside the club, they would not give him eyes inside the men's room. He entered a reasonably clean stall and carefully dropped his pants while holding the small phone. He sat on the toilet and set the handset down on top of the toilet paper dispenser.

"Hurry it up, Detective," Randall's voice crackled.

"Yeah, well I have a little business to do," Mike replied. He carefully scooped up the phone and clicked the icon for text messages, which brought up a box for the number of the receiving phone. Mike tapped in Jason's cell phone, which he knew by heart, then began emptying his bladder as loudly as he could manage while tapping his message:

911 maspeth now mike

He pressed the SEND button and watched the loading icon spin endlessly. Mike had to hold himself back from swearing, knowing that Randall was still listening. The device apparently was not able to send text messages while the phone line was active. He hoped that when the line was disconnected the message would send, but he would need to figure out how to disconnect the call without triggering retaliation from Randall.

Mike tore off some toilet paper, completed his business on the toilet and flushed. He picked up the phone from its perch on the dispenser and decided to take a chance. He dropped the phone, shouting out "Fuck!" as it clattered to the tile. He quickly reached down to pick it up and tapped the red box to end the call. Within seconds, the phone vibrated and Mike swiped across the screen to answer the new call. "I'm sorry, I dropped the phone," Mike quickly said before Randall could speak. "It was an accident, I'm sorry. Damn. I'm still here."

"That was very careless, Detective!" Randall shouted. "I think I should call this off and just kill Doctor McNeill."

"No!" Mike shouted back, not caring who might hear. "It was an accident. Don't hurt her! I'll do whatever you want."

There was silence on the phone. Mike could hear his heart beating loudly in his ears. He waited, saying nothing.

"There will be punishment for this, Detective. But for now, please immediately exit the club, turn right out of the door, and stop at the corner. You have twenty seconds."

Mike hitched up his trousers quickly and sprinted out of the bathroom, past the bar, and out the door. Panting, he rushed to the corner and stopped, holding the phone to his ear. "I'm – here," he said in between breaths.

"Good. Now walk along the side of the building down the street for three blocks to the stoplight. Keep the phone line open."

Mike started walking, slowly feeling his breath returning to normal, but his heart thumping in his ears and chest. He did not speak and did not hear Randall. He listened for anything on the other side of the phone line that would help him place Randall's location, or for Michelle's voice, but there was nothing. When he reached the corner, he said "I'm here."

"Turn left and walk until I tell you to stop."

Mike turned and started walking. He glanced at his watch. It was after 10:00. His stomach rumbled, reminding him that the dinner he and Michelle were supposed to have never materialized. He walked and wondered whether Jason had received his text.

Chapter 48 – Deception

A T THE SAME TIME that Mike was exiting the Greek restaurant, Jason and Angela were getting ready to head out from the war room when FBI Agent Simpson called. The killer had posted on his blog. With only a day to go before the next expected murder, the Task Force had decided to risk checking the blog more regularly, more worried about missing a post than about tipping him off that they were watching. Randall had put up a new post at 7:20 p.m.

October 26

The Day of Judgment is upon Centurion and I shall have my vengeance. The evildoers who have met their end at the hand of the Lord through my actions had no idea that their doom lay upon them. Centurion, however knows that the sword of Yahweh hangs over his head. He will be more vigilant and careful than the others, and so I shall surprise him. I have observed his routines and movements and when he emerges from his cave, I shall swoop down and pluck him from his perception of safety under the very noses of those who seek to provide protection.

Circumstances have conspired against me and have cut short my divine mission. Haman may yet face justice at the hands of the mortal authorities, but alas I shall not be the one to rain fire upon his head. Indeed, my epic shall not be completed, it seems, due to happenstance and the interference of the federal police. My sanctuaries have been defiled. I have retreated to safety and now my days of glory are limited. And yet God's justice must be meted out.

I have planned carefully, as the Lord has shown me I must, and I am confident that precision shall prevail in this instance. Tonight, there shall be no succor for Centurion.

The sound of trumpets shall ring through the Heavens on this night. I shall look over the dark waters and see the reflection of the moon as the eye of the Lord watching over me, and watching the demise of God's enemy.

"He's going for Forrest," Angela said as soon as she finished reading. "The reference to the moon on the water has to be the river. He's going to try to take him out when he goes out for his evening run along the river!"

"I'll get some units over to his apartment building," Jason said, "without lights. We want to be watching but we don't want to tip him off."

"I'll get some extra agents up from downtown and tell Forrest not to go out running until we have the team in place," Angela chimed in. "Call Mike, Mason, and Berkowitz and let them know to meet us there."

Jason decided to forego the phone and dashed down the stairs to Captain Sullivan's office to tell him what was happening. Sully, who was getting ready to leave for the day himself, told him to get going and that he would dispatch some black & whites to the area. Jason then tried calling Mike's cell, but it rolled immediately to voicemail. Either the phone was off or he was on the line. Jason sent Mike a text, then called Berkowitz and told him to get his ass and Mason's to the East Side. He met Angela in front of the precinct building, where they piled into an unmarked sedan and headed out with a uniformed officer driving.

"Try calling Mike again," he said as their driver popped the siren once to get through a clogged intersection. "I tried but got his voicemail."

Angela got out her phone and scrolled to Mike's cell number. After thirty seconds, she punched the END button. "Same for me – right to voicemail."

"He can't have turned his phone off," Jason muttered in a confused voice.

"Well, he might just be on his phone."

"Yeah, but who would he be talking to besides us?"

"Maybe his date is running late and he's politely talking to her while she's in a cab?"

"You're such a romantic," Jason deadpanned.

As they approached the neighborhood where Forrest's apartment was located, Jason slowed down and pulled up next to a parked squad car. He got out to compare notes with the uniformed officers. Angela tried Mike's phone again, but got only his voicemail. She left a quick message asking him to call her right away and that it was urgent. Then she got out and walked to where Jason was standing next to the officer.

"What do we have?"

"They have a perimeter set up from here to the river and three blocks north and south. Your FBI guys are inside the lobby and placed around the streets. So far no sighting of Randall."

"Is there any kind of command post?"

"This is it. Apparently, they were waiting for us."

"OK. We need a space where we can monitor communications."

The moon was just above the skyline as Jason stared toward the blackness of the East River in the distance. The wide concrete walkway along the river was illuminated by streetlights every twenty yards, and by the general glow of the New York night. Jason fixed a pair of binoculars on the iron railing separating the strolling couples and dog-walkers from the river, as if he would spot Randall walking down the path. Cars honked as they squeezed past the bottleneck in the street caused by the double-parked police cars. He crossed his arms over his chest and sighed. "Where the Hell is Mike?"

Chapter 49 – Treasure Hunt

MIKE WALKED for about twenty minutes until he came to a multi-way intersection. Unsure of which way to go, he spoke into the phone. "I'm at the intersection of Maspeth and Maurice. Which way?"

The line was silent. Mike stood on the edge of the curb and glanced up and down the wide avenue, watching the pedestrian signals count down to the next red light. He scanned for any passing police cars or people he could flag down without speaking. There were no other pedestrians on the street, which he guessed was normal for the industrial area.

"Continue following Maspeth Avenue," Randall's voice said at last.

"Do I need a bodyguard down there?" Mike asked seriously.

"Probably. Start walking."

Mike complied and continued down the narrowing street with sparsely spaced streetlights. In between the dim lights, Mike figured that Randall could not really see him, even if he had a camera somewhere on the street. He looked down at the phone's screen and swiped his finger until he found an icon he recognized as a flashlight function, and pressed it. A bright light shot out of the top of the phone next to the camera lens, lighting up the sidewalk in front of him. Randall did not react, suggesting to Mike that he was not under surveillance. If challenged, Mike would say that he needed the light to avoid the potholes in the crumbling sidewalk. He hoped that the flashlight function would suck battery life out of the phone.

At the next intersection, Mike paused and asked Randall which way he should go.

"Straight," was the terse response.

Mike kept going, crossing over 49th Place, then slowing down to take stock of his surroundings. The main avenue he had been on earlier at least had a few restaurants and bodegas that were open and had lights on. This side street was deserted and flanked by the drab cinderblock walls of large buildings that looked like warehouses or factories. He could not see any signage and there were no cars parked along the curb, which was marked by "no standing" signs. It felt to Mike like he had to be getting close. Why send him down a side street like this just to run him around?

"I'm doing what you want, Randall. Why not let Doctor McNeill go now? You'll have me exactly where you want me in a few minutes, so you don't need a hostage anymore."

Mike listened for a response or reaction, but got only silence. He puzzled over the killer's lack of a snappy retort for a few seconds, then grunted and smacked his left palm against his forehead. Idiot! He had used Randall's name. Up to that point, Randall did not know Mike knew his real identity. Mike had tipped him off, and now Randall was thinking about whether this information was important – whether it compromised him at all. Mike tried to get him talking.

"Hey! Are you there? Come on, are we doing this or what?" Mike stopped walking so he could listen more intently without hearing his footfalls on the sidewalk.

After another pause, Randall's voice came through in its usual calm manner. "I am here, Detective. I must, however, decline your suggestion. The lovely doctor will remain my guest for the present. I would suggest that you resume walking."

Mike shrugged and continued down the sidewalk. He wondered whether Randall had him under visual surveillance or just had a GPS tracking device in the phone. Looking around at the barren landscape and the dim lighting, he thought it unlikely that he was on camera. He decided to test the theory by reaching his free hand into his pocket and pulling it out, then staring at his palm and pretending to dial a phone. He held his palm up to his ear as if making a call, waiting to see if Randall said anything to scold him or to instruct him to stop, but there was no reaction. He was still walking, so Randall was apparently content to track his movement without having eyes on him. Mike wondered whether there was any way to let Jason track the GPS signal from the phone. But, even if he could get a message to Jason, he did not know how to find the information in the phone for the GPS. He knew it was possible, but he could not do it without some IT geek walking him through it. "Sucks being the old guy," he thought to himself.

At the next intersection, he kept walking straight ahead. A chain link fence on the far corner was illuminated by a dim street light. Mike could almost make out an empty space behind the fence, either a vacant lot or a parking lot – he couldn't be sure in the dimness. Another dark, warehouse-looking hulk of a building rose up behind the empty space, windowless and menacing. Mike scanned the corner for possible camera locations, but saw none that looked like much of a candidate.

"Turn right at the next corner," Randall's voice ordered.

Mike slowed his pace, trying to take stock of the neighborhood. The large, dark building on his right obstructed any view of the rest of the block. On the opposite side of the street, the dark waters of a creek or estuary lapped up on the muddy edges of a vacant lot. The nearly full moon shone down and shimmered on the murky surface. The moonlight added a tiny incremental light to the shadowy scenery. There were no markings or signs that he could use as landmarks. He did not want to stop moving, but was not in a hurry to get to the end of this particular treasure hunt.

Chapter 50 – Finding Centurion

THE TASK FORCE and their FBI backup had been on high alert for more than ninety minutes and everyone was starting to think they had been led on a wild goose chase. Then the call came over the radio. One of the FBI agents positioned on the walkway near the river had spotted their suspect. He was wearing a black New York Yankees windbreaker despite the unusually mild temperature, along with a matching baseball cap pulled down low over his eyes. He was sitting on a bench with his back to the river. The bench was in between streetlights, making it hard to get a good look at the man's face, but he seemed to be watching the path that led from Agent Forrest's apartment building to the river walk. According to the report, the man was just staring at the path like he was waiting for someone.

That was enough to send the team into motion. Two agents were dispatched to cut off his exit routes to the north and two more took up positions to the south. Two uniformed officers and a backup car were positioned on the street in front of the building, cutting off the immediate route out into the city, while two more were sent to monitor the building lobby and direct residents to exit in a different direction while the operation was running. All the agents and officers were careful to stay out of the sight line of the suspect.

There were two uniformed officers with Jason and Angela at the command post. One of them, a tall white guy with a crewcut who looked to be no older than twenty, turned to Jason and asked, "Why don't we just bust this guy if we think he's the Menstrual Killer?"

Jason was annoyed by the question, but then softened his attitude, realizing that this was just a young cop who didn't know any better. He pondered how Mike would handle it and decided to give out a little training to the rookie. "We could grab him, of course, but the problem is that we don't have any evidence that he's our killer. We didn't find any incriminating evidence in his apartment. We have him on camera at the building where the last murder was committed, but no physical evidence links him to the actual kill. He had a company with an office in the building, so he had a reason to be there. Sure, he was using a fake name, and we have him on a tapped phone call setting up a meeting with the dead guy using a different fake name that happens to match the fake name used by the guy we think probably poisoned another of the victims, but it's a lot of circumstantial stuff that a good lawyer would shred apart in court. We need to catch him doing something that will incriminate him. We're hoping he'll make a play for Forrest and we can bust him in the act."

The officer, whose name plate read "LaBlonde," nodded. "I don't know, it seems like maybe we should just let this kook keep taking out these scumbags. So far he's doing a pretty good job of picking people I'd be happy to put a bullet in."

"We're not here to decide who gets to kill whom," Jason snapped. "How would you feel if his next victim was your mother?" Before Officer LaBlonde could reply, the earpiece in Jason's right ear sprang to life. Agent Forrest was being directed to go for his evening run and he came bounding out of the building wearing his usual track suit with a heavy sweatshirt despite the relatively warm evening. He had a Kevlar vest under that sweatshirt but he loped easily down the path to the river walk. He jogged right past the bench where the man in the Yankees windbreaker was sitting. A dozen agents and cops watched as the man turned his head to follow the jogger, but he did not move from the bench. Agent Forrest passed under a street lamp and then disappeared into the darkness before reappearing in the pool of light twenty yards or so farther south.

Jason and Angela listened to the chatter of the agents from their position at the command post. They figured that their killer might recognize them if they made an appearance at the stakeout. So, as frustrating as it was to just sit and wait, they had no choice. The agents were keeping tabs on Forrest, who was under instructions to run his normal route. It took him south along the river for 1.55 miles and then back again, and would normally take him between twenty-four and twenty-six minutes. It was already after 9:30. Jason chewed on an energy bar while Angela sipped a tepid coffee. According to the surveillance, their suspect had not moved from the bench.

Jason reached for his phone and dialed Mike for the tenth time, then punched the END button as soon as the call rolled to voicemail. Then he dialed a different number. "Hey, Phyllis, it's Detective Jason Dickson, ID number 35953. I've been trying to contact Detective Mike Stoneman. He hasn't been answering his cell phone. Can you ask the command center to check the GPS for his phone and see if they can get a twenty on him? . . . Sure, I'll wait." Jason paced along the curb next to the squad car that was blocking the street from oncoming traffic. After two minutes, he stopped pacing. "Queens? Where? . . . OK, can you please dispatch a black & white to that location? . . . Yes. Consider it an 11-99. Thanks." Jason hung up and turned to Angela with a puzzled expression.

"What was that about Queens?" Angela asked.

"I ran a trace on Mike's cell and it came up in Maspeth, Queens."

"That's weird. Did he say anything to you about going to Queens tonight?"

"No. He was supposed to be meeting McNeill for dinner. He

told me that he didn't want to be out late since we're going to be on kill watch all day tomorrow."

"Did you try calling Doctor McNeill?"

Jason scowled at his phone and dropped his chin. "No. I didn't." Jason searched his phone until he found the doctor's number, but realized that it was the number at the lab. "I don't have her cell," he grumbled, then dialed dispatch and asked the operator to track down the Medical Examiner's cell phone number and call him back.

"Any idea what he might be doing in Queens?" Angela asked.

"None."

The voices over the surveillance radio crackled in Jason's ear. Agent Forrest had turned around and was heading back north. The suspect was still on the bench. "Twelve or thirteen minutes until he gets back," Jason sighed. Then his phone buzzed.

"Dickson . . . Yes . . . Can you connect me? . . . Thanks." Jason pressed the phone against his left ear while he continued to listen to the surveillance chatter through the earpiece in his right. After a pause, he spoke into the handset. "Doctor McNeill, it's Jason Dickson. It's important that I contact Mike, so if you get this message please call me back." Jason noted the time as 9:56 and left his cell number before hanging up.

"They both have their cell phones turned off?" Angela said with a sly smile.

"I'm not happy about this," Jason said much more seriously. "It's not like Mike to be out of touch this long. If his phone is really in Queens, then either it's been stolen from him, which is not likely, or Mike is in Queens, which makes no sense. If he's not with Doctor McNeill, then why is she not answering her phone? She's the M.E., so she has to be available in case of an emergency situation. If she is with Mike and neither of them are answering their phones, then why would they be in Queens? It's all wrong."

"What can we do?"

"I already dispatched a squad car to the location of his phone and told them to treat it as an 'officer needs help' situation. We'll see what the uniforms find there."

Before they could continue the conversation, the surveillance team crackled to life over the radio. Their suspect had moved from his bench and was walking south. Forrest was still several minutes away. "He's on an intercept course," one of the agents said. "We're following behind. Send a unit down to 59th Street to cut him off from that direction."

Jason turned to Angela. "Forget waiting," he exclaimed as he started jogging in the direction of the river walk. He knew they would not be able to catch up to their killer, but he wanted to be close by when the bust went down. Angela followed, keeping up remarkably well in her heels.

They both listened to the radio chatter while they hurried toward the action. The suspect was still walking south along the river walk. Agent Forrest was still jogging northbound and was about two minutes from meeting up if the suspect kept up his current leisurely pace. The two agents who had been monitoring the southern edge of the stakeout area fell into step fifty feet behind the suspect, who was walking with his hands in his jacket pockets. One of the agents murmured that he might have a gun or a knife in one of those pockets. Two more agents reported that they had taken up positions south of Forrest and were now following him up the river walk.

Forrest continued to jog north. "Move in!" came the call over the radio as the two figures came closer together. The agents hustled forward toward the suspect, not wanting him to be in proximity to Agent Forrest without an escort. The suspect made no move toward Forrest, who made eye contact with the agents whom he could see right behind the man in the Yankees cap and jacket. He was ten feet away, then five. Then he passed by the man and skidded to a stop right behind the two surveillance agents, who stopped to catch him from falling down. When they turned around, the Yankees jacket was still walking south, seemingly oblivious to the activity taking place behind him.

"Do we take him?" came the question over the radio.

"Yes! Go! Move in!"

All of the agents, including Forrest, ran toward the jacket. The agents coming from the north arrived first, tackling him from behind. One agent planted a knee into the suspect's back while the other pulled his gun and stood five feet away.

"Stay down! Stay down! FBI! You're under arrest!"

The two agents approaching from the south panted up to the scene, guns drawn. They took up positions surrounding the suspect, as the New Yorkers who had been out enjoying the warm October evening backed away far enough to be safe, but close enough to see what was happening. The agent perched on the suspect's back cuffed his hands behind his back and patted down the jacket, but found nothing resembling a weapon. He rolled the man over onto his back and straddled his chest, gun pointed at his face. A dark patch began to spread around the suspect's crotch. The agent stood up, still keeping his gun pointed at the man's head.

The man in the Yankees cap had closed his eyes and was sobbing. "Please don't shoot me! Please don't shoot me!"

The agent backed away a step and left the man on the ground, hands cuffed behind his back with four FBI agents surrounding him. The agents remained at full alert as Jason ran up to the scene, huffing from the run down the river walk. Angela followed twenty yards behind.

He walked to the man on the ground and shouted down at him. "What's your name!"

The man blubbered, "Don't shoot me, please don't shoot me!"

Jason motioned to the agents to step back and lower their guns. The man did not seem to be much of a threat in his present position. "OK, OK, fine. The guns are down. Nobody is going to shoot you." Jason lowered his voice and changed his tone from angry to soothing. "You're alright. My name is Detective Jason

Dickson, NYPD. Tell me your name."

The man stopped crying and took a few breaths. He looked up at Jason. "M-M-Marshall. M-M-My name is M-Marshall. Marshall Johnson." The man's lip quivered as he looked up at the menacing Black cop towering over him.

"Where do you live, Mister Johnson?"

The man looked confused. "I'm . . . well . . . I don't have . . . . I mean I live on the street, sir."

Jason frowned. "You live on the street? You mean you're homeless?" The man nodded.

Jason looked closely at the man's face. It was mottled and dirty. A few wisps of stringy, grey-blond hair dangled from under the ball cap. Jason reached down and removed the hat, revealing a matted tangle of hair that appeared not to have been washed in some time. The hat itself, however, had a holographic, metallic sticker attached to the bill and looked off-the-shelf new. "Where'd you get this hat and this jacket?"

The man, who now looked even less like Ronald Randall, looked up with fear on his face. "A guy. He gave me some money and some clothes. He told me not to tell. I was in the park, see. He told me to come over here tonight and he was gonna meet me and give me some more money after I did what he said. I didn't do nothing wrong. I didn't do nothin'."

Jason scowled and took a step back, stretching his back. He turned to the nearest agent. "Take this man back to the precinct and hold him there. He's not our guy."

The agents dutifully hoisted Johnson off the ground, careful not to touch the urine-stained area of his pants, and led him off in the direction of the black & white that was parked on the street a block away. Jason turned to Agent Forrest. "You good?"

"Sure," the agent responded. "What the Hell just happened?"

"I'm not sure," Jason said, removing his ear piece. "You should go back to your apartment. You guys go with him," he ordered, gesturing at the other two agents who had chased the suspect down minutes before. "Keep your eyes open. Randall seems to have created a diversion here, which we fell right into like putzes. He may still be here somewhere, waiting to catch us when our guard is down."

The agents began walking northward toward Forrest's apartment building. Then Angela came over to Jason's side. "What's Randall playing here?"

"You tell me. You're the expert on psycho behavior."

"Well, he's certainly trying to throw us off. Do you think this has anything to do with Mike being out of communication?"

Jason nodded, reaching for his phone. He planned to call dispatch to see if they had heard from the cruiser he had sent to Mike's phone's location. When he looked down at his screen, however, he noticed a text message waiting. He touched the icon to reveal the text:

911 maspeth now mike

"Holy shit," Jason mumbled.

"What?"

Jason handed the phone to Angela so she could see the message for herself. "We need to get out to Queens."

Jason turned to start moving back toward where their car was parked. Angela, however, grabbed his arm to stop him. "How do we know that the text message is really from Mike? We know that this guy is a tech wiz. What if he is sending us this message to pull us away?"

"How can we know for sure either way?" Jason asked. "It seems like the kind of message Mike would send if he was in a hurry. If it's a fake, then it's a good one."

"Let's go, but let's not abandon this location. I'll keep the agents here watching Forrest. We don't want to leave him vulnerable if Randall is really here."

"Fine. Let's go."

Chapter 51 – Reeling in the Fish

MIKE MADE THE RIGHT TURN at the corner, around the windowless building he had been skirting for the past several minutes. This street was darker than the last one, with lights spaced farther apart and somehow dimmer. The ambient light from the rest of the neighborhood and the moon cast eerie shadows. Mike peeked at his watch. It was past 11:00.

Then it hit him. In a little while, it would be Saturday. All this running around Queens was as much to kill time as to make him anxious and tired and to ensure that he was not being followed. By the time he got to the kill site, it would be the last Saturday of the month. It seemed to Mike that this was as good a time as any to try to get Randall talking. He pressed the phone against his face and spoke as casually as he could.

"Why the last Saturday of the month, Randall? What's the significance of that? I can see that it's almost midnight now, so soon it will be Saturday, which is the day you kill, but it's been bugging me that I can't figure out why. I know that you are a religious man and the Bible means a lot to you, so is it as simple as that? It's the biblical Sabbath? Is that it?"

Mike stopped walking, waiting for a response. He wondered how close he was to the kill site, and whether Randall had a camera on him here on the dimly lit sidewalk. He knew that Randall was tracking the GPS on the phone and would figure out that Mike had stopped moving, but at this point he was pretty sure that his adversary would be focused on getting him to whatever location was the final destination of this forced march. Randall would not give up now that he was so close. He knew this, and yet his stomach was still in a knot over the miniscule possibility that he could be wrong and Michelle could still be in danger. He wished he could consult with Angela.

"The Lord's work ceases on the Sabbath, Detective, yet the Angel of God does not rest."

"Is that an answer?" Mike was trying not to be unnecessarily provocative, but he wanted this guy to start interacting with him. He needed to find something that might give him an edge, or some information. Right now, he was flying blind and Randall had all the advantages.

"It's as much of an answer as you're going to get, Detective Stoneman."

"Why don't you just call me Centurion?"

The phone line was silent, but Mike thought he could hear Randall breathing. Although Mike had been stopped on the sidewalk for several minutes now, the killer had not mentioned it or instructed Mike to keep moving. Either he was not paying attention to the GPS blip, or he didn't care. Mike did not fill the silence. That was one of his five pillars of interrogation technique. Once you have asked a question, let the silence intimidate the witness – let them feel uncomfortable with their absence of a response. Silence bothers people. He hoped that Randall was susceptible to the ploy. But the phone line stayed silent. Now it was a game of chicken to see who would speak first.

"You do not know the significance of Centurion, Detective." Randall's words were clipped; his voice seemed slightly angry.

"I understand that Centurion is different from your other victims. The others all deserved to die because they were evil people. Meting out the plagues of Egypt upon them was justice in your eyes, right?"

"I am so pleased that you recognize the divine plan. You must understand that what I do, I do as the agent of the Lord."

"But Centurion is different. Centurion is not a bad person. I wonder whether you really have your heart in this one. Maybe you don't really want to kill Centurion." Mike was encouraged that he had Randall talking. He needed to turn the conversation to information that might help keep him alive.

"Death is a part of life, Detective. When God decrees that one must die, no man can stay the scythe. It is not for me to judge. I am but the hand of the Lord."

Mike took a breath, trying to maintain a calm tone. "And you have done your work, but now it's time to stop. Now it's time to rest, Lieutenant Randall. You don't really want to kill me, or Doctor McNeill. You kill for justice, not for spite or for protection. When the world reads your story, you want them to understand that you were working for the greater good, not that you were a cop killer."

"The greater good cannot be fulfilled if I am not permitted to complete my tasks. You and your FBI helpers have diverted me from the true path."

"You have already accomplished so much," Mike said, hoping to feed the man's ego. "You have eradicated six bits of garbage from this world. I know you planned to continue on to complete the group of ten, but perhaps you should rest, as the Lord did after six days. Perhaps this is the time to stop."

"Perhaps you will best me in combat. Perhaps not. Only the Lord can know. The time has come to find out. Come, Detective. Come to me and find your destiny. Walk forward to the next intersection and you will find your doctor."

Chapter 52 – On the Scent

JASON AND ANGELA grabbed a ride in a black & white squad car, which crawled across the Ed Koch Bridge, despite its flashing lights. The address where the command center last had a fix on Mike's cell phone was a Chinese strip club on 58th Street in Maspeth.

"You were right, Jason," Angela said softly.

"About what?"

"About Mike possibly being Centurion."

"Yeah. Great. I've been right about a few things during this case. I'd rather be wrong."

The squad car weaved through traffic, shaving off a few minutes from the slow trip across the bridge. The uniformed officer in the front seat called in their destination to the dispatcher, who advised him that another patrol car would meet them there.

Angela studied a map of Queens on her phone. She worked outwards from the location of the strip club, looking for a likely hiding place for their killer and knowing that it was a fantasy that she would just see something jump out at her from Google Maps – maybe a building labeled "criminal hideout."

Jason's phone rang and he quickly swiped to answer. "Dickson . . . Yes . . . Okay, we're already en route. Did he give a name? . . . Of course. Thanks."

"What?" Angela asked as soon as Jason punched the END button.

"Dispatch got a call, anonymous, from a driver saying he had a cop in his car who told him to call 9-1-1. Says he dropped off the cop, named Stone, in Maspeth at the same location where Mike's phone was last known to be."

"What time was that?"

"Just before 10:00."

"I guess that settles the question of whether the text message was really from Mike."

They pulled up to the curb next to another squad car with its lights flashing. Angela and Jason spoke briefly with the uniformed officer standing outside the door to the windowless façade, who informed them that Mike was not inside. Angela suggested that they question the manager and staff to see if anybody had seen Mike, but once inside, it became clear that finding someone who spoke English and who was willing to cooperate was not going to be easy.

The manager came out of a back room after a wait of several minutes. He was a short, thin man of Chinese extraction, with small eyes and a scar running down the left side of his face from ear to mouth. He seemed to understand what Jason and Angela were saying, but said he knew nothing, saw nothing, and declined to act as a translator so that Angela could interview the waitress and bartender.

"How would you like to have a health inspection every week for the next year?" Jason asked angrily.

"Go ahead, we serve no food here," the manager shot back without seeming to be concerned.

"You have cameras in here?" Jason demanded.

"Sure," the manager admitted with a shrug.

"Let me see the video from tonight."

"Fuck you," the smaller man said, puffing out his chest. "You got a warrant?"

Jason raised his hand as if he was going to strike the manager, but held back. The little man did not flinch.

"Let's get some air," Angela suggested, tugging Jason in the direction of the door. She pulled him back outside, where Jason promptly hit the padded door with his open palm, landing the blow with a loud smack.

"Even if we saw some video and confirmed that Mike was here, how would it help us?" Angela said. "Let's assume he was here. The real question is, where did he go? Either his phone is off or the battery is dead. We have no location based on that. If he left, it had to be either on foot or in a car."

"He had to get here in a car," Jason said, pacing back and forth in front of the club's massive door and planting a punch into the padding each time he passed. "If Randall got him here in a car, why have him get out if he was going to get into another car? If it were me, I'd have him walking from here."

"Agreed," Angela said. "He has to be somewhere within walking distance. That may be wrong, of course, but it's the only theory we have, so let's go with it. What time is it?"

"What?" Jason threw out his left hand to pull back his shirt cuff and looked down at his gold-colored Citizen watch. "It's a quarter to twelve."

"So, it's almost midnight. That means it's almost Saturday."

"Right," Jason said, blowing out some breath into the October night. "That makes sense. Should we have the squad cars start cruising around the side streets?"

"Can't hurt," Angela said without much enthusiasm. "Needle in a haystack, but that's all we have."

Jason went back to the squad car in which they had arrived. Before he could ask the officer to call dispatch, however, the radio crackled and the dispatcher put out a call for any units in the vicinity of 49th Place in Maspeth that were available to respond to a fire alarm. The officer in the front seat punched the call button and asked for the attention of the dispatcher. Then Jason grabbed his arm.

"How close are we to that alarm call?"

"Beats me, Detective. I work Manhattan," he responded. Then he called out to the officer on the sidewalk from the other unit. "Hey, Scott — how far are we from the alarm call that just came in?"

The officer paused, thinking, then called back, "Maybe two miles or so. Why?"

Jason looked at Angela. "Needle?"

"Why not?"

Jason slid over in the back seat of the patrol car to make room for Angela and called out to their driver. "Let's go check it out."

Chapter 53 – Showdown

WHEN MIKE ARRIVED at the next intersection, he saw another large, squat building that looked like a warehouse on the far corner, with a long wall extending down the block to his right. Ten feet or so from the corner of the building, a single light glowed above a doorway, illuminating a white sign reading: "NiDi Exports, Ltd." The name rang a bell somewhere in the back of Mike's brain, but he couldn't place it. Mike could see light peeking out from the interior. The door was ajar.

"Come and get me, Detective," Randall's voice said through the phone.

Mike pressed the red button on the phone's screen to end the call. Then he quickly dialed 9-1-1, but the call did not connect. He looked at the screen and saw "no service." Could Randall have somehow killed the burner phone remotely? Could he be blocking cell service at this location? Mike tossed the phone onto a scrubby bush next to the sidewalk. He didn't want Randall tracking his movements through its GPS.

As he neared the corner and approached the open door, he reached inside his jacket and pulled out his service weapon. All evening, he had wondered why Randall had allowed him to keep his Glock. Surely, he was smart enough to know that Mike might have his gun with him. Perhaps Randall wanted Mike to have a gun. Why? Was he planning to stage a duel? Was he so confident that he could kill Mike that he didn't care if the detective had a weapon? Whatever the explanation, Mike was happy to feel the metal in his hand.

As he slowly approached the building, Mike held the Glock at his side, elbows stiff with both hands on the smooth handle. He went past the doorway, keeping himself twenty feet or so away from the side of the building. He tried to scan the interior through the small open space between the door and the jamb, but he could not see anything. When he got about fifteen feet past the door, he scampered to the wall and pressed his back against the cinderblocks. Then he scuttled back along the wall until he reached the door.

"This has to be a trap," Mike muttered to himself. He moved away from the door and walked back to the scrubby bushes where he had tossed Randall's burner phone. He had to get down on his hands and knees, but he eventually saw a reflection off the glass screen and scooped it up. Then he hustled back to the wall next to the entry door. He carefully placed the thin phone on the ground in the crack between the door and the jamb. He hoped it would block the door from locking behind him after he went through.

Mike took in a deep breath and held it, then reached out and pulled open the steel door. He darted through, gun raised, his eyes scanning the scene. He could feel the throbbing of his pulse in his ears and felt a trickle of sweat meandering down his right eyebrow. Without a spare hand with which to wipe it away, he ignored it. He paused with his back against the inner wall, letting his eyes adjust to the sudden brightness.

The room was a cavernous warehouse space with no interior walls or partitions. It was lit by several banks of fluorescent lights high above the bare white floor. Mike noticed an EXIT sign above a door on the far side of the room that looked to be similar to the one he had just come through. Next to the far door a huge, shiny, square of corrugated metal ran from floor to ceiling, fully twenty feet across. Mike assumed this was some kind of access door for merchandise to flow to the rear portion of the warehouse, probably carried by fork lifts. For now, the gateway was closed. Looking up, Mike could see windows along the top of the interior walls, perhaps fifteen feet off the floor, but they were blacked out. He could make out a few cracks around the edges where the painters had not been careful to fill in every centimeter.

There was random debris scattered on the white floor, as if there had been an organized installment here once that had been packed up and moved out. In the center of the space, a platform rose off the floor two feet or so like the dais in a banquet room. Mike figured that the far door was the most likely path to Randall, but he also knew that Randall was not stupid enough to make it easy to get there. The door was at least two hundred feet away across the expanse of open space. There was no possible cover inside the warehouse.

"What am I doing here without backup?" Mike muttered to himself. Randall was a planner. He would not have picked this location at random or hastily. He would have figured out all the angles and have backup plans and escape routes. "He knows this building. He has a big home-field advantage," Mike whispered to an imaginary partner.

There were no other doors except the one at the far end of the main vault. Mike didn't want to be exposed by rushing across the open expanse of the room, so he carefully started moving to his left, away from the door he had just come through, keeping his back against the wall and his gun out in front of him. Randall may have the home-court advantage, but he wasn't going to sneak up behind Mike. When he was twenty feet or so away from the door, the lights went out and the door slammed shut. The room was thrown instantly into inky darkness. Then Mike heard a voice, amplified and coming from all around him as if there were speakers on all sides of the room. It sounded like the voice of God in the otherwise silent space.

"Welcome, Detective Stoneman," the voice boomed. Mike chose not to return the greeting. He opened his eyes as wide as he could, hoping that his pupils would dilate enough for him to see something, but he could not even make out his gun at the end of his arm. "This was supposed to be used as the location for the ninth plague – darkness." Randall's voice filled the expansive space, echoing off the bare walls. Mike had no way of getting a fix on the location of the speaker, if he was even in the room. "It is fitting that the place where Abel carried out his tainted trade should be the site where another of his evil compatriots would meet their end. Here, where there is only darkness. But I am now forced to employ the darkness as the setting for this final encounter between the two of us."

"Show yourself, Randall!" Mike shouted into the void. "Come out here and meet me like a man." Mike wasn't sure Randall was even there, but he couldn't just listen quietly any longer. He knew he was giving away his position by speaking, but he figured Randall probably already knew where he was. If Randall had set up a lightless room as a kill site, he had to have night-vision or infrared goggles so that he could see his target. The question was whether Randall was watching him from some vantage point outside, or if he was in the room, somewhere nearby.

"I am not a man, Detective. I have a purpose far beyond being a mere man. I am the Angel of the Lord. You have prevented me from fulfilling my destiny. You have chased me and while you cannot catch me, you have thwarted me. I am ready to end the quest for now, but first the Lord has commanded that you pay the price for your blasphemous interference. You shall substitute for Haman and you shall succumb to the darkness."

Mike stopped moving, listening carefully for any sound of Randall breathing or moving. He heard nothing. He still could see nothing. "I'm not evil like Abel, or Napoleon, or Pilate. I haven't done harm to the world. Do you truly think that God wants my death? Do you believe that the Lord will be happy with you if you kill me?" Mike fell silent, again listening for movement. Instead he got only the loudspeaker voice.

"God has commanded me, and my actions can't be other than divinely controlled. You shall die and I shall be forced to flee and finish my quest in the future. The time has come."

"Like Hell it has," Mike mumbled as he made a dash back toward the door. He held his right hand against the wall as he ran until his fingers felt the door jamb. He slammed his shoulder into the door and it gave way with a creak and a crunching noise. When the door opened into the Queens night, there was enough light for him to look down and see the mangled wreckage of the cell phone, its screen shattered and the body bent nearly in half to conform to the shape of the door that had smashed into it. But the little unit had done its job. Mike hurried through and allowed the door to slam shut behind him, wedging the phone back into the opening.

Mike turned and put his back against the outer wall of the warehouse, breathing hard from the exertion. He brushed the sweat out of his eyes with his jacket sleeve as he pondered his next move. He could run and try to find a phone and call for back-up, but by then Randall would surely have escaped. And what about Michelle? Randall had not injured any bystanders so far, but if he was pissed off at Mike for spoiling his kill, would he take it out on her? He couldn't risk that. He dropped his arms, letting his gun dangle in his right hand. The muscles in his elbows and forearms ached from holding the weapon at attention for so long. He flexed each arm, easing the tension.

Then Mike moved past the doorway along the edge of the building until he reached the corner. He peeked around, looking down the long side of the warehouse. In the dim ambient light, he could make out a long swath of what was once grass, but was now a wasteland of garbage and clumps of crabgrass. The place had not been tended for a while. Beyond the field of detritus, Mike could make out a stretch of concrete. He crept silently along the cinderblock wall until he could make out the indentations of loading docks. The concrete Mike had spied was a ramp that sloped down toward the metal loading bay doors. There were at least fifteen bays for semi-trailers to back into and receive their freight.

At the far end of the loading bays, Mike thought he could make out a twin to the concrete wall where he was now standing. Mike had seen such loading zones in action and knew that there would be separate doorways for humans to enter the interior, probably on both ends of the loading dock and maybe even in the middle since the dock was so long. He estimated the distance he had traveled along the exterior wall and then tried to picture where the far doorway was inside the cavernous room he had first entered. It seemed likely that the door shielded the forward room from the loading zone that lay behind these loading bay doors. If Randall had been monitoring him from outside the large main room, it was probably from somewhere on the loading dock side of that door.

Mike dropped down over the wall at its lowest point and then hugged the concrete against his left shoulder until he was standing directly under the first loading bay with his head resting against a large rubber bumper. Then he ducked his head just below the level of the loading dock and hustled down the line toward the far end. He hoped to enter the building from the opposite side, as far away as possible from where Randall had likely set up shop. He was out of breath and sweating profusely again by the time he reached the far end, where the steel door bore the number 16. He clambered up a four-rung ladder affixed to the side of the bay and up toward the dock.

Once on the dock platform, he was exposed and had no time to hesitate. He slid toward a doorway next to the last loading gate. As he moved, he glanced up at the corner where the overhanging awning of the loading dock met the main building and froze for a moment. He could make out a tiny red light atop a small black box mounted in an iron cage. A security camera. This building had been uninhabited for some time, but that red light indicated a live feed. Mike flinched slightly. His first instinct was to raise his gun and shoot out the camera, but then he thought better of the idea.

He averted his eyes, hoping that Randall might not have seen his glance toward the corner. There was no way to avoid being seen by the electronic eye, and there were probably many others around the building, but maybe if his adversary thought he was oblivious to the security system, Mike could catch him being overconfident.

Mike slowly approached the human-sized door next to the loading bay and pushed gently, then harder against the long bar in the center, but the bar did not depress and the metal sheet did not budge. He looked for some kind of entry plate or security pad and found it to the left of the door. Mike had no hope of hot-wiring the door lock. He looked down to see whether there was any kind of lever he might use to pry open the door and noticed a small gap between the bay door and the floor of the dock. It was the kind of door that rolled up on wheeled casters like a garage door. Mike wedged his fingers under the rubber padding at the bottom and pulled up, expecting to need a great exertion of effort to force open the edifice. But the metal slid easily upwards at his first tug, throwing him momentarily off balance as the thin aluminum made a grinding sound, followed by a loud clang when it reached the end of its track. The sound echoed in the otherwise silent setting. Mike dashed inside and put his back against the wall next to the pedestrian door, raising his gun in front of his chin.

Mike could immediately see the skeleton of the abandoned warehouse operation. Rows of metal conveyors lined the loading dock bays, two leading to each opening. Ten feet inside the bay doors, the conveyors with their rows of metal rollers curved into a spider web of similar belts, spreading out like a bizarre roller coaster. This was where merchandise would travel from distant shelves toward transportation. Beyond the conveyor lines were rows and rows of industrial shelving like the ones used in the big warehouse shopping stores, except that they were all bare of product.

In the dim interior light, Mike could not see the far end of the aisles between the massive storage shelves. He could imagine dozens of workers busying themselves shuttling packages off the shelves and onto the conveyors toward the trucks. He wondered what kinds of goods were shipped from this warehouse in past years, but then he shook his head to clear his thoughts. It didn't matter. What mattered was finding Michelle – and Randall. Mike hoped again that Michelle was only bait for him tonight, and that Randall did not actually intend to hurt her.

In an operation like this warehouse, there must be a manager's office somewhere, Mike thought. It was probably elevated so the boss could survey the whole operation. If he were a killer setting a trap, that's where he would go. It was also where the monitors would be for the security cameras.

He looked around but could not make out the walls of the building or any elevated offices. Unlike the room at the front of the building, the back end was only dimly lit by sporadic overhead lights, casting barely enough illumination for safe movement around the machinery. There was not a breath of air moving inside the abandoned space, nor any sound save for Mike's heavy breathing and footsteps. He walked in between two conveyor lines toward the empty shelves. After a few steps, he stopped and listened. He heard, very faintly, the whirring of a small motor and the purr of hydraulics. He made a huge effort not to look in the direction of the sound, but recognized it as a pan-tilt-zoom security camera being re-positioned somewhere above his left ear. Randall was adjusting his camera to follow Mike's movements. Mike turned away, trying to seem unaware of the silent eye, and kept moving between the conveyer lines.

He reached the edge of the rows of empty shelves and strode into the nearest one until he reached a point where he could see the far end, then stopped. He looked above and around and guessed that there would be no cameras pointed here. Then he stepped up onto the lower platform of the row of shelves on his left and ducked under the second level, emerging on the other side in the next aisle. He continued through the middle of the rows of shelves, like cutting through the rows of stalks in a cornfield, in the direction of the front of the building. He was banking on Randall not being able to track him here. When he reached the last row, Mike paused.

Through the steel superstructure of the shelving, he could see that beyond the last row was another aisle about six feet across. Beyond that was a cinderblock wall painted red from the floor to a line about five feet up, and then gunmetal gray above that as far as he could see. More importantly, he could see light coming through two large windows at a second-floor height. Mike wondered whether he had any element of surprise. If he were the mastermind here, he would certainly make sure that the entrance to the upper offices was covered by a camera. Even if Randall did not know exactly where he was at that moment, Mike was sure that as soon as he found his way to the stairs leading up to the lighted windows, he would be seen. But maybe not with a lot of advance notice.

Mike stepped into the interior of the shelving unit and crept toward where he figured the stairs up to the offices would be. He stepped over metal supports and across the plywood shelves, trying to remain reasonably quiet and hidden from the security cameras for as long as possible. He had holstered his gun in order to use both hands to steady himself as he navigated the jungle of metal. His heart was still racing and the sweat was trickling down his face and down his back into his beltline. The sleeves he used to wipe it away were now damp. As he approached the end of the row, he saw the dark indentation of a recessed doorway in the cinderblock wall.

Taking a deep breath and drawing his gun, he jumped out from the steel frame of the unit and dashed toward the opening in the wall. He expected to find a door, but instead he faced a concrete stairway leading upward in one straight flight. There was a door at the top of the steps, blocking any view into the upper room. He had no time to wait, so he leapt up the stairs two at a time. At the top, he threw caution to the wind and threw his shoulder into the door as he pushed down on an iron handle, bursting through with a loud bang, hoping that Randall would not have sufficient time to react, even if he saw him coming. He was slightly surprised that the door was not locked, but had no time to ponder the significance of that fact as he held his gun in front of him and scanned the room.

Mike squinted in the sudden bright light and took in the scene in a split second. The space was about ten feet square, with desks pushed up against the wall on one side and bright florescent lights in long spans overhead. Directly across from the door were two office chairs with pale blue fabric. In one chair sat the slumped figure of Michelle McNeill, seemingly unconscious. Both her arms were held to the armrests with layers of duct tape and her ankles were taped together and secured to the chair's central base. Her black hair was matted to her forehead. Mike rushed across the room, knelt in front of the chair, and patted the doctor's cheek. She was warm to his touch and stirred at his intrusion on her sleep. Her eyes blinked open, then gaped wide in recognition that it was Mike's face in front of her. Then, Mike saw her eyes dart past his shoulder toward the door behind him.

Michelle raised her eyebrows and tilted her head forward as she grunted through the duct tape that covered her mouth. Mike got the hint and swiveled around as quickly as he could, but he was unable to entirely avoid the blow that struck his shoulder and sent a searing pain down his left arm. The gun was still in his right hand as he turned and fired in the general direction of his attacker. He got off four quick, low shots that ricocheted off the walls with loud pings as he rolled to the ground. He heard the door slam closed as he bounced to his knees, his gun extended in front of him. Randall was gone – down the stairs, but likely not far. Mike struggled to his feet and glanced at his left shoulder. There was a gash in the fabric of his suit jacket and shirt, both of which sported dark blood stains. Mike couldn't feel his left hand and the arm hung useless at his side, numb with pain and possibly nerve damage. Mike could only guess what kind of knife had done the damage. It had felt heavy, like a butcher knife or a machete.

Ignoring the pain in his haste to deal with the immediate danger, Mike scrambled back to Michelle's chair. He put his gun into Michelle's right hand, which was tethered to the chair but otherwise free enough to shoot in the direction of the doorway if necessary. Then he reached up and ripped the duct tape off the doctor's mouth.

"Ahhww!" she screamed as the tape ripped away the skin from her lips. "He wants you, Mike. This whole setup is so he can kill you."

"Does he have a gun?" Mike grunted through the pain in his arm.

"I don't know. I haven't seen one."

Mike nodded, without any need for further conversation. He reached into his pants pocket, and extracted his boy scout knife. He used his teeth to open the blade and quickly sliced the tape that held Michelle's left hand to the chair. Then he handed her the knife and took back his gun. "Find a phone and call 9-1-1 – tell them an officer needs backup." Mike spat out the instruction while looking at the dark door at the far end of the small room. Then he looked at Michelle and saw her eyes wide with fear and a tear trickling down her cheek. He had to remind himself that she wasn't a cop and was not used to such situations.

He slowly placed the back of his right hand against her face and said, "It will be all right. You can do this." He then kissed her quickly and turned toward the door, charging ahead even as the blood dripped down his limp left hand and splattered on the linoleum floor.

Mike paused only briefly at the top of the stairs, then leapt down to the bottom in three strides. He slumped against the far wall with his right shoulder and peered out from the opening toward the interior of the warehouse. Seeing no movement, he risked moving around the corner, his gun extended. Mike's left shoulder was starting to ache and he knew he was bleeding pretty badly, which only made him want to act more quickly while he still could.

To his right was a corridor, at the end of which stood a doorway that he guessed was the same one he had seen from across the big open room when he originally entered the building. The door was closed and he moved cautiously in that direction. Just before he reached the door, he saw a small room with a glass window on his right. Inside, a bank of television monitors showed images from the building's security cameras. He stopped to look inside, hoping that Randall's image would show up on one of the small screens, but saw no movement. He did not have time to stalk Randall electronically. Instead, he moved forward, carefully pulled open the steel door just a crack, and looked into the cavernous front chamber. The lights were back on, but Mike could not see much through the crack.

Just then, an alarm bell jolted through the silence from the direction of the loading dock, causing Mike to jump and allow the door to slam shut in front of him.

"Good girl," he mumbled to himself, "you pulled the fire alarm." He smiled at Michelle's quick-wittedness and returned his attention to the door in front of him.

Again, he cracked open the heavy sheet of steel and peered beyond. He could see the exit sign above the far door that led to the outside world. There was no movement inside the room. Randall could have gone the other way, toward the loading dock, but Mike had no time to search the entire warehouse. He pulled the door open again and carefully entered the room. When the heavy door closed behind him, the sound of the fire alarm dimmed. Mike considered whether to wait for the fire department's arrival, but there was no time to waste. Randall might try to run again and Mike was not going to lose him a third time. He was starting to feel lightheaded from the blood loss. He wondered whether he should have had Michelle provide some first aid and stem the bleeding before he charged after Randall. She was a doctor, after all. But no, he had to rush off to save the day. It had been a dumb move.

As Mike scanned the room, he saw something move. It was Randall. He was dressed all in black from head to toe, and had some kind of helmet on his head. When he turned, Mike could see that he had goggles, pushed up onto his forehead. Mike took three quick steps forward toward Randall and shouted, "Freeze!" as he raised his gun and sighted.

Then the lights went out. Mike heard a loud click from the direction of the door. Mike fired three quick shots into the total darkness, toward the location where he had last seen Randall. The sound of the shots was amplified by the echoes off the walls. When the blast of the gunfire finally subsided, all was silent and Mike was disoriented. He reached out his hand into the blackness and groped for the wall. His gun clicked against a hard surface and he felt his way back toward the door. When his fingers felt the door frame, he turned and pulled on the handle, but the door was now locked solidly. "Damn!" Mike whispered to himself. If he had thought about it he probably could have found something to prop that door open.

Mike carefully stepped forward, keeping his right shoulder against the wall. His immediate plan was to try to work his way around the room to the other door. He hoped that it was still propped open by the smashed cell phone, but even if it wasn't, when the fire department arrived it was probably where they would enter and he wanted to be nearby. And he did not want to make an easy target for Randall by staying in one place.

Mike heard a faint sound, like a book sliding across a table, followed immediately by a stabbing pain in the left side of his abdomen an inch above his belt buckle. Mike jumped back, away from the invisible knife. He could not see his attacker and was blinded by the pain, but raised his Glock and fired in the direction he thought the attack had come from. After two shots, he paused. The explosions from the gun had included brief flashes of light, but not enough to really see by. He took a step back, listening again. Had he hit Randall? There was no indication.

Then Mike remembered the blacked-out windows all around the top of the room. He turned back toward where he thought the wall was and felt in front of him until his Glock again clicked. Then he turned so that his back was against the wall and guessed at where those windows were at the top of the far wall, which should be facing the front of the building if he was properly oriented. He pulled off four shots, each one slightly higher than the last. He heard three pings as the first three bullets ricocheted off the cinderblock wall, and one crash as the last bullet penetrated a pane of glass.

In the complete darkness of that room, the small, shattered square of glass from that one window was like a candle. Mike looked to his left and saw a shadow move. He pivoted and emptied the remaining bullets in his magazine in quick succession, trying to lay down a diagonal pattern from upper right to lower left across his field of vision. When the echoes of the shots quieted, Mike fell to the ground, half as a defensive move and half out of pain.

He listened for the sound of movement, not really knowing what he would do if Randall came at him, but he heard only the persistent ringing of the fire alarm in the distance. He lurched onto his right elbow and then sat back onto his butt, wincing at the pain in his belly, which now superseded the throbbing in his shoulder. He held out his gun at arm's length, despite knowing that he was out of ammo. He could hear the labored breathing of a person somewhere in front of him, but he could not see enough to know whether Randall was just mildly wounded or down for the count. Mike pressed the button to eject his spent magazine from the Glock, which clanged on the hard floor.

Mike set the gun down as he reached into his jacket pocket for another magazine. Using only his sense of touch, he slipped the fresh ammo into the gun and slammed the butt down on the floor to jam it in. Then he looked up at the dim light filtering in through the broken window and took aim, emptying another full magazine into the windows to the left of the one that he had already broken. Seventeen bullets more or less found their marks, punching holes in some and shattering others as more and more light seeped into the darkness.

Mike had one more magazine in his pocket and he dug it out, once again using only his right hand to eject the spent cartridge and slamming the new ammunition into the gun by banging it on the floor. Then, he struggled to his feet and carefully walked forward toward the sound of the heavy breathing. In the faint light filtering into the space from the broken windows, Mike was able to make out the outline of a man lying on the ground with one hand pressed against his stomach. Even without real lights, Mike could see a dark stain on the white floor next to Randall's prone form. Next to Randall's outline lay the silhouette of a large knife. Mike recalled the heavy blow his shoulder had absorbed and winced. He looked down at the shadowed face of the man who had been at the center of his waking mind as well as his dreams for the past three months.

Randall slowly reached a hand to his face and slid his infrared goggles up from his eyes onto his forehead. He blinked a few times, looking up at Mike, who was standing ten feet away holding his gun at arm's length. Then Randall smiled. "You are the victor," he said in a calm voice. "I yield to you. The chase is done."

"Who the fuck *are* you?" Mike grunted, trying to steady his gun despite the pain in his gut and the continuing bleeding from his left arm.

"I am the Crusader, the Avenging Angel, the Deliverer."

"You're fucking crazy." In the distance, over the continuing din of the fire alarm, Mike made out the sound of a siren, which was getting louder.

Randall looked up at Mike with his eyes wide. "You are now the captor, and I the messenger of the Lord. I shall tell the world of the works I have done and my great deeds. You shall be exalted, Detective Stoneman. You, who have fought evildoers for so long. You shall be glorified, as will I. I look forward to our collaboration."

Mike now heard more sirens in the distance and could distinguish the horn of a fire truck from the wail of a police cruiser approaching. Now it was Mike's turn to smile. It would be at least a few minutes before the firemen and police arrived. He hoped an ambulance might also join the party. His left shoulder throbbed and he was light-headed and starting to feel nauseous. He wasn't sure he could retain consciousness until the cavalry got there.

"I don't think that's going to happen," Mike said softly.

One minute later, Mike could see the flashing of blue and red lights filtering in through the broken windows as the sound of the sirens became louder than the fire alarm, which was still clanging away beyond the door in the loading dock area. Mike dropped to his knees, fell on his right side, and passed out.

When Jason burst through the exterior doorway into the dark room, he couldn't see anything and couldn't hear anything over the din of the sirens and the fire bell. Two uniformed officers stormed through right on Jason's heels with their guns drawn. Angela came in a few seconds later behind the second wave of officers. Jason pulled out his phone and clicked on its flashlight function, casting a beam of light in front of him as the officers pulled out their combat flashlights and began clearing the room.

Jason was the first to come upon the two figures lying on the floor. Mike was unconscious, but was warm and breathing. Beyond Mike's slumped figure lay a man Jason presumed was Ronald Randall. He was wearing all black clothing and had a helmet on his head with bulky goggles that looked like miniature binoculars pushed up above his eyes. The goggles were splattered with blood from the gaping wound in his face where his nose once was. His black shirt was also soaked with blood from a wound in his abdomen. Jason didn't have to check carefully to determine that the man was not a threat and didn't need to be cuffed.

"Get those EMTs in here, now!" Jason called out. "I have Mike here and the killer. The room is secure, so tell the firemen to go check out the alarm."

The ambulance team came in, along with several more uniformed officers and some firefighters. Nobody could figure out how to turn the lights on, so the space was illuminated only by a swarm of flashlights. The EMTs worked on Mike as two officers and Angela held their lights on him. The other officers swept the entire room, which took extra time given the darkness. While they were working, Jason patrolled the scene around Randall's body by the light of his cell phone's flashlight app. He found two empty magazines on the ground near the wall, which he presumed came from Mike's gun. He left them alone and kept scanning the area. He got down on one knee to make a closer inspection of the area around the corpse, noting a large blood-stained knife on the floor a few feet away.

Then Jason found Mike's Glock, near where Mike had fallen, about fifteen feet away from Randall. Jason took a handkerchief from his pocket and picked up the gun, which was still warm and smelled of recent discharge. He ejected the magazine from the Glock, careful not to leave any of his own fingerprints, and examined it. Then he reached down in the semi-darkness and picked up a shell casing, also still warm. He dropped Mike's gun, the magazine of bullets, and the shell casing into his jacket pocket.

By that time, the EMTs had Mike on a gurney and were wheeling him toward the exit. Jason instructed the officers to secure the room so that the forensics team could go over everything later, then hustled toward the door so he could ride with Angela to the hospital.

As he climbed into the back of the ambulance, Jason glanced at his watch again. It was after midnight.

Chapter 54 – Partners

November 5, 2018

*T*HE NEW YORK TIMES ran a front-page story the day after Randall was killed under the headline: "**Serial Killer Taken Out By Hero Cop**." There were no details about the confrontation in the Queens warehouse. The dead man was not identified, but was confirmed to be the killer known as the Righteous Assassin, who had been stalking New York since April and who was believed to be responsible for at least six murders. The cop who killed him was identified as well-known NYPD detective Mike Stoneman. There was no mention of Medical Examiner Michelle McNeill being involved or present, although Stoneman's partner, Detective Jason Dickson, was mentioned by name as being the first officer on the scene.

What the article lacked in detail about the events of the prior day, it made up for in amazing and sensational details about the killer's six murders, which were sourced to a journal written by the killer and provided exclusively to *The Times*. As Dexter Peacock later recounted, he had received an email from an anonymous address that included a detailed account of the killing of Justin Heilman along with a link to the website containing the killer's journal. The article did not publish the URL of the blog, which was later taken down by the host site, but a follow-up article noted that *The Times* would publish its content on the paper's website. The

Righteous Assassin's journal quickly became the most read online article *The Times* had ever published.

Special Agent Manning was assigned to lead the public relations effort on behalf of the FBI in the immediate aftermath. She made the rounds on the television news shows, where she praised the work of the NYPD, and in particular detectives Dickson and Stoneman. She also mentioned the contribution of Donyell Jackson, the teenager who had first stumbled across the killer's blog and alerted the police. And, he had kept it confidential, which was essential to the success of the investigation. Angela suggested that young Mr. Jackson would make a great cop someday if he wanted to pursue that career. The city paid the $10,000 reward to his mother, and the John Jay College of Criminal Justice offered Donyell a scholarship, even though he had not yet finished his sophomore year in high school.

The FBI had no problem identifying Randall based on his fingerprints. The Army, quite understandably, was not in a hurry to make it a big story that an ex-soldier who received a psychological discharge had become a serial killer.

The police started trying to track down a next of kin, only to find it a difficult hunt. His parents had died before he enlisted, and his only sister had married, taken a different last name, and moved with her husband to England. She turned out to be his only living family and she did not want to have anything to do with him.

Meanwhile, Mike spent a week in the hospital. Randall's knife had severed his deltoid muscle and torn through both his rotator cuff and labrum before glancing off the glenoid bone in his shoulder. The deep gash had bled profusely and might have killed him if the paramedics had not arrived when they did. The damage was surgically repaired during a three-hour operation at the Hospital for Special Surgery. Mike sent a bottle of McCallan 18 to the surgeon, Dr. Frank Cordasco. He was finally allowed to go home, but had to put up with a nurse coming in every day to check on him. Berkowitz pointed out that he could now pass himself off as a former major league pitcher who had rotator cuff surgery. The wound to his belly had bled a lot, but the blade had missed any vital organs. The doctors had to cut away several pounds of flab from Mike's abdomen while stitching him up, which Mike joked was the police department's new liposuction alternative.

The day after Mike got home from the hospital, Jason and Angela visited his apartment. His left arm was encased in a black brace of metal and cloth, including a semi-circular metal arc around his waist that extended his elbow outward six inches from his side. With physical therapy, the doctors said he should recover his strength and range of motion within about six months. For now, Mike sat reclining in a lounge chair, sipping Diet Coke through a straw from a paper cup held in his right hand.

"Hey, Mike."

"Hey, Partner," Mike replied with a nod.

"Partner?"

"Well, I think it's about time, Detective."

"Thanks, Mike. I appreciate that. Is that what it takes? Saving your miserable life from a piece-of-shit murderer? Is that all?"

Mike took a swig from his straw and stared at the younger detective seriously. "No, Jason. It takes showing me intelligence and good police skills. You saved my life by following that fire truck and calling that ambulance. A few more minutes and I might have bled out. You did what a good cop does. I appreciate it. Thanks."

Jason stared at his mentor and then just smiled. "I can be taught," he deadpanned.

"Good, because there's a lot more for you to learn."

"Does that mean I can still take your classes?"

"Sure," Mike said, "just as soon as I get back on my feet."

"I'll look forward to that, Mike."

Angela then spoke for the first time. "I heard that there are two different production companies racing each other to put together a movie based on Randall's blog."

"Yeah," Mike grunted. "I'll take a pass."

"So, you're not going to sign on as a consultant, then?" Angela egged him on.

"Hell no!" Mike shot back. "I'm just happy the bastard isn't going to make any money off of his story."

"Well, his sister doesn't want to claim any of the rights, so his blog is public domain. The Son of Sam law doesn't apply because he's dead, so only the production companies are going to get rich."

Mike put down his cup and waved his right arm derisively. "And the newspapers. Don't forget the muck-raking newspapers. They are full of stories about the bastard, every damned day. They're recounting the crimes and offenses of his scumbag victims and some of them are saying that he should be considered a hero and not a criminal. He's a cash cow for them."

Jason shrugged. "What the hell? Let them make a buck, they need it."

Mike looked at Angela, who was standing with her arms crossed and looking glummer than Mike could remember. "What's eating at you?"

Angela shook her head and let her arms drop. "Sorry, I'm just not very good at saying good-bye."

"You could stay. I'll put in a good word with Captain Sullivan for you."

Angela chuckled at that. "No, sorry. I think I'll have to take my chances with the Bureau. As a matter of fact, I already have a new assignment, in Phoenix. I have to go home to Virginia, do a month's worth of laundry, and pack up again."

"Good time of year to be heading to Arizona," Jason offered supportively.

"Yeah, I guess the serial killers think so, too."

"Good luck to you, Special Agent Manning," Mike said, giving her a half-salute with his right hand.

Angela stepped forward, bent down over his chair, and gave

Mike a soft hug, being careful not to jostle his injured shoulder. "It has been a pleasure working with you, Mike. And you, too, Jason." She gave Jason a full-body hug, then stepped back. "I really have to go now. I'll look you up the next time I'm in New York." And with that, she turned and walked to the door, closing it behind her without looking back. After a few moments, Jason broke the silence.

"How's Doctor McNeill doing?"

Mike paused. "She was pretty shook up by the experience. The bastard was not gentle with her, but she wasn't seriously hurt. She had the sense to pull that fire alarm, and afterwards she got released from the hospital in an hour. She came by this morning to check on me. I think she'll be okay, but you never know with trauma."

"You think she'll want to put some distance between you two?"

"I hope not," Mike said with a sigh. "What about you? Any post-traumatic stress disorder?"

"Is that a serious question?"

"No. I think I know what you're made of. You gonna keep my desk clean while I'm stuck here?"

"Captain says that after the inquiry is done, he's going to put me with McMillian until you're ready for duty. I can't stand that dude. He never stops talking."

Mike laughed out loud, then winced and grabbed at his shoulder. "Try not to make me laugh, Jason. The doc says I need to keep the shoulder still as much as I can."

"I can do that," Jason smiled. "But before I go, we have to talk."

"Sure," Mike said, taking a serious tone. "What's on your mind?"

"Well, Mike –," Jason paused and looked out the window. All he could see were the windows of the building on the opposite side of the street. "Remember how you told me that you had this guy figured out? You said that what he wanted was attention, and that he wanted to get caught eventually so that he could tell his story, right?"

"Agent Manning said that same thing," Mike pointed out.

"Well, if Randall had survived, the trial would have been a circus and the media would have totally eaten up the story of the Angel of Death. Randall would have been a world-wide celebrity. Which is exactly what he wanted, right?"

Mike nodded again.

"You knew that. Manning confirmed it, but you called it, too. That's why he didn't kill Michelle, or Slick Mick's granddaughter, or anybody else except his intended victims. He didn't want to sully his reputation. He wanted to be a hero. I'm a little surprised he didn't try to give himself up to capture so that he could have his Ringling Brothers trial, do his television interviews, publish his crazy anthology, and then do life in the loony bin. You had that all figured, didn't you?"

Mike just stared straight ahead.

"So, Mike, I have to say that you were absolutely right, but it leaves me with a problem. We don't really know for sure the exact sequence of shots that killed Randall."

Mike stared at his partner for a full thirty seconds in silence. "That's good, Detective. You left the question hanging in the air, and then let the suspect fill in the silence. Good technique."

"Who said anything about you being a suspect?"

"You didn't have to. I know how things work in internal affairs, and so do you. Shots were fired. A man was killed. There's always an inquiry. So, what did you tell them?"

"I told them that I didn't see anything and that by the time I got there it was all over."

"That's all? That's what you said?"

"Yes, sir," Jason responded.

"May I ask what happened to my gun?"

Jason frowned and turned to the side, shielding his face from Mike. "You were on the ground and bleeding. When the paramedics arrived, I helped roll you over and I picked up your

Glock and eventually returned it to the station. You'll find it in the evidence room when you return to duty. The forensics guys wanted to give it a once over before they release it back to you. Or maybe they'll just keep it there and give you a new one."

"I was kinda attached to that Glock."

"I know, Mike, but sometimes you have to let go of things."

"True. And if I do go collect my old gun, will I need to also retrieve the mags? I think I might have gone through a few that night."

Jason stood facing the wall. "I found two empty magazines on the floor near the wall, about twenty feet away from where you collapsed. You must have ejected the last empty one after you shot out the windows, before you passed out."

"Yes, I must have." Mike sat in silence, waiting for the next question, but it didn't come.

"You know, it's a lucky thing, really," Jason said as he walked over to Mike's chair and looked down at the man who taught ethics to newly minted detectives. "In the dark there, without being able to clearly see your target, you laid down a pattern hoping to wing the guy. The forensics team found the bullets that missed him embedded in the far wall. You hit him twice; once in the gut and once right in the nose, under his infrared goggles. What are the chances?"

Mike stared up at his partner. "I don't know, Jason. I'm a cop, not a mathematician."

"And those goggles were pushed up onto his forehead, I guess by the impact of the shot to his face."

"I suppose that could happen."

Jason leaned down slightly so that he could look Mike in the eye. "The pattern of the missed shots formed a diagonal line. It seems pretty likely to me that as you were shooting at a subject you couldn't see, you would likely have started high and worked downward, rather than starting at his feet and sweeping upward. Just an assumption, of course."

"A valid and reasonable assumption, although I would have to say that I have no specific memory of exactly how it happened."

Jason nodded and then continued as he paced across the small living area. "Of course, if the pattern had been high to low, the slug that hit him mid-face and blasted away most of his nasal cavity would have sent him falling backwards, making it pretty unlikely that you would also hit him in the gut without any other bullets striking the body."

Mike raised his left eyebrow and nodded slightly. "I can see how you could draw that conclusion, although you never can tell how a body will fall in such a situation. He could have been moving at the moment of impact and fallen in the direction of his inertia, putting his body in the path of another shot."

"And I guess," Jason continued haltingly, "once you hit him square in the face, and again in the gut, there would have been no reason for you to put a fresh magazine into your gun, especially since you were injured pretty badly yourself."

"Well, Jason, remember that I couldn't have known for sure whether Randall had a gun as well as a knife in the dark there. I also couldn't have known for sure whether I hit him or whether he was dead or alive, so it would have been prudent for me to reload."

"True," Jason responded. "You might have shoved that last mag into your gun. But there would not have been any reason for you to fire again at that point, since Randall was already down and out."

"I suppose that's probably right," Mike agreed.

Jason then reached into his pocket and removed a fully loaded magazine of bullets for a 9mm Glock pistol. He placed it on the end table next to Mike's cup, where it clacked against the wood.

"That looks like one of my mags," Mike observed.

"I think you may be right about that," Jason responded blankly.

"Where did you get that?"

"I'm not entirely sure. I found it in my jacket pocket – the jacket I was wearing that night at the warehouse in Queens. I put it on today, and there it was in the pocket. I guess it must have accidentally ejected from your Glock when I put the gun in my pocket."

"So, when you turned my gun over to the boys down in the evidence locker, it had no mag in it?"

"No, it did not."

"You didn't put the gun in an evidence bag when you picked it up in the warehouse?"

"No, I didn't have one on me."

"And you didn't notice, at the time, that the mag was in the gun when you picked it up, but wasn't there when you turned the gun in?"

"I guess not."

"That's not good crime scene procedure, Detective," Mike scolded.

"I know. I'm sorry. Oh, and I reloaded that magazine for you, so it would be full the next time you need it. It was short one slug."

"You don't say?"

"Yes. You should be more careful to make sure that when you load the mag you put in all seventeen bullets."

"I'll take that to heart, Detective. Next time." Mike paused and looked into Jason's eyes, which betrayed no emotion. "Do you happen to know how many shell casings the forensics team recovered from the crime scene?"

"Yes," Jason responded. "I checked the report. Thirty-four casings were officially recovered between the office where Doctor McNeill was held captive and the big warehouse room."

"Exactly two full mags of bullets," Mike said.

"Exactly." Jason then reached into his other pocket and pulled out a spent 9mm shell casing, slightly bent from the impact of being fired. He placed it beside the magazine on the table with another metallic clack.

"Is that mine?" Mike asked.

"I think so. I found it on the floor near your gun, between you and Randall. I figured that you might want it back."

"Thanks," Mike said without emotion. "And was that casing counted among the thirty-four that were found at the crime scene?"

"I'm pretty sure it wasn't," Jason said calmly. He nodded toward Mike, then turned and walked toward the door.

Just as Jason turned the knob, Mike spoke again. "Jason, it's nice to know that you have my back."

Jason stopped and replied, without turning around. "You can count on it." He then opened the door and walked through without another word. Mike listened for the sound of the ker-chunk as the heavy metal door latched into place.

Mike reached out his right hand and picked up the spent shell casing, examining it carefully. Then, he struggled up from his chair, wincing as his shoulder brace failed to maintain total stability of the joint, sending a small jolt of pain down his left arm. He shuffled to his small kitchen, opened the cupboard under the sink, and dropped the casing into the garbage bin.

"Good-bye, Lieutenant Randall," he said softly to himself.

The End

Thank you for reading *Righteous Assassin*. I hope you enjoyed it. Whether you loved it, liked it, didn't particularly care for it, or hated it, I would most appreciate it if you would post a review on Amazon and/or on Goodreads or Bookbub. Reader reviews are the best way for others to evaluate whether to purchase the book. They also help me understand what worked and what didn't work and make me a better author. I want to have as many reviews as possible – including tepid or even negative reviews (really). I also welcome comments and conversation about the book on The Mike Stoneman Thriller Group on Facebook or on my website at KevinGChapman.com. By visiting my author site, you can also find out a little more about me and find links to my other books, including the FREE short story where Detective Mike Stoneman was born. *Fool Me Twice* was written in 2012 as a submission for a legal/crime writing competition sponsored by the New Jersey Corporate Counsel Association. The story won first prize, and when I started working on this current novel, I decided to draw upon that character again. Please enjoy the free short story, which you can also download from all major book selling websites.

The Mike Stoneman Thriller Series continues with *Deadly Enterprise*. Like *Righteous Assassin*, book #2 was named one of the top 20 Mystery/Thrillers of the year (2020) by the Kindle Book Review! *Deadly Enterprise* begins with Mike in rehab, following his shoulder surgery. While Mike is out on short-term disability, Jason is reassigned to a different partner, and they are tasked with an investigation that has political sensitivity after a Hispanic shopkeeper in the Bronx is killed. Keep turning the pages and you'll find an excerpt from *Deadly Enterprise*.

The series then continues in book #3 – **Lethal Voyage**. After the exciting conclusion of *Deadly Enterprise*, the New York press is all over Mike and Jason. The Commissioner suggests that they take a vacation – to get out of town and be totally unavailable for comments. Luckily, Michelle and Rachel Robinson are able to book them all on a last-minute cruise to Bermuda. Sounds relaxing, right? Well, a dead body can ruin a vacation. When the wife of a Broadway producer falls to her death from a balcony, Michelle is convinced it was no accident. The ship's head of security wants nothing to do with a murder investigation, so Mike and Jason take it upon themselves. So much for a relaxing vacation. On this Bermuda cruise, the onboard production of *Chicago* isn't the only venue for murder. . . . . Enjoy the trip by purchasing **Lethal Voyage, winner of the 2021 Kindle Book Award**.

Then, just back from their cruise, Mike and Jason investigate the murder of the Black starting quarterback of a New York NFL team in **Fatal Infraction**. Was it a racist attack by an angry teammate, or could it have something to do with a point-shaving scheme? Mike and Jason need to solve the mystery before the case tears the team – and the City – apart.

Finally, come with Mike and Jason to Las Vegas as they are dragged into an investigation of a murdered drag queen. It's a family affair close to Jason's heart, and the suspect may become the victim if they're not careful. The only way to avoid disaster for everyone may be Mike's **Perilous Gambit**.

No matter what, keep reading books by independent authors!

Kevin G. Chapman – April, 2022

Acknowledgements

I have many people to thank for their help in creating *Righteous Assassin*. First, of course, is my wife, Sharon. Our discussions and arguments over plot points and characters always showed me that she really cares about my fiction. I also need to acknowledge that this book would not be anywhere near as good as it is without the tremendous work of my editor, Samantha Chapman. The fact that she's also my daughter does not diminish the fact that she did a fabulous job with the draft I submitted to her and her corrections, notes, suggestions, and re-writes resulted in a final product so much better than what I had before she dove into it. She is truly talented. If you're an author or anyone else who needs written words edited, you should look up Samantha at www.SamanthaChapmanEditing.com. Finally, and not at all least important on this list, I want to thank Peter O'Connor at Bespoke Book Covers, who designed my cover. Having tried before to self-design a book cover, I appreciate how important it is to have an eye-catching and appropriate cover and that the pros have the tools to make it pop. Peter did a great job and any commercial success this book has will be substantially thanks to the work of Peter and his team of designers. Find him at www.BespokeBookCovers.com.

If you are reading as part of a book club, consider the discussion questions on the next page.

Discussion questions for book clubs

1. Nobody will say that Ronald Randall was a moral person, but by the time he executed his sixth victim how did you feel about the "righteousness" of his selection of targets?
2. Be honest, did you make the connections about the first four kills being linked to the Plagues on Egypt before Mike and Michelle ?
3. In an otherwise all-male environment, how do you think Angela handled her role on the task force?
4. Were you offended by the term "the menstrual killer?" If so, why? If not, why not?
5. How did you feel about the relationship between Mike and Michelle, and how did it influence your overall impression of Mike's character?
6. How did you feel about the explanation of Ronald Randall believing that his killing was a mission from God? Would you have felt differently about him as a character if he were Muslim rather than Christian? If so, why? Do you feel that the character makes any particular statement about Christianity, or religion in general?
7. Would you have visited the website set up by *The New York Times* and read the entire journal of the Righteous Assassin? Do you think a newspaper is being responsible by publishing it?
8. In the final scene – what happened? Are you confident that you know what happened in the Queens warehouse?
9. The relationship between Mike and Jason started out tense. How do you feel about their relationship by the end?
10. How do you think the relationships will develop going forward: Mike and Michelle? Mike and Jason?

Note to book clubs: If you give me more than two weeks of advance notice, I will be very happy to join your discussion about any of my books – by video chat or phone (unless you are in Central New Jersey, in which case I'll come in person). Contact me at Kevin@KevinGChapman.com to let me know the date and time for your book club's meeting.

About the Author

Kevin G. Chapman is, by profession, an attorney specializing in labor and employment law. He is a past Chair of the Labor & Employment Law Network of the Association of Corporate Counsel, leading a group of 6800 in-house employment lawyers. Kevin is a frequent speaker at Continuing Legal Education seminars and enjoys teaching management training courses.

Kevin's passion (aside from fantasy baseball, golf and tournament poker) is writing fiction. Kevin's first Novel: *Identity Crisis: A Rick LaBlonde, P.I. Mystery*, was self-published through Xlibris in 2003, and is now available via Amazon.com as a Kindle e-book. His second novel, *A Legacy of One*, published in 2016, was a finalist (short list) for the Chanticleer Book Review's Somerset Award for Literary Fiction. *A Legacy of One* is a serious book, filled with political and social commentary and a plot involving personal identity, self-determination, and the struggle to make the right life decisions.

Kevin has also written several short stories, including *Fool Me Twice*, the winner of the New Jersey Corporate Counsel Association's 2012 Legal Fiction Writing Competition, which was the genesis of Mike Stoneman. *Fool Me Twice* is available as a stand-alone short story at https://BookHip.com/LQMRWJJ -- or on amazon, Google Play, Kobo, Nook, and other ebook retailers, or get it directly from Kevin's website. He has also written one complete screenplay (unproduced so far) and has another screenplay and two more novels currently in the works.

Kevin lives in Central New Jersey and is a graduate of Columbia College (class of '83, where he was a classmate of Barack Obama), and Boston University School of Law (magna cum laude '86). Readers can contact Kevin via his website at KevinGChapman.com

Deadly Enterprise (Mike Stoneman #2)

Chapter 1 – A Very Bad Date

THE GIRL ON THE FLOOR in the skimpy red dress groaned softly and rolled her head to the side. The corner of her right eye was caked with dried blood. A gooey scarlet trickle ran down toward the dirty blond hair hanging in unkempt wisps around her ear. One of the thin shoulder straps of her dress was snapped off, allowing the shiny material to peel down, exposing the top half of her small breast. A knot on her forehead the size of a golf ball throbbed an angry shade of red with each heartbeat.

"We should dump her in the river," a male voice said, without a hint of anxiety. He sat casually on the edge of a bare wooden desk in a Spartan room lacking any semblance of charm. The bed, covered with a drab brown comforter, was pushed up against the wall in front of an imitation leather headboard with large buttons holding in the padded surface. Next to it, a nondescript lamp glowed on a stained nightstand. There was no art on the walls and the floor was industrial-grade carpet with a swirling pattern that hid most of the remnants of prior visitors. The air smelled of musty sweat and industrial-strength disinfectant. The calm man, by contrast, wore an expensive suit and a gold Citizen watch. He was tall and fit, with graying black hair that was carefully groomed. He looked decidedly out of place in the dumpy room.

"She might not drown, though," a different voice replied. "She's not hurt that bad. Look, she's coming around." This second voice was agitated and came from a much shorter man, who paced within the cramped space. He was thin and wiry. He ran his hand through a head of brown curls, pondering his next move. He wore blue jeans and a plaid button-down shirt. His gaunt face looked like it was pushed together from the sides, with large eyes and a bent nose. "We'll make it look like an overdose, but make sure she's dead. We don't want her ending up in an ambulance like the last one."

"Not many people accidentally go in the river, Eddie," the first man said, still without emotion.

"She's an addict. She can OD, then there's lots of reasons somebody might toss the body in the river."

"All of those reasons involve somebody trying to hide something."

"Yeah, I know, but what other options have we got? She was gonna run. She knows who you are, so sending her into lockup ain't gonna be safe."

The first man stood up, stretching his arms above his head. He was much bigger than his companion and thick, like the trunk of a sturdy tree. He looked down at the girl, who had brought one arm up to her head. She was clearly going to open her eyes in a few moments, but she was no threat to jump up and run away. "I don't want to get in the habit of just shooting up every girl who gets out of line."

"Nobody has said boo about the others," replied Eddie, who stopped pacing. "I can go upstairs and get it from the doc." He glanced nervously down at the girl, then back up at his comrade. "I'll go right now." The taller man nodded, and then Eddie scurried to the door and disappeared into the dimly lit hallway beyond. The heavy door slammed behind him with a loud thump.

The girl partially opened her eyes, then blinked several times. Once she focused on the tall man, a shadow of fear passed over her expression and she started to cry. "I'm sorry," she sobbed, her body shaking, causing the remaining fabric of her dress to fall completely off her left breast. "Please. I won't say anything. I promise. I'll be good. I'll be—"

Her voice was snuffed out by the man's vicious kick to the side of her head, which then lolled in the opposite direction as her eyes re-closed and she sank back into unconsciousness.

The tall man looked down, dispassionately. "You'll be dead, Sweetheart."

Chapter 2 – Physical Torture

Wednesday, Feb. 6, 2019

MIKE STONEMAN'S FACE was contorted in a mask of pain. "Aaaahhoooww! No more!" he groaned, a tear forming in his right eye as he turned his head to that side. He was laying on his back on an elevated table; his feet were strapped down to prevent movement. The man on his left, wearing a plain white t-shirt and sweat pants, held Mike's left wrist in a vice-like grip with his left hand and pressed his right hand into Mike's elbow, keeping the arm straight and pushing upwards. Pain shot through Mike's shoulder and down his arm, making his fingers tingle. He could feel the sinew in his labrum stretch to the breaking point and heard the pop and crunch of scar tissue ripping. He gritted his teeth and held his breath as long as he could stand it, before shouting out again "Stop!"

Mike felt the pressure relax slightly, allowing him to catch his breath. He blew out three quick puffs of air as he looked up at Terry Kramer with malice in his eyes. Then the pressure returned as the man once again pushed against the limits of Mike's flexibility.

"You can take more," Terry said, pushing a little harder this time, until Mike cried out again. "What's the PIN to your ATM card?" Terry shouted over Mike's groans.

"You'll never get me to . . . Aahhh . . . talk, you bastard!" Mike grunted out. Then the pain subsided slightly as the big man eased his grip on Mike's wrist and relaxed the pressure. Mike sighed, then cried out in pain again as his arm retracted down toward his side. He panted as he lay on the soft tabletop, sweat running down his forehead and dripping onto the vinyl surface. "I hate you," Mike said softly, slowly regaining his regular breathing.

"Good," Terry replied as he released Mike's legs from their straps. Mike sat up with some struggle, careful to keep his left arm immobile as much as possible at his side. He swung his legs over the edge of the table and looked across the therapy room, where his recovery partner, Dolores, was doing arm curls with a giant blue rubber band while standing against a full-length mirror. Terry smiled. "You got up to sixty degrees today, Mike. I'm proud of you."

"Hmmff," Mike grunted. "You're going to rip all my pins out and send me back to surgery."

Terry laughed robustly and slapped Mike on the back with a solid open palm. "Like I don't know how far I can push you without doing damage? C'mon, Mike. Trust me."

Mike was now fourteen weeks removed from being stabbed in the shoulder in a Queens warehouse by former Army lieutenant Ronald Randall, dubbed the "Righteous Assassin" by the New York press. After his surgery, he spent six weeks in a brace to keep his arm immobile, and then started physical therapy in mid-December. Now, it was the middle of February and struggling into his parka was an ordeal, but the New York winter would not permit Mike to get away with just a light jacket or a zip-up hoodie. At least the abdominal knife wound was fully healed. He had a scar that looked like he had given birth by Caesarian section through his belly button, but his abs looked pretty decent due to the exercises he had to do for his post-operative recovery. Overall, he was down fifteen pounds since the fall. At least that was a plus.

"I'm gonna shoot you," Mike replied with a smile. He took a deep breath, then hoisted himself off the table and walked slowly toward the far wall, where Dolores had finished her arm work. She was a traffic enforcement agent who had injured her shoulder in a kayaking accident while on vacation in Florida. She was a thick Black woman just over five feet tall, but she had disproportionately slender calves and ankles. Her upper body was dominated by a huge bosom and a pile of black hair mounted on her head in a never-ending variety of styles. Today she wore a 70's afro that increased her apparent height by a good six inches. She also sported a set of bright white teeth that were nearly always smiling. Her perpetual good mood sometimes caused Mike to be even more curmudgeonly than normal, as if it were a competition to see whether Dolores could get him to smile back. She had a torn labrum and a torn rotator cuff and had her surgery one week after Mike's. They had been in rehab together since just before Christmas and were basically on the same regimen of exercises.

Terry, the physical therapist at the NYPD athletic and medical facility, had scheduled them for simultaneous sessions so that he could maximize his efficiency as the two patients traded off time on the table with time on the exercise equipment. Mike and Dolores had a running wager on who would complete rehab and get to a full range of motion first. As Dolores sauntered past, Mike whispered, "Sixty."

"Ooohh," Dolores said with a twinkle in her eye. "You are making progress. I better get busy!" She laughed and hopped up on the table so that Terry could manipulate her arm and shoulder, as he had done with Mike moments before. The therapy included strengthening exercises and also manual stretching to push the now ultra-tight muscles, ligaments, tendons, and cartilage back to their normal range of motion and flexibility. Terry forced the joints to move despite the fact that the surrounding muscles and tissue had been sewn together and locked down tight during surgery, then allowed to sit immobile for six weeks while the cuts healed. Now, stretching the joints back out involved more pain than the original injuries. Dolores took it all with her usual smile and good cheer. Mike was just sore.

Mike went to work on the rubber bands, lifting his arm up in front of his body as far as he could before the pain stopped him, then down. Ten reps with his injured left arm, then ten with the right, just to keep both arms in shape. Then side-to-side, then from the floor up to his waist, then pressing his side against the wall and stretching his left hand upwards as far as he could. This was his eighth week of physical therapy. He could see the progress. When he started, he could not lift his arm more than ten degrees, even without weights or resistance from the rubber band. Now he was at sixty degrees. He still had a long way to go, and progress was agonizingly slow. He was sure that if he were twenty years younger, he would be recovering faster. As always, he thought, it sucks to get old.

Dolores hopped off the table, fresh off her torture at Terry's hands, but Mike did not recall her screaming even once. She flashed him her bright teeth and whispered "Sixty-five," as she passed him by, on her way to grab her coat and purse from a hook on the wall. Mike congratulated her as sincerely as he could, dropped his last resistance band, and waved to Terry that he was also calling it a day. They were actually several minutes beyond the official end of their time, but Terry always allowed them to stay as long as they wanted to keep stretching. Mike grabbed his own winter coat and pushed through the glass doors of the PT room. He waved at the elderly receptionist who scheduled the appointments and exited out into the general gym portion of the facility. Mike thought that, on the one hand, it was great that the NYPD had its own physical therapy facility so that the recovering cops did not have to fight with the general public for appointment times. On the other hand, it was unfortunate that the police had so many injuries that its officers could fully book an entire physical therapy operation, to the point that it was difficult finding open time slots and officers had to double up with the therapists. At least he had been able to set up a reasonable schedule.

Mike waved to Dolores as she walked toward the subway, while Mike headed south down Amsterdam Avenue, bending his head down against the chilly wind. He fished a knit hat out of the pocket of his jacket with his right hand and managed to get it on his head one-handed, since he could not get his left arm up that high. He had twenty blocks to walk, but he needed to keep up the exercise. It was still impossible for him to jog because the pounding jarred his injured shoulder too much, but walking was fine, so he had been walking everywhere, even through the snow and slush of the city. His plan was to stop by the precinct on 94th Street for a while, then continue on to his apartment on 68th Street. That would be close to fifty blocks of walking by the end of the afternoon. He wished he were back on active duty, but he was mollified somewhat by Captain Sullivan's willingness to let him visit the precinct, consult on pending cases, and work on his training class materials while he was drawing disability pay. This was not strictly permitted under departmental rules, but as long as nobody from the downtown brass or the benefits consultants came in to check on him, Sully would swear he was never there. Mike limited his appearances to about once per week, just in case.

After several weeks of bitterly cold weather, which the reports had referred to as the "polar vortex," the temperature had shot up in to the low 40s, which seemed like spring. It was nearly 4:00 p.m. when Mike turned west on 94th Street and saw the line of black & white cruisers lined up in the parking spaces in front of the precinct house. He climbed up the four steps of the building that was once a brownstone residence and pushed open the heavy wooden door with his right arm, nodding in greeting at two uniformed officers who were exiting. He climbed the stairs to the third-floor bullpen, where the detectives had their desks, and waved at his comrades. He scanned the room for his partner, Jason Dickson, but didn't see the big man anywhere. Jason was the only Black detective in the Homicide division and he was also always the best dressed cop in the room, so he stood out in the crowd. Mike called out a greeting to detective Steve Berkowitz, who grinned widely and yelled back that Mike should demand a new contract with the Mets, now that he had a surgically repaired left arm.

"I'm leaving for Spring Training in the morning," Mike quipped back.

"Hey, Mike!" came the booming voice of Jason Dickson from the foot of the stairs. Jason came bounding into the bullpen and charged toward Mike with his arms extended as if he were going to tackle the older detective, or put him in a bear hug. Mike crouched quickly and held out his right palm, signaling for Jason to stop. Jason kept running right up to the point of contact before stopping short and softly giving Mike's right hand a high-five. Jason towered five inches and easily fifty pounds of muscle over Mike's five-foot, ten-inch frame. "A little late for work, aren't you, Detective?"

"I make my own hours now," Mike deadpanned.

"While you're here, do you have a minute?"

"Sure. I got nowhere to be."

Jason turned and yelled across the room, "Hey, Ray!" as he waved at detective Raymond McMillian, who was filling in as Jason's partner while Mike was out on disability. Ray rose from his desk and slowly walked in Jason's direction. Ray was in his early thirties and tried to look even younger, sporting a Fu-Manchu beard and moustache combination and combing back his flowing brown curls into a wave. He was shorter than Jason and stockier, but still bigger than Mike. He swaggered across the room with an attitude not generally seen from the newest detective in the group.

"Hey, old man," Ray said with a smile. "How's the broken wing?"

Mike scowled at the man's familiarity. "It wasn't broken, Kid. If you survive in this job long enough to reach my advanced age, you can tell me how your body's doing."

"OK," Ray said, only slightly chastised, "I'll be sure to look you up in the rest home to tell you."

"Great. Maybe you'll pass my evidence handling class by then."

That shut Ray up for a moment and let Jason insert himself between the two of them. "Ray, I want Mike to join us on the call with the M.E. on the floater. Let's go into the conference room." Mike raised an eyebrow at the mention of the Medical Examiner,

Dr. Michelle McNeill, who was a veteran of many homicide investigations and a frequent witness in high-profile trials. She was also the woman with whom Mike was spending most of his nights, now that he was able to sleep in a reclining position again after his surgery. Dr. McNeill had also been present in the Queens warehouse when Mike was injured. Mike and Jason exchanged a knowing look, passing between them the understanding that Ray McMillian was not clued in to Mike's relationship with the doctor.

The three men huddled around a small wooden table in a cramped, windowless room, which passed for a conference area in a Manhattan precinct where space was always at a premium. An ancient telephone with a black cord snaking to a large silver speaker box sat in the center of the pock-marked tabletop. Mike glanced toward a credenza at the far side of the room where an urn of coffee sat next to a stack of paper cups and a bowl of sweetener and creamer packets. A red light glowed over the black spigot, indicating that the coffee was brewed and ready to drink. There was a small pile of paper plates on the opposite side of the wooden surface, along with a leaning tower of white paper napkins, but the rest of the space was bare. Mike raised an eyebrow and asked, "No donuts today?"

"He hasn't heard?" Ray asked.

"I guess not," Jason replied. "No donuts, Mike. No food at all. We've got a rat issue."

"Issue?" Mike said with another raise of his brow.

"Yeah. We had one running around the bullpen a few days ago. The exterminators came in and said they found droppings all over the place and a bunch of bags of candy and crackers had been chewed open. They say we have to clear out all the food in the building until they get the infestation under control, so Sully has banned all food. We can have coffee, but that's it. Anybody caught eating in the building will do hard time."

"That sucks," Mike said, stating the obvious. "What about lunch?"

"We have to go out of the building to eat. We've turned the squad cars into makeshift food trucks, since it's too damned cold to stand around outside."

"I guess you do what you gotta do."

"It's a pretty poor reflection on the city's building maintenance program," Ray cut in.

Mike and Jason just stared at him without speaking. Jason shot Mike a look to say, "This is what I have to put up with from this guy," then reached for the phone without further comment. He picked up the receiver, then paused. "Ray, please brief Detective Stoneman on the case before we call the M.E."

Ray looked up, slightly flustered at being put on the spot. He quickly recovered his composure, sat back in his chair, and began his summary. "Well, Mike, it's pretty routine, I think. Some jogger reported seeing a body floating in the East River. The uniforms and the EMTs fished her out, but she was way dead. We got prints and we're running them through the national database, but her fingers were pretty bloated, so we're not sure about getting a match. She was naked except for a pair of red silk panties. Looked to be early 20s. Bruise on her head, but other than that no obvious signs of injury." Ray looked at Jason, seeking approval for his recitation.

Jason looked at Mike. "Any questions?"

"Not yet."

Jason dialed the phone and punched a button at the bottom of the ancient device, which blinked once, then stayed lit. The line connected and rang several times before being answered.

"Medical Examiner," came the voice through the tinny speaker.

"Doctor McNeill, it's Jason Dickson from Homicide. I'm here with Detective Raymond McMillian and Detective Mike Stoneman. You sent me a note that you wanted to talk about the Jane Doe that you've been examining."

There was a pause on the line and the detectives could hear the sound of footfalls. Mike pictured Michelle walking across her examination room to her neatly organized desk, extracting a file from her desktop, and then walking back to the phone. He smiled at the thought, and remembered that he needed to pick up something he could make for dinner at Michelle's downtown apartment later. "I have the file, gentlemen."

Mike said, "Go ahead, Doctor."

"We have a Caucasian female between eighteen and twenty-three. Cause of death is drowning. I'd say she was in the water between twenty-four and thirty-six hours. Deceased has a large contusion on her left forehead consistent with a blunt force blow, which occurred several hours before death. She has other assorted scratches and bruises that I can't say for sure existed before she went into the water. Most importantly, she had a large quantity of opiates in her system, and a single needle scar on her right arm consistent with an injection of heroin shortly before her death. When her system shut down, she stopped metabolizing the drug, so I was able to detect about how much she had in her at time of death, which was pretty significant. Her teeth and nose showed signs of recent use of crystal meth, but the tox screen didn't find any of that in her system. Her stomach was basically empty. She had semen in her vagina but no indication of trauma or tearing, so it does not look like sexual assault."

When Dr. McNeill stopped talking, Mike spoke up. "Anything else to suggest foul play, and not just an overdose and an accidental or intentional dive into the water?"

The doctor was silent for ten seconds before responding. "You know that I can't speculate. That's your job. But I've seldom seen an overdose case with just one needle mark."

"What do you mean?"

"This girl had one needle scar in her arm. Nothing in the other arm, and no other indication of heroin use. So, if she accidentally overdosed, she did it on the first hit, or at least the first hit in a very long time. That's not normal for a heroin addict, in my experience. The big bump on her head, which did not happen when she went into the water, suggests that she took a significant impact, and then a few hours later, high as a kite from a big dose of heroin, she ends up in the river. And it's February and freezing cold, so she's not skinny dipping. She may have been wearing something when she went in, but it wasn't anything warm, which would have stayed attached to her. So, either she walked in light clothing to the river while really high, after taking a serious blow to the head, and jumped or fell in, or somebody clubbed her in the head, before or after she took the drugs, and then helped her in where she was sure to drown."

"Thank you, Doctor," Mike said, determining that McNeill was done. He then looked at Jason. "Any other questions?" Jason shook his head. Mike turned to Ray, who leaned forward, but then waved a hand to indicate that he had nothing to say. "Okay, Doctor. Thanks for the report. We'll get back to you if we think of any other information we want. By the way, are her fingerprints more legible now than when she came in?"

"Yes, I think so. Her bloating has subsided some. I'll take another set of prints and send them up for processing."

"Thanks again." Mike reached out to punch the lighted button and end the call. "So," he said, looking at Jason, "you're treating this as a homicide?"

"We're treating it as a possible homicide," Jason responded. "Let's see what we get once we have an ID on her and take it from there. It's still possible that she went into the river because she was so high she didn't know any better. Stranger things have happened to junkies."

"The M.E. just told us that she doesn't think she was a heroin addict. I must say that I tend to agree – it's pretty rare for an addict to have no track marks."

"She can't know that for sure," Ray broke into the discussion. "The lady said there was evidence of crystal meth use, and she was high on the smack for sure at the time. Let's not make her out to be Cinderella yet."

Mike frowned, but chose not to respond. Ray was not wrong. Mike would have supported the M.E. loudly, but he didn't want to seem like he was too deferential. He was pretty sure that Jason got the message. "It's your case, gentlemen. What can I do to help?"

Ray started to say something but Jason cut him off. "What do you think, Mike? Where would you go from here?"

"Well, you don't know where she went into the river. It could have been anywhere on the Manhattan or Brooklyn side. Without an ID, you have no idea where to look or who to talk to. I'd say you work every angle you can to find out who she was and go from there. Until you have that, you have nothing."

"That's what I was gonna say," Ray blurted out.

"That's good, Detective McMillian," Mike said, nodding at Ray. "We're on the same page. Now see what you can do to get a positive ID on the poor girl."

"How would you suggest we do that?"

"You look like a smart guy, Detective. I'm sure you can figure it out." Mike stood up slowly, careful not to put weight on his left arm as he pushed up from his chair. He shook hands with Jason, then waved in the direction of Ray, who was sitting on the opposite side of the table and who did not stand up when Mike did. Jason walked Mike to the door of the precinct and watched as the older man climbed carefully down the four slippery stone steps to the sidewalk, turned left, and walked away toward Broadway.

When Jason went back inside, Ray was still sitting in the conference room. "Can we talk about the Sheffield case?" he asked when Jason came in.

"You think there's nothing else to do about our unidentified floater girl?"

"Nah. Let's wait to see if the fresh prints come back with an ID. No point spinning our wheels over this junkie until we know something."

"You've decided you don't like her already?"

"Hey, I see a lot of these strung-out losers on the street over in Robbery. They are suspects in a lot of the snatch-and-grab cases – just trying to snag enough for their next fix. They're disgusting. Maybe the crazy bitch wanted to kill herself. Maybe she fell in. Maybe she thought she could fly and jumped off the bridge. Maybe a lot of things. I'm not losing any sleep over her."

"Is there anything that makes you lose sleep, Ray?"

"Not really."

"I didn't think so." Jason turned toward the door to the conference room. "I tell you what. I'm going to go home. We can work Sheffield in the morning. You do what you want."

"I always do," Ray said smiling and leaning back as he clasped his hands behind his head.

Jason turned and walked out, muttering, "I know."

CPSIA information can be obtained
at www.ICGtesting.com
Printed in the USA
LVHW041542110723
752161LV00001B/58